BORROWED TIME

Also by David Mark

Novels

THE ZEALOT'S BONES *(as D.M. Mark)*
THE MAUSOLEUM *
A RUSH OF BLOOD *

The DS Aector McAvoy series

DARK WINTER
ORIGINAL SKIN
SORROW BOUND
TAKING PITY
A BAD DEATH *(eBook only)*
DEAD PRETTY
CRUEL MERCY
SCORCHED EARTH
COLD BONES

* *available from Severn House*

BORROWED TIME

David Mark

Severn House Large Print
London & New York

This first large print edition published in Great Britain and the USA in 2021 by Severn House, an imprint of Canongate Books Ltd, 14 High Street, Edinburgh EH1 1TE.

First world regular print edition published in 2020 by Severn House, an imprint of Canongate Books Ltd.

British Library Cataloguing-in-Publication Data
A CIP catalogue record for this title is available from the British Library.

ISBN-13: 9781780291864

MIX
Paper from responsible sources
FSC
www.fsc.org   FSC® C013056

Typeset by Palimpsest Book Production Ltd.,
Falkirk, Stirlingshire, Scotland.
Printed and bound in Great Britain by
TJ Books, Padstow, Cornwall.

For Marcel – un homme bon,
beacoup manque

'You must be proud, bold, pleasant, resolute,
And now and then stab, when occasion serves.'

Christopher Marlowe

Prologue

Dedham Vale, Essex
October 9th, 2007, 3.48 p.m.

It is a cold, grey, excessively English day.

A uniformed constable in a bright yellow coat stands shivering at the side of this quiet country road, holding a clipboard to his chest as if it were a hot-water bottle. He has his back to the great tangle of damp woodland that clusters in behind him; an impenetrable mass of rotten trunks and twisted branches; splintered timbers pushed deep into wet, fetid earth. This is a place of muted browns and sepia: a pattern in bloodied fox fur and damp soil. There is no greenery here. Whatever feeds the tree roots does not provide the nutrients for colour. In his rain-soaked blues and fluorescent coat, the officer is a bruise on rotten flesh.

This part of England is known as Constable country, in tribute to the great painter. PC Goodwin has yet to get the joke.

'Better here, Goody,' he mumbles to himself. 'Better here than there.'

He doubts any of his colleagues would disagree. Better anywhere than 300 yards into the damp murk of the forest. Better guarding the perimeter than standing by the water's edge, looking at the thing beneath the tarpaulin; the assemblage of white bone and rotten meat; the wire and tendons and steel. The surroundings have unnerved him. He jumps at every sudden sound. The slam of a distant van door nearly folded him into a ball. He keeps expecting to see something cloven-hoofed and terrible stalk purposefully towards him through the trees.

Above, a bird takes off in a flurry of damp, frantic feathers. Goodwin's head disappears into his collar and his hands become fists in his pockets.

'Fucking hell,' he mutters, as he reappears, slowly, like a rising sun. Then, for emphasis: '*Concentrate, you prick!*'

He checks his watch. Grimaces, sucking spit through his teeth. Huddles inside his waterproof and wonders how quickly the warm relief of pissing himself would be replaced by the ghastli-ness of standing in sticky wet trousers. Wishes he'd done what the old traffic cops used to do on cold days and worn a pair of tights beneath his uniform. Wishes he had a hot Pukka pie in each pocket: two meaty hot-water bottles, like his dad used to carry on bitter match days. Coffee with a brandy in it would be nice too. And a hat. He'd kill for a proper hat . . .

He turns at the sound of footsteps; expensive leather shushing through the fallen leaves. Goodwin stands a little straighter. It's Bosworth. Detective chief inspector with the Serious and Organised Crime Agency. She ticks both boxes of the job description. She's shed her white foren-sics suit and now looks inappropriately chic in her vintage duffel coat, flannel trousers and sturdy

2

boots. The fringe of her short hair peeks out damply from beneath a boilerman's cap. If the weather were kinder, Goodwin would probably be able to find the energy to dislike her for being attractive, ambitious and capable, but he's too cold to find the enthusiasm. She hands him a takeaway cup. Hot chocolate, with a shot of something sickly. He wonders where she found it – whether her team is so elite that it has the funding for its own on-call barista.

'Seriously?' He's surprised. Embarrassed, even. He feels like a little-known neighbour has sent him a Christmas card. 'Thanks, ma'am.'

Bosworth gives a tight smile. 'I don't like ma'am. *Guv* makes me feel like a football manager. I'll accept Cass.'

'Yeah? Brave new world, isn't it?' He thinks of something to say to demonstrate his capabilities; to reassure her she was right to pick him from the team of on-call constables and send him to guard this particular patch of muddy road. 'Was there a mix-up with the Home Office?'

'Sorry?'

'Wanted a barrister and they sent you a barista . . .'

'That's funny. I'll remember that one.'

'You're not laughing.'

'No.'

Her eyes move over him like a metal detector. He sips his drink. Spills some, and decides not to notice.

'You look like you're about to die,' she decides, without much obvious sympathy. 'If I was a doctor and you asked me how long you had to live, I would start counting backwards from five.'

He considers her. Enjoys the view. She's small, but he fancies he'll remember her as taller.

'I'll survive,' he says, smiling. 'I'm tougher than I look.'

'Me too,' she replies. 'How much longer are you manning the perimeter?'

'Until somebody gets sent to replace me. Or I die.'

Bosworth turns away, staring off down the curve in the road. She pulls a phone from a pocket and taps out a message that likely won't send until she's in a better signal zone. It's likely a cry for help. Bosworth's got a lot to process and Goodwin can't blame her for needing a few moments away from the sheer raw horror of the crime scene. Goodwin knows what's in the woods. Knows what's beneath the white, rectangular tent, oozing into the earth, trickling back down to the water: a syrupy mass of organic matter – meat slipping from bone like rotten fruit.

'Any ID yet?' he asks, teeth clicking like castanets.

'They've found the hand,' she says, quietly.

'Left or right?' he asks, making conversation.

'Does it matter?'

'Right for spite,' he says, and winces. He eyes the DCI carefully, just in case she's looking at him like he's a twat. He's relieved to see her staring off into the distance again, all thoughtful and grey.

They stand in silence for a time. Goodwin looks up at the crumpled clouds, coiled like damp rope.

4

Thinks of ash and salt and gunpowder. Watches the frost sparkle in the silvery-blue air: wisps of vapour rising from the ground.

'Gangland, you think?' he asks, at last.

'That's why we're here,' says Bosworth, taking off the hat and rubbing at her short, dark hair. 'We didn't just look at the weather and decide it would be a nice spot for a picnic.'

Goodwin finishes his hot chocolate. Hopes the cup will keep its warmth. Wonders whether it would be a sackable offence to grab the hat from her hands and ram it down over his ice-cold ears.

'Bleak spot,' says Bosworth, waving vaguely. 'Might not have bothered if I'd known it would be like this.'

'We'll be bringing back memories for the locals, I reckon,' says Goodwin. 'There'll be a granny or two wetting their pants with excitement that we've just found Jack the Hat.'

She shrugs, meaningfully. 'Anybody old enough to remember those days is probably half a day away from Alzheimer's already. And selective amnesia has always been a problem in this part of the world.' She blows out a breath, tired and cold. 'This is where they buy their pubs, isn't it? Where they join their golf clubs and set up their taxi firms and try to pretend they're normal people instead of killers and thieves. Where the old gangsters go now that Margate's full and Spain doesn't cooperate the way it used to. Throw a rock in the air and you'll hit somebody guilty – that's what my boss says.'

Goodwin decides not to reply. Bosworth is a shooting star; a fast-tracked graduate destined for a career filled with headlines. Her unit deals with gangland crime. People trafficking. Drug smuggling. Some days, she gets to run the rule over the local CID when a body turns up that might have links to active cases. Dedham Vale is known by the locals as Dead Man's Vale, in tribute to the bodies rumoured to have been planted here by warring crime families in the 1960s and 70s. Bosworth's unit was notified not long after the initial 999 call. It had been made by a local man; an endurance athlete with an inexplicable desire to accustom his body to immersion in bitterly cold water. The experience had also proved useful from a cardio perspective, having very nearly stopped his heart. Naked, shivering, he had been front-crawling through the tangle of pondweed, brushing his knees on moss-slimed rocks, when his fingertips had touched something waxy, cold and dead.

'Your sergeant says you're local yourself,' says Bosworth, looking up at him. 'Essex born and bred.'

Goodwin takes a moment before he nods, wondering what else she might have heard. Decides to play it straight. 'Mum's house is about ten minutes away. I should have called in for a second pair of socks.'

'So you'll know the story, yeah? These woods?'

He wonders what she's heard. Keeps his face straight lest a smile betray him. He suddenly wonders whether she's sought him out because of something she knows, or whether he's being overly suspicious. He's been accused of paranoia before, and reckons far worse is muttered behind his back.

6

'They say this is where the Richardsons used to dispose of rivals,' he says, in the tone of somebody who isn't sure whether to believe the rumours. 'No proof of it, not as far as I'm aware. It's not somewhere you play after dark. There were always stories about the ghosts of gangsters slithering in the trees. You know when you hear the leaves rustle? My grandad used to joke that it was all the old faces warning each other that snitches get stitches.'

She doesn't smile. Just nods. Sucks at her cheek and listens to the flapping of the tape.

'It's not that old, is it?' asks Goodwin. 'The body. I thought he was still pretty fresh. I heard the forensics lot talking. Said it would be hard to tell but it didn't seem like somebody from the old days.'

'Recent. Weeks, not months.'

'That normal, is it? To be in that state?'

Bosworth nods. 'Try leaving a chicken breast in a pan of cold water. See what it looks like after a week.'

'And the barbed wire? The nails?'

'A lot of it was done before he went in the water,' says Bosworth, leaning back against a tree. 'No ID but we're getting there. There's some markings on the hand that are looking promising. Not many other distinguishing features. The axe saw to that.'

'Christ, was it an axe?'

She stares past him, talking to herself. He's good at this. Has perfected the subtle art of getting people to talk without realizing how hard he is listening.

'Ligature marks. Back of his head caved in. Went at him with something sharp. Would still be down there if our swimmer hadn't got lucky.' She shakes her head, disturbed at the very notion. 'You ever tried this wild swimming lark? Can't say it appeals. Least of all here. Water's black as ink.'

'How is he?' asks Goodwin. 'The swimmer, I mean.'

'Still shivering. I reckon he'll be having nightmares for a while.'

Goodwin stays quiet. Imagines the sensation of clammy dead skin touching his own bare flesh. He gives another stab at being helpful. Entertains a fantasy of impressing her and somehow inveigling himself onto her team. The Serious and Organised Crime Agency could use a man like him. He has contacts. Friends in low places. He could do more than guard a perimeter and sign names on a soggy clipboard. Besides, knowledge is valuable, and he has always wanted to be a man of means.

'Local lad himself, is he?' asks Goodwin, and a fleck of spitty rain spurts from his lower lip. 'I mean, it's an odd spot, like you say. I can ask around, if it helps. I'm on-call for as long as you need me and I'd be glad to stay involved.'

Bosworth is playing with her phone, barely paying attention. She thumbs out a quick text and gives him a flash of smile. 'Help, you say? See if your old mum knows anybody likely to spend their evenings swimming through filth in the middle of a forest, you mean?'

'I've got contacts . . .'

'I'll keep that in mind,' she says, cutting him off before he can make a further prick of himself. 'I should head back in. Rain's forecast later and our forensics lot want to get him out of here before it starts.'

'Let me know if you need anything . . .'

'You're doing a great job,' says Bosworth, indicating the absence of gawkers, tabloid journalists or grieving relatives at this section of the perimeter.

'I'm here if you want to offload anymore,' says Goodwin, an urgency creeping into his voice. 'Seriously, what's the surname? I might know the family . . .'

Bosworth looks up at him, disappointed. Manages a tight smile and turns her back. He watches her walk away, cursing himself. He'd been doing so well.

When he's sure she's gone, he pulls the mobile phone from the pocket of his big coat. There's only one number stored in its memory and he knows that after he's made the call, he will have to dispose of the device. Another will arrive within days – another number programmed into the memory. He feels his heart rate speed up as the call connects. Hears a change in the quality of the silence.

'It's definite,' he says, and the words come out in a whispered rush. 'Found by a wild swimmer – I'll have the name soon enough. Recent. Too recent to worry you, though somebody's worked him over in a way you might recognize. They don't know who he is yet, but they will.'

Goodwin waits for a reaction. When none comes he starts gabbling.

'They've got SOCA on this. Bosworth. Do we know her? Is she staunch? She was asking questions. I might have said too much already. I need more for this to be worth my while . . .'

He stops talking as the man at the end of the line clears his throat.

'Is your life valuable?' he asks.

'What . . . yes, but . . .'

'Then you're already well paid.'

The line goes dead. It gives PC Jon Goodwin a glimpse of things to come.

Part One

One

Stanhill, Charlwood, Surrey
October 14th, 2007, 9.01 p.m.

The rain has started coming down hard, here: on this unremarkable B-road not far from Gatwick Airport. It blackens the tarmac, which twinkles like iron ore, in the light of the big peroxide moon. The raindrops slap fatly into the leathery leaves of evergreens, then trickle and tumble into the muddy, glass-jewelled surface of the car park.

For years this bar was called The Rose. It did a decent Sunday lunch. It won a few awards from the Real Ale people and its roast potatoes in goose fat were mentioned by a reviewer in a broadsheet food column. It made just about enough money to give its licensees, Robin and Emily, a pleasant life. It never made anywhere near the kind of cash required to support Robin's appetite for gambling. Nor did it put enough in Emily's purse to stop her from falling in love with an air traffic controller who wooed her with tales of exotic places like Dusseldorf and Bruges. Their divorce was a messy affair and Robin began tipping most of the pub's wine cellar down his throat. Standards slipped. Staff quit. The police were called by concerned customers who could not convince themselves that Robin was joking when he said he planned to blow the whole place up. It closed

13

a year ago. Robin is living in a bedsit somewhere in Bermondsey. Emily has yet to see Bruges. And The Rose is now in the hands of a private property developer and venture capitalist called Nicholas Kukuc. He recently began work on turning the old coaching inn into the sort of upmarket bistro that serves raw veal cheeks and deep-fried badger snout on planks of wood. He plans to put a lot of money through the business. If it does well, he will be able to launder at least ten per cent of his actual yearly income. It's a front, but Kukuc still hopes it will be a success. He isn't accustomed to accepting second best.

Tonight there are two cars in the car park. An off-road vehicle is neatly tucked away next to the lock-up at the far end. The other is the comfier kind of hatchback, a sporty number; shielded from the road by the curving line of trees and from the pub windows by a brick outbuilding.

A door opens. A middle-aged woman climbs out, a little awkwardly, as if she is used to travelling in bigger, better vehicles. She wears a short black dress, exclusive boots and a fur-lined leather jacket. She is a little overweight; her tummy a swollen lip that presses against the wide red leather of her elasticated belt. She has expensive breasts, a feathery haircut eight shades of blonde, and well-tended nails. Arty rings bookend the clustered diamonds on her fingers. She is Alison Jardine. She carries the name like a gun.

The driver's door slams closed and Alison is joined moments later by a tall, well-built man in his thirties. He smells of cigarettes and petrol.

'He'll be mob-handed,' mutters the man, as

14

they head towards the door. 'Kukuc. Probably got an army in there waiting for us.'

'I told him two, maximum.'

'And you think he'll listen? He does what he wants, and he likes putting on a show.'

'We're partners. It's a matter of courtesy. Any more than two would be rude.'

'But you've only brought me.'

'You're enough, Jimbo. You're a walking orgy.'

'We should have brought him.'

'Him?' asks the woman, cocking her head.

'Tim. He needs to cut his teeth . . .'

The woman stops. Turns to the younger man. Looks through him with eyes that burn like cigarettes.

'That sounded a lot like advice, Jimbo. And I don't need advice. Not from anybody. Not from you. You're here because you look the fucking part and because sometimes, when I'm lonely and I get that itch, I let you rub me where I'm tender. But that's the limit of your *responsi-fucking-bilities*. The day I choose to talk to you about my son is the day you know I've lost my mind.'

Jim knows better than to reply. He stuffs his hands into his pockets and trudges on ahead, sulkily. Alison stands still, letting him put some distance between them. If a gun barrel were to poke out of the darkened front windows, she'd like Jimbo to be standing between it and her heart.

When he's far enough away not to hear, she lets out the breath she's been holding. It comes out in a tremble. The hairs on her arms rise. She

15

keeps a strip of sandpaper inside her left boot and uses it now to grind against her naked sole. It hurts, but stops the fear. Instead she focuses on the pain. Feels the adrenaline and the endorphins. Rides it like a wave. Feels herself slow down. Becomes her father's daughter.

At the door, Jimbo looks back. Drinks her in. She has her mouth open, a perfect black circle, as she traces the outline of her lips with her finger. Only when her lipstick is immaculate does she follow him to the door. She allows her rump to brush his groin as she slides past and into the warm, half-darkness of the bar.

'Good boy,' she whispers, all cigarette smoke and Chanel.

There is only one light on in the shadowy expanse of The Rose. A lamp with a pink shade has been plugged into the wall and sits on a round wooden table in the centre of the empty bar. Most of the fixtures and fittings have been ripped out and the floor is covered with equipment left by the builders and decorators assigned to give the building a facelift. Two men are seated at the table. One is Nicholas Kukuc. He looks as though there is some Indian in his background. He's olive-skinned with brown eyes and a neat beard. He's younger than she is but not by much. He's wearing a blue suit with a striped shirt. The man to his right is broad-shouldered and wears his black hair in an unfashionable cut: short on top and long at the back. He wears a black jacket, zipped up to the neck. There are tattoos on the back of his hands. Alison would like such a man to work for her but she has heard he is loyal to

16

his paymaster. She admires such loyalty; even while rueing the fact that it will necessitate his inclusion in what is to follow.

'Alison,' says Nicholas, staying seated but making the effort to give her a smile of welcome. 'Good of you to come so far out of your way.'

Alison returns the grin; a gleam of expensive dentistry. 'It's not so far. We're a lot closer than you think. And we needed a chat.'

Nicholas nods his assent. Unbidden, the man beside him stands and crosses to Alison. Rolling her eyes she puts her arms out to the side and allows herself to be professionally frisked. She half expects him to linger on her buttocks or breasts but he is interested in nothing save for doing his job. He repeats the process with her companion, then takes a position behind Nicholas, nodding his confirmation that Alison is not carrying a gun.

'How can I help?' asks Nicholas, sitting back in his chair and inspecting the backs of his hands. 'You know I live to serve.'

Alison takes a moment to settle herself. She takes care to keep her expression inscrutable. She doesn't want him to see what's going on beneath her surface. Doesn't want him to know that she knows.

'Things are going well between us, Nicholas,' says Alison, briskly. 'I had my doubts about whether we could put the bad blood behind us but I'm happy to concede that you've proven me wrong. You've paid on time, we've shared resources, we haven't strayed onto one another's territory and more importantly, we're making good money.'

17

'I'm pleased you're pleased,' replies Nicholas with a smile. 'I'm told you are a hard woman to satisfy.'

She sneaks a glance at the hole in the ceiling. Her thoughts are running like water. She focuses her gaze on the bridge of the man's nose; a guaranteed way to give the illusion of eye contact without having to actually maintain it. Her father taught her the trick when she was still a girl; taught her how to intimidate people even as she felt her knees shake with fear.

'Dedham Vale,' she says, flatly. 'There's a body in the water. A body that shouldn't be there.'

A look of bewilderment rushes across Nicholas's features. 'Dedham Vale? This a trip down Memory Lane, love? We going for a stroll around Bethnal Green and having a pint in the Blind Beggar? History lesson, is it? Why are we talking about that?'

Alison leans forward. She places her palms flat on the table. 'Nicholas, I know how many bodies were in that stretch of water. I know who put them there. And I also know that they were removed in 2001 when we got wind that somebody was interested in buying that patch of woodland. There wasn't much left of them, but they were dealt with. Dealt with professionally. Still, rumours do leak out. People like to tell tales. And everybody knows the stories about my dad, Nicholas. Anybody looking to make things difficult for me and mine would only have to drop a corpse into that fucking pond and every snout in London would know what it meant. It would mean you'd upset the Jardines.'

18

Nicholas shoots his associate a look. Gives his attention back to Alison. 'You're rambling, love. I don't know what you're banging on about but if I'm honest I'm a bit fucking offended you'd waste my time.'

'The body,' says Alison, ignoring him. 'We've made our enquiries. Coppers are too. He was a private investigator out of Portsmouth. Name of Larry Paris. Somebody trussed him up. Skewers and barbed wire. We both know my father's an honest, decent businessman, but those who've had unkind things to say about him in the past, well . . . they've often found themselves in a similar pickle. Are you starting to see why I'm feeling a bit miffed, Nicholas?'

Nicholas shrugs. 'You're a mystery to me, love. Due on, are you?'

Alison turns as Jimbo moves towards the bar. She raises a hand; tells him to hold his position.

'Tell me it's nothing to do with you and we'll have a drink and say no more about it. How's that for a proposal?'

'I'm getting bored, love,' says Nicholas, shaking his head. His face has taken on a nasty, toothy aspect, like a rat emerging from a too-tight drain.

'I know you've got something to tell me,' she continues, inspecting the backs of her hands.

'Have I? Jesus, you've got some front. Your dad at least used to put on *hors d'oeuvres* and lap dancers when we had get-togethers. And unless you're going to tell your pretty boy over there to drop his trousers and give us all a wiggle, I'm going to say goodnight and we can pick this up again when you start making fucking sense.'

19

Alison stares a hole through him. 'The lock-up on Lawrence Road. Your lock-up. The warehouse where you unload and where your boys are paid very well to keep things low-key. The warehouse Dad used to use. The one you were gifted as part of our agreement.'

Nicholas pulls a face. 'This is what I'm here for, is it? This is what I've given up my night for? I've told you enough times, love, we can buy what you've got left and there'll be no penalties. You'll have done Daddy proud. What other way is the future going to go for you, love? Your boy's hardly going to take over, is he? Can't tie his shoelaces – even if he gets his trainers on the right feet. And don't give me your bullshit about your boogeyman. If he's still alive he's a fucking geriatric.'

'I'm not hearing much in the way of an apology,' says Alison with a tight smile.

Kukuc pushes back from the table, shaking his head. 'You fucking Jardines. You think you've got some God-given right to power just because your dad used to frazzle people's bollocks for the Richardsons. I've given him respect. Every outfit on the Christian side of the river gives him their respect. But you? You think you can come here with one muscled-up prat and intimidate me? I don't know anybody called Paris. I've got my own disposal sites. I wouldn't waste the petrol to get to Dedham fucking Vale. I'm not as tied to the past as you are. I don't need to prove I could have mixed it with the Krays. I already know who I am and I'm fucking good at what I do. You think I haven't worked out what you're

20

up to? Buying up all those properties, cosying up to councillors, using your old friends. Your dad tried to do the same thirty years ago, when you were still playing lacrosse and asking him for a pet fucking unicorn. Canning Town's mine, love. Newham's mine. I'm not going to play nice any more . . .'

'Did you kill him, Nicholas?' asks Alison, quietly. 'Kill him and dump his body in the place where Dad used to deposit our inconveniences?'

'Are you listening to yourself?' asks Kukuc, balling his fists.

'You look very het up,' says Alison, sweetly. 'You look as though you're eager to kick the stuffing out of Francis Jardine's daughter, if I'm honest. I hope I'm wrong. Because that would be absolute fucking suicide, mate.'

He pushes his hands through his hair and closes his eyes. Alison thinks he might be counting backwards from ten. When he opens them again he seems calmer. He even flashes a tight smile. 'I get carried away,' he says, sitting back down. 'The wife's got me listening to whale song and drinking bottled water. Thinks I should go vegetarian. She wants me to get a yoga trainer.'

Alison softens her body language. Places her hands, palm-up, on the table-top, as if asking for her fortune to be read. 'Start again, shall we?'

Nicholas looks past her at the man by the door. They share a smile. He reaches across the table and Alison takes his palm as if she were a fortune teller.

'Like calfskin,' she says, and her eyes seem to glaze over as she stares into him; lustful and

21

dreamy. It unnerves him and she feels him start to withdraw his hand. She grabs his wrist, her fingers wrapping around the black ink upon his pulse. His eyes widen in surprise as she pulls the flick-knife free from its bindings inside her belt and rams it down through the back of his hand; pinning skin and bone to the table like the body of a mangled spider.

'Bitch!' hisses Nicholas, through locked teeth. 'You fucking bitch!'

He swivels away, blood leaking into the table, as his bodyguard lunges forward and tries to pull the knife from the back of his employer's hand.

Alison pushes herself backwards from the table and covers her head.

Bang.

Bang.

Bang.

Both men look up as the ancient timber ceiling joist shrieks free from the low roof and swings down like a falling tree. Nicholas throws up an arm to protect himself but the wood is centuries old and hard as ice. It falls across the back of his neck and he is crushed beneath its weight as it crashes to the floor in a shower of dust and splinters. His hand remains pinned to the table and there is a terrible popping, crunching noise, audible even over the sound of falling plaster and stone, as the limb is yanked out of the socket. Great gouts of blood and gore squirt out of his ears, his eyes, his nose, his mouth, as the timber crushes him into an inhuman shape; a rat crumpled beneath a paving slab.

Spitting, groaning, the bodyguard pulls himself

up from the floor, bleeding from the head, his employer's crimson insides splattered across his face. He shouts something unintelligible and tries to pull his gun from inside his jacket. The hatch in the floor swings open and a shape appears in the dark rectangular void. There is a flash of flame and smoke and then he is collapsing in on himself, the remains of his head hanging from his neck like a twist of orange peel.

The man by the door is reaching for a gun in an ankle holster. Jim grabs a bottle from the bar, smashes it across the brass rail, and sticks it into the other man's neck, carving a jagged trench down towards his windpipe.

The sounds of destruction fade away. The timbers settle. Brick dust falls. Nicholas's corpse slumps sideways, his hand still pinned to the table.

Alison takes a second to compose herself. Slows her breathing.

'Well done,' she says, to the room in general. Then she stands. She tugs her knife from the back of the dead man's tattooed hand. She wipes it on the hem of her skirt and slips it back into her belt. It means a lot to her, this knife. It was a present from her father when she turned sixteen.

She turns back to the bar. In the darkness of the open cellar hatch, a patch of shadow delineates into a human shape. The man called Irons emerges. He's a monstrous thing; all scars and twisted skin, as if half his face is made from cold spaghetti and cheap leather. He is tall and broad across the shoulders and despite his years his movements are effortless.

He nods at Alison. 'Boy done well,' he says, his voice a pained whisper, as if his throat has been sawed open and stitched back together. He jerks his head in the direction of the broken ceiling. 'Done as he was told, once he shut up.'

'Praise indeed,' smiles Alison, enjoying herself.

Irons looks down at her. His eyes have leaked pinkish tears for the last thirty years. He has no eyelids. Beneath his eyes, the skin is so translucent that she sometimes thinks she can glimpse bone. He slips on his big brown sunglasses. Zips up his coat. He looks like the Invisible Man. 'Those things he said. About your boy. It don't serve to dwell.'

Alison reaches up and puts her warm palm on the ruched flesh of his face. She has known him all her life. She owes him almost everything. He has kept her family in business and alive for the best part of half a century. And yet she still has to fight a shudder as she touches his ruined flesh.

'You think it was him?' she asks, looking at the broken body of her recently deceased business associate. 'You think he was trying to frame Dad? Frame me?'

Irons shakes his head. 'He seemed genuine enough. Doesn't matter either way. Whoever put that body there isn't long for this world. And we owe them a thank you, in a way. It's the excuse you needed. Nobody will argue. Nicholas broke the ceasefire – that's the story people need to hear. You dealt with it. And the only people who'll be angry are the people who you're going to make rich. Don't give it another thought. I swear, your dad will be proud.'

24

The lie hangs between them like gunsmoke. Both know that Mr Jardine is too far gone on his medication to even recognize his daughter or his closest ally. Tumours eat into his pancreas, spleen, liver and brain. He should already be dead. Alison does not wish it so, but she is ready to grieve. She has even picked out the dress she will wear for his funeral.

'This Paris,' says Irons, thoughtfully. 'Office is Portsmouth registered.'

'South coast?' she asks, closing an eye, as if to better focus on a blurred memory. 'You and Dad had business there, didn't you? I remember the signs on the side of the van . . .'

'Don't look too hard at that memory, girl,' says Irons, softly. He is the only person allowed to talk to her with such familiarity. 'You worked too hard to forget.'

Alison's thoughts are already starting to accelerate. She remembers a friend, long since turned to ash. Remembers the bad thing that happened, and how far her family fell as a consequence. She looks at Irons, and realizes he is thinking it too.

She considers the corpses around her and feels mildly aggrieved. She had expected to sleep soundly tonight having removed a nagging irritation. Now she cannot imagine herself finding serenity before the morning. She looks up into the ceiling cavity. She glimpses a ratty, freckled face; a smudge of facial hair across a sweaty top lip and a baseball cap screwed down hard onto short, gelled hair. If she didn't love him, she'd find the sight of him repulsive.

'Those things he said,' she whispers to her son, wrapped in darkness and dust. 'That's what they think. Out there. Be better. Be a fucking Jardine.'

She glances back to Jim, leaning by the broken door. Looks again at the dead men. Thinks of that ugly night, and the things that were done to the only friend she's ever had. Feels the rage build, and looks for a place to hurl it. Irons, as if sensing it, rolls up his sleeve and hands her his cigarette. She crushes out the burning tip upon the dead skin of his forearm. He doesn't make a sound. Alison smells burning meat, and breathes deep. She nods her thanks. Irons retrieves the cigarette butt and places it in his pocket. Rolls down his sleeve without a word. He is already slipping away into his memories; remembering the last time he'd had business on the south coast and all that it cost him. He raises his hands and touches the wrinkled, ruined skin of his face. 'Pamela,' he says, and a pink tear runs through a channel in his cheek. He doesn't feel it. Feels nothing, save a grief almost forty years old.

Two

Derby Road, Stamshaw, Portsmouth
October 23rd, 2007, 7.04 a.m.

This bedroom is a pencil sketch: all fuzzy edges and blurred lines, as though a photographic negative has been smudged with a careless thumb. A watery yellow light dribbles in through a gap in the curtains. It illuminates a ragged, joyless square: discarded clothes camouflaging a threadbare carpet; half-empty bottles stacked up like bowling pins beneath an avalanche of charity-shop books. Condensation, flavoured with cigarette breath and dry white wine, lends a sequined shimmer to the high, honey-coloured walls.

Adam Nunn splurts into wakefulness as if emerging from a lake; heart pounding, skin goose-pimpled, wrapped in a headache.

'Stop . . . *stop!*'

He cannot remember where he was. Who he was. Why they were doing such things to him . . .

The pictures recede like the tide.

In moments he cannot remember anything at all. He is left with a mild sensation of residual disquiet; the faintest recollection of having been briefly ill-used.

He centres himself. Places himself. Breathes until his pieces reassemble.

Considers the world beyond the glass. A city

27

drawn in charcoals and dirt: a place of suet-faced pensioners, of teenagers in baby clothes; of egg-shaped women and puddled men; big middles and conical legs. He pulls the blue bedcovers over his head. Wraps himself in the musk of their mingled scents. Considers himself. He is so tired it feels like paving slabs have been laid on his chest. He tries again to remember the dream. Something about rabbit fur and the taste of old keys. It's shaken him. Left him feeling a vague unease, as if he has done something wrong.

He reaches out and feels Zara's warm, bare shoulder. Eases himself gently behind her. They fit together well. Her, a shade over five feet tall; him a quiff under six. She lifts her head and his arm slides beneath her jawbone. His knees slot behind hers. This is the best he will feel today.

'Stay asleep,' he whispers, softly, and is relieved there is no tremble to his voice. 'Dream something pretty.'

She stirs, nuzzling against him like a cat. 'I was in a circus,' she says, opening one eye. 'An old-fashioned one. Tigers. A ringmaster with a big moustache. I was a trapeze artist. You were there.'

'Clown, was I?' says Adam with a smile. 'Exploding car and custard pies?'

'It's fading,' she says, concentrating on the memory. 'You were my partner. You had to catch me after my double flip. You were dangling upside down, arms outstretched.'

Adam holds her tighter. 'I'll always catch you.'

'I'd catch you too,' she replies. 'Even if it

yanked my arms off, I'd keep hold of you. You're never getting away.'

Adam smiles, kissing her neck. 'You should put that on Valentine's cards.'

'I liked being in a circus with you,' she says, and pushes herself against him. 'I think there was a bearded lady.'

'That'll be Mum,' he says, in her ear. 'You had to spoil it.'

They lay in a rare moment of silence, breathing in tandem. He tries to think of something funny to say; something to maintain the nice mood she has woken into. Decides that for once, silence will serve him best.

'My arm's gone to sleep,' Zara says, after a time. She sits up, allowing him a glimpse of her extravagant skin. He grins, absurdly pleased that he belongs to somebody who looks like this. She is a marble canvas, adorned with flowers, fairies and butterflies. Her back is a frame of bluebells and angel wings, spread as if in full flight. Two hummingbirds dance on her flat tummy, and a sun surrounds her belly-button. Blue flowers and green vines wrap around her wrist and onto the back of her left hand. Roses bloom on her ankles.

'Come here,' he says, reaching out for her. 'You are such a poem . . .'

The door to the bedroom bursts open without a knock, and a small superhero explodes into the room. It's Jordan, Zara's son, dressed in the Batman costume he received for his ninth birthday, complete with muscle definition and utility belt. He is grinning wildly, singing a theme tune from a show that Adam has never heard of, but which

29

has nothing to do with Batman. He is holding his schoolbag in a gloved hand, and the part of his face not covered in black fabric is stained with the chocolatey residue of his breakfast cereal.

Adam bursts out laughing, pleasantly baffled, as Jordan stops still and stares at him for approval, both hands on his hips and jaw firmly squared.

'I own the night,' he says, and gives in to a peal of giggles.

Zara, swivelling to face the door, lets out a burst of laughter. 'Wow, Jordan, that's so much more than I can process right now . . .'

'Do you like it? I'm Batman. Or I'm half of him, anyway – I can't find the trousers so I'm wearing some of Selena's leggings. They're a bit flappy.'

Zara looks to Adam, hoping he'll be able to offer an answer. He's too busy laughing.

'Looks ace, buddy,' he replies with a smile. 'One of your ears is a bit flat though. You could always be Flatman . . .'

'Ha! Flatman!'

'Why are you wearing that?' asks Zara, confused.

'Children in Need,' says Jordan, as though this explains everything. He performs a dive-bomb onto the bed between them. 'I'm in need, actually. We're out of Coco Pops . . .'

'Is it a charity thing?' asks Zara, still confused. 'I didn't get a note.'

'You can wear your own clothes,' says Jordan, excitedly. 'For a pound. It's Pirate Day.'

'Pirate Day?'

'Yeah. So I'm Batman.'

Adam lets out a little laugh and slaps his forehead with his hand. Zara looks at her youngest child, eyes narrowing. 'This is going to be a Jordan thing, I can tell. We're going to laugh about this in years to come.'

'Can I have a pound, please?'

'Jordan, why are you going as Batman if it's Pirate Day?'

'I don't understand.'

'What's Pirate Day?' asks Adam as tactfully as he can manage through the laughs.

'You can wear your own clothes. Come in a costume, y'know. For charity.'

'So why's it called Pirate Day?'

'Because you can come as a pirate.'

'Is everybody coming as a pirate, Jordan?'

'I think so.'

'So why are you dressed as Batman?'

'Because it's Pirate . . .'

Zara, half-laughing, lets out a squeal of frustration as she grabs him by his costumed chest and presses her forehead to his. 'I can feel myself getting dimmer!' She pulls him to the door, shaking her head, pulling on one of Adam's T-shirts as she goes. 'Come on, you halfwit. I'm turning you into Captain Hook.' She turns to Adam, exasperated. 'There's a test for this. If it turns out he really is a moron we qualify for benefits . . .'

'He's special, I'll give him that,' laughs Adam.

'Come on you,' she mutters to her youngest. 'Let's start by teaching you how to say "arrrr".'

'There's a breadknife in the sink,' yells Adam,

as he listens to them giggling their way down the stairs.

He sits on the edge of the bed for a while, smile fading like a dying bulb. Slowly, predictably, he feels his spirits fade. He always loses the will to be cheerful when she's not near him. Can't feel a reason to be sunny on his own. He sometimes worries that it is this fear of how he would treat himself on his own that has stopped him from ever being single. He's been in relationships for twenty years – always with a brief period of overlap. He falls in love a lot. He never knows what it is he's searching for but there is something about the passion and possibility of new relationships that intoxicate him. He's fallen hard for Zara. She's older than him, which helps. Prettier too. She reminds him of one of the mature students he saw hanging around the art department when he was a student; all piercings and baggy clothes, bare midriffs and Doc Martens. He sometimes wonders whether he is trying to recapture his youth. He never made it all the way through university, dropping out of his Biological Sciences degree at university before he had to take his final exams. He'd been in a bad place. Made some mistakes over a girl and could barely get himself to class without taking a double dose of diazepam. He'd headed home rather than risk failure or a 2:2. Mum and Dad had been happy enough to have him home. Told him he just needed to get his head right and then he could go back and take his final exams. Fifteen years later, he's still in Portsmouth. Criminal record to his name, a bank account in the red, and a personal life as tangled as a bail of barbed wire.

He broods on the thought for a while. Rolls it around. Feels himself drift into well-worn grooves of introspection. Money. The future. What he's for. How much longer can he do all this without it all coming down around him. He's still making the same mistakes he made as a young man. Still throwing himself – body, soul and bank balance – into love affairs that never seem to fill the gaps within him.

Adam sits up in bed, angling himself so the light from the window illuminates his lean, wolfish face. He's slim. Dark-eyed. Stubbly, no matter how close to the bone he presses the razor. People always tell him he looks like his dad. The thought used to be comforting. Now it crushes his heart like a boot.

Slyly, guiltily, Adam reaches down for the cheap blue laptop, tucked away beneath Zara's robe and his own inside-out trousers. His neighbour recently spent a fortune installing wireless internet and Adam, dropping off a parcel and accepting an invitation to join him for a glass of wine, had spotted the password on a Post-it note, stuck to the fridge with a magnetic banana. Adam now enjoys the almost magical benefits of being able to use the laptop without having to crouch by a skirting board.

'Come on, Larry,' he mutters, opening the screen and calling up his email. 'How hard can it be?'

He refreshes the screen twice. Checks each folder in his mail. Chews at his cheek, nervous now. The only new email is from a charity he'd contacted months ago – back when the wound was still gaping and he hadn't known how to put himself back together. He'd filled in an online form, jotting down the paltry details he'd known for certain about himself. Membership of the site had allowed him access to their facilities and regular updates about their work. He truly wishes he'd stayed on this path. If he'd done things properly, if he hadn't tried to avoid the unpleasantness of painful confrontation, he might have answers by now. He clicks the link on the email, navigating his way to a list of new case studies. Feels the lump grow bigger in his throat as he reads the plaintive words of mothers and children reunited after decades of separation. Scans the accompanying links for new appeals. Has to suppress a shiver as he pores over the desperate, heartfelt pleas. He indulges himself in fantasy for a moment, his eyes hot, palms clammy. Considers what he would do if he stumbled upon a notification from a mother searching for a child given up in 1971. Imagines the wording. Her regret. Her apology. Her wish that things had been different and her certainty that there has never been a day in which she has not missed and loved him. He blinks, hard, as he considers it, and has to cuff himself across the cheek lest disloyal tears start to fall.

He sits quietly, now, wondering what the day will bring. Thinks of the infinite possibilities. He'll have to see Dad later. Will have to sit in the grey-green room and listen to the old boy rasp away his final breaths.

And all the time, the question will be there on his tongue, burning like a hot coal.

Without wanting to, Adam pictures the old man, and the words he had wielded like a cutlass. Sat there in his armchair in his paisley pyjamas, red lines marbling his eyes, glaring daggers into his son. The words had come from behind bared teeth, frothing onto the stubble of his grey chin.

We should have sent you back. If you were a toaster I'd have kept the fucking receipt. Could have had anybody and we got you. You were the puppy with the biggest eyes – the one your mother had to have. Should have left you in the cage. Taken a pedigree – not some shabby mongrel. Worst investment of my fucking life.

Adam had never heard his dad swear before. Never seen him lose his temper.

The words seemed to come from somebody else entirely, as if the frail old man in the armchair was a conduit for something else. Adam had been too stunned to reply. Just sat there with a silly look on his face, listening to the tick of the clock and the ugly rasp of his dad's breath as he turned away from him and closed his eyes. On the sofa beside him, his mum was stiff as a dead bird. *He didn't mean it*, she said, when they were alone. *Doesn't know what he's saying, half the time . . .*

Adam tries to make himself feel better. Thinks of the people around him; the people he loves, the countless reasons to feel optimistic and grateful.

His thoughts drift back like a kite on a string.

He wonders if today will bring answers.

Wonders if today, Larry Paris will call and tell him who he really is.

Three

Inside the unmarked police car, DCI Cass Bosworth tries to suppress a yawn as she listens to the soporific tones of her boss, oozing down the phone like treacle. Bosworth has never mastered the art of staying entirely *present* when dealing with Detective Superintendent Mick Gray. Drifts off a lot. Makes shopping lists in her head and ranks the skills of ex-lovers when she's supposed to be making notes and absorbing facts. He's not dull – he just manages to sound like he's reading a bedtime story, his words soft and perfectly enunciated, his pauses large enough to drive a truck through. He's got a lullaby of a voice, even as he's highlighting the parts of a post-mortem examination most likely to cause the listener's breakfast to make a U-turn.

'. . . had the hand in a Lysol bath . . . not much of the chest left to work with . . . from the amount of blowfly larvae and the volume of maggots that seethed out of the chest cavity he was definitely on the ground for a period of time before going into the water . . . definitely dead . . . twenty-nine major pieces of skull – exceptional work, taken a digital reading but they did things the old-fashioned way . . . sorting, drilling,

36

wiring the bits back together, bit of a jigsaw puzzle but the hole we're left with is almost certainly a hammer, though the indentation suggests it may be wooden with a metal binding, so it may be antique . . . so, factor that in. You have enough officers, yes? It's important we follow the new protocols . . .'

Bosworth realizes it's her turn to speak. She opens her mouth wide and is rewarded with a satisfying crack at the hinge of her jaw. Beside her, in the driver's seat, her detective sergeant winces. Inside the warm, moist vehicle, it sounds like a gunshot.

'More than enough,' says Bosworth. 'Honestly, it's overkill, sir. I'm sure the local CID will be grateful for using our resources but I don't really see why this is something for a DCI . . .'

'I hate ticking boxes as much as the next man . . . woman, sorry . . . if there's a link to ongoing case work it shows we're across this – the database is working, we're an asset, not a nuisance . . .'

'It'll be a pissed-off husband, I'm sure of it. A private eye, snooping around, irritates the wrong person and pays the price . . .'

'Perhaps. But we've taken four separate tips from registered informants indicating that Kukuc is suddenly out of the picture . . .'

'I don't see the connection.'

'The pattern of injuries, the location of the body, they all point to somebody with know-ledge of crime scenes identified between 1968 and 1972 . . .'

'Anybody with the internet or a library card

37

could find that out,' says Bosworth, testily. 'I don't see why that leads me to sitting in a damp car in bloody Portsmouth.'

'It's more a case of showing willing . . . we asked to be given first refusal and it would be churlish to suddenly decide we're not that interested after all.'

'You're the boss.'

'Well, that's not really the philosophy I want to be associated with. We're a team. First among equals, if I have a title.'

'That's one of the things we call you, yep.'

There is silence as he digests this. Gray is guru-calm. Bosworth's never heard him raise his voice and he can deal with catastrophic news without a flicker of distress crossing his features. He's been on a lot of courses. He takes the mental health of his workforce seriously and has managed to secure a 'mindfulness budget' from the accountants to ensure that HQ is festooned with greenery and that the canteen serves organic fruit and vegetables. He has dehumidifiers at both ends of the office and has insisted that one interview room be set aside as a 'safe space' in which his staff can spend time formatting their thoughts. A private counsellor is on-call, and he's trying to secure the services of a masseuse to provide neck and shoulder relief for the office staff asked to do more than a standard shift. Bosworth likes working for him, even as she counts down the days to his complete nervous breakdown and practices pulling the correct facial expression upon being asked to take over the unit.

'I just don't know if I see it myself, Mick,' she

38

says, enjoying the novelty of using a superior officer's first name. 'I can do a damn sight more back in London talking to informants. If somebody's made a move on Kukuc, that's big. The fact that a dead man's car is parked near his warehouse, well, to me that kind of shows there's no connection. Kukuc knows what he's doing. He would have had it crushed by now if he was involved. And as for this chap I'm door-stepping . . . remind me his name . . .'

'Nunn.'

'Small time, wouldn't you say? He's got convictions but a different judge on a different day would have given him a reward instead of a record.'

'I know it's a pain . . . you're appreciated, I promise you. You'll be mentioned by name in the memorandum to the Home Office. It may not seem it, but it's jobs like this that will secure the future of SOCA . . .'

Bosworth nods, eyes closed, knowing that this is all part of the game. Show willing, she tells herself. Be an asset. Play nice up until the point you have to play nasty.

'Of course, Mick. Who knows, it may still pay off.'

'Thank you. We'll talk again later.'

Bosworth hangs up. Looks to her number two and gives a theatrical roll of her eyes. Then she nods at the house they have been watching since before the sunrise. 'Poor sod,' she says, begrudgingly. 'No way out of it. Let's go ruin his day.'

Four

Adam pulls on a pair of jeans, a grandad shirt, and shrugs himself into his pinstriped linen jacket – a pale, wrinkled affair, like a deflated brain. He fishes out a pair of yesterday's socks from under the bed and pulls them on with the practiced soundlessness of somebody used to slipping away unnoticed at two a.m.

Checks his phone again. A jaunty 'good morning' from Grace, complete with a blow-by-blow account of how their daughter managed to sleep for three whole hours in her cot last night before persuading Mummy to let her climb in with her. Adam smiles as he pictures Tilly's persuasion tactics. She can make a noise like no other two-year-old: an intense and monstrous shriek that Adam thinks he could only replicate with the aid of a horny fox and an industrial blender. He blows a kiss into the air and hopes it finds its way to her cheek.

'. . . *these are meat shears, Jordan – they're not scissors, why are they up here? Oh for God's sake, pass them here . . .*'

Adam can hear bangs and thumps and shouts coming from Jordan's room. It had been Adam's study until a little while ago. Now it's Jordan's room. Adam's old walk-in closet is now

40

Selena's room. His kitchen is now Zara's excuse for an office. He feels a tremor in his chest; the hot ash of rising panic, and shakes his head like a dog bothered by a wasp. Distracted, he bumbles his way downstairs. Selena, in her sensible school uniform and smelling of freshly-brushed teeth, is standing holding a mug of coffee, smiling at him like he's Justin Timberlake.

'Morning, Adam.'

'Morning, poppet. You look nice.'

'I don't. But thanks.'

'You make the best coffee.'

'It's all to do with the stirring. Anti-clockwise is best.'

'I had an Auntie Clockwise, once. Total wind-up merchant.'

'Was that a joke? I can laugh if it was a joke.'

'You are a horrible person. Well done.'

Adam kisses Zara's teenage daughter on the top of the head as he passes, losing his face in her mess of curls. He gets on well with Selena. They do a lot of clandestine eye-rolling and he likes the way she talks to him. She always seems interested in learning new things. She asks him questions in the unshakeable belief that he will know the answer. She's too old for hand-holding but she sometimes pokes her wrist through the loop of his arm when they're pushing the trolley around Tesco. They have fun together, making each other laugh as they pursue the woman with the pricing-gun as she shaves pennies off the cost of perishables fifteen minutes before closing time.

'Are we in mourning?' asks Adam, nodding at the closed curtains.

41

'Sorry, forgot,' mutters Selena, and pulls back the drapes. 'We never used to open them at our old house. Mum said the sunlight showed up the dust.'

'Well, this is Portsmouth – it's not a problem we often have.'

Adam smiles, imagining his mother's contribution to such a discussion. He doesn't think he can picture her without an apron and a duster. As a child, the house was so mercilessly disinfected that every time he went outside he caught a cold. His immune system still hasn't recovered.

There's a fine mist of rain speckling the pale blue light. Adam squints out past the overgrown front garden; the small two-bed semi across the road.

'That car's there again,' says Selena, at his side. She nods towards the spot where the street curves away towards the main road. A black Mercedes is tucked in behind the white telecommunications van that has recently taken up residence outside number 17.

'Don't worry,' says Adam, automatically, and squeezes her forearm. 'You're safe, I swear.'

Selena has answered the door to more than her fair share of unwelcome visitors. Bailiffs and enforcement agents called more often than family and friends when they still lived in the flat in Southsea. She can't see a white van without worrying that there will be a knock on the door from some intimidating specimen in a black uniform, wearing a lanyard like a medal. She's paid them off with her birthday and babysitting money. She's set up repayment plans in her mum's name. She's hidden behind the sofa, her hand over Jordan's mouth, crying into the floor and praying for an earthquake. When she sees an unfamiliar car she knows it means trouble.

'*Garr!*'

Adam turns at the sound of an enthusiastic pirate taking the stairs four at a time. Jordan is radiating equal amounts of glee and menace. Zara has cut the sleeves off a checked shirt, drawn an eyepatch on his face with felt-tip pen and turned some random piece of material into a bandana. An old pair of school trousers has been given a zig-zag hem with a pair of scissors and his pale legs poke out like sticks. Adam's relieved to see she hasn't sawn his leg off for authenticity.

'Excellent,' says Adam, warmly. 'You look champion, buddy.'

'Best I could do,' says Zara, following on. 'I reckon the other kids will walk all over him – he's such a plank.'

'You've done a great job, darling,' he says to her, kissing her on the top of the head and hoping he sounds complimentary rather than patronising. 'Genius.'

'It'll do,' says Zara. She's wearing a little skirt and a hooded sweatshirt that smells of yesterday's cigarettes. She takes a slurp of Adam's coffee and glances behind him. 'Car's there again,' she says, quietly.

'I'll go have a word,' he says, stroking her cheek with the back of his hand. 'Let me just wake up a bit.'

Zara doesn't reply. She plods through to the

kitchen and begins searching for clean crockery. Through the open door he sees her pouring cereal into a blue Tupperware box. She pours the milk without sniffing it first, which Adam takes as proof that she's definitely distracted by other things.

'Have you done your reading?' shouts Zara, from the kitchen. 'Jordan? Have you done your reading?'

Jordan, who is swinging from the front-door handle as though it is the rigging of a ship and making swipes with an imaginary cutlass, looks up at Adam, pleadingly.

Adam sighs, and shouts back, 'I promised him he could read to me on the way to school.'

'You're OK to take them, are you? I didn't like to ask . . .'

'You're flashing,' says Jordan, pointing to the duty coffee table by the electric fire where Adam's mobile phone has been charging overnight. He picks it up and glances at the screen. Four missed calls and a couple of voicemails. The first is from his infant daughter, all giggles and squeaks and a song that might be 'Twinkle, Twinkle'. The other is eight seconds of near-silence; quiet breathing and the whispered sensation of movement, like air rushing past an open window. Adam checks the caller info. The call came at a little after midnight, the number withheld.

More out of habit than anything else, Adam rings his mum. She answers on the second ring, the way she always does – snatching the phone from the cradle by the kitchen sink and saying the telephone number, complete with area code.

'Morning Mum.'

44

'Oh, hello son. Sleep well?'

'I don't know, I was asleep.'

'You're always taking the mickey out of me.'

'You make it easy.'

Adam could talk to his mum for hours without ever once really engaging with the conversation. He makes her laugh when he can. Tells her nothing of any great seriousness. Chats to her like a local radio DJ trying to get the best out of a recalcitrant guest.

'How's Dad?'

'Better than yesterday. He was asking for apple pie and custard.'

'Did he ask for it or did you suggest it?'

'Does that matter?'

'Probably not.'

Adam's dad is dying. His mind is disappearing in tiny increments. Some days he is lucid: funny, cantankerous, clever. Others he is a child, unsure of himself, his wife, unable to recognize his own son – lashing out at the district nurse as she wrestles with the tube that slurps the green slime from his rasping lungs.

'I'll be over later.'

'Only if you're free . . .'

'Cheap. Never free.'

'You are a one.'

He hangs up and savours the moment. Wishes he could say 'I love you' without feeling like a prick. Wishes he had the balls to demand answers.

It took Adam a month to ask his mum the question that he'd kept locked away for as long as he could remember. *Am I really yours, Mum? Am I adopted?*

45

If she'd said no, he would have accepted it. He'd have kissed her and left it alone. He could have swallowed down his suspicions the way he had since he was a boy. But she'd refused to answer. Refused to engage with it. Refused to be in the same room as him while he asked such terrible things. That was when he'd known. Thirty-six years old, and suddenly his mum wasn't his mum and his dad wasn't his dad and everything he thought he knew about himself was a lie.

He glances at the phone. Still nothing from Larry. It's been five weeks since they last spoke and Adam is growing more anxious. Each day that goes by without answers adds another layer to the fantastical story that Adam is stewing inside his skull. Each day he concocts fresh narratives about his origins and bloodline. He makes believe that he is a Gypsy prince; the heir to a forgotten fortune; a foundling fished from a river in a wicker basket. He isn't entirely sure he wants to have such fantasies replaced with truth – even as he yearns for some form of contact from the elusive private detective upon whom Adam has invested his last three grand.

'Car's gone,' says Selena, peeking out through the curtains. 'Probably nothing.'

Adam breathes out, slowly. He's grateful. He doesn't really like confrontation. He's been a doorman, a debt collector, and a security consultant but he'd rather hide in a cupboard than endure unpleasantness. He's broken up with his last three partners rather than chide them for imperfection. He wonders whether it runs in the family.

'I suppose we should be . . .'

Adam doesn't finish the sentence. The knock at the door is hard. Official.

Jordan opens it before Adam has the chance to tell him not to.

There are two of them. The man is pushing fifty. Plump, with iron-grey hair and the burst capillaries and vampiric lips of a red wine drinker. He's scowling, half a step behind his companion. She's small, with dark hair cut short and eyebrows that reach a marked point above her blue eyes, making her seem quizzical; disbelieving.

'Hello there,' she says, seemingly unperturbed at being greeted by a small pirate. 'I'm a police officer. So's my friend here. Oh yes we *arrr*. I'm looking for Mr Nunn? Is he home?'

Adam, tucked out of the way, is tempted to conceal himself behind the curtains. He fancies he could stand here, listen to the conversation, then take a view on whether or not to ever emerge.

'Yeah, he was here a moment ago . . .'

Adam clicks his tongue against the roof of his mouth. Shoots a look to the kitchen, where Zara stands in the doorway, panic pinching her features. Automatically, he twitches out a smile. *Don't worry*, it says. *It's nothing. Whatever they think I've done, I didn't do it . . .*

'Hi,' he says, gently removing Jordan from the doorway and giving both officers his best smile. 'I'm Adam Nunn. What's this about . . .?'

The woman smiles at him, an oddly incongruous expression. She looks like she's trying to sell double-glazing, or initiate him into a cult. Either way, he's not buying.

47

'Mr Nunn? Oh that is a relief. You haven't answered any of the phone calls to your mobile – we were starting to worry.'

Adam rubs a hand through his hair. 'I get a bad signal. And I do ignore numbers I don't recognize. How can I help?'

Bosworth seems to be using her tongue to work something free from her teeth. She gives a sudden grin of triumph, evidently successful. Then she gives Adam her full attention. Cocks her head, and turns to her colleague. 'You reckon?' she asks.

The older man glares. Shrugs. 'Could be.'

Adam looks from one to the other. 'I'm sorry, what's going on?'

'Could we come in please, Mr Nunn?'

Adam crosses his arms, unsure whether to play this out like Hugh Grant or Ray Winstone. He can play both roles – the floundering Englishman, and the cocksure bruiser. 'Why?' he asks, settling on a middle ground that emerges sounding like a Waitrose Bob Hoskins. 'You both look very serious. What's happening?'

'I'd rather explain inside . . .'

'I've got to get the kids to school . . .'

'I'd really rather get in out of the rain.'

'Then tell me what you're after.'

The senior officer looks disappointed in him. 'Mr Nunn, my name is Detective Chief Inspector Cass Bosworth of the Serious and Organised Crime Agency. I'm investigating a murder. I've driven a long way.'

Adam grimaces. SOCA are new. They're the UK's answer to the FBI. He doesn't want to

48

be on their radar. He doesn't think he's done anything wrong recently but he can't say for certain. A picture bursts in his imagination; a memory of past misdeeds and more recent indiscretions. Most have been performed at the behest of Larry Paris. He pictures him. A loud shirt; slick curly hair, gelled into waves and question marks, a dark frame around a fleshy pink face.

'A murder? Whose murder?'

She gives him a look that's hard to read, her features as inscrutable as a dinner plate. Sucks her teeth. 'Do you know a Larry Paris?'

Fuck.

'Larry? Why?'

'I'd prefer it if you let me ask the questions, Mr Nunn.'

'Yeah, I'd prefer it if you'd brought croissants, but it looks like we're both disappointed.'

Behind her, the older policeman tenses up. Bosworth gives a tight smile.

'Do you know him, Mr Nunn?' asks Bosworth, again. She sounds as though she could keep asking all day.

Adam can feel waves of panic rising inside him. Feels grief, too, before it is replaced with a sudden, ugly burst of self-interest. Larry has his money.

'Jesus,' he says, quietly.

'No, otherwise he'd have walked on the water. Now, Mr Nunn, are you going to start cooperating? How did you know Mr Paris?'

'We've done some work together,' says Adam, vaguely. He wishes he had a solicitor to call. Wishes he was all the things he's claimed to be.

49

'Christ, that's awful. Awful. I mean, he's a mate, of sorts.'

Bosworth keeps her eyes on him, staring into him as if examining an oil painting for brush-strokes. 'Mr Paris was found dead last Saturday morning. We are treating his death as murder.'

A picture flashes. How many weeks ago? Three? Four? He sees Larry. Sees him waving with his short fat hand, gold at his wrist and on his fingers: gesturing royally through the open window of his unremarkable Volvo. He'd made the signal with pinkie and thumb – the international gesture for a phone call. They'd parted on good terms, hadn't they? Adam down to the pennies in his pockets and Larry three grand richer. Their goodbye had been sincere. Friendly. Larry, promising him that whatever he turned up, it would be good value for money – the outline of the envelope full of cash visible in the top pocket of his Hawaiian shirt.

'Larry?' Adam says it again, feeling daft. He lets his real feelings take hold of his features. 'Jesus, that's awful. What happened? Did you say he drowned?'

'Inside,' says DCI Bosworth, more pointedly.

'No, no, I've got things to do.' He wishes he'd let them in when they first asked. Now it's a matter of stubbornness; of pride.

'Really, Mr Nunn, your attitude isn't helping this situation.'

'Neither's yours, love. Now, tell me about Larry.'

The other detective moves forward and Bosworth steps into his path. She looks at Adam with

50

something like pity. She reaches out to put a hand on his arm and he jerks back as if she were a leper. 'It would be better if we started all this again,' she says. 'There are matters you might prefer to discuss in private.'

Adam's temper frays, then snaps. 'I want you off my doorstep,' he growls. 'You're lowering house prices.'

DCI Bosworth clicks her tongue again; a noise like a horse pulling a hoof free from deep mud. She looks past him, almost apologetic in her manner. 'That's how you want it, is it? Fair enough. Mr Nunn, I'm arresting you in connection with the death of Mr Larry Paris . . .'

Adam doesn't move until the uniformed officers start piling out of the back of the telecoms van. Doesn't start to protest until the fat cop puts his hand on his arm.

Then he lashes out.

Hits and hurts and hits and hurts until there are three of them on his back and his face is being pushed into the cold, dark ground.

Only then does he remember the dream. Only then does he recall that in the moments before he woke, he had known, somehow, what today would bring.

Five

Adam is seated in a blue chair, at a grey desk, in a room the colour of sour milk. On his cheek, a bruise is turning purple. There's a crimson line where his split lip is knitting back together. He's leaning forward as if in prayer, or on the toilet. His knees hurt where the uniforms tackled him to the ground. It's his left hand that stings the most. There's some kind of friction burn making his fingers glisten shiny pink. The wound seems to sing with pain. He can't help wondering whether there could be a compensation claim in all this. He feels oddly high, as if he's drunk too many cans of sugary drink. His legs are jiggling up and down; a peculiar smile twitching across his features even as he tries to look like he's done this enough times not to care.

Larry, he's thinking, and it takes an effort not to start kneading at his temples with his thumbs. *Poor sod. What were you doing? What had you found out?*

Then, like a drum: *This might be your fault.*

'None of that was really necessary,' says DCI Bosworth, testily, seated across the desk.

'Murder cops on your doorstep – best to play nice.'

Adam looks from Bosworth to her colleague.

52

'Was that an apology?' asks Adam, keeping his voice steady.

'Sorry, Mr Nunn?' asks Bosworth, tilting her head.

'That's a start, I guess,' he replies, through gritted teeth. 'It doesn't sound very genuine.'

'I meant I can't hear you very well. Could you speak up, for the benefit of the recording.'

Adam raises his head. Sings the opening bars of 'Old Man River', then stops when nobody laughs. 'Sure. That better?'

'Perfect.'

'You think? You're not so bad yourself.'

'I was saying, that this could have been handled very differently.'

Adam sits back, slipping down the chair so it looks as if he's watching the football on a comfortable armchair. 'I'm sure it could. I'm sure with the benefit of hindsight you wish you hadn't come to my door mob-handed and kicked the shite out of me in front of my kids.' He reconsiders, looking at his bruised knuckles. 'Tried to, anyway . . .'

DCI Bosworth shakes her head. Beside her is a grey-haired man in a dull suit. He'd been introduced as a detective sergeant but Adam had been too busy brooding to register his name. The other person at the table is a solicitor who was introduced to him while he was being seen by the medical examiner. He's a slick, stylish Asian whose facial hair has been styled into such perfect angular points that Adam wonders whether the design was done on computer. He's barely spoken since the interview began.

53

'We hadn't planned on making an arrest,' says Bosworth. 'You're a person of interest. We had the back-up there because of your record. Protocol. *Guidelines.*'

'What record?' asks Adam, giving a look somewhere between a smile and a wince. He knows where this is heading. Knows he isn't going to like having his failures, his indiscretions, held up for inspection.

'You have a conviction for aggravated assault . . .'

'I was twenty-one . . .'

'You attacked a Mr Gordon Strange, aged forty-one, in May 1998 . . .'

'He started on my mate. I was sticking up for her.'

'And you received a suspended sentence five years ago for demanding money with menaces . . .'

'No, that's not how it was . . .'

'You were providing debt collection services for a telephone company based in Northampton. You told a creditor of the firm you could make it go away if they gave you a cash sum instead of paying the total to your employer . . .'

'It wasn't like that,' says Adam, and he still can't be sure if he believes the story he gave in mitigation. Had he really been trying to help? Had he really been trying to stop a single mum having to pay back a debt she could never even make a dent in? He'd wanted to help her, not add to the list of people taking advantage. He'd have gotten away with it, too, if her husband hadn't found out and jumped to the wrong conclusions.

'And there was an incident at HMP Hull while you were briefly on remand. You put an inmate and a guard in hospital. It would have been an attempted murder charge but no witnesses could be found. You're quite a dangerous man, Mr Nunn.'

Adam looks down at the bland trainers they'd given him in the custody suite. He wonders who else has worn them. Who else has worn the jeans and T-shirt they gave him as they bagged up his clothes.

'I don't know what you want from me,' says Adam, and it sounds pitiful to his ears. 'I've done nothing wrong. I'm trying my best. I'm a family man.'

'The children belong to your partner,' says Bosworth.

Adam looks hurt. 'Don't be cheap about it, I love them like they're my own.'

'You have a daughter, yes? With a woman called Grace Senoy?'

Adam glares at the other detective. 'And?'

'Complex family set-up,' says Bosworth, pursing her lips.

'I'm a complex man,' he says, bitterly. He doesn't want to have to start explaining himself. He doesn't understand his own life – he just lives it.

'Tell me about your relationship with Larry Paris,' says DCI Bosworth, looking down at the folder which lays open on the desk in front of her.

'Larry? He's my mate, like I told you. Are you sure it's him? He's OK, is Larry.'

'He's not,' says DCI Bosworth. 'He's dead. His body was found in a stretch of water in an area of woodland in Dedham Vale, Essex, on Saturday last. Did you not hear about it?'

'I don't listen to the news anymore,' mumbles Adam. His mind is racing. Essex? Could Larry have been there for any other purpose than the task he was performing for Adam? He feels a sudden, unnerving impulse to pray.

'It took us a while to identify him, of course. Things had been done to him. Bad things. We couldn't identify him from dental records because there weren't many teeth left.'

'Jesus,' says Adam, quietly.

'When did you last hear from Mr Paris?'

Adam closes his eyes, focusing on the memory. They'd only met briefly, sheltering from the rain in Larry's crappy car, overlooking the harbour. Larry was giving him his full attention, scribbling down notes, nodding his head so that his curly hair flopped forward onto his glossy face. Adam had been trying to be glib about it all – trying not to show much in the way of sincere feeling in front of a man he's only really known in a professional capacity, and to whom he has just entrusted a confidence. He can hear Larry's voice, telling him that it shouldn't be difficult; that adoption records are his bread and butter and that he knows a guy who can have an answer inside a few days. If he concentrates hard enough, Adam can feel Larry's sweaty hand gripping his own. He can hear Larry telling him not to worry. That he's doing the right thing, and that all he has to do if he wants him to stop his enquiries, is give him a call. Some chance of that, thinks Adam, testily. Larry had stopped answering his calls within days of taking his money.

'I don't remember. A few weeks.'

'Where was that?'

'The harbour.'

'What was the nature of that meeting?'

Adam pauses. It feels like his head is full of wasps.

'He's a private investigator. A good one. I thought I might have some work to put his way. That's what I do, I guess.'

'You've worked for him before?'

'I've worked for a lot of people,' says Adam, awkwardly. 'He's used my company in the past.'

DCI Bosworth smiles at that. 'Your company? You mean yourself. We've checked with Somerset House. Your "company" was wound up three years ago. You've paid no income tax since then and you owe £54,000 in unpaid company tax. You owe more in VAT. You're still registered as living at your mother's address.'

Adam tries to smile, to show her that she's not getting to him, but he's never really been very good at playing this game. He shrugs, out of moves. 'Yeah? Bloody bureaucracy.'

'What do you do for Mr Paris's firm?'

A good question, he thinks, chewing at the inside of his cheek. He realizes the borrowed trousers are pulling at his leg hairs. Shifts, uncomfortably, as he mumbles a weak 'no comment'.

'Are you familiar with his business partner, Angus Lavery?'

'Aye, we've shared a few drinks. I've done

57

surveillance work for him. Tracked down a few people . . .'

'I understand that you've done no actual tracking down. I understand that Mr Paris or one of his colleagues does the complex aspects of the searches, and you are the muscle who goes and knocks on the door.'

'Why are you bothering me?' asks Adam, dejectedly. 'I'm just trying to get by. I'm trying.'

'Have you been to Essex in the past six weeks?' asks Bosworth, opening her folder and glancing at him. Adam glimpses a crime-scene photo. Sees a face split down the middle; all bone and putrid meat. Sees matted twine cutting deep into a rancid, bloodied neck.

'I haven't been to Essex in years.'

'When was your last communication with Mr Paris?'

Adam looks from one detective to the other, suddenly exasperated. He's as keen to know if he's to blame as they are. 'Tell me what's happened to him, please. I mean, we weren't best mates or anything but I liked the guy. I trusted him. He doesn't deserve that!'

'And who does?'

Adam looks over at the tall man in the good suit. 'Sorry?'

'You're saying some people might deserve that.' He nods at the picture in the file. 'Who?'

'What? No, I don't mean that . . .'

'I hear you,' he replies. 'Some people bring it on themselves, don't they?'

Adam looks around for help. He's feeling picked on.

Bosworth looks across at her colleague. He gives a tiny nod and she leafs through the pages in her file. She holds up a piece of paper and turns it around for him to examine. It's a hand on a dissection table, cut off at the wrist. It lays there, bloated and white, like the belly of a cod. On the palm, written in black ink, is a sequence of letters and numbers.

'Is that Larry's hand?' he asks, the colour draining from his face.

'Removed with an axe,' says Bosworth, breezily. 'Sniffer dog found it, best part of half a mile from the rest of him. We're still looking for the other one. Feet too.'

'Jesus . . .'

'And that number on his palm, Mr Nunn – that's your National Insurance number, yes?'

Adam looks up, desperate now. 'I gave him that! Called him with what he needed from me. Maybe he scribbled it on his hand, I don't know . . .'

'Mr Paris was last seen seventeen nights ago, Mr Nunn,' says the DI. 'He left his home address and drove east towards Guildford, where he parked in an NCP and bought a return ticket to King's Cross. From there, he took a taxi to Canning Town. Shortly afterwards, the signal from his mobile telephone went dead. We have CCTV footage of a man matching his description trying to access warehouse premises in Lawrence Road at 7.17 p.m. on the same day, though that hasn't been confirmed.'

'My head's spinning – slow down, please,' says Adam, pitiful to his own ears.

'Do you know a Francis Jardine?' asks Bosworth, lobbing the name like a rock.

Adam starts to stutter. 'Jardine? No . . . oy, yeah, he was in the *Guardian* a while back, wasn't he? Trying to prove he wasn't a gangster . . .'

'How about a Nicholas Kukuc?' asks Bosworth, without pause.

'Kukuc?' Adam scrunches up his face, trying to show willing. His mind is racing and he can feel the fingers in his throat again; the dream rising up from wherever it retreated when he woke.

'A man in your position – he would surely know one of those names . . .'

'Maybe,' says Adam, floundering. 'Look, you're throwing stuff at me like they're punches. I didn't take my medicine this morning. Can we stop for a bit?'

Bosworth glances at her colleague, a Paxman-mask of scorn creasing her features. 'You reckon he's genuine?' she asks. 'You think he really is this far out of his depth, or he's just putting on a good show?'

The other detective shrugs, refusing to commit. 'Maybe he's malfunctioning. Maybe he's just realized what he's got into and his software has crashed. Maybe we should reboot him, what do you reckon?'

Adam looks from one to the other. He suddenly realizes how serious this is. Realizes what a mess he's made of things for himself. He could have let them in. Could have answered their questions. Instead he let his temper out. He knows he had nothing to do with Larry's death. He'd liked him well enough but the last thing he wanted was for him to be hurt. He'd paid him in advance for a start. His thoughts start grinding together. Why had his number been on his hand? Was it something to do with the investigative work he'd undertaken on Adam's behalf? He wonders if he should just tell the whole truth. Just look into the camera and say it. I'm adopted. I paid Larry to find my birth parents. I don't want him dead because he still hasn't delivered the information I was after and I can't afford to hire anybody else . . .

'Mr Nunn?'

Adam realizes he's been asked a question. It's the big cop again, his voice gentle. 'You're in a safe place, Mr Nunn. You're among people who want to help you. I know you're not telling us the truth. Why did you meet with Mr Paris?'

Adam shakes his head. He doesn't know if he's being stubborn or strategic but he suddenly realizes that every step he's taken has made things worse for himself. What had he promised last time he'd been in trouble? That he'd keep his mouth shut. Say nothing. Make them work for their bloody money. He shakes his head.

'No comment.'

'Mr Nunn, that's the wrong approach to take . . .'

'No comment.'

'Mr Nunn, you're not helping yourself . . .'

'No comment.'

'We can do this all day, Mr Nunn . . .'

61

Adam forces himself to relax. Feels a peculiar sense of calm descend upon him. Wonders, briefly, if this sensation has a name.

He lets himself smile, and feels the scab on his lip tear open. 'So can I.'

Six

Alison Jardine considers her reflection. Her silk robe is Chinese; a riot of peacocks and cherry blossoms, all plum and purple and teal. It was a gift from Dad, boxed and tied in ribbon red as blood. There were dried flowers and a lavender bag inside. Waves of tissue paper and sugared almonds. He'd written the card himself.

To My Favourite Son, with all the love I can find.

She'd smiled at that. It's their private joke. Mr Jardine has four children but Alison has always been her father's favourite. Her three brothers have all let him down in their own way. Two are in prison and the other went to sea at sixteen, changing his name and never looking back. It is Alison, his eldest and best, who makes sure the name Jardine still means something. Alison who's been taking care of things since the old man's health took a turn for the worse and he started to spend more and more time at home: a big country house in an eye-wateringly expensive

63

pocket of rural Essex. Alison moved back in six months ago. It's a big, drafty museum of a place: just her and Dad and a couple of trusted helpers.

Alison angles her head. Takes herself in. She's never seen herself as a stunner but she's always been happy enough with her looks. Small, a little fleshy, she's had plenty of time to get used to the idea of being attractive rather than beautiful and she takes a perverse pleasure in the knowledge that her tall, willowy contemporaries are descending into their advancing years with considerably more distress. She likes to imagine all those golden-blonde, size eight bitches, sobbing as they inject Botox into their foreheads and splurge their life savings on surgeries and rejuvenation procedures; their skin puckering, spines beginning to curve, veins rising like lugworms on their shins and the backs of their age-mottled hands. Alison doesn't see herself as cruel, but she comes from a family that understands the natural order of things. In the end, everybody gets what's coming to them.

She turns from the window. Seats herself at the table and kicks one of the antique chairs into a position she can use as a footstool. The nail polish crowning her tanned toes is a shade of red that makes her think of London buses. Dad doesn't like it. *Slag red*, he calls it, though he says it with that smile of his: lopsided, teeth clenched, as if accommodating an invisible pipe.

Alison sips her coffee and feels the warmth seep into her. The kitchen isn't much changed from the days when servants and butlers busied themselves pleasing their betters: plucking fowl

64

and kneading bread, faces a mask of flour and sweat. The modern table in the centre of the cold room looks out of place, as does the giant, flat-screen TV on the wall by the entrance to the larder, wires dribbling like a rat-tail down the cracked surface to the plug by the skirting board.

'Afternoon.'

Alison shivers. Goose pimples rise from her ankles to her armpits.

'Afternoon,' she says, disguising her disquiet with a gulp of coffee. It scalds her lip, already swollen from Jimbo's rasping stubble, his sandpaper kisses.

The creature called Irons passes silently into her field of vision.

Black coat, scarf, cap, sunglasses. Jeans and work boots. Always the same. Never any alteration to the adornment of his giant, scarred, looming presence. And always that smell. A stagnant pond, concealing a forgotten corpse. An air of something dark. Something putrid. Something dead.

'Alison,' he says. 'Sleep well?'

'I hate waking this late – messes up my body clock.'

'Your father? How's his chest?'

'Well enough. You should go and see him.'

'He doesn't need me bothering him.'

'He asks after you.'

'No he doesn't. He wouldn't want me seeing him when he's poorly. He has enough on his mind. My face doesn't make people feel better, Alison.'

'Now that's just silly. He's never cared about that kind of thing.'

'I have.'

Irons looks at her over the top of his glasses. His face is a butcher's window, all pink and red, meat and offal: a rag-rug of ruined flesh. He still has to apply lotions five times a day to stop his cheeks tearing open when he laughs. Not that Irons laughs often. He's a quiet man. Hasn't engaged in much chit-chat since the brothers went to work on him with a bayonet, a blowtorch and a claw hammer.

Alison drains her coffee. Watches as Irons pours himself a mug of hot water and takes a sip. He leans with his back to the counter. Looks at her in a way that Alison isn't used to being looked at.

'We've had word. Definite. Not one we missed. Fresh.'

'Right.'

'And word's out that Kukuc won't be coming back.'

'That was always going to happen.'

'It troubles me,' he says, quietly. 'There's no chance of coincidence. Somebody did it to point the finger at you. At me. At your father.'

'And we dealt with him, didn't we? He's not much more than mince now. He'll be lining somebody's drive before the week's out. It's done with.'

Irons pauses. Blows on his hot water. 'I want to be satisfied.'

Alison pushes her hair back from her face, sweat beginning to prickle her skin. She works so hard not to let her anxieties show but Irons has always seen through her layers of protection.

66

'Now isn't the time for things to start coming apart,' she says. 'We're so bloody close.'

'Yes. That's why we need to make sure.'

Alison looks out through the glass. Broods on just how much she has to lose. She and a select group of associates have invested huge sums of money in the Docklands project. Alison has ploughed the entirety of the family fortune into buying up old buildings and parcels of land in the derelict swathe of waterfront where work will soon begin on building the stadiums which will host the finest athletes in the world when the Games come to the capital in 2012. Her dad, delirious through pain and medication, has approved the scheme in part. He'd tried something similar in the seventies, back when London was bidding to host the 1988 games. He was part of a consortium that spent colossal sums on the same forgotten warehouses and crumbling real estate: his contacts ensuring that the planning applications sailed through committee without hiccup. Alison believes he would approve of the resurrection of the scheme. There has been minimal bloodshed. Some of the old faces haven't wanted to sell, but she has good men at her disposal and those who have not bent to her will have broken instead.

'Larry Paris,' says Irons, gravel in his throat. 'You want to hear?'

Alison wraps herself in her robe. Nods, all business.

'Larry, to his mates. He's small-time. Business partner is ex-Army. Military Police. Done time for half-killing a Provisional but he's been clean

67

enough since setting up the business in '96. They do surveillance work. Paris started off in cyber security, back when computers were the size of your living room, and then did some consultancy jobs for big firms running checks on employees. Pretty straight. Put a few noses out of joint but that's the business, isn't it?'

'So why was he looking into Nicholas Kukuc?'

Irons wipes a pink tear from his cheek. 'I don't know if he was.'

'No? He was at Nicholas's warehouse, wasn't he? I mean, that's what you said. Why we did what we did . . .'

Irons sips his hot water, waiting for her to stop talking. He takes a breath. Behind his glasses, his eyes close.

'I think he was looking for us, Alison. Or your father, at the least.'

Alison looks confused. 'A private dick from Portsmouth fronting up to Dad? Who'd be daft enough?'

'I've got a lad on the edges of the investigation of the team,' says Irons, softly. 'He's sent me chapter and verse on his last movements. Every premises he visited or called in the days before he went to the warehouse – they've all been owned by your father.'

'But that doesn't mean . . .'

Irons flashes her a hard look and Alison stops talking. He nods, grateful. 'We did business out of that lock-box on Lawrence Road for a while. The one we gifted Kukuc. Quiet. No interruptions. People knew we were there. If this Paris was hoping to find Mr Jardine, it's a place

68

people would point him to in exchange for a few quid.'

Alison rubs her arms, suddenly cold. 'And what? Kukuc didn't like him poking around – saw a chance to make life difficult for us. Did him in and dumped him where he knew people would make the connection to us?'

Irons looks past her. It's a cold, grey afternoon: the sun a broken promise; the sky a lid of hammered tin. Incongruously, a jet of water arcs from the mouth of the plump, libidinous mermaid who lounges, green and gold, upon the lip of the pond. Koi carp suckle, wetly, among the great lily pads that catch the tumbling droplets as they arc back down into the water. Irons looks as though he could stare into the distance forever. His thoughts seem far away.

'I want to see his computer records,' snaps Alison, colour rising in her cheeks. 'His phone. I want to know everything about him. Wife? Kids? Who do we step on?'

Irons readjusts his sunglasses, waiting for her to stop talking. 'Whatever they know, we'll know soon enough. They took somebody in this morning. Bosworth . . .'

'The skinny bitch who thinks she's a Fed?' snorts Alison.

'A bloke that Paris and his business partner use from time to time. Couple of minor convictions. Clever lad but a bit of a fuck-up. Name of Nunn.'

'Means nothing to me,' says Alison, and begins opening drawers looking for her cigarettes. Irons hands her one of his own.

'I know the name,' says Irons, softly. He taps

69

his head. 'It's all up here. I just can't find the page I'm looking for.'

Alison sucks smoke into her lungs. 'We've done nothing wrong,' she says, reassuring herself. 'Whatever Paris was looking for, it can't be anything to do with the Docklands. We're watertight there. And this bloke that Bosworth's picked up – what's he to us? Done time, has he? Any cellmates we should be contacting? Maybe he's picked up some pad-mate gossip and thinks it's worth a few quid . . .?'

Irons places a cigarette between his own lips; two scrawny lugworms; a slash in the proving dough of his face. 'I'm going to go talk to him,' he says, in a plume of grey smoke. 'Do what needs to be done.'

Alison pauses before saying anything. She wonders what would happen if she told him not to go; to tell him that his job is to be here, with her. To run things. To keep things sweet. To keep her safe.

She grinds out her cigarette on the glistening marble of the worktop. Nods her assent.

'Make it go away,' she says, flatly. 'All of it.'

Seven

It's damp inside the car. Adam watches the steam rise from his clothes, his jaw bulging with the effort of keeping his teeth locked together. He smells of the cell they kept him in while they were processing the paperwork. Smells like the manky carrier bag they had kept his clothes inside. The whole thing is fading like a dream. He keeps having to centre himself. Has to stop erupting with small, private exclamations of amazement at the direction his day has gone. He'd been arrested! Been questioned in connection to a murder. Been grilled about names he only knows from gangland memoirs and lurid headlines. Then just as quickly he'd been let go. No apology. No explanation. He found himself blinking in the rain at the front of the police station, a dozen missed messages from Zara on his phone. He'd called her back before he did anything else. Laughed it off. Apologized for the kerfuffle and told her he'd try to pop by the restaurant later if time allowed. He told her he loved her, and meant it.

Here, now, he isn't sure what to do next. The man he hired to find his birth parents is dead. Before he died, he'd taken the time to scrawl

71

down a number implicating Adam. But Adam knows he's done nothing wrong. He's hurt people in temper, but he is a better man now than he has ever been and he's got too many problems without adding to them by killing a man to whom he has just given three grand.

He wants a drink. His liver is kicking like a foetus. He wonders if he is feeling excited or scared. He's never been sure. Taking shallow breaths, he buzzes the window down another centimetre and peers out at the terrace of squat brown houses. It doesn't help. There's a smell of Indian takeaway; a sticky scent, heavy enough to taste. It serves as a deodorant of sorts in this part of the city; a spicy cologne above the background miasma: that juicy stench of rotting cardboard and ammonia. The breeze seems gleeful as it sweeps into the car, displacing papers, scattering parking permits, riffling the clip full of receipts that hangs from the rear-view mirror. On his knee, the cigarette paper lifts off like a kite, scattering tobacco into the footwell.

'Jesus,' mumbles Adam, and suddenly feels unbearably lonely.

He glares out through the glass, wishing he could afford air con, or a radio that played more than static and soft rock. The windows of the car are dribbly with condensation and every time he smears his hand across the windscreen he only succeeds in making things worse. He can barely make out the genders of the people at the bus stop at the end of the road. He grins, madly, as the scene comes into focus. A mum with a yanked-back ponytail has ordered an offspring to lean over so she can roll a cigarette on his back.

A shape appears at the window beside him. Angus Lavery is a giant of a man. He's fiftyish: all beard and hair and yellowed false teeth. As he pulls open the passenger door and thrusts out a colossal hairy arm, Adam winces in readiness for the ritual finger-crushing that he associates with shaking the big man's hand. As ever, the hand that closes around his is warm and soft and slightly damp. Adam gives him a quick once-over. He wears jogging trousers and a short-sleeved shirt, which struggles to contain his rotund, hair-carpeted gut. There is a clatter as he throws his walking stick into the car, then plonks himself down. The chassis groans in protest as twenty-five stone of ex-Army Scotsman makes himself comfortable on the threadbare seats. Adam pushes himself back against his own door, trying to accommodate the great mountain of flesh that has just invaded the too-small space. He looks down and glimpses the black, specially made shoes that protect his ankles. He looks like he has his feet stuffed into baby seals.

Adam stays quiet until the big man has lit his cigarette. He knows Angus's quirks. He likes to get himself settled; to let his breakfast settle and to get his phlegm level in his lungs before he suffers himself to speak.

'They gave you a walloping, so I heard,' says Angus, his voice a low Glaswegian rumble. 'Brought it on yourself, like as not. Told you before, your temper does you no favours.'

Adam barks out a laugh. 'So says the man

discharged from the Military Police for taking a shovel to a paramilitary.'

'Touché,' says Angus, and it sounds peculiar in his accent.

Adam starts rolling himself a cigarette, wondering whether the big man is going to punch him in the side of the head. He has fists like basketballs.

'Why didn't you ask me?' says Angus, at last. 'I wouldn't even have charged you.'

'There's always a price, Angus,' says Adam, with a note of regret. 'You'd have waived the bill but banked the favour. You'd have had me doing something I don't want to do.'

'That's what you're good at, boy,' says Angus, turning dark eyes on him. 'You're right, though, I would have. But you'd be two grand better off and my partner wouldn't be dead.'

'Two grand? I paid three.'

Angus gives a low chuckle. 'Even dead he's got his hand in my fucking pocket.'

They sit in silence for a time, Adam wondering whether he should pretend to know more than he does, or just wait to see how things play out. He'd known Angus would call from the moment that Bosworth mentioned Paris's name. It was Adam who suggested this quiet side street, not far from where the big man takes his lunch most days, and where the waiters know better than to let the stack of poppadoms at his elbow slip to an unmanageable level. There's a faint smell of garlic and cardamom coming off him and Adam thinks he can see a whole cube of diced lamb hiding in the strands of his beard.

'I didn't need this,' says Angus, grinding out a jalfrezi-flavoured belch.

'Neither did Larry,' mutters Adam. 'How's Val?'

Angus tugs at his beard. 'Weepy. He was insured, but it will take an age to sort it all out. They were still on good terms. He wasn't bitter about the settlement. Gave her what she wanted without complaint, so if Bosworth starts thinking she's a suspect then she really is out of her depth.'

'He didn't deserve what happened,' says Adam. He looks uncomfortable. Winces, as if he's having a splinter removed from somewhere tender. 'Was it me, you reckon? Was he there for me?'

Lavery softens his features. He can look a lot like a young Father Christmas when he isn't scowling. 'If he was, that's not on you. He was doing what you paid him for. Off the books, might I add. If he hadn't been trying to trouser that extra bit of cash, maybe I'd have known what he was up to. Maybe we could have done things properly. But no, he never could resist the old cloak-and-dagger. Always saw an opportunity, did Larry. I can see it now – his eyes lighting up like Chinese lanterns the second he stumbled on the name Jardine.'

Adam pushes his hair back from his face. Watches as the windscreen wipers carve a likeness of the Sydney Opera House into the rain-jewelled glass.

'Bosworth mentioned that name. Kukuc, too.'

Angus picks at a stain on the leg of his trousers. Looks at Adam pointedly, as if waiting for more. Then he laughs, an exasperated,

75

bass-note chuckle, and his accent changes back to broad Glaswegian.

'Jesus, Adam, are you buttoned up the back? You really are a fucking chancer, aren't you? Are you playing us all or are you really clueless about all this?'

'All what?' asks Adam, unsure whether to look like he is sitting on a secret he'd rather not share. 'Look, this isn't how I wanted any of this to play out, y'know? My dad gets sick. Starts losing his marbles, tells me I'm not their real son. Then him and Mum clam up. And I try to forget it but I can't. So I ask Larry to dig into it for me. To make enquiries. And then he goes quiet on me and the next thing I'm being handcuffed and Larry's been murdered and dumped in Dedham Vale.'

'You know that name, at least,' says Angus. 'Dead Man's Vale, to those in the know.'

'Course I know it – anybody who's read a true crime book knows that once Epping Forest got too full, the London firms went upmarket. Started dropping bodies in the countryside.'

'And you know the names, yeah?' coaxes Angus.

'Mad Frank. The Brothers. The Richardsons. Billy Hill.'

'Keep going,' growls Angus. 'You'll get to Jardine eventually.'

Adam frowns. Thoughts drop into his gut like coins into a slot. 'I knew I knew the name.'

'Yeah,' says Angus. 'Now you're on it.'

'But that's nothing to do with me, is it?' asks Adam, scratching nervously at his chest. 'I just wanted a copy of my birth certificate and maybe an answer or two. I didn't send him off to this, Angus.'

Angus breathes out, heavily: his nostrils two shotgun barrels emitting great gouts of smoke. He reaches into the pocket of his short-sleeved shirt and retrieves a folded square of paper.

'Bosworth's got all our tech equipment. Every computer. Every laptop. Every phone. Turned up with a warrant the same time she told me Larry was dead. I barely had a chance to press delete on a few choice files before her team were carting stuff from the office. I was in his office when they came in, trying to find out where the sod had got to and why he hadn't been answering my calls. He always liked the cloak-and-dagger, like I said. Wouldn't buy a desk unless it had a secret compartment. Spent many a happy day gluing documents into the pages of old law books and hiding them away on his bookshelves. But I worked with him long enough to know that the important stuff was always hiding in plain sight. This was taped to the underside of his desk.'

He hands the piece of paper to Adam. It's a list of addresses, handwritten in fountain pen, and a photocopy of an 'In Memoriam' placed in the *Newham Recorder* in September, 1996. At the top, written in fountain pen, a name; at the bottom an address and more notes.

Adam.
Garner, Pamela. September 17, 1971.
Always loved and remembered. Your
presence we miss, your memory we

treasure, loving you always, forgetting you never. Time slips past, but memories last. With such sadness and love, your friend, Alison. Xx

Marketfield Road.
Potters House
West Green Road
Marinello. S?
Garlands Lodge, CA1
Highgate Cem – registrar, Bronwen Moorhouse, 0208 347 2471

'Mean anything?' asks Angus. 'I called the number. Mousy wee thing answered the phone and said the usual registrar was off sick. I pushed. She recognized Larry's name. He'd been asking questions about a plot. Early September, this was. He was trying to find out which funeral company arranged the burial. Pamela Garner. Died, aged fifteen. No headstone. She gave me more than she probably should have. I got the impression she was expecting a handout so Larry must have already paid for whatever he got.'

'And what did he get?'

'Funeral was paid for by Muirhead Storage. A warehouse firm, offices in Lawrence Road. Company director, one A. Jardine. That would be Alison, I reckon. I've run that search through a few websites. Makes interesting reading.'

Adam stares out the window, watching the people at the bus stop. Feels unfathomably sad. 'I only wanted to know who I am,' he says, quietly.

78

Lavery tugs at his beard. 'Alison Jardine. Bloody hell.'

'Makes sense that it would be on SOCA's radar,' muses Adam, wondering.

'That's who Bosworth's gunning for, don't you think? A result like that and she's queen of SOCA. You're going to be collateral damage, Adam. Going to get in the way. Fucking hell, lad – three grand and you've bought yourself a shitstorm you could see from space.'

Adam stares at the piece of paper. Thinks of Larry. Wonders whether he was alive when he went into the water. He realizes he is shivering. Can taste pond water and dirt. There are fingers in his throat and eels sliding down his gullet, coiling around his lungs, as he leaks black blood into the blacker water.

He looks again at the names. Blinks, until it comes into focus.

'I'd leave it at this, if I were you,' says Angus, fatherly. 'Go see your missus. Go see your mum and dad. They're your parents, no matter what they may have said. Forget this. No comment your way through the interviews. I'll even try and get you your money back. You're a cocky wee shite but I like you. Let this go. You don't want any part of the Jardines.'

Adam nods, trying to look grateful for the well-intended advice.

Quietly, a soft voice, right inside his head: *Maybe I do.*

Eight

Grace Senoy holds the plastic spoon to her daughter's lips and makes a last, desperate attempt at an acceptable choo-choo train noise. 'Tunnel, Tilly,' she says, pleadingly. 'Show me the tunnel.'

Tilly's lips remain steadfastly pressed together. Just for the badness of it, she turns her head away from the spoon, leaving a smear of cold, clay-like Weetabix smeared across her mouth and cheek. It's not much of an evening meal but Grace has rather given up on trying to get her to eat anything else. She smiles up at Mummy with the confidence of one who knows, even at this young age, that she is sufficiently adorable to be forgiven for pretty much anything.

Grace stands, and lifts Tilly down from the table. She gives her a chocolate biscuit. 'Go play,' she says, beaten.

Tilly gives her mum a victorious smile, then runs off into her playroom. Grace crosses to the window and pours herself another black coffee from the percolator. She stares out through the grey light and the drizzle at her front garden, with its neat, paved driveway and crew-cut grass. She catches sight of her reflection in the kitchen window, and winces. She still hasn't lost the baby

80

weight. Round shoulders and big hands. Size fourteen, for most of her life. Tight in a sixteen, now. She's taken to wearing her pyjamas until lunchtime, when she changes into slouchy jogging pants and baggy jumpers. Some days she wishes she were like the perfect mummies at playgroup, with their six-pack stomachs and gleaming skin. It just seems an extraordinary amount of effort, and she finds the thought of life without Maltesers unpalatable.

A low, yellow light suddenly blinks through the veil of the tall privet hedge which guards the property from the rest of the quiet street; all terraced houses and bay windows, where two-car families play complex games of vehicular Tetris, backing in and out of driveways and rolling their tyres over muddy grass verges.

The big silver car pulls into the driveway and Grace catches a glimpse of Adam's profile as he parks up. She steps back from the window. 'Tilly,' she shouts. 'Daddy's here.'

Tilly lets out a shriek of happiness and runs to the front door. There is a gentle knocking on the double-glazed panelling, and Tilly leaps up and pulls the handle down. She's big enough to do that now, thinks Grace. Better start locking it. She'll be off. Running down the street in her Dora slippers, looking for Daddy.

Adam bends down and scoops his giggling daughter into the air as he steps inside. Blows a raspberry on her tummy. Wriggles his hand up her T-shirt and tickles her under the chin. She screams with laughter and kicks her feet. Adam pretends to put her down, then scoops her up again.

81

'Where's my kiss?' he asks her.

Tilly puckers her lips and presses them against Adam's. They rub their noses together, saying 'mmm' and giggling, then break apart. Tilly shouts 'again, again' and they repeat the process.

Eventually, Adam looks up and sees Grace. She smiles.

'Evening,' she says. 'How's your day been?'

Adam finds himself laughing. Feels all the tension and stress and confusion of the past hours leave his body in a rush, as if the sight of his friend and his child have opened a valve somewhere inside his chest. She's always made him feel better. She was the only one of his university pals who stayed in touch after he left. Even moved to Portsmouth a few years back when a friend of one of Adam's associates tipped him the wink about a position opening up at a private school nearby. They lived together for a while, every bit as platonic as when they'd been housemates at Lancaster Uni. The night they tumbled into bed together had been dismissed an aberration, a true one-off, when Grace discovered she was expecting his child. The smile on his face when she told him the good news lasted just long enough for her to commit it to memory. Then it was pummelled flat by the weight of obstacles facing them. In the end they agreed to be parents, to stay best friends, but not to force themselves to be a couple unless it happened naturally. He'd been at the birth. He'd held her hand throughout. He'd kissed her and held her and done everything she could have asked of him and more. He just never let his kisses reach her mouth. And then he met Zara.

'It's been one peach of a day,' he says, bone-tired, but laughing.

Grace and Tilly smile too. They don't know why, but they like it when he laughs. It doesn't happen often and he's been so very cold, so very quiet, these past few weeks. 'What's so funny?' asks Grace, squeezing his forearm and making him look at her. He has had manic episodes in the past. Bought too much; made poor investments, got himself giddy on new possibilities and lost himself to exploring the honeycombs and elastic walls of his mind. She stares into him. Sees the man she knows and nothing more.

He sits down. Bounces Tilly on his knee. Tells her all of it. About Larry. Angus. DCI Bosworth. About his arrest. He only pauses to drink the coffee she has brewed, and to retrieve the bottle of Tia Maria from his daughter as she pretends she's a pirate and swigs from the bottle. When he mentions the name Jardine, Grace's eyebrows head north. She likes her true-crime books. Has a bedside table crammed full of lurid tomes by Mad Frank, Dave Courtney, Lenny McLean and just about every crook or headcase who ever met the Krays. She retrieves her laptop from beside the sofa, her look of concern replaced with excitement.

Adam falls silent as her fingers move over the keys.

'I've not met Larry, have I?' asks Grace, absent-mindedly. 'Doubt I will, now.'

'He may have come to the house a couple of times when we were sharing,' says Adam, pretending to drop Tilly and then swooping her back up, giggling. 'You'll have been at work.'

83

'Did he leave the smell?' she asks, looking up. 'There was a man used to visit sometimes – wore an aftershave that was almost a perfume. Smelled like geraniums.'

Adam nods. 'Larger than life,' he says, and his face falls as the poor choice of words hits home. He retrieves the sheet of paper that Angus had given him – the one he can't help thinking he should memorize and burn. If Bosworth comes back to pick him up, he doesn't want anything to do with Larry Paris about his person. He hands it to Grace.

'Marinello,' she reads, frowning. 'That's a cherry.'

'I don't think it is,' he smiles.

'And the registrar – unavailable?'

'Like I said.'

Grace types again at the laptop. Before Tilly came along she was working at a secondary school on the outskirts of the city. Most of her job involved child welfare. She was the Designated Safeguarding Lead: sifting through conflicting parental statements and persuading pupils into her confidence – looking for evidence that those in her care were being treated poorly. She got good at the investigative side of the job.

'Francis Jardine,' she reads, her eyes flickering over a page of text. The story is from the *Independent* and is dated April, 2002: illustrated with a photograph of a small, wiry man in an expensive coat. A lawyer, clutching a crocodile-skin briefcase, is holding the door of a palatial court building and even though the image is still, his posture suggests he is in no hurry to get inside.

Grace turns the screen. Adam moves closer and nods, curtly. He recognizes him. Grace does too.

'We watched that documentary together,' she prompts. 'The Irish presenter – the one who went undercover to expose football hooligans.'

Adam nods again, his lips pursed. 'Real deal,' he mutters.

'"People stand up when he walks in",' reads Grace, turning the laptop back towards herself and using her best newsreader voice. '"It's like having a pop star or the pope in the room. He's got an air of super-confidence about him, and there's good reason for that. He behaves the way we all would if we knew with absolute certainty that there will be no repercussions. He's been around long enough to be as close to bulletproof as you can get in this game. The numbers are silly when you try and get a handle on what he's worth. The last estimate was north of £300 million, but how do you know for sure? On paper he runs a business selling warehouse space and dabbling in waterfront property. In reality, he's got a finger in every pie worth biting in London . . ."'

'Nice quote,' says Adam, begrudgingly.

'". . . does the things that other people just threaten to do. Rumour has it that most of the Mockney gangster movies are based on the legends that have sprung up around him. He's a big fan of electrocution as torture, though word has it he likes to use barbed wire most of all . . ."' She stops, eyes wide. 'Bloody hell, no wonder he sued!'

'Sorry?' asks Adam, quietly.

'The piece is from a Court of Appeal hearing. A broadsheet newspaper was fighting for the right to call him a gangster. He was trying to block it. Most of this stuff came out in open court so it's covered by the ruling. According to Mr Justice Farrell, Jardine's everything the journalist claims, and more. Here, come look.'

Adam purses his lips as he considers the image. 'Certainly looks the part. If Bosworth's looking for somebody to pin Larry on, he's a better bet than me, don't you think?'

'Untouchable,' says Grace, tactfully. 'That's the point of this piece. It's a profile called "The Rise and Rise of The Untouchable Gangster". That doesn't suggest that many people have been able to catch him – even if he is involved in this.'

'Thanks for your encouragement,' says Adam, pulling a face. 'Should I pack a bag for prison now or later?'

Grace ignores him and continues to read out choice snippets from the article. '"Born in Canning Town in 1933, father Billy a petty criminal who served time for bank robberies. Francis was a promising boxer, trained at the same gym as the Krays . . . running his own firm by the age of twenty-three . . . name appears in police reports when the twins were at war with the Richardson brothers . . . avoided prison, began running extortion rackets, armed robberies, drugs, alleged involvement in a blackmail scam that earned him a colossal pay-day from a minor royal and senior members of the House of Lords . . ."'

'Oh brilliant,' mutters Adam, laying back on the carpet, beaten. Tilly, dutifully, imitates him.

He turns and presses his forehead to his daughter's.

'Daddy. Hug.'

'All I wanted was some answers about my biological parents,' he says, softly, holding Tilly as if she is about to float away.

Grace, deep in thought, doesn't register the catch in his voice. She ploughs on, thinking aloud. 'Well, his eyes are green and yours are blue, so if Larry was working on something sensational, the biology might not work . . .'

Adam sits up. 'Don't be silly,' he says, with a forced laugh. 'That's not even . . . why would you say that?'

Grace shrugs, embarrassed. 'It would be so much easier if you just spoke to your mum and dad,' she blusters.

'My mum will stand still and say nothing,' sighs Adam. 'And Dad's not even sure what day it is.'

'But they must have some paperwork. A birth certificate . . .'

'That's what Larry was supposed to be finding for me. I mean, we celebrate my birthday on September 24th, so he should have been able to find it . . .'

'But that's not necessarily your real birthday,' says Grace, a little sadly. 'I mean, that's what your mum always told you it was, but what if it's not?'

Adam rubs his hand through his hair. Grace can see he wants a cigarette but he would never roll up or light up in her house, and never in front of his daughter.

'September 24th,' she says, and reaches over to grab the piece of paper Larry had left under his desk-lamp. 'You were born '71, yes?'

'Yeah,' he says, then shrugs. 'Two years younger than you, remember.'

'And seven years younger than Zara,' says Grace, automatically. Her voice drips with disdain as she says it. 'Pamela Garner,' she adds, before he can offer reprimand. 'Died on September 17th, 1971. That's a week after you were born.'

'Yeah, I worked that out,' says Adam, and pulls Tilly closer. He kisses her head, wearing sadness and bewilderment like a well-cut suit.

'I'll check,' says Grace, her fingers swift on the keys. She types the relevant names into Google. 'Garner, Pamela. Francis Jardine. Should I put in Kukuc? Yes, I will . . . here we are . . .' She shakes her head. 'Plenty on Jardine. Kukuc is mentioned in an article on a true-crime website – a man called King Rat. He's written books on all the famous names. Hang on . . . there's a blog and a forum, loads of people arguing about who'd win in a fight between Lenny McLean and somebody called Gypsy Joe. All men – what a shock. Somebody here called Dabbler22 – he says Kukuc has lost his bottle, done a runner. Did Angus mention that to you. God, these people are obsessive . . .'

'My brain's hurting, Grace,' says Adam, and Tilly puts her small, warm hand upon his head. Adam reacts like a happy cat.

'I could ring him,' says Grace, brightly. 'There's a mobile number here.'

'For who?'

'This King Rat. He seems to know his stuff. He might recognize the name – maybe shed some light . . .'

Adam laughs. 'Grace, I appreciate that you want to help but it's specialized work. You're a teacher. And I'm, well, I'm not anybody really . . .'

'But you've paid money to find answers. And it's possible that looking for those answers cost Larry his life.'

Adam pulls a face. 'I don't want that to be true.'

'No, but it's possible. And it's also possible it's going to cause you problems. You got arrested, for goodness' sake.'

'Only because I was a prick about it,' he says, feebly.

Grace picks up her mobile from the windowsill and starts typing in the number. Adam waves his hands. He doesn't seem to want things to move from this position; seems happier letting every possibility exist. She realizes she is enjoying this a little too much. She's excited. Pointedly, embarrassed with herself, she puts the phone down.

They brood for a moment, then Adam says, 'Fucking hell,' and drains his coffee. He pulls himself up and Tilly lets out a squawk, overcome with fear that he might leave. Grace isn't sure whether to spare him the torture of confirming his daughter's fears. She could be the bad guy here – could tell their child that Daddy is needed elsewhere and that she shouldn't make him feel bad for working so hard. But to do so would make her a liar. Adam only works hard in the sense that he manages to stay one step ahead of the problems he causes for himself. If he could only tolerate reality; if he could handle a domestic set-up and the shackles of fidelity, he could be here, with her and his child, all the time. At once, she feels bad for thinking such disloyal thoughts. Grace can see him struggling to digest all of this information. She knows how hard this is for him. She knows what his family, his real family, mean to him. Despite her enjoyment that he has shared his confusion with her these past months, she is angry that he is having to endure such feelings. His father's words did more than pull the rug out from under him. They buried him up to his neck in guilt and bewilderment and left him gasping for air.

'Shit, it's Mum,' says Adam, as a buzzing noise emanates from his back pocket and Tilly points out that his 'hone' is going '*bzz*'. He takes the call, trying to sound bright. 'Hiya. Yeah, I'll be there. No, no of course not. Same old, same old. Just with Tilly. Yeah. You can talk to her if you want . . . okay, another time . . .'

As he talks, Grace picks up her own phone. She smiles at Tilly, who has picked up a Lego creation and is talking into it like a mobile, keen to be part of the gang. Quickly, she types out a text message and sends it to the number on the bottom of the website.

Hi – I'm a researcher. I'd like to know about a girl called Pamela Garner who died in 1971. There may be a link to Francis Jardine. Would you be able to help? On the QT, of course.

90

She sends it without a second thought, rather pleased with herself for striking the right tone. Then she turns her attention back to Adam, convinced he will see that she has done the right thing. He's still talking – tickling Tilly with his foot as he stands, awkwardly, staring out the window as if planning an escape and holding the phone to his ear.

'. . . of course I remember him, he was Dad's, wasn't he? Sorry, partner. Aye, loudmouth but one of the good ones. Okay, whatever. Right, I'll see you when I'm looking at you . . . ace. Bye. Bye.'

Adam hangs up and gives Grace a knowing look. She has long since stopped teasing him for the sickeningly insincere way he speaks to his mother. He treats her like she's made of glass and rose petals, though she supposes he learned that from his father. If she were to think about it at all, Grace would probably admit that she thinks of Adam's mum in a fond, bemused, kind of way. Bit dotty. Bit flighty. Frail and high-pitched; good-natured and kind. She doesn't know what to make of his dad. Strong. A big man. Loud. Solid. Down-to-earth, but clever with it, before his mind started to slip last year. Something about him, though. Something harsh, underneath the smiles and the old-fashioned shades of chivalry. He is always civil to her, though, in their rare meetings. Offers tea. Asks her about her work. Had given her a kiss and a cuddle when she and Adam told him she was pregnant.

'I thought you were just friends,' he'd said.

91

'We are,' Adam had replied. 'It just happened.'

She'd wanted him to say something more powerful, more lusty and romantic, but all she heard was apology. He'd been OK about it all, though, for a man of his age. Didn't disapprove when they said they were going to lead separate lives. Said his son would have his blessing no matter what he chose to do or whom he chose to do it with. Good with Tilly, too. Good with all kids, Adam had said. Used to have half the neighbourhood in his house when Adam was growing up, making them Roman swords and shields amid the sawdust and poster-paint of his shed; spinning tales about adventures after the war. Grace found it all strangely disingenuous, now.

'I should go,' says Adam, shyly. 'An old colleague of Dad's has been round, or he's coming round – she's in a flap. Needs biscuits and the right kind of milk, or something. Look, thanks for letting me offload on you, and yes, I realize how mucky that sounds. Honestly, you're the best. I don't know what I'd do without you.'

Grace grins, madly, and accepts the cuddle that he offers. She fancies that he may have sniffed her hair as he held her. Certainly she took the chance to press her nose into his neck. Tobacco. Soap. Clothes dried in a too-damp room. And something else, too. Something animal and raw, that makes her want to rake Zara's eyeballs out of her stupid bald head and squish them between her toes.

'I'll call you,' he says, as he makes a fuss over Tilly and tells her to be a good girl.

'Nooo . . . Daddy stay . . .'

'Please, Tilly . . .'

'Peeese, Daddy . . .'

'I can't, baby girl . . .'

'Can. Can!'

'Oh Jesus, fine . . . Grace, can I take the car seat?'

Grace nods, grateful that she has not interceded. She cannot commend her daughter's emotional manipulation skills, but she will admit to being grateful for their efficacy. She looks away in case her smile should betray her, listening as Tilly starts shouting 'woo-woo' and 'shoe-shoe' as Adam wrestles her into her outdoor clothes. Blurrily, her eyes land on the screen of her phone. It's a reply from King Rat, written in capital letters.

FREE TO TALK NOW. IF YOU'RE A MATE OF LARRY PARIS, I'M SORRY FOR YOUR LOSS. IF YOU'RE NOT A MATE OF LARRY PARIS, YOU WONT GET A CHANCE. HA HA.

For once, Grace is pleased to see the back of the man she tries so hard not to love.

Nine

Under a canopy of grey, his feet sinking into sodden grass and coffee-dark mud, Irons stalks purposefully through the woods. The strong wind, which has ensured his isolation on this afternoon walk, seems to split around him, like water around a boulder. He has his phone to his ear, and each word spoken seems to drive another nail into his wounded skin.

'Say that again,' he growls. 'Say it like you would if I was standing over you.'

The bent copper at the end of the line has a tremble in his voice, as if he's talking while being observed by a slavering pit bull.

'Bosworth's briefed the unit. This Nunn, the one they picked up and let go at lunch – he's saying that he hired Paris to look into a personal matter for him. Says they do a bit of work together – he handles odd jobs, dirty work, all the off-book stuff. He didn't blink at the mention of our, erm, mutual friend. Nor the other one – the dead one, though Bosworth's already hearing rumours on that front . . .'

'Leave that to me,' growls Irons, stomping his booted feet harder into the damp ground.

'They've done a proper trace on Paris's phone, bounced the signals off all the towers – his route went through half a dozen premises all associated with our mutual friend . . .'

'You told me that already.'

'The post-mortem,' he says, urgently. 'They had to bring in an expert from the university because the pathologist couldn't be sure but it appeared as though somebody had gone to great lengths to make it look like he'd been in the water a very long time. The skin is in a state completely inconsistent with being submerged for such a short time. It was like he'd been parboiled before going in . . . we thought we had something from decades ago when he was pulled out but it couldn't have been there any longer than twenty-three days. The skin samples show he was in contact with a substance called methylene chloride – do you know what that is?'

'Of course I fucking do,' he snaps.

'Paint stripper,' says the copper, urgently. 'That's as much our mutual friend's calling card as barbed wire and a car battery.'

'Cause of death?' asks Irons, without emotion.

'Multiple injuries, but there's a hole in the skull that looks like it was put there by a fucking Viking.'

Irons says nothing. A faint whisper of regret is starting to reverberate inside his head. He didn't speak up when Alison suggested using the discovery of Larry Paris's body as an excuse to take out an ambitious rival, Nicholas Kukuc. It's what her father would have done, were he able. But now he is beginning to wonder whether or not she may have accidentally stumbled onto a truth. Somebody seems to be trying to point the finger at the Jardines. And by extension, they're pointing the finger at him. Mr Jardine rarely wielded the weapons himself. He was happy enough to stand there and ask his questions and smoke his cigarettes but it was always Irons who made the men scream on his behalf. Always Irons who sank the barbed wire into their fleshy parts and connected up the battery. It was Irons who had to spend a godawful night in the woods at Dead Man's Vale, pulling out body parts, barbed wire and old bin bags from the soft mud at the bottom of the pond where he had dumped half a dozen old friends back when the world was a more psychedelic place. It had been unsettling, seeing them all again. Some of them seemed to have aged better than he had.

'I can't keep sneaking away like this,' comes the voice in his ear. 'Bosworth's heading back to London so if you're going to lean on Nunn, now would be the time. This is worth something, yeah? Only I think she got suspicious, and . . .'

Through the trees he sees them. Two young men and a girl. They're all skinny. All got bad skin and eyes that never seem still. Timothy Jardine, his pal Logan, and the girl they seem to share as if she were a bag of pick-and-mix. She's dressed for Malibu despite the chill and bluster of the day: a tiny top showing jewelled midriff and a skirt short enough to wear as a hat. Her bare legs are the colour of cheap ham. Even so, she could do better than Tim and Logan. Were it not for his surname and the money in his trust fund, Timmy would struggle to attract anything further up the evolutionary ladder than a macaque.

Irons stands still and watches. This little clearing, half a mile from his own quiet cottage, seems to have bypassed autumn and gone straight to winter. It's bitterly cold, and the rain blows in from every angle. Timmy is lounging on what used to be a boundary wall, but which has settled into the damp earth in the decades since Mr Jardine bought the estate and told the tenant farmer they were about to retire to somewhere warm.

From behind the mossy trunk of a big sycamore, Irons considers the young man. He was already a tearaway when Irons had been released from prison for gutting Tommy Dozzle. Six years old and getting expelled from expensive schools for sticking pins and needles into the fleshy places of pupils he didn't like, and rubbing himself against the legs of those that he did. Irons does not claim to understand the complexities of raising a child but from what he has seen, Alison has done her best with her parcel of damaged goods. She's been through tough times herself and has never been a natural mother. Irons, in his moments of introspection, wonders whether the thing that happened to her best friend had also, in some unfathomable way, happened to her too. She had lost the only person who understood her. She had seen the vulnerabilities in her father's armour. The man who knocked her up had no doubt enjoyed bragging to his mates that he'd fucked a Jardine. Franco had personally put him in the water at Dead Man's Vale. Alison had agreed to it.

Turned her back on some of her bad ways in exchange for coming back into the fold, and allowing her dad to bind her lover in barbed wire and smash in his skull with a caulking mallet.

Irons looks again at the boy. He'd done okay the other night, out at the airport, hiding in the loft hatch with his gun. But he'd enjoyed it a little too much. Irons knows what it is to take a life. He understands the magnitude of it. Timmy seems positively hungry for opportunity.

He watches, silently, as Logan passes Timmy the clear polythene bag and the aerosol. Watches him suck throatily at the solvent, then lay back on the mossed stone as if in ecstasy. The girl takes the bag from his hand. Treats herself to a hit, then starts to tug at his jogging trousers. Her eyes are dead.

Irons turns away. He has no appetite for seeing young girls degrade themselves. Were Tim's surname different, Irons would plant him where he lays. But he is kin to the man he serves, and the only time he has gone against an order it cost him eighteen years of his life.

He experiences a moment's weakness, his resolve faltering for just long enough for the memories to reach out for him.

Inside, he hears her voice. The angel's song.

He can almost see her, hovering just out of reach.

Can almost feel her hair tickling his still-handsome features as she giggles into his blue eyes.

Can almost see Pamela.

Pam.

Can almost see the child he couldn't save, and whose desecration haunts him like a burned church.

Pain stings his chest and he savours it. Pain means his heart still beats, and where there's life, there's still hope for a man who deals in death.

He forces himself to move. Turns his back on the clearing and trudges on through the woods towards the road. He half hopes that the fresh air will blow away some of the corruption in his lungs. All the people who've tried to take him down and it'll be his own metastasizing cells that will kill him. He hasn't had time to think much about the doctor's diagnosis. Six months, she reckons, though he won't let it get that far. He'll go once Mr Jardine has slipped away. It seems right that they enter the next world together. They've always walked side by side through this one, and he fancies that he will need an ally in the afterlife. He fancies Mr Jardine will be running Hell within the year. If not, he doubts the fire and brimstone will hurt any more than the wounds he has experienced in life.

Thoughts of his own mortality cause a vision of Alison to flash inside his mind. He should tell her, he thinks. Should start making contingency plans. She's tough and capable, but she's not her father, and neither Jimbo nor her halfwit son are capable of doing the things on her behalf that he has done, without flinching, for as long as he can remember. Even when the twins went to work on him, he took what they dished out without once letting the family down. His kind of loyalty is absolute.

The woodland thins out as Irons pushes through the tangle of trees and emerges in a clearing, criss-crossed with deep tyre tracks. His new vehicle is waiting for him, the keys in the ignition. He pulls open the door of the eight-year-old Toyota pick-up truck. Checks beneath the passenger seat to ascertain that the other items he has requested are where they should be. He slides his gloved hand along the blade of the bayonet and is gratified to feel the soft leather slice like ripe fruit. He doesn't check that the gun is loaded. Nobody would be fool enough to double-cross him.

He turns the key and eases the car forward. He fiddles with the radio and finds a classical station. The vehicle fills with the angelic sounds of an aria from *La Bohème*. He hopes it's just starting. He has a couple of hours of driving ahead of him and he has always found opera to be a soothing soundtrack to a journey. It always drowns out the screaming in his head. He hopes, too, that something similar will be playing on the drive back. He fancies that there will be fresh shrieks to soothe.

Ten

Grace glances at the clock above her fireplace. King Rat has now been talking, without interruption, for forty minutes straight. She feels as though a snooker cue is being inserted, one millimetre at a time, into her ear.

'. . . *wouldn't know a proper gangster if he was sitting on his chest with a hacksaw and a sock full of batteries, but he gets the money, y'see, because he looks the part and he's got the wonky nose and the gold chains, whereas I'm more sort of, well, a bit Timothy Spall, if you catch my drift . . .'*

Grace now knows more about King Rat than she does about anybody else. Almost all of what he has shared has been about himself, his underworld connections, and how he's the only author that the gangsters really trust. He'd have been boss of his own firm by now, if he hadn't met the wife. Bad lad. Proper tearaway. Ran with them all. Had to get pretty shirty with the brothers one night in Tangiers in 1968 – had to tell Ronnie he wasn't like that and that he'd only worn the extra-tight trunks to show off his flat gut. Knows them all, now. Doesn't fear repercussions because there are people who would do time in order to show they had his back . . .

Grace has given up trying to get a word in. She

hopes that he will eventually run out of breath, though so far, he hasn't given any indication that he's preparing for a pause.

'. . . but that leads me to your boy Larry, of course,' he says, his accent a mess of mangled vowels and missing consonants. Every 'u' is an 'a', every 'h' absent without leave. 'Poor bastard. I got the call twenty-five minutes after the cops did. Body in Dedham Vale? Thought I was having déjà vu . . .'

'You know the place,' says Grace, pleased to find her voice still works.

'You'll have seen the documentary, of course,' continues King Rat, and it's not a question. 'It was only on one of the satellite channels but it got good numbers. Had me looking proper moody, pratting about in the cold. I thought maybe they'd blur me out but to be honest that would have defeated the purpose of the exercise. I've got books to sell, love. That's why I called you back. Researcher, you said. BBC, is it?'

Grace ignores the question. 'You knew at once I was ringing about Larry Paris. How?'

'I watch the forums,' says King Rat, with a smile. 'Bit of software they make in Korea – gives you the IP address of every casual observer of the chatrooms, unless they've got the software installed to block it. Yours is Portsmouth. Larry Paris is Portsmouth.'

'I'm sorry for your loss,' says Grace, automatically.

'No real loss,' says King Rat, breezily. 'We weren't pals. I do feel like a bit of a prick for not warning him off, but he was a grown man.

I swear, I wouldn't have wanted to go through what he went through at the end. If whoever did this is trying to make it look like it was Effie, they'll have needed a strong stomach.'

'Effie?' asks Grace, reluctant to waste the pause for breath.

'Just a nickname, love – in case the one he prefers isn't one he'd thank me to have in my mouth.'

'Who are you talking about?' she asks, hoping she still sounds like a researcher for a TV company and not a stay-at-home mum who's worrying about her best friend.

'You don't know very much, do you,' he says, without malice. 'Dedham Vale is where Jardine used to dump bodies. Dead Man's Vale, that's what the locals call it. Wouldn't want to go there after dark – I reckon the place is crawling with the ghosts of dead gangsters, but I won't say that on air if you think it's too much. Anyways, I've got it on good authority there's no dead men there any more. Jardine's men cleared it out when it was being touted for sale as a private woodland. Grim job for some poor bastard—'

'I'm sorry,' interrupts Grace, her head spinning. 'If I could just steer us back on track – exactly how did Larry contact you? And why?'

'Oh, did I not say? Bloody hell I'm getting old. Same as you, love. Google search led him to a Wikipedia page and that led him to my homepage. He got himself on the forums, I checked him out, called him back – put the wind up him a bit when I said I knew all about him. That's me, love. Knowledge is power, and all that. Anyways, we got talking, he said he was looking for information on Pamela Garner, same as you. I made a couple of calls on his behalf.'

'For a fee?'

'There would have been, though I doubt it'll be paid now. It wasn't a hardship. I've got old pals in every borough in the East End so it's never a big job finding stuff out.'

Alison suddenly realizes there's a gap in the conversation. King Rat seems momentarily unsure whether to press on with his story.

'Pamela Garner,' she says, quietly, trying to make it sound like they both know a secret that the world does not. 'I think we're on the same page.'

Something like a sigh of relief crackles out of the receiver. King Rat seems far happier with noise than silence and Alison hasn't had to push very hard to get him to continue talking.

'Tragic case was Pamela,' says King Rat, and his sadness sounds genuine, even through the cigarette smoke. 'Big pals with Alison when she was a nipper. Went to the same posh school as she did, even lived in their big house out Dunmow Way. Close as sisters, the way I heard it. Bloody horrible what happened to the lass.'

'Well, of course . . .'

'Like I told Larry, he might be as well to leave that one alone. Whoever did for Pamela will have already had their punishment, mark my words. To do that to a girl of that age? They won't have stopped killing him for months. Jardine's a ruthless cunt, and I mean that with all due respect. And Effie – well, he's a fucking monster.'

Grace frowns, trying to disentangle it all. 'Sorry,' she mumbles. 'For clarity, you're saying you think Larry upset the wrong person?'

A laugh snuffles down the receiver, as if somebody is tickling a pig. 'Hell love, I just throw the theories in the air and see who shoots them. But if Larry went wading in, knocking on doors, trying to stir up memories, well it's no surprise it cost him, though I'd have given one whole bollock and half an arm to know what he found out before it all went tits up. Will you want me to say all this again on camera, by the way? Telly, was it? Which channel?'

Grace realizes her leg is jiggling up and down. She's sweating across her shoulders and back.

'Have you spoken to a DCI Bosworth about this?' she asks, surprised at herself for remembering the name.

'The shooting star? No, I don't go out of my way to help the coppers – my reputation depends on it. I'm not a grass. I know a lot and I'm not frightened to tell the truth but I don't go out of my way to make new enemies – least of all when there's this new breed coming in who don't seem to respect the rules. You'll have heard Nick Kukuc has done a bunk, have you? Greasy little weasel. He won't be missed. Wouldn't surprise me if he's in the ground somewhere, though plenty say he's in Witness Protection or sunning himself somewhere pretty. Alison's her old man's daughter. She won't have thanked him for making waves, though I doubt he had the brains to do Larry in and make it look like Effie did it. Besides, he'll be too old for that caper now anyway. Must be seventy-five if he's a day.'

Grace takes a moment to pretend to glance at her notes. 'Larry visited various properties owned by a firm with links to Alison Jardine . . .'

'Silly bastard. Well, that's that, then. Probably saw a chance at an easy payday. Did he have a wife? Kids? Not that it makes it any worse, mind – everybody who dies is mourned by somebody. Maybe not Effie. Respected, yes. I doubt he was ever loved.'

'I presume you wouldn't recommend me trying to speak to Alison Jardine about her old friend, would you?' asks Grace, and there is a catch in her voice.

'What's the worst that can happen?' asks King Rat, laughing. 'Of course, I said the same to Larry, and now he's on a slab, but he was a private investigator with a habit of lining his pocket. You might get further. Tell me again, was it ITV? It's just I've a book coming out in the New Year and if you use me as a talking head I'm going to want the title in the caption, yeah? If you hang about I'll find you a number for the snooker club.'

'Snooker club?'

'If you're wanting her that's where she is – unless she's down Bayswater having her nails done or her fanny waxed or whatever it is she does when she's not buying up great bloody chunks of Canning Town. I swear, she's going to be richer than her old fella. Would make him proud, if he were still well enough to know about any of it.'

106

Grace writes the number down. Bluffs her way through a thank you and a promise to call him back. Then she hangs up.

Only then does she let out the breath she has been holding.

Adam, she thinks, and the thought is full of tears.

Eleven

Dysart Avenue, Drayton, Portsmouth
7.36 p.m.

'Coming into money,' says Pat, counting the bubbles in the top of Adam's mug. 'That's a fortune I've poured you.'

'Thanks,' he says, from behind his hand.

'You can stop covering up,' she says, over her shoulder. 'I spotted the split lip. Fingers too. I'm sure you had your reasons. Least said, soonest mended, eh?'

'Thanks, Mum.'

Pat puts the teapot back on the work surface and begins putting biscuits on a patterned plate. She hums to herself, nervous, fingers nimble despite the arthritis; fussing and fidgeting and smoothing down her apron every time she bends down or stands back up.

Adam takes the opportunity to look at her properly. Stares at her looking for something familiar – some curve of jaw or hereditary protuberance that might suggest they share the same blood. Sees nothing. Doesn't know whether to feel depressed or relieved. She has aged a lot recently, looking after Billy. The skin beneath her neck and arms looks loose and dangly, and her back, which has begun to curve in recent years, is now positively humped. She's dressed today in a pleated beige skirt, blue jumper and cardigan, and has recently decided to stop dyeing her hair. The last of the bottle brown she has branded herself with for the last four decades now flecks the tips of her curly grey perm.

'What about the little one?' she asks. 'I got some of those Froosh Toots when I was at Morrisons. Does she still like them?'

'Fruit Shoots, you mean? Yeah, she loves them.'

Pat makes a low grunt of exertion as she bends down to the cupboard by her knees and pulls out a bottle of flavoured water, which she hands to Adam. He takes the top off and calls Tilly through from the front room, where she is playing with building blocks in front of the TV. She takes the bottle with a smile and a ''nk you' then toddles off back to her game.

'She's got lovely manners,' says Pat.

'We try.'

They stand in silence for a moment in the kitchen of the tiny bungalow, with its neat gardens and double glazing and its wall insulation and its four-bar electric fire and its geriatric neighbours. Knackers Yard, Pat called it, before she began to sense that such things upset her son. God's Waiting Room.

Adam feels his spirits settle, like lime juice sinking to the bottom of a glass of soda water. He nods at the wall which divides the kitchen from the guest bedroom. 'Any improvement?'

They consider the invalid in the next room. Billy Nunn is dying, they both know that. The asbestosis in his lungs is turning him the colour of a garden statue: all cracked greys and streaky, rain-lashed greens. His dry smoker's cough, so familiar to Adam in his youth, is now a wet, nauseating thing filled with lumps of phlegm and cherries of blood. He's shrunk, too. His big, imposing frame is slowly deflating, and he lays beneath the clean sheets of the guest bed like a cold sausage between slices of white bread. It'll get him soon, the doctors say. He won't be here much longer.

'They were talking about the hospice again,' says Pat, shaking her head. 'Cheek of it.'

'Do you really feel up to this, though, Mum? You look exhausted. And he's only going to get worse.'

'I've looked after him these past months, haven't I? And besides, he's on the mend.'

Adam, looking up at the clock on the wall-mounted microwave, allows his mother the lie. They both know that Billy's mind is unravelling. It began years ago, when he became convinced he had a hair on the end of his tongue. He would sit for hours, worrying at his mouth with his thumb and forefinger, trying to catch the end of the non-existent irritation. Then the library in his mind started misfiling people. Family members suddenly exchanged names. Children were suddenly old friends. He would ask after work colleagues who had been dead thirty years. Then last year he got up at six thirty and started making his bait for work. Pat had found him in the kitchen, grumbling that there was no luncheon meat for his butties and telling her he had planned to be on the road for seven. Pat, frightened and confused, had to tell him he had been retired more than ten

110

years. He'd got cross with her, then. Told her he wasn't in the mood for wind-ups. Told her to give Adam a kiss for him and then he'd gone outside. He'd been back in, moments later, furious, flustered, telling her the car had been stolen and to phone the police. Saying that he couldn't ask Mally Santinello to cut him any more slack on his time-keeping.

That was the start of the ugly, slithering descent that had grabbed Pat by the ankle and threatened to pull her down too.

'Are you going on through, then?' she asks, pointedly. 'He might be waking up right about now and he's better about this time.'

Adam knows he can't put it off any longer. Knows he has to face him, even as the name 'Francis Jardine' kicks away at his insides. He wishes that Billy Nunn would get better just for long enough to give him some advice on what the hell to do next. Billy's always been a capable man. Does what has to be done. Decent, hard-working, easy to chat to. Adam's always been proud to call him 'Dad' and seeing him so reduced only makes it harder not to be grateful that his own blood may have sprung from another source. God, how he wants to ask him.

He changes so much every week, he tells Grace. It's like seeing photographs of the stages of deterioration. Every time I open that door, he's shrunk a little and his face has sagged a little more and his colours gone a shade more sickly.

Adam takes a breath, like a nervous smoker sucking on a filter tip. Pushes the door. Into half-light and a fog of hospital smells . . .

Against the white of the pillow, Billy's face is the colour of butter that has melted and reformed. His eyes are closed, but his expression changes in accordance with the different sensations that stab at his guts and grate at his lungs. To Adam, he seems like a newborn baby; his world turned inwards, his countenance a mirror of his hunger and thirst, his pain and irritation.

'Dad?'

'I can hear every bloody word, y'know,' rasps Billy, not opening his eyes. 'These walls are made of spit and paper.'

Adam closes the door behind himself and leans against it. He's smiling, because his dad is behaving like his dad, and not the crazy man who has been wearing his ever more ragged skin these past months.

The room is half-dark, the way Billy likes it. A lamp sits on a chest of drawers, a handkerchief over the shade to drown the glare of the bulb. The curtains are open no more than a crack. A bedside cabinet serves as a plinth for Billy's necessities. There's a sewing kit, emptied of needles and thread, and filled with his daily doses of pills, divided into compartments, and neatly labelled with times and doses. His 'sweeties', Pat calls them. They sit beside an untouched cup of tea. A jug of water and a half-empty glass. The grey mask that the doctor will plug into the oxygen cylinder when he calls this afternoon. Billy's cream, rubbed into his skin each day for more than thirty years, cooling the burn and salving the broad pink fossil on his chest and shoulder. A picture of Billy and Pat, trouser legs rolled up, jumping waves on the beach at

Lytham; each holding one of Adam's plump, toddler hands.

'You feeling well enough to grouse then, are you, Dad?' Adam finds himself stumbling over this word, now an impostor on his tongue.

'Feeling well enough to give you a bloody good hiding,' says Billy. His voice is like parchment rustling.

Adam sits on the foot of the bed. The old man's hands lay on top of the blankets, and he wonders if today he will reach out and take one of them in his own. He knows he will not.

'Where's the pain?'

'Every-bloody-where. I feel like I've been wanting a shit since May.'

'Maybe you have.'

'You seen the size of me? I let this one go I'll drop to under a stone.'

They sit in silence, until eventually, Billy turns his head and opens his eyes. They're wet and rheumy. Grey-green.

'Do I hear the little one? Young whatshername?'

'You know her name.'

'Aye, but I'd rather not use it. Who would give a little one that cross to bear?'

'It's a lovely name. It rhymes with Billy, for God's sake.'

'So does Willy and Silly and both of them go better with Nunn.'

'Dad . . .'

'It's a bloody good name, Nunn. Goes back generations. Why can't you just marry that darky and then you can call her what you want?'

Adam sighs and lowers his head. He half hopes

that Billy will slip into his usual confusion so they can drop this. So he can go. Leave. Continue his betrayal. Find himself a father to replace the crinkled lump in the bed.

Billy will never understand why Tilly has got Grace's surname. Nor can he fathom why Adam lives with somebody else, with kids that aren't his. 'You're in a pickle, son,' he says. 'One grandchild you give me, and she's got somebody else's name. Then you shack up with another one and they aren't Nunns either . . .'

A cloud drifts across his face, blocking the sun. He's gone again.

'They like the scar,' says Billy, suddenly. 'All the women like the scar.' Billy's eyes snap open and he begins to pull down the bedcovers. 'You seen it?' he asks.

'Only every day for my whole life, Dad,' says Adam, standing, trying to stop his father; wondering why, suddenly, he seems to want to show everybody a wound he spent so much of his life covering, greasing, soothing, hiding.

'Saw my own skin peel off,' he says, proudly. 'Still had hairs on it as it unrolled and lifted off, like a sheet of asbestos. Could smell my own flesh burning. That's what I think Hell smells like, don't you . . .'

Billy is unbuttoning his pyjama top, now, eyes still closed. Adam is standing up, leaning over him, trying to pin down hands that feel and look like dry twigs stripped of bark. Billy tears the top button off his striped top and Adam glimpses the top of the wound that has branded his father for half of his lifetime.

114

'Was lighting a cigarette in the wind,' he's saying, wheezing, his words almost a cough. 'Forgot I'd been using turps. I was covered in white spirits, I was. Ducked out for a fag, couldn't get it lit. Lifted my coat over my head, struck a match. Went up like a bloody volcano, I did. Put myself out. Didn't find me for hours. I was in a hospital bed, wrapped up like a mummy, stinking like a bacon sandwich, and Mally walks in and says, "Billy, that Nunn of yours must have been looking down on you . . ."'

Billy's hands suddenly contort as a cough kicks him in the chest and he starts hacking and bringing up great handfuls of phlegm. It runs down his chin and neck like slime.

Adam stands, repulsed, confused, feeling hopeless and guilty and useless, until the door opens and Pat comes in, matronly, a box of tissues in her hand, and she takes Billy's hands, and wipes them, and then his face, and she strokes his lank, white hair back from his face, and whispers to him, and holds him until he gives a shudder, like a dying animal, then gives in to unconsciousness.

Pat turns, smiles weakly at her son. 'He'll be out for a while, I'd say,' she whispers, motioning for him to follow her outside. 'Maybe try another time with the little one.'

In a voice of shattered glass, Adam calls for Tilly, and she bumbles through from the living room all excited and eager. He crouches down to her, needing a kiss, something pure and soothing. His daughter stops, holds up a tiny pink finger for inspection, and says, 'Sore.'

Adam smiles, leans down. 'Magic kiss,' he

115

says, and plants his lips on the wounded digit. Tilly smiles, and throws her arms around her father. She kisses his cheek, unbidden, and Adam's heart begins to slow.

Pat is fetching Tilly's hat and coat from the cupboard, and fussing over them both. She wants them to go, so she can start looking forward to the next time they visit. Everything is an intrusion, now. Her life is taking care of Billy.

Adam kisses his mum on her warm, comfortable cheek. He wants to tell her. Wants to ask if she knows Francis Jardine. Wants to apologize for what he will make her endure these coming months, heaping more miseries on a back that is already buckling. He wants to tell her that this morning he was arrested in connection with a murder. Instead he says, 'Let me know if you need anything.'

'Of course, of course,' says Pat, manoeuvring them to the door with her clucking and fussing.

'Bye,' says Tilly, as instructed. 'Ee oo 'oon.'

Pat smiles at her granddaughter, the way an old woman should, and watches them safely into the car. She waves as they pull away, and catches the heavy, double-glazed door on her slippered bunion as she closes it. The dam breaks, and her tears fall.

Twelve

Adam fiddles with the car radio, searching for distraction. Nothing seems to satisfy. The classical station is too funereal. Each concerto is suddenly a dirge, a tribute piece to a fallen general or lost love. He flips to a commercial station. Somebody is singing about their heart being in a headlock, and Adam wishes, not for the first time, that ears were fitted with the same benefits as eyes. He wonders whether ear-lids may be the next evolutionary step. He switches off, angrily, and listens to Tilly sing a song of her own. She's bouncing around in her car seat, holding aloft a Happy Meal toy she has found, smiling at herself in the mirror.

'. . . mold Ocdonald ee-i-o . . . tinkle minkle starr . . .'

Adam wishes he could just stay put in the moment. To catch his daughter's eye and make her laugh until bubbles pop from her nostrils. Instead he keeps drifting back to Larry. To the questions the confident little DCI had thrown his way; about the apocalyptic words his father had stuffed down his throat all those months ago. He feels suddenly disgusted with himself. He doesn't want to look too closely at the thought, but he knows on some level that a man is dead because he, Adam Nunn, was too shit-scared to have a proper conversation with his parents. He gave three grand to a private investigator rather than push his own mum about how he actually came into the world. He tries, again, to fathom himself out. He feels a fool. He completed more than two years of a degree in biological sciences and yet he had never questioned a damn thing about his own blood. He keeps thinking of all the forms he's filled in over the years; medical histories, with their sections for hereditary conditions. He's been worrying for months that his own future contains the same vascular dementia as his father. Worrying about diabetes and angina. Every time he's lost his temper he's heard his mother's voice ringing in his head: *You're just like your father.* He feels as though the last few strands of rope anchoring him in place have frayed down to nothing. Feels adrift, unsure even what to hope for.

'Daddy. Daddy – man. Man!'

Adam glances to his right. A seventy-something man is waving at him from the pavement as the car sits, immobile, at the junction. He's wearing a three-quarter-length wool jacket, black trousers with a neat seam, and polished shoes. He looks well-to-do. He's waving at Adam in a way that suggests he wants his full attention rather than an acknowledgement. Adam squints. Too old to be a copper. A threat? He looks capable enough, despite his years.

'Daddy. Who man?'

Adam glances around. The estate is quiet. No traffic. No noise save the breeze and the gulls.

118

He could drive away. Put his foot through the floor and screech off in a plume of smoke. Instead he checks his mirror then winds down the window. 'Help you?' he asks the man.

'He any better?' asks the old man, bright and perky, as he crosses the space between them.

Adam looks blank. He frowns. Suddenly recognition dawns. 'Mr Santinello?'

'Malcolm, please,' he says, his voice betraying more than a hint of accent. 'I told your mum I'd pop round.'

Adam's head fills with half-remembered images. Mr Santinello. His father's boss. His friend, too, for the best part of forty years. He took over his immigrant father's construction firm in his mid-twenties, and turned it into a thirty-man operation. Billy Nunn worked his way up from apprentice to foreman-fitter, and eventually, took charge of the sub-contract teams that Santinello used on jobs further afield. They were close. Loyal to one another. He'd paid Billy's wages even during the eight months he was off sick with his burns, and invented him an office job close to home while he convalesced. He was a frequent visitor to Adam's home as a child, and was always full of funny stories and enthusiasm. Adam hasn't seen him since his father's retirement party (a lavish affair that Santinello had funded and hosted, and turned into the social event of the season) but the sight of him is suddenly a warming, cheerful thing.

'I've been meaning to catch up with you,' he says, leaning in. 'Your mum. She told me.'

Adam isn't sure how to reply. Told him what? 'Sorry, mate – you've got me there.'

119

'Said your dad was getting things mixed up. Saying things he shouldn't. Upsetting people. Upsetting you, I mean.'

Adam turns down the radio and gives the older man his full attention. 'I don't take anything he says seriously,' says Adam, managing a smile. 'Like you say, he's confused.'

Santinello doesn't seem satisfied. His hands, gripping the frame of the open window, are white at the knuckles. 'He's a good man, your dad. Doesn't deserve to be thought of as anything else.'

'I don't think of him as anything else. He's old. Poorly. But I come see him nearly every day and if I could do more then I would.'

'That's good. Family's what matters, Adam. Don't ever forget that.'

Adam nods, as if the words are some piece of revolutionary philosophy. He notices the gold medallion dangling at the older man's neck and feels an odd frisson of jealousy. It's gold and chunky and matches his designer labels. Adam would like such a piece. He wishes it were around his own father's neck; an heirloom awaiting collection. At once the thought repels him. He fights with his warring emotions, trying to push down the two halves of himself as they kick and scrap within him.

'Working hard, are you? Always were a clever one. I know you've had your problems but you're looking well. Family of your own now, I hear. Good for you, mate. Did I hear you're in security or something? Your mum always sounds so proud of you. I always hoped you'd come work for me

120

some day but your father, he said you had your own plans. Good for you, my friend, good for you . . .'

'Daddy! Man funny. Meet Tilly.'

Santinello looks past him, to the back seat. His face pleats into a huge smile when he sees Tilly. 'Oh, bambino – you are a poem!'

'Yes,' says Tilly, nodding, solemnly. 'Am.'

'I bet your dad adores her,' says Santinello, giving his attention back to Adam. 'She's a true beauty. Bet you're proud.' Then, pointedly: 'Got your father's eyes.'

Adam manages a nod of thanks. He doesn't know why Santinello flagged him down or what his words really mean. Is he referring to the adoption? His real parentage? He can't imagine his mother ever opening up to anybody about her deepest and darkest secrets but her friendship with Santinello goes back to before Adam's birth. He would surely have been aware of what was happening. Adopting a child is a lengthy process. There would be meetings, paperwork, endless forms, a paper trail. Adam feels a sudden urge to be direct. To simply ask him.

'It's typical, you seeing me like this,' laughs Adam, ruefully. 'I'm a wreck – creased to high heaven and desperate for a bath. It's been a hell of a day.'

'Oh yeah?' asks Santinello, making goo-goo eyes at Tilly. 'Work, is it?'

'Mix-up with the police,' says Adam. 'Don't mention it to Mum though, you know how she worries.'

'Coppers – honestly you do have the luck,'

121

says Santinello, shaking his head. 'Been misbehaving?'

'Friend of mine. Business colleague, I suppose. Suffered a mishap. Coppers needed some background. I had nothing much to give them.'

Santinello takes a breath. The silence of the estate hangs heavy as a shroud.

'Trying to get some answers for me actually,' says Adam, staring straight ahead. 'Some of the things Dad's said since he's been poorly – they've wriggled about in my brain a little. He was trying to find some answers for me. I feel like the worst type of bastard if it led to him getting caught up in something that cost the poor sod his life.'

Santinello nods, not really listening. Turns his attention back to Tilly as if Adam hasn't spoken.

'Least said, soonest mended,' says Santinello, quietly. 'One of your dad's mottos, that. Had it tattooed on his chest before the fire. All come off now, of course. Well, you've seen for yourself. Goodness he was a tough nut. Barely shed a tear, even as he watched his skin fry like bacon.'

Adam decides to shut up before he wastes any more time. He's getting nowhere. He's due back at Grace's and he wants to take a couple of turns around the ring road to make sure there are no coppers following him. He doesn't need to be here, trying to nudge an old man into revealing memories he's kept locked up since 1971.

'He'll be pleased to see you,' says Adam, trying on a smile for size. 'You've always made him laugh. Mum too.'

'Good woman, your Pat.'

'Thanks. She can be hard work but her heart's in the right place.'

'They all can,' laughs Santinello, looking more relaxed. 'My daughters say I'm a dinosaur, old-fashioned; a relic. All because I revere women? How does that make sense? How can I be sexist for thinking women are better than us? I mean, they're different, of course, but definitely better.'

'I'm not sure you've understood the whole message . . .' begins Adam, and is relieved to feel his phone vibrate in his pocket.

'I'm pleased I'm an old man,' grumbles Santinello, warming to his theme. 'I don't understand the world the way it's going. Ladies behaving like trawlermen: drinking and swearing and shagging; blokes signing off work for weeks because they're sad and need to watch daytime telly until they're better. Nobody gets a slap any more – not even when they deserve it, and if you try to solve somebody's problems they tell you you're denying them their chance to work through their pain. Whole world's going to the dogs. My Angelina, now – God rest her – she was a real lady. Dressed nice, looked the part, cared for me and the kids, didn't nag, smiled when she got a present and held my hand when things were tough. And now my daughters say she was a fool; that she was downtrodden and I dominated her. Dominated her all the way into a bloody big house and three holidays a year, I said. But that was wrong too . . .'

Adam gives an obliging smile, though he's not really listening. He has a text message from Grace. An instruction to call her at once. She thinks she may have done something impulsive and silly.

'I'm sorry, I'm going to have to shoot,' says Adam, as politely as he can. 'It's been good catching up. We should have a proper chat some time.'

'I'd like that,' says Santinello, and seems to mean it. 'I make my own wine. Not very strong but very tasty. And I've some old photos of your mum and dad in their glad rags that you might want to keep for the little one. I'll let you get on. Ciao for now.'

Adam nods again and pulls away from the kerb, flicking the headlights back on to carve two great yellow circles in the darkening air.

'Home to Mum?' he asks, looking at Tilly in the mirror.

'Daddy home?'

He just smiles. Pretends not to understand what she wants.

Thirteen

Waldo's Snooker Club takes up the whole top floor of an old art deco building on the main drag through Romford. It doesn't look as splendid or luxurious as it did when the interior boasted crushed velvet upholstery and curtains thick enough to stop bullets from a drive-by shooting, but it's still got plenty of character. There are scars on the parquet floor that were put there in the Sixties by men who fought one another with bayonets and coshes. A forensics team could come swab the skirting boards and find themselves a who's who of household names. Alison Jardine enjoys having access to this quiet office. It isn't a grand affair – just a pleasant, green-painted square with a big desk and an Anglepoise lamp, watched over by black-and-white photographs hung haphazardly on the wall. The guy who runs the place always makes himself scarce when Alison comes to do the rounds. Leaves her a black coffee in a thermos and empties the bin before he leaves. Doesn't even straighten the photos unless they somehow mess with her feng shui. Alison is grateful for the gesture – for his acquiescence to the natural order. Things belong to other people, up until she wants them for herself.

'That can all be taken care of,' says Alison, smoothly, into her mobile, sitting back in the battered swivel chair. She's talking with an associate from Silvertown: a friendly money launderer, who's struggling to persuade a sitting tenant off his land down Silvertown way. She feels at once like his priest and psychologist – absolving him of guilt while convincing him he doesn't deserve the bad things that happen to him. She hears herself talk, and realizes afresh just how very good she is at what she does.

'He's bitten off more than he can chew and he just needs a way out that allows him to keep his dignity. He's been sold a pack of lies. We're all reasonable people, aren't we? Compromise isn't a dirty word. And he may have a point – he has been on that land for the past nine years, and while I know you're going to say that it's not your fault you got sent down, it does leave us in this tricky situation. But look, we'll talk to him. He'll see sense, don't you worry. Keeping the peace means a lot to me – my father too. Come back to me when you have a figure in mind and we'll take it from there. You look after yourself now. Be lucky.'

She hangs up. Rolls her eyes. Lights a cigarette and tunes back in to what her son is saying. He's lounging against the wall; jogging trousers and a muscle vest, chunky gold chains and a baseball cap with a flat brim. He has earrings in both lobes and a tattoo of a bird of prey on his neck. It was done by his mate, against Alison's advice, and looks to Alison like a tubby parrot rather than a majestic eagle. It's distinctly boss-eyed and she

126

feels it looking at her wherever she goes, as if it were the Mona Lisa. Alison has heard it said that a mother's love is blind, but she has never been short-sighted when it comes to her only boy. He's an ugly, rat-faced, little specimen who, at twenty years old, has yet to master the art of having a conversation without thrusting both hands down his jogging trousers and cupping his gonads. She loves him, but not in any way that makes her want to touch him, look at him, or spend time breathing him in.

'. . . all this pretending to be a businesswoman – makes me fucking sick. Just go in there, wrap the cunt in barbed wire and plug him into the wall! Hints are no good. We don't need subtlety. Put me on it, Mum, I'll sort the fucker . . .'

Alison sighs as she considers her boy; questioning, not for the first time, whether the doctor threw away the best part of him when they disposed of the afterbirth. He has always been difficult. Even in the womb he used to feel as though he were wearing football boots. He was born with fingernails like a pop star and clawed her to ribbons on the way out. Wouldn't sleep as a nipper. Late to walk and talk. Tantrums like an animal. Forever getting sent home from school for bullying the other kids; for torturing the class pets; for telling the teachers he was going to torch their cars, then making good on his promises when they dared doubt him. He would have been expelled were his surname not Jardine. He's always appreciated the special treatment that the moniker ensures. These past couple of years, since he buddied up with a group of boy racers in souped-up muscle cars and baseball caps, he's been acting like he's untouchable. Telling everybody he's Old Man Jardine's grandson. Then, when it means nothing, telling them just who Old Man Jardine is. It makes Alison question where she's gone wrong with him, and Alison doesn't like to doubt herself. He doesn't get it, that's the trouble. Born too rich. Doesn't understand the art of things being understood, but left unsaid. He even brings his friends back to the house to bother the old boy and try and talk him into sharing stories. Offering to help him. To join the team. Go on the pay roll.

Timmy pushes himself away from the wall and picks up the snooker cue from the floor. He starts twirling it between his fingers like a martial artist. Alison lifts another stack of envelopes from the open leather bag at her feet and places them on the table, then unlocks the desk drawer. It contains two fountain pens, a letter opener, two porn magazines and a wodge of cash the size of a house-brick. She picks out the blade and starts opening the post. She's spent the morning driving between her various business concerns, picking up mail, showing her face, arranging deliveries. She likes this part of the job. Likes the look on the big blokes' faces as they wait for her words of approval. She matters, and she's mattering more by the day. She's cost people loved ones and built a boat of broken bones without ever admitting it to herself. She worries, sometimes, what will happen when her father's illness finally claims him. Who she will be. Whether Irons will still be there. Whether the boys at the clubs will start pinching her arse and calling her 'darling' and the envelopes they hand over will grow thin. It's a thought that troubles her, so she doesn't address it. She does what she can, while she can, and when her worries get her hot under the collar, finds that fanning herself with a stack of fifty-pound notes relieves the worst of the tension.

Timmy is rambling about some lads who tried to race him last night. Two souped-up Peugeots full of rowdy bastards who reckoned they could force him off the road. *Sorted 'em*, he's saying. *Burned 'em off. Met 'em again later in Burger King car park and got in their faces. There was more of 'em than us but they were shitting themselves. Spat on the bonnet of their cars and they didn't say a word. I reckon they knew. Knew who I was, like . . .*

Alison mutters words of feigned interest as she slices open the envelopes. He did her proud the other night at The Rose but her hopes of him learning from the experience and behaving like less of a twat, appear to have come to nought. She wonders whether he has told any of his ridiculous friends about what he did. Wonders, if it came down to it, whether Irons would remove the risk if he ever thought Timmy was too much of a liability. She curtails the train of thought. It's unhelpful. Turns her attention back to the paperwork.

There are a few bills, some legal documents, offers of credit cards. A notice to stop work on one of their building projects due to health and safety breaches. A letter from the council warning her father, still the named proprietor, that the new

129

smoking ban was compulsory and that there had been complaints from a punter thrown out of his bar in Limehouse. Usual stuff. Problems to be solved but nothing to worry about.

She reaches across and presses 'play' on the answerphone; a light winking on and off as if in code. She hears a voice she doesn't recognize: nice accent and a bit out of breath, as if she's talking on a treadmill. Alison falls silent as the message plays.

> Yes, hello. I hope this is the right number – I'm working my way through a long list. Erm, I'm looking for a Miss Jardine. My friend, well, he's more than that, I suppose, but look, my friend found something out about himself a little while ago and I think, or at least I hope, that maybe you could help him find some answers. He's looking for his birth parents, you see. And we've heard the name Pamela Garner and – well, correct me if I'm wrong, please – but I heard you were close. Look, this is all a bit messy. Maybe I've made a mistake. Yeah, I'm pretty sure I have. Look, sorry. I'll call back, maybe. I'm Grace, by the way. My friend is Adam Nunn. Right. Sorry again. Bye.

Vomit rises in Alison's throat. There is movement in her belly; a constriction at her chest. Her skin feels hot and prickly. Memories flood her; wash away the present and pitch her into a churning sea of yesterdays.

130

Guilt.

Shame.

Images of two girls laughing and plaiting each other's hair. Practising kisses and doing one another's make-up. Seeing how many jelly sweets they can fit in their mouths at once. Holding Dad's hand. One each. Riding in the big car and writing their names in the condensation on the windows.

That night.

1971.

Her, and what was done to her. Being taken away. Dad closing in on himself, folding inwards like petals at night-time. The child she only learned about through snatches of conversation. The screams coming from the gamekeeper's cottage in the woods as nine pounds of red, screaming infant clawed his way into a world that didn't want him.

Pamela's having a baby, poor lass.

How could she love that thing? After what happened?

Best thing would be to drop it in the river with a brick.

And her face! How will she get a man looking like that?

Jardine does his best by her but every day she's there it makes him look like he's making up for something.

Like he's soft, or guilty . . .

'. . . a tonne would do it, Mum, I reckon,' says Timmy. 'See me through.'

There is no reply. He looks at her. Her face has gone pale and there is wetness on her cheeks.

'Mum?'

Alison looks up and her eyes are red-seamed. 'Nothing. Just a spot of bother.'

'Let me sort it,' he says and straightens his back, fixing his face into hard-man mode.

'No, it's nothing. Just a problem to be solved . . .'

She stutters into silence. She can feel her heart, hear her blood. Her mind is swimming with trite phrases and clichés. *Can of worms. Old wounds. Skeletons in the closet. You can never go back* . . .

'That message, was it?' asks Timmy, nodding. 'I wasn't listening. Give us his name and we'll sort him.'

'It's . . . it's nothing like that,' she begins and stops when she hears the tears in her voice. She picks up the fountain pen with fingers that can barely grip and copies the telephone number onto an envelope. She takes the letter and folds it into four, tucking it inside her bra. She needs a drink. A cigarette. Time to think. Her brain is pounding like a jackhammer.

Pamela.

Pamela.

Pamela.

Like a daddy-long-legs bumbling along a skirting board she clatters out of the room, light-headed, stomach churning, looking for Jimbo and his fags, heading for the optics behind the bar.

Fourteen

Timmy scowls at his mother's backside until she's out of sight. 'Bitch,' he says under his breath. Then, louder, for his own enjoyment, he repeats it. He likes saying 'bitch'. It's a punch of a word, meaty and impactful. He says it a lot when he's hurting people. Says it more when he's taking his turn with the girls who like to hang around within kissing distance of his wallet.

He walks over to the desk. Slides open the unlocked drawer and takes a half-inch of notes from the pile. Slips them into his pants and enjoys the feeling. He likes the way paper money feels. It's one of his favourite sensations. Not his *absolute*, not a cataclysm of sensuality, like bringing down something hard on something soft, but definitely on the list.

He casts his eyes over the paperwork on the desk. Looks at the phone; old-fashioned and plastic. Plays the recording again and listens to the message. A smile creases his unpretty features. They always try and push him to one side. He'd shown them, hadn't he? Lay in the dark in the loft of The Rose, sweating and cramping up and desperate for a piss. Had done what Irons told him to and hadn't hesitated when the moment came to release the old ceiling joist. He'd known

133

there'd be no remorse. No guilt. His mother and her geriatric bodyguard think it was his first kill, and Timmy has no plans to educate them. He likes being underestimated. That was, nobody ever sees him for what he really is until it's already too late. Keeping himself from going mad, that's the hard part. Killing time until it's his turn to take over. He likes the blood and crunch of confrontation. Likes how it feels when a person comes apart in his hands. He'd love to perform such a service for his grandfather, but in the meantime, he's trying to be the best version of himself he can be. That means taking care of things that need taking care of. And the voice on the phone certainly seemed to have ruined his mother's day.

He picks up the pen and writes the names on his hand, then sits back in his mother's chair, still warm from her arse, snooker cue resting across his knees.

Opportunities keep falling into his lap. He's making a habit of being in the right place at the right time. The Old Man needs men like him. His mum's good at the business side of things but she hasn't got the stomach for the rough stuff. He hadn't liked seeing her flaunt herself in front of Kukuc. Doesn't like hearing the noises that come from her room when she lets Jimbo stay over. And she'd looked white as sour milk as she'd hurried from the office, all upset and undone by a voice that doesn't sound important to him.

He lets himself revel in a memory. The voice at the end of the line. The frightened, half-mad plea

134

for help. Something had gone wrong. He needed to call in a favour. He needed Mr Jardine . . .

Timmy had stepped up. Done what was needed.

He reaches into his trousers and cups the money with one hand.

The other makes a fist around the cue.

He's going to make the family proud.

'I don't know what I wanted to happen. Maybe I was ready to leave things alone . . .'

'You said you wanted to know! I'm sorry. I thought I was doing the right thing.'

'No you didn't, you thought this was all exciting and wondered what you could find out while you didn't have Tilly strapped to your leg. Well, well done you. I'm so impressed.'

'Don't be like that, Adam. I hate it when you're cross with me. We know now. At least we know . . .'

Grace is trying not to cry. Adam is doing his best not to shout. Tilly, still strapped into her car seat, plonked like a throne on top of the coffee table, is watching the back-and-forth like a tennis umpire – occasionally offering helpful phrases from her limited vocabulary: *shurrup, mine* and, somewhat incongruously, *ham.*

'You had no right!'

'I was trying to help, Adam! I'm sorry, but you wanted answers . . .'

'And I've got them now, have I? Now you've had a chat with some plastic gangster who can't keep a secret if his life depends on it? Now you've phoned a snooker club and spilled the beans to whoever's fucking listening . . .'

135

'Please, don't be cross, I was thinking of you . . .'

'What a fucking day. What a fucking day!'

'*Shurrup.*'

'Tilly, don't say that – it's rude.'

'*Ham.*'

'Jesus.'

'No, ham.'

'*Hone . . .*'

'What's that word?'

'Hone? Oh, phone. Phone!'

Grace, grateful for the distraction, fumbles with her mobile. She puts it on speakerphone so that Adam will stop yelling at her.

A London voice, cocksure and young, crackles through the speaker. 'Yeah, you left a message on the answerphone? Is that Grace?'

'Yes,' she mutters. Then, louder: 'Yes.'

'Nice one, nice one. Look, seems a tricky thing to chat about over the phone. Why don't you tell me where you're based and I can come see you. I work for the family, you see, and as you can imagine it's a sensitive subject. If we could have a little meeting – what do you call it, a tête-à-tête? Ha, yes, then we could progress things from there.'

Grace looks at Adam, his face pale, eyes dark. He gives the tiniest of nods.

'We could come to you. London, yes? It'll just be Adam, of course. I'm not sure I'll be able to attend personally . . .'

'Oh, what a shame . . .'

'But Adam would be keen to find some answers, if that's convenient . . .'

'Can't wait. Give me half an hour and we'll arrange something. At our expense, of course.'

'This is so good of you – I was frightened I'd made a terrible mistake . . .'

'Not at all. Cheers.'

The silence is heavy, crackling with the forked lightning of things unsaid. It seems like an age before Adam crosses to where she stands and puts his arm around her shoulders; pulls her close and kisses her cheek, her forehead, the edge of her mouth.

'Thank you,' he whispers. 'Thank you.'

Fifteen

'You like him for it?'

DCI Bosworth takes a moment before she replies. Just keeps staring at the screen of her laptop. Adam Nunn glowers back at her, unshaven, dark-eyed, his expression captured somewhere between angry and afraid. She can't read him. Can't work him out. He's good-looking, in a dishevelled sort of way, but she can't imagine giving him a second glance if she passed him in the street. He has the look of somebody without a destination, but in a hurry.

'Cass?'

She ignores the voice, focusing on Nunn until the pixels spin and blur and swim in her vision. She can't even make up her mind whether she finds him charming. He'd done his best to act the hard man during the interview but it had seemed curiously affected, as if he'd learned the role from watching gangster movies. He'd only seemed true to himself in his moments of concern. He'd seemed genuine in his unhappiness at Larry's death – had looked positively ashamed when she had read out his list of convictions, all but patting at the air and urging her to keep her voice down lest somebody should hear about his

138

indiscretions, even while attempting to revel in the role of thuggish enforcer. She finds it easier to imagine him reading bedtime stories to his offspring than taking an axe to an enemy, but she's been in the job long enough to know that few people have murder in their eyes. 'Cass?'

She glances up at the rather bland mass of Detective Sergeant Pat Deakin. He's Irish, middle-aged, and his prematurely grey hair gives him the look of a judge who's forgotten to take his wig off. He's wearing a blue pinstripe suit over a checked shirt and the clash of patterns strikes Bosworth as one of the main reasons for her repeated headaches since inviting him onto her unit. He's holding out a beige plastic beaker full of something that might be tea.

'Twenty pence from the machine,' says Deakin, pulling up a chair and plonking himself down beside her. 'Tastes like tramp piss but you can't argue with the price.'

Bosworth takes a sip. It's wet and warm and helps rid her mouth of the taste of stale air. She's been sitting in this little interview room since before lunch and her tongue feels too big for her mouth. It's a despairing cube; the ceiling tiles eaten through in places and patterned with damp in others. The carpet feels like cold toast against the soles of her bare feet. The bosses here at Portsmouth nick are accommodating them as commanded, but offering up the minimum of comforts. She's considered asking to be moved to a cell.

'You briefed him yet?' asks Deakin, nodding at the mobile phone on the table top.

She purses her lips and blows out a sigh. She hadn't had much to tell their boss and he's never been great at keeping his disappointment out of his voice. Nunn had seemed like a decent suspect. He'd been the reason she had made the drive from their London HQ to this knackered old town on the south coast.

'I emailed it over but he rang straight back,' she says, rolling her eyes. 'Prefers to listen than to read – you know how he gets. Too many words and he drifts off. But I gave him the bullet points.'

'And they are?' asks Deakin.

'He's a viable suspect, but until we can pin down a time of death he's got alibis aplenty, and he's got a perfectly good reason why that number should be on the dead man's hand.'

Deakin pulls a face. 'Does he, though? I mean, Paris did a job where you'd be in the habit of keeping proper notes, don't you think? Just strikes me as odd.'

'It's only odd when you view it as a copper,' says Bosworth, grimacing as she sips her tea. 'On a normal day, to a normal person, scribbling a number down on your hand doesn't instantly point to its owner being a murderer. It's just something you do.'

Deakin makes a face. 'Did you get the message from Gray? He's got enough for a briefing note for the Home Office so he's happy to let us slip away. Too late to go tonight but there's a hotel by the harbour . . .'

'I don't like doing half a job,' mutters Bosworth, and the sentiment feels genuine. She thought this might be an easy case. Something with a bit of glamour and glory. Instead it is making her feel positively sad, and she left CID to get away from such inconveniences.

'Can you imagine?' she asks, half to herself. 'Finding out you're not who you think you are . . .'

'He went to university to study science,' scoffs Deakin. 'Must be half blind if he didn't spot the inconsistencies.'

'Must be hard, that's all I'm saying. I'm tempted to go ask the parents, but in all honesty, what's the good? In terms of our own brief, we're onto a loser. No point being twats for the sake of it.'

'Maybe forensics will come up trumps,' says Deakin. 'A partial print. A skin cell. God, we could find the hammer and put the whole thing to bed.'

'You think that's likely?'

'Well, no . . .'

'The boss said the same thing,' mutters Bosworth, slumping in her seat and staring up at the ceiling.

'We could lean on the missus,' continues Deakin. 'Or the mum. Get him to stop playing silly beggars.'

Bosworth looks back at the man on the screen. Glares into the dark pupils and sees herself looking back. She reaches out and pointedly minimizes the image. 'I take it you don't like him,' she says, stretching.

'Too cocky by half,' says Deakin. 'Good punch on him, I'll give him that. Local plod's having his jaw wired.'

'It was the wrong approach,' concedes Bosworth.

141

'Turning up mob-handed like that. We'd have got more out of him with a conversation.'

'He's the one who lost his temper. Guilty conscience, I reckon.'

Bosworth shrugs. 'I reckon we're onto a loser here, Pat. It's lost a little of its flavour.'

Deakin nods. They'd leapt at the chance to take over when the body was found at Dedham Vale, both half convinced that they'd found a gangland corpse from long ago. They hadn't been prepared for looking into the murder of a private detective from the far side of the country. Their brief is to investigate organized crime, and while the investigation has thrown up a possible link to the Jardines, both officers' careers would be better served by finding the absent Nicholas Kukuc. Adam Nunn is small-time in comparison, and Bosworth likes to think big.

'We going to throw it back to CID then?' asks Deakin, jerking a thumb over his shoulder as if pointing the way. 'Keep a watching brief, make sure it comes back our way if anything, well . . .'

'If it gets juicy,' says Bosworth, smiling. She can't see the point of being able to pick and choose her cases if she can't throw back the ones she tires of. 'I think we're as well heading back to HQ. We've got Nunn's DNA swabs but they'll not be processed for a few days. Until then, I don't know what good we are here.'

'There's nothing to compare it to anyway,' says Deakin. 'Forensics can only do so much.'

Bosworth chews her cheek. Closes an eye. Decides to take a leap. Reaches forward and enlarges the image of Adam. 'Am I going mad here, or does he remind you of somebody?'

Deakin looks at the image. Leans forward in his seat. 'I thought that myself,' he says, under his breath. 'In the interview. When he cocked his head. It's the eyes.'

Bosworth glances behind her. Returns her attention to the screen. Her fingers move over the keys as she logs in to the secure database that the Serious and Organised Crime Agency has spent an ungodly amount of money installing, and which is slightly less effective than the cheap one she used to use as a detective constable. She calls up a black-and-white image: a police mugshot from 1964. It shows a tall, dark-haired man: big collar, tattooed chest, somebody else's blood on his lapels. Handsome, in a dishevelled sort of way, his eyes staring up from beneath neat brows; a little angry, perhaps a little afraid.

'Before he lost his looks,' says Deakin, under his breath. 'Before they went to work on him . . .'

'Somebody told me it was pigs . . .' she muses.

'No, that was the Geordie lad. This poor sod got carved the old-fashioned way. Bayonet, ground glass and a psycho with a temper. Never said a word.'

Bosworth says nothing. She calls up the next image in the file. Francis Jardine, in his heyday, small and wiry and tough as old leather. It's a colour image, but his beady eyes are black as ink.

'Would be nice, wouldn't it?' says Bosworth, softly. 'Headline-grabber.'

Deakin considers the suggestion. Shakes his

143

head. 'No,' he says, flatly. 'No, it fucking wouldn't. It would be like finding out you'd just pissed off the devil.'

Bosworth weighs it up. 'It's their MO,' she muses. 'The location; the wounds – that's why we're here, after all. And if the old man's still alive, why not his monster? He's no spring chicken but we don't know he's dead. And even if not, just because we've got nothing on Alison doesn't mean she's clean. That name carries a lot of weight.'

'We go to the boss with this and we'll be laughed out the building,' says Deakin. 'Money laundering. People trafficking. Who's buying up Newham and what do they want it for? That's the brief. This is what comes with cherry-picking, Cass. Francis Jardine's off-limits. Daughter too. And certainly not that . . . thing . . .'

Bosworth drains her tea, a bad taste in her mouth. She imagines the front page of the *Evening Standard*. Imagines a Queen's Police Medal around her neck. 'Your snouts and mine, they all say the same thing. Big man. Scarred. Old. Kills like cancer . . .'

'I'm not making the case, Cass,' says Deakin, flatly. 'Not telling the boss we're interested in interviewing the boogeyman.'

Bosworth gives a snort of laughter, and the impulse to do the right thing fades away. She closes the laptop, decision made. She's going to leave things alone. Larry Paris's death is somebody else's problem. Adam Nunn, and whatever secrets he's hiding, have nothing to do with her investigation. If she's lucky, Nicholas Kukuc will turn up dead and she'll be able to make a case that he was responsible for this particular corpse, and no doubt a few others as well.

They stand, grateful to have reached an understanding.

As they head for the door, neither takes the time to look up. Were they to do so, they would perhaps glimpse the tiny black device secured to the flickering strip-light on the dirty ceiling. They might trace the transmitter to the adjacent interview room, where a digital transmitter relays it on to an unregistered mobile phone: confidential information pouring in like water.

As Bosworth closes the door, laptop tucked under her arm, she feels a moment's disquiet, as if she has shirked a duty, or chosen the easy path. She forces herself not to indulge in the sensation. She is paid handsomely to make such choices. She does what is best by those who pay her wages. And she is certain that to pursue Jardine's monster would cost the taxpayer dearly. The funeral bills alone would amount to a fortune.

Part Two

Sixteen

*The 11.42 South Western service from
Portsmouth Harbour to King's Cross
October 27th, 12.48 p.m.*

Visibility is down to yards. The view from the
window is blurry, dirty. The landscape flashes by
too quickly to be anything more than colours and
shapes. *House, barn, house, village, dark green,
light green, water, industry, house, house, a new
development of red bricks and brown roofs,
house, graffiti-daubed siding, deserted station,
pocket of trees, birds speckling the sky like tea
leaves in an empty mug, a scattered handful of
livestock, green, green . . .* The countryside
swishes by in frames of paper snowflakes and
black doilies; through the twisted, patterned arms
of bare, soot-darkened trees.

Adam sits and tries to read the newspaper one
more time, but the words are as vague as the
landscape and his eyes just seem to blur and
sting. He looks at his watch. Not long now.
Wishes it nearer. Wishes it further away.

He gets up and walks like a cross-country skier,
holding onto backs of chairs and headrests, to
the toilet. Checks his reflection, and doesn't mind
it. Not showy. Not deprived. Not making a statement, other than casual indifference. Grey suit
trousers with a neat seam, black vest, zip-up black

149

cardigan, matching suit jacket and expensive, Crombie coat. Fifty-pound shoes with embroidered tongues. Hair the right side of messy. Dark eyes.

He texts Zara. Apologizes for his quietness these past two nights, staring at the wall as if stripping off the paint, lost in his thoughts – too preoccupied to return a kiss.

I love you, Zara. You make me the best version of myself. I know I'm hard work. I promise, I'll be worth it. I'm working through some stuff but you're my certainty, I swear. xxx

He returns to his seat, and fidgets.
Texts his Mum.

Sorry if I've been a bit off with you. You're the best. Love you.

Deletes it without sending.

Thinks. Chews on his lip. Cleans his fingernails with his fingernails. Tries to check his teeth for crumbs in the reflection of the window, but finds his near-transparent image uncomfortably weak and inconsequential. Looks at the time and curses.

House, farm, town, green, green, field, pocket of trees, red bricks and brown roofs . . .
On . . .
On.

Raindrops jewel the lenses of Alison's sunglasses and plaster her hair to her face. She makes no

150

move to wipe away the droplets or to push the lank strands behind her ears. A rat-tail of fringe has worked itself behind the arm of the designer specs and hangs like a sodden shoelace against her damp cheek, blotched with hastily applied make-up and a mascara splatter-pattern.

The walk in the bracing rain has done nothing to clear her head. Her brain feels muddy. Her insides fit to burst. She walked through the snooker club with her practised swagger, but when she made it to the office she toppled over, reaching the desk for support and hauling herself into the chair. She's been lost to herself for days. She's failed to return important phone calls; let debts go uncollected, palms ungreased. She's been lost inside her own head, running down corridors and trying the locked doors of rooms she has worked so hard to forget.

'Pam,' she mumbles, the way she has countless times since the voice bled out from the answerphone. She had an extra slug of gin in her orange juice at breakfast time. Sent Jimbo out to pick her up a bottle of Mateus Rosé from the shop on the corner, then had to shout at him and send him away when she uncorked it and took a sniff. This was always their drink. This was what she and her best pal used to neck while they listened to T-Rex and did each other's make-up and called each other silly names.

'Call her back,' she mutters, glaring at the telephone, eyes unfocussed. 'It's probably bollocks. Probably lies. A copper, trying it on. Some chancer. Think bigger than this. Come on. Be who you are.'

151

She hears her own voice as thin and far away. She is a teenage girl again, asking Daddy what has happened to her friend. She is standing still as a cardboard cut-out, listening to the screams carry across to the big house from the gamekeeper's lodge. She is listening as Daddy tells Irons to hold himself together: to leave the Dozzles alone; that there are alliances to be considered before something as simple as revenge can be entertained. And then she is looking into the tear-filled eyes of Priya, the personal nurse hired by Mr Jardine to look after all of Pamela's needs. And she is telling her the grotesque, painful truth.

'She couldn't take it. There was too much sadness in her to go on. I'm so sorry, jaanu. She swallowed her bandages – stuffed them down her throat and swallowed and swallowed until she couldn't breathe . . .'

Alison sits with her chin cupped in her hands, nibbling the expensive glittered beads from the tips of her pink-and-white fingernails, wishing she had somebody to talk to. Her friends are ladies of a certain age who don't really know how to talk to her. Her eyes glaze over as they criticize the men in their lives; as they compare the prices of Bahamian holidays and fantasize about the masseur at the private clubs where they have themselves pampered and preened to some foul approximation of beauty. Perhaps she could call up an old school acquaintance, eager to pretend their teenage years were more fun than they really were. The men in her life are fleeting, and purpose-picked for their lack of sensitivity. She feels utterly alone.

152

Alison jumps as the phone on the desk rings, loud and bright, cutting through the low base thump of the rock music, which blares through from the snooker hall.

Sniffing, wiping her eyes, she picks up the receiver.

'Snooker club,' she says, drowsily.

'Hi, look, I hope this is the right number. It's stored in my phone.'

'Yes?'

'Look, this is Adam Nunn. I'm on my way up. I tried phoning the number that your text came from but got no reply, so I'm trying this number. I just wanted to say the train's running a wee bit late so don't think I've bottled out or anything . . .'

Alison feels the world tip; a buzzing in her head. She squeezes the phone.

'I don't understand . . .' she begins.

'So I'll see whoever's meeting me at the station, yes? Is that right?' The phone crackles and cuts out for a second, before the voice reappears, faintly.

'I'm not sure what you mean,' she says, panic rising. 'Did somebody contact you? Who was it?'

'I'm sorry, you're cutting out . . .'

'Was it a man?'

'I'm losing you . . .'

'A young man or an old man?'

Silence.

'Hello?'

Alison drops the phone and pushes herself back from the desk, her hands in her hair, her mouth half-open. *Him*, she thinks. *Pamela's boy. You spoke to him.*

153

For the first time since she embraced the reality of who she was and stepped into her father's shoes, Alison doesn't know what to do.

'Ladies and gentlemen, this train will shortly be arriving at Leigh-on-Sea. On behalf of myself and the rest of the team, I would like to thank you . . .'

The train slows, and Adam blunders his way to the door. He leaves his paper on the table. He likes to travel light. Unencumbered. He was always the same at school. Pen in his top pocket; Portsmouth FC shirt under his uniform on PE days.

The train rattles to a halt and Adam looks through the grimy windows at a bleak vista of grey pavements and metal railings; a constellation of pinched cold faces and feet clad in sensible shoes. He pushes the door handle. Nothing happens. Pulls. Nothing. Pushes again, and out, with force, left foot first, onto the platform.

The wind cuts like a Stanley knife. The hairs on his arms rise up like the topmasts of a ship-in-a-bottle. Adam thrusts his hands in his pockets and sets off through the dozen or so passengers and guards in a direction that looks like it's the exit. He catches himself mumbling, asking himself questions about where he should be going. Up some stairs, across a platform, down some more, past pigeons and chewing gum, graffiti and litter, through London accents, past kisses hello and goodbye, feelings rising in him like a bruise, and then into a softer, more natural light, oozing through from a high window. He walks past the ticket office, feels the air grow colder, fresher, wetter, and emerges onto the street in front of the station.

Three taxis sit in the rank in front of the station. The car park is half full, and the main street beyond is a damp, flickering tableau of young mums and pushchairs, old ladies under umbrellas, well-wrapped couples holding hands, shivering office workers holding greasy bags of pastry and running back to desks. Adam feels like shrugging. Lighting a cigarette. Stamping his feet.

I'm here, he's thinking. *Now what?*

Three doors swing open on a white Golf GTI in the car park. Four people get out. Three young men, one young woman. The men can't be older than twenty, and are dressed like a boy band on its arse. Tracksuit tops over polar necks, or stripy T-shirts. Tracksuit bottoms tucked into white socks, which feed into whiter trainers. Two wear baseball caps, another, who got out the driver's seat, wears a woollen hat over curly blonde hair. His tracksuit has a more expensive sheen to it, a fancier label. None have shaved, or look like they need to very often. The girl is dressed similarly, but her tracksuit bottoms are pink and her jacket is a white, hooded waterproof. Her hair, the colour of sunflower oil, is scraped back to reveal dainty ears skewered by large golden rings. She is carrying an empty bottle of Dr Pepper, and holding it as if it were a child. All are smoking cigarettes, and with the doors of the vehicle open, a cloud of smoke is curling upwards to freedom from the inside of the car.

The doors close, and the four communicate

155

something important to each other with a series of shrugs, grunts and nods of the head. They see Adam, and there is more muttering. Then they approach, slouching and furtive.

Adam would not let these people into a nightclub. Were he Prime Minister, he would not let them breed.

The one in the bobble hat accepts the girl's hand in his and they take the lead. Getting closer, Adam realizes they are both good-looking, but senses that this will change before they hit twenty-five.

'Hi,' says the young man in the woollen hat, smiling, showing nice teeth and extending his hand. 'We've been asked to collect you.'

Adam pauses for a moment. Something feels wrong. He doesn't like to make snap judgements about people but there's nothing about this group of people that suggests they are in the employ of an untouchable crime boss. They look as though they should be standing at a bus stop, eating a sausage roll and sharing a joint.

'You all right?' asks the leader, jerking his head back as if tugged by a string. 'Staring like a goldfish, you are.'

Adam closes his mouth. Fixes on a smile. 'Much appreciated,' he says, taking the youngster's hand in his. It is soft, and warm. 'I'm Adam.'

The four smile and shrug and look at each other, then the girl says, 'You're quite nice looking.'

'That's sweet,' says Adam, surprised and pleased. 'You're a bunch of stunners yourself.'

Nobody smiles.

'Shall we maybe make a move?' asks the lad, gesturing to the car, and Adam hears the same accent that he heard on the telephone. His vision of a lawyer in a business suit evaporates.

'We're going to see Mr Jardine?'

The others giggle, and there is much smiling between themselves. Adam licks his lips, his throat feeling uncomfortably dry. He's beginning to feel anxious. There's a crackle of static in the air, the taste of iron on his tongue. The enormity of the situation suddenly threatens to overwhelm him. It's a struggle not to give in to laughter – to erupt at the sheer absurdity of where he finds himself. He considers his options. He can say no, get back on the train, and end this now. But he knows that he won't. He's in the grip of this thing now. He needs to know more. Needs to understand. More than anything, he doesn't want to be rude. He gives a shrug. 'After you.'

The lad in the woollen hat leads them back to the car and opens three of the doors. The others return to the doors where they exited, save Sergio Tacchini, who stands behind Adam, at the rear offside, while the other lad in a baseball cap reaches across from inside the car and opens it. Adam winces into the teeth of the gale as the rain blows in slantwise. Looks up to see a brutish, thick-necked gull glaring at him from atop a razor-wire fence.

Adam senses it before there is any movement. There is a stiffening of the wind, a thickening of the air, and then the lad behind him is on his back, something cold and light and plastic rustling against his face and a hand stiff, bony, on his face and neck. Adam feels strength in the boy's arms, feels his own lips burst. His instincts spread out from his centre as rays from the sun, and he jabs back with an elbow that catches his attacker in the sternum, with a sound like somebody slamming an encyclopaedia on a wooden desk.

Adam turns his head as the boy staggers away, his hat askew, the bin bag in his hand trailing on the floor. He sees no immediate threat from this side and turns back to the car, just as the wind grabs the half-open door and slams it into Adam's knees. With a grunt, he bucks back, as the other lad inside the car reaches out and grabs him by his coat, pulls hard . . .

The other lad, angry, sore, struggling to get his breath, shoves Adam again, hard in the back and he pitches forward, banging his jaw on the car roof. He is shoved and pulled, leg banging against the car door, his hands grabbing at the webbing around the roof, and he feels more hands, reaching through from the front seat, dragging, tugging, wrenching him into the space in the tiny car, and he is trying to find room to swing his fists, jaw aching, neck starting to stiffen, adrenaline white water in his veins.

Another shove, a kick to the knee, and then he is inside, weight on his back, shouts and swear words in his ears, a girl's shrieking laughter, and they are doing fifty mph in second gear, tearing into the traffic on two wheels, one door still hanging open, one boy hanging out and shrieking for help. Adam, thrashing, elbowing, lashing out, sucking the bin liner into his mouth and almost choking as it is wrenched down past his eyes, and his world becomes a dark, angry place.

Adam feels as though he has been turned inside out. The darkness inside himself closes over his face, is pulled tighter, closer, tighter again, until he feels like a made thing, a Christmas cracker toy, a vintage wine bottle melted down and melded, with inferior glass, into something larger and less beautiful.

The blow comes, hard and final. The doors close, the car finds the right gear, and Adam, because nothing else occurs to him, lets his eyes close, and his body fall still and silent.

The only thing he cannot mute is the voice, deep in his head, in an accent at once naughty-schoolboy and ministerial.

Is this what you wanted?

Is this exciting enough for you?

Seventeen

The bag comes off with a flourish, as though a magician is revealing his showpiece. Adam blinks out at a small, cheap bathroom, with dirty blue tiles and white walls and a shower over an enamel bath which is streaked with grey dirt and errant, curly hairs. The room is lit with a bare bulb, and the frosted, small window is ajar. There are strange dark blobs floating in the air in the top left corner of the room. They move as Adam tilts his head. He blinks and they disappear before flooding back like ink dropped on plain paper. When the pain comes, it's bearable. He feels more numb than anything else – dizzy, disorientated and sick.

He tries to move. Pain climbs up his arms and grips the back of his skull. He realizes his hands are tied behind him and he is sitting on the hard plastic seat of the toilet.

'Morning, princess.'

Adam raises his head as his attackers congregate in the doorway. The room is only a few feet square, and there is not enough space for them all to stand inside, so the girl, and one of the baseball caps, loiter outside.

The driver has removed his hat to reveal flattened curly hair, and is kneeling down in front

160

of Adam, holding a screwdriver, blade pointed inwards, like a dagger. Sergio Tacchini has stripped down to T-shirt and tracksuit trousers. He is holding a kitchen knife in one hand, and some sort of Oriental weapon, made from three wooden cylinders held together with links of metal chain, in the other.

Adam starts to come back to himself. He feels fear, there are aches and pains, but his overwhelming sensation is of confusion and . . . perhaps, victimization. He feels picked on. Overloaded. His mind clings to a sense of injustice, a bleating thought: *You've been through enough. There's enough on your plate. Like there wasn't enough to deal with? Single spies and battalions, eh lad? Never rains but it pours. This isn't fair!*

'Wake up, you twat,' says the driver, and stands up, giving Adam a kick on the shin.

'I'm awake, you prick,' says Adam, teeth bared. 'If you're after money, you've really backed the wrong horse . . .'

Sergio says, 'Shut yer mouth,' and steps forward, but the driver holds him back.

'Mine,' he says, then fixes Adam with a look he has seen so many times on so many Saturday nights. It is the Hollywood hard man, the malevolent glare, the granite face practised in front of mirrors. It is the scowl of the pretender.

'Why you bothering Jardine, eh?' he asks. 'You want to get in a legend's face, do you? You want to harm the big man, eh? Think you're something? Look at you. You're fuck all. Fuck all.'

'What are you talking about?' he asks, screwing

161

up his face and feeling pain erupt in his temples. 'I'm here because I was invited. He doesn't want me here, I'm gone.'

'See the hard man now?' asks the driver scornfully, looking at his friends for approval, and getting it. 'Wetting his pants. Wants to go home. Should have thought of that before you came up here.'

'You asked me here!' shouts Adam, pissed off. 'You asked me!'

'I know what I hear, and I know important people don't want you bothering Jardine.'

'Fine! You could explain that verbally! Could have put it in a letter! You were on the phone to me last night! Why go to all this bother? I'm not that fucking interested.'

'Yeah, yeah. You're shitting yourself. You're shaking all over.'

'Am I?'

'Just stay away from him. That's what she wants, that's what I provide?'

'Who's she?'

'Never you mind.'

'This is bloody stupid. Untie me and I'll get back on the next train. You think I need this? Do you know anything about my life?'

'I think you need a lesson first. I think Mr Jardine would approve of us giving you a lesson.'

'What are you fuckin' . . .'

The driver lunges at Adam. This is the bit he has been looking forward to. He hits him hard across the forehead with the handle of the screw-driver, while kneeing him in the chest. 'Stay away from Francis Jardine,' he shouts, as he lays into

Adam, to the whoops of delight from outside the room, against an accompaniment of 'Go on, son' and 'Kill the bastard!'.

Adam tries to make his body as small as he can and tucks his chin into his chest. The blows to the head hurt, but not intolerably, and the driver is wasting energy with his kicks, which cannot contain any real power in such a small room, and at such an angle. Angry, but professional, Adam kicks out and his right leg thumps into the shin of his attacker. He drags his boot down the leg, grating flesh from muscle and bone. The driver yells in an indignant voice unaccustomed to pain, and he hops back, yelping. Sergio darts forward, cleaver raised, and Adam kicks out again, wriggling his hands and wrists, feeling his bonds tear. He frees his left arm just in time to block the cleaver, and sees a frayed school tie hanging from his own wrist. He kicks again, hitting Sergio on the kneecap with a satisfying crack, pulling his other hand free and trying to stand.

There is noise on the stairs, as the other baseball cap tries to open the door and it bangs into the face of the driver, who is bent over, trouser leg rolled up, examining his leg, trying to stick the skin back down over a strip of oozing blood and shredded flesh. He staggers back, hurt, cursing, and bangs into Sergio. They fall, almost into the bathtub, teetering on the brink, and Adam takes a moment to try and untie his right hand, still held fast behind the toilet . . .

The girl, shrieking, asking what the fuck is happening, banging at the door, suddenly falls silent.

163

Adam hears a whimpering, a garbled apology, then nothing. The baseball cap, half in, half out of the door, turns to face something on the stairs, and his expression turns to fear, a genuine, primal terror. It is not the face of a naughty boy, an impertinent teen. It is the face of a man who can taste death on the air.

The room seems to grow colder, the cries of the two young men struggling on the verge of the bathtub are sucked into nothingness by a silent explosion, a burst of utter noiselessness, that cascades into the room as the door opens, slowly, inexorably . . .

An old man stands in the doorway. He is big around the middle and the muscles in his limbs run to fat, but there is a strength to him, a sense of concealed power. His face is monstrous. White skin, albino white, marbled with red: scaly burns across nose and cheeks, like uncooked meat stretched across a frame. His head is concealed beneath a flat cap, and Adam sees the slope of his skull as a duck egg steeped in onion skins.

There is no malice in his expression as he looks at Adam. He takes him in, emotionless, then turns to face the two struggling youngsters. In a stride he crosses the bathroom, his arm brushing Adam's as he moves. Adam can smell damp earth, rotting vegetation, the mulch and algae of untended ponds, and he shivers and flinches from the touch.

The man grabs the driver by the throat and with one hand pins him against the wall behind the bath, his feet drumming on the bathtub; squirming, in both pain, and at the sensation of this thing's skin on his own.

He leans in, and opens a toothless mouth.

'Your mum is going to go fucking spare,' he says, and drops him.

The man turns and nods at Adam. He looks at Sergio, sprawled on the floor, clutching his kneecap, and his milky eyeball fills, for a moment, with crimson blood. He blinks, and a red tear runs down his cheek, leaving a gory trail over the sores and scales. He extends a hand to Adam, before experience makes him withdraw it. He nods again.

'I'm Irons,' he says. 'Come with me.'

Eighteen

Adam's body language speaks in swear words as he sits hunched in the passenger seat of the red Toyota Hilux, twin-cab, scowling out of the window, his back turned on the creature in the driver's seat. He's scared and sore and wants to go home. He wants to rub his bruised jaw, but pride won't allow him to show he's suffering. He doesn't know if he's been saved from a beating, saved from a stabbing, or saved from jackals by a hungry bear.

Music drifts up from the radio, almost lost over the drone of the tyres on the wet road. It's early Cliff Richard, a jaunty number called 'Blue Turns to Grey'. The big man taps his gloved hands on the wheel, enjoying the rhythm.

'Met him once,' he says, nodding at the stereo. 'One of the brothers had a warrant out on him. Handsome, wasn't he – our Cliff. When they liked the look of somebody they'd put out what they called a "W". It meant whoever got them together would get a nice few quid. I had the chance to deliver. Saw him down Catford, if you can believe it. Decided against it. Seemed all right, did Cliff. Wouldn't have been right serving him up like that.'

Adam feels as though somebody has reached

166

inside his skull and squeezed his brain for firmness. He wouldn't be surprised to feel pulped cerebral cortex running down his cheeks.

'You like Cliff Richard?' he asks, quietly.

'Lovely voice,' says the driver, a little snippily.

The song changes. Adam wonders if his life could get any more surreal, then stops, lest Fate be listening and open to temptation.

'He's just over-eager,' says Irons, suddenly. His East London accent is gravelly with cigarettes. 'The boy, I mean. He wants to impress his mum. His granddad. He thought he was helping. He hero worships Mr Jardine. Wants to be just like him. Try not to be too upset.'

Adam can't bite back the laugh. 'Try not to be too upset? Would you be upset?'

The driver shrugs. 'I've had worse and got over it. Forgiveness is a beautiful thing.'

He glares out of the window, trying to slow his pulse, watching as the council estate, with its boarded-up shops and spray-painted shutters, slowly bleeds into detached homes and oak-lined avenues, bistros and boutiques.

'My name's Irons,' says the driver, quietly. 'You can add a mister, if it feels less odd. But Irons will do. I don't give out my name very often, so I hope you appreciate the gesture and what it means.'

Adam looks back at him. 'You know who I am, I'm guessing.'

'I know your name. I know you got arrested a few days back after losing your temper with some coppers. I know you did a bit of work with Larry Paris. I know you're a long way from home.

167

After that, I don't know very much, but finding things out is one of my specialities. I don't have many others.'

Adam pauses. Clicks his tongue against the roof of his mouth. 'I had nothing to do with Larry's death, you know that, right?'

'None of my business,' says Irons, with a sniff. 'If I thought it was you, and that you'd put his body somewhere it caused problems for me and mine, then we'd be having a very different conversation.'

'I don't doubt it,' mutters Adam.

Irons takes his hands off the wheel and lights an untipped cigarette from a gold packet. Adam runs his gaze over him, hoovering up details. He is wearing polyester-blend grey trousers, black shirt, thin black tie, and a heavy, zip-up, leather jacket. He is somewhere between sixty and seventy, but with his sores and diseased features, he looks to Adam as though he could have died years ago and simply not been informed.

'We can drop all this, if you like,' says Adam, trying to keep his voice light. 'Drop me at a station, I'll shoot off home. I had enough problems already without, y'know, all this . . .'

Irons gives something like a smile. 'Don't wet your pants. You're not in bother.'

Adam looks sceptical. 'Would I know if I was?'

'Yes.'

Adam grinds his teeth. He wishes he could open the window and gulp down some fresh air. The smell in the car is making him feel sick, reaching into his throat, stroking his thorax, climbing into his belly.

'So?' asks Adam.

'So what?'

Adam waves his arms. 'So what just happened?'

There is a foul noise as Irons sucks his cheek. 'Look, Mr Jardine isn't as young as he was. Alison's very good at the business and Timmy sometimes feels a bit of a spare part. He's always up at the house with those friends of his. Mr Jardine's made them a room of their own with those computers they like and videos and whatnot, and he doesn't mind them hanging around, but they keep asking him about the old days. About before. They've read all the books and the papers and heard all the stories about who he was. They want to impress him, that's all.'

'So why did they think doing me over would impress him?'

Irons looks vaguely apologetic. 'I do as I'm asked, son. And I was asked to make sure you didn't get hurt.'

'Asked by who?'

Irons glares at the road. 'Just keep your powder dry. It's worked out well. You're getting an audience with the queen.'

'The queen?'

Irons sighs, a plume of grey. It might be smoke, or the last dregs of his soul. 'No more questions, eh? You sound like a copper.'

'A copper? You must be joking.'

'I am, actually. I know you're not a copper.'

'How do you know?'

'Feel your pulse. It's still pulsing. So, take that as proof.'

'My brain is hurting. Seriously, let's call it a day . . .'

'Shush, lad. Be a good boy.'

They drive in silence a little while longer, through ever smaller towns and down windier, tree-lined roads. Adam broods and worries and thinks, briefly, about trying to make a call with the mobile phone in his pocket. One glance at Irons is enough to dissuade him.

Five minutes later, the car is turning right through black, wrought-iron gates onto a gravelled drive, hemmed by bare trees and bushes with thick green leaves. The driveway opens onto a large forecourt, which borders an immaculate green lawn, lush with dew and fine rain.

Against the darkening sky, sits the house. Opulent. Extravagant. Broodingly wealthy and eccentrically frayed around the edges.

'And they say crime doesn't pay,' says Adam, quietly.

'They're wrong,' says Irons. 'But Mr Jardine isn't a criminal. He's a businessman.'

'They all say that,' says Adam.

'No, they don't,' says Irons, pulling up beside a yellow VW Beetle with flowers painted on its side, in front of the steps which lead up to the house. 'I'm a criminal, and I admit it.'

'What they get you for?' asks Adam, fizzing with energy. He tries too hard to be funny. Fails. 'Fashion Police?'

'No, son,' says Irons, taking the last inch of cigarette out of his mouth and turning his black, shark-like eye on Adam. 'I'm a killer.'

170

Nineteen

A curvy, middle-aged woman in an expensive dress, black raincoat and leather boots emerges from the double-doors at the front of the house. She has blonde hair running to grey, cut into a layered bob. There is a softness to her face that suggests a melted kind of beauty: that if she could just be twisted and bound at the scalp, she would pass for twenty-five. She wears enough fake tan to offer decent protection in the event of a punch to the jaw.

The woman stops as Adam gets out of the car. She stands completely immobile, the wind tugging at her clothes, one hand on her hip, the other pushing her hair back from her eyes. Her lips, a shade of pink that is too young for her, part slightly, as though receiving the sacrament. She looks at Adam as if he were a risen martyr.

Irons, his strange aroma hanging ripe on the air, sees something in the woman's expression. He turns and looks at Adam, again. Adam feels as though he were enduring a living autopsy: as if he were pinned out, skin folded back, a subject for dissection and analysis. It is all he can do not to pull his jacket over his head and hide.

'Hi,' says Adam, unnerved. He feels silly. Out of place. Doesn't know what to say or hope for.

171

The woman seems to shake herself out of her trance and walks towards Adam. He can feel her eyes on him like an X-ray. He has never been devoured this way before, never been consumed so entirely in a gaze. He is self-conscious, as though undergoing an inspection, an assessment. He feels tested, weighed, on the scales of her stare.

She leans in as if to kiss him, then checks herself, extends a hand adorned with jewellery. Adam takes it, and feels her hand tremble in his.

'Hi,' she says, on a voice that dances on the air like a dandelion seed. Then, more firmly: 'I'm Alison Jardine. I understand there was a mix-up?'

He gives her his best smile. 'Nice to meet you,' he says. 'I'm sorry about all this.'

'All this?' she asks. 'Probably my fault. Blundering about, causing mischief . . . Well,' she continues, and rubs her hands together as if she's cold, 'all sorted now, I hope.' Then, to Irons: 'Was there any trouble? Where's he at?'

'Off in a sulk,' says Irons. 'Apparently we don't know what he's capable of.'

'Oh we do,' says Alison, showing teeth. Her gaze zeroes in on the bruise on Adam's cheek. She glances at his hand, checking for signs of violence. She nods to herself.

'I don't really know what's going on,' says Adam, his guts filling with dirty water as he looks from one to the other. He wants to call home. Hear his daughter's voice. Wants to call his mum. 'It's a lovely place you've got here. Been here a while, have you? I've got a little semi-detached. Portsmouth. It's okay, I suppose. Kids have kind

172

of wrecked it but it makes it feel more homely. Rent it, of course. I did own a place but I signed it over to the mum of my little girl. Tilly, she's called. The girl, not her mum . . .'

Adam stops talking, embarrassed with himself. Irons lights another cigarette. 'We need to chat,' he says to Alison. 'I think I'm missing a piece of this story.'

'I'll explain later,' says Alison, chewing her lip and returning her eyes to Adam's face. She drinks him in as if through a straw.

'I reckon I'm just about caught up,' growls Irons. He gives Adam his attention. 'Alison here doesn't let many people come to the house. Her business is her business, and I don't ask more questions than I have to, but when she asks me to give her son a slap and to keep you safe from harm, and then to bring you home for a nice little chat, some part of my brain gets all fizzy with static. But I'll leave you be. I've got things to sort out. Thoughts to roll around in. I won't be far away though. And I can move faster than you'd think.'

Adam fights the urge to look away. He meets his own reflection in the mirrored surface of Irons's glasses. 'I'm grateful,' he says, and means it. Then he forces himself to put out his hand. After a moment's hesitation, Irons takes off his right glove. His hands are covered in tattoos: black-blue ink, cobwebs and sea-beasts, twisted and snarled on great stony knuckles. Adam doesn't clinch at the connection. Feels Irons' fingers close over his; registering the warm dry roughness of the older man's palm against his own. Irons' breath seems to stick in his gullet. An unexpected gasp catches in his throat. He coughs, painfully, and breaks contact, punching himself in the chest with his hand.

'Irons?' asks Alison, reaching out a hand.

'Are we done?' wheezes Irons.

'Irons, we'll talk later . . .'

'Are we done, Alison?'

Alison nods her permission. He stares at Adam, the same searching gaze that Alison had given him as she emerged from the house. He's beginning to feel there is a treasure map drawn in his freckles and wrinkles.

'We cool?' asks Adam, feeling daft.

Irons turns away. Walks off across the forecourt, onto the grass, and out of sight, down the garden and into the trees. The whiff remains on the air, a heat haze of wet vegetation.

'He's a very intense man,' says Adam, trying to lighten the mood. 'Irons. It suits him.'

Alison gives him her attention. She smells of orange juice and grenadine. 'He's a good man, is Irons. I know he looks a bit . . .'

'Like a leper who shaves with a potato peeler?'

'. . . a bit, funny, I was going to say, but he's done a lot for my family. He means the world to my father. He was away for a long time and I know how he missed him. Been friends for years.'

'Does he live in a cave in the woods?'

'No, no. He's got the old gamekeeper's cottage. It used to . . . never mind.'

'So, Mr Jardine is your dad, yes?'

'For my sins, yes.'

They stand looking at each other, buffeted by

the wind, their clothes growing damp on the misty rain, the darkness sliding towards the ground like a screen. Even this, this discussion of Alison's origins, seems to tweak something inside them both, some reminder of why they are here, now, in the forecourt of the big house, too afraid and too curious to open themselves up.

'This hasn't really gone as I planned, you know,' says Adam, with a half smile. 'Not that I planned anything, really. I just had to know. When my dad, my adopted dad, I mean, when he told me the truth, I just . . .'

'I can't imagine it,' she says, and seems to shudder, as if in pain. It seems for a moment as though the action is a response to her own words, a manifestation of the voice inside her which says, *Yes, you can. You've imagined it all his life.*

'This is all kind of doing my brain in,' says Adam, and wishes he could find a more impressive, articulate turn of phrase. He feels like he might shiver at any moment.

'Me too,' she says quietly, and Adam wonders again, if this might be her. If his reunion with a woman he did not know he had lost has come here, in the half-dark, in the shadow of a gangster's mansion.

He searches her face for familiarity, a feature he knows as his own, an expression he recognizes from his reflection. Perhaps the mouth, he thinks. The full lower lip, the smile's sternness in repose. The eyes? The dark beneath. Is the blonde real?

They catch each other staring, and smile, give in to a shared moment that pricks the balloon of

175

anxiety, and they deflate a little, smile again, and roll their eyes.

'Weird, this,' she says, laughing.

'You reckon?'

'Just a little. Look, shall we take a walk?'

'If you like. You've seen one stately home, you've seen them all.'

'Oh, it's not that stately. Costs a bugger to heat. Would cost a fortune if we bought it today.'

'It's nice. Very secluded.' Then, tentatively: 'Is your father inside?'

'Yes, he doesn't get out much any more,' she says, and takes her eyes from Adam's for the first time. 'He doesn't know you're here. He's old. He doesn't need those feelings again. I wasn't even sure if I should respond . . .'

Adam looks up at the house, its stained glass and leaded windows, its sloping eaves and sturdy brick. In this light, it is a sinister place, a fairy-tale castle on a hillside. Adam sees Jardine stalking the corridors of his vast home, torn with guilt and regret, remorse over past deeds. He wonders where the image comes from.

'There's so much I need to know,' he says, softly. 'And I don't know why I have to. I wasn't exactly living the dream before I knew, but now? I'm lost.'

Alison steps closer and looks up into his face with a tenderness, and perhaps a flicker of something more.

'Let's take that walk,' she says, and he feels her warm hand through the thick cloth of his coat.

'Fine,' he says, blinking, slowly. 'It's nippy, though. Are you warm enough?'

Alison looks at her best friend's lost son, and gives a grin that warms her through. 'I'm fine, thanks,' she says, and links her arm through his. She steers him off the gravel and onto the path, paved with wood shavings, which leads into the woods, and down to the stream. She holds him tighter than she means to, and wonders if she holds him close enough, it will be possible to feel Pamela again.

Twenty

Were anybody watching, it would appear that the big, scarred man in the living room of the drafty cottage were having a heart attack.

He is on his knees before the fireplace, gazing up at the savage strokes; the scars and swirls of lurid paint which pattern the wall.

His hands clutch at his chest, as though he is trying to pull a stone from inside his ribcage.

His face, never pretty, is now a tortured, writhing thing. It is as if the mask of his features is mirroring some anguish within.

Irons sees his breath upon the cold air. It rises as a cloud, and in the sepia glow of his melted eyes, it takes shape, and becomes a veil, draped across the images which adorn the chimney breast: the paintbrush having been wielded with enough force to scar the brickwork and plaster.

He sees *her*.

He clutches at his chest and inhales, deeply, sucking back his own breath.

One thought, thumping the inside of his skull. *Pamela.*

He falls backwards inside his mind, crashing through layers upon layers of stacked memory. Halts that cold, pretty night in the spring of

178

1971. Sees Pamela. Sees the night it all went wrong . . .

She's barefoot. Happy. She emits something between a wriggle and a shiver as the grass folds her feet inside a lovely, damp embrace, and takes the sting from her mucky soles and painted toes. She holds her high-heeled shoes in her hand. She could not have afforded to buy such shoes herself, with their sleek black straps and teardrop crystal studs, and she intends to keep them as pristine as the white cardboard box (with its waves of pale blue tissue paper, scrunched, elegantly scrumpled, a breaking wave) in which they arrived, and which she now keeps under her bed, filled with her paints, her charcoals and oils. She does not mind getting mud on her feet or legs. They are her own. They are trifling things. They were not a gift from Mr Jardine, and as such, require less care.

The fine rain feels gloriously cool on her bare arms, as she had known it would when she slipped away from the party to wrap herself in the oily dark. Her eye make-up is smeared, having been sweated into paste during the last dance. The white dress, with its tapered waist and its bulbous bottom of scrunched-up silk, is a very grown-up affair.

The girl is too young to dress this way, but allowances have been made because it is a special occasion, and because Mr Jardine will look after her.

The girl, who is called Pamela, feels like a princess. She has felt this way most of the time since

179

Mr Jardine decided that his daughter could use a sister, and took in the clever, pretty orphan girl.

Beneath the damp leaves, beneath a sugar-dusted blackboard of stars, Pamela stands in the darkness and listens to the faint noise coming from the party in the big Georgian manor house behind her. The DJ is playing 'Puppet on a String', one of Alison's favourites. Pamela can't imagine the other guests are enjoying it as much. Mr Jardine, despite tonight's good mood, is more of a jazz man, and the big men in suits and expensive coats who are standing at the bar and drinking champagne and laughing and slapping backs, don't seem like big Sandie Shaw fans.

Pamela wishes Alison had come outside with her. Though she likes the dark and the rain and the fresh air, and the dark shapes of the hedgerows and the trees and flowerbeds in the plush gardens, she would like to have somebody to talk to as she stands on the wet grass beneath the big weeping willow and catches her breath. She wonders if Alison will kiss Thomas tonight. She wonders if she will dare. She and Alison have practised kissing on their pillows and on the backs of their hands, and even tried kissing each other before they started giggling, but she knows she would be too afraid to let somebody like Thomas put his tongue in her mouth. It seems gross. Thomas is sixteen, and with his smell of cigarettes and Brylcreem, he seems to her more like a man than a boy, and she associates men with big underpants on washing lines and proud after-dinner farts. The only men she exempts from this harsh categorization are Mr Jardine, and Irons. Mr Jardine has a

180

graceful kind of firmness about him. An unim-
posing solidity. A strength contained. He is the
equator of her world. Irons is something else.
Something cold and pale and nameless. He is a
shiver. A handprint on a condensation-speckled
mirror. He is the shadow at the window. The sen-
sation behind you. Never smiling, but always
watching. Alison doesn't know the full details but
she told her the story of how he got hurt. How
they tied him to a chair and super-heated a sharp-
ening iron in a brazier. Held it to his face and
made him listen to his own sizzling flesh; to smell
himself cooking. Alison doesn't find his face fright-
ening so much as interesting. She enjoys his
company. He's quite clever, when he lets himself
talk. Nice manners, too. Always thanks her when
she pops over to the cottage and reads to him, or
sketches him a picture of one of the wildflowers
from the woods behind the house.

The light from the half-moon glints off the
bonnets of the big expensive cars in the driveway,
and Pamela takes a pride in knowing she arrived
in the finest one of all. She lets herself remember
the journey here with Alison and Eva. It was sixty
miles across dreary countryside, but the comfy
seats and the low hum of the radio made it pass
in a snooze.

Pamela feels cool enough now. The sweat she
worked up dancing has dried on her body.
She hopes she doesn't smell. Although she is
enjoying herself, she feels a little out of place,
here, in this big hotel. The other guests all have
that whiff of money about them. She recognizes
some of them from the newspapers. Alison told

181

her that the tall man in the pink shirt and the white tie is a footballer. Ace Somebody. Ace-hole, she jokes. There are politicians, too, drinking honey-coloured liquid from big, goldfish-bowl glasses. There are policemen, dressed in more luxurious suits than their salaries alone could provide. They orbit Mr Jardine like flirty moons.

Rubbing her chicken-skin arms and checking the soles of her feet for dirt, she turns to walk back into the party. She hopes she hasn't been missed. She fears Mr Jardine will be cross if he knows she has been outside on her own, and his fondness for her makes her feel special, and almost as pretty as Alison, and enables her to come to big houses with beautiful gardens like these, and to dance to pop songs with her friends. She hopes to slip back to her table without being noticed. She decides to tell anybody who asks that she was busy sketching. Immortalizing the moon, the petrol-black of the cloudy sky, the heat-haze of rain against the forest. Mr Jardine likes her sketches. Says she will go far, if she works hard. Even presented her with the most beautiful set of oil paints she had ever seen, when he hosted her birthday party at one of his snooker clubs last year.

Pamela takes a step towards the house. The darkness around her becomes alive. A patch of charcoal air becomes a blunt black mass, and it steps forward and lashes out. Pamela feels something cold and hard strike her above her left eyebrow, and everything suddenly tastes like money smells, and she feels as though she's being sucked down the plughole in the bathtub and she swirls into unconsciousness.

182

The shape leans down and picks her up like a mannequin. It hoists her as though she were weightless. One of her shoes slips off as it carries her, soundlessly, through the trees and the darkness and across the grass. The sounds from the party fade away.

The lights from the road grow brighter, and the shape becomes a man. His face is red with excitement and exertion. He is wearing jeans and white trainers and a black jumper and a waterproof coat. Pamela is slung over his shoulder, her arms hanging down his back. The man fancies she is trying to touch his bottom, and he smiles, showing teeth, and his breath begins to come in a stutter.

He reaches the low dry-stone wall at the edge of the stately gardens. He drapes Pamela's body on the top of the wall, and climbs over it himself. He lifts her into his arms, the way he would comfort a crying toddler and walks with her down the kerb of the quiet country road to the passing place where he has parked the van. He opens the unlocked back door and with a grunt, tosses Pamela inside. She lays on her back, arms outstretched like a snow angel, one leg drawn up, a gash and rapidly swelling bruise on her forehead. Her lips move, wordlessly, and her eyelids, fluttering like leaves, make the man wonder for a moment if she is having a fit.

The man climbs into the back of the van, and pulls the door closed behind him. His trainers leave a muddy print on the paint-splattered dust sheet he has laid out like a tablecloth. He pulls two large, black torches from the metal toolbox behind the door, and switches them on. Two garish circles of light illuminate the darkness within the van. Coils of rope and rolls of gaffer tape appear snake-like on their hooks on the van walls. The hard hat, donkey jacket and luminous waterproof on the back of the door are suddenly human-like, standing mute witness as the man begins to remove Pamela's clothes. When she is naked, he places his face close to her bushy vagina, and breathes deeply. He repeats the process at the armpits, neck, mouth and feet. Then he begins to remove his own clothes.

The man lifts a World War Two gasmask from the toolbox and slips it over his face, before unfastening his jeans, pushing them down, and kicking them off with his trainers and socks. His penis has been hard all day, but now juts from his body like a lance. Each breath now comes with a faint grunt.

The man steps out of the van and feels the faint rain on his skin. He walks, naked, to the driver's door, leans in, and switches on the ignition. The radio comes to life. He walks back to the rear of the vehicle, and climbs inside once more; his breath warm and fetid on his cheeks as he sucks hot air inside the gas mask. In the hours that follow, the mask will fill with spittle and hot air, and his eyes will grow wide, and he will skin his knees, shins and toes. Pamela will see her own frightened face in the reflective eyes of the gas mask. She will be reminded of the giant squid that attacked the submarine in the black-and-white film she saw on her washed-out TV. She will see her freckly, rounded features, twisted and tear-streaked, stretching away on a neck of

184

straining tendons, as if trying to get as far away as possible from the hot, burning squelching pain between her legs. She will know her rapist only from the grey-black of his hair and the patterned ink on his chest and forearms.

When Pamela stops resisting and appears to let her mind leave her body, the man will feel cheated, and visit fresh atrocities upon her. He will place a sharp blade across her cheek as he enters her, and slash jagged scars into her eyelid and earlobe. He will cut through the epidermis of her face down to the jaw-bone. He will drop the blade in his ecstasy and his fingers, scrabbling and clawing at her skin, will find the puncture wound and tear at her face, as though removing old wallpaper from a damp wall.

The skin will hang from her jaw like veal.

A winter will enter Pamela soon. Parts of her will simply cease to operate. Neural pathways will lock themselves. The best parts of her will die.

Later, Mr Jardine's men will find her at the roadside: naked, blood-soaked. Even the strongest of them will feel heat prickling at their eyes and a coldness in their guts. Mr Jardine will cry for the first time since Alison was born, and despatch death.

Nine months from now, Pamela will give birth to a son. She will not cry out during labour. She will save her tears for the moment he is plucked from her embrace, and given to the lady from the agency. She will cry then, until her soul is dry, and then never again. A week later, she will stuff tissues into her mouth until she chokes to death.

Then her benefactor will sell her son.

185

Twenty-One

Lower Drayton Lane, Portsmouth
10.58 p.m.

Adam sits at Grace's kitchen table, his coat still on, both hands wrapped around the mug of coffee that Grace has insisted he drink. The mug is unpleasantly hot against his skin, but has no desire to release it. He listens to the faint sound of Grace's lullaby as she shushes Tilly and strokes her to sleep in the Little Mermaid bedroom upstairs. His phone keeps pinging with messages from Zara. He can't find any words to reply with.

It's dark in the kitchen, lit only by the dim bulb of the extractor fan above the oven. He wishes it were brighter, but knows that if the room were light, he would long for dark.

Footsteps grow louder, and Grace comes into the kitchen. She has put her pyjamas on, to convince Tilly it is bedtime, and is wearing a grey, Snoopy-motif outfit underneath her black dressing gown.

'Dead to the world. Snoring like a docker.'

She starts clucking as she busies herself picking up Tilly's toys and moving dirty plates onto the draining board. She looks at Adam intermittently, smiling, in case he should turn his head and catch her looking. He does not look up. He simply

186

stares into his coffee, and watches the galaxies of cream swirl on its surface.

He is thinking of Alison Jardine. He'd expected her to be hard as nails. Had expected her to order that he strip to his underwear before she would even consider sharing confidences with him. Had thought that she would be difficult to read: face inscrutable as a dinner plate. Instead she had spoken to him as if they were old friends. She spoke as if she owed him an explanation. At times, he had felt that she was talking to somebody else, her words directed at some other figure, somewhere just outside his peripheral vision, watching and listening and passing judgments as they sat on the stone bench and watched the rain and told one another how they had spent the past thirty-six years.

'She held me,' says Adam, quietly. 'Back then, I mean. Two days old. She said I had lots of hair and she thought my nose looked like a little mushroom. Irons held me too. I could fit in the palm of his hand. 6lb 1oz. Smaller than Tilly.' He pauses. 'I don't think she ever did.'

'She?'

'Pamela. It was a bad birth. She wasn't well. And the nurse thought it wouldn't do her any good to let me latch on. Out of sight, out of mind.'

'Oh, Adam . . .'

'She thinks it was done for the right reasons. She was still a girl. Pamela. Just turned fifteen. And her injuries. What he'd done to her. Nobody even thought the pregnancy would come to full term. He hired a live-in nurse. Tried his best by

187

her, or so Alison says. It wasn't enough. She stayed alive long enough to have me. And then she did what she felt she had to.'

'I'm so sorry, Adam.'

He stares into his mug. Thinks of the picture she had shown him. A single snap. Two girls, grinning for the camera, patterned dresses and big hair. He'd seen himself in her, just as Alison had. In the almond shape of the face, the line of the jaw. They had the same hands. Big palms and slim fingers.

'What kind of man . . .?' he begins, and his face creases. He makes a blade with his fingers and stabs it at his chest. 'What's in here? In my blood? Fuck, Grace, I'm rotten all the way through . . .'

'No, Adam, you can't think that way,' she says, gently, as she puts her hand on his. She means what she says. He is Adam. Wherever he came from, whoever his parents were, he is Tilly's father, and a good man.

'It changes everything,' hisses Adam, and places his mug down so he can use a hand to massage his brow. He has repeated this action so many times, the skin is becoming raw.

'You're you. You're your own person. A wonderful person. A great father. A good man. The rest is just circumstance . . .'

They sit in the dark, listening to each other breathe, to the sound of their lips on the coffee mugs, the mugs on the table, their chair legs on the floor.

'There's no doubt?' asks Grace, and there is a well of hope echoing in her voice.

188

'None,' says Adam. Then, again: 'None.'

'Can you tell me? Can you?'

'I have to get it out of me or it'll choke me, Grace,' says Adam, and he wishes he could cough up the apricot stone which is wedged in his throat. His head is spinning, as the alcohol seeks out his vulnerability, washes over it, picks it clean, leaves it bare, its nerve endings exposed. 'They found her in the early hours of the morning. Her face was hanging off. She was just a puddle of blood. You could see the bone around the orbit of her eye . . .'

'She told you this?'

'I made her. I needed to hear it all. She was barely conscious. Pamela, I mean. Some of the party guests drove her to hospital, and that's where they found out she'd been raped.'

'But she was naked? I mean . . .'

'Yeah, yeah, you know what I mean, the doctors told them the full details. Everything that had been done to her.' Adam stops, grimacing.

'What did the police do?'

Adam glares at the floor. 'Mr Jardine didn't want the police called. She said he already knew who had done it, and that it would be dealt with.'

'Jesus . . .'

'Pamela didn't speak about it for weeks. She was too messed up. They had to stitch her face back together, she lost the sight in one eye. Looked like she'd been mauled by a dog. When she came to, she could barely even speak. Just managed to tell Alison it had happened in a van. That there was music, and that he'd worn a gas mask. From the war. She couldn't tell them all

189

the things he had done to her, but they know from the medical reports.'

'God, that's horrible . . .'

'Then they tell her she's pregnant.'

Adam makes a sound that Grace thinks is the start of tears, but which becomes a hollow laugh.

'That's me,' he says. 'The icing on the fucking cake.'

'But she kept you,' says Grace. 'She didn't have an abortion . . .'

'No, no. Wasn't on the cards apparently, although everybody around her wanted her to get rid of it. Asked her how on earth she could stand to look at a baby brought into the world like that.'

'Oh, Adam,' says Grace, filling up with tears, shivering inside her dressing gown. She cannot imagine how this feels for him.

'So how did you end up with your mum and dad?' she asks, gently.

Adam stands up from the table, walks to the cupboard by the sink and pulls out a bottle of white rum. He sits back at the table and puts a large measure into the cold, half-empty coffee cup, then drinks it down. He feels the acid burn his stomach, the pain inside him, and thinks, for a moment, he can hear a demon inside him shriek in indignation. He takes another drink and then stares directly at Grace.

'She said it was a standard adoption. There was talk of raising me themselves but they wanted to give me the best start they could. Without me knowing what I was.'

'Adam, you're still you. You're a good man . . .'

'Yeah, course,' mutters Adam.

190

'But there's no paperwork, is there?' asks Grace, cautiously. 'I mean, you're taking a lot of this at face value . . .'

Adam waves a hand. 'The things he did to her,' he says, and screws up his face. 'To a child.'

'I'm so sorry, Adam.'

He licks his dry lips. Takes another drink. 'Pamela said it was a man. A man with graying hair and tattoos. A gas mask. A man with rough hands and dirt under his nails.'

He stops. Drops his eyes to the floor as if his head is too heavy to hold up.

'What about Larry?' asks Grace, softly. 'Did they know him? Had he been nosying around?'

Adam swallows, his jaw aching. 'She didn't know the name until after the body had been identified. Didn't know my name until you rang her snooker club and left a message. It's been hard for her. Knocked her for six.'

'I'm sure she's tough,' says Grace.

'Yeah,' says Adam, only half there. 'Soft too, though. You could see she wanted to cry but wouldn't let the tears fall. And she was fighting with herself – like she wanted to hug me but wouldn't give in to it. She tried to give me money too.'

Grace pulls a face. 'Guilty conscience?'

He shakes his head. 'Don't say that. She was okay, you know. She was kind. Wanted to see pictures of Tilly. Zara. You.' He manages a smile. 'Said you sounded like a trouble-maker, but she meant it in a nice way. Reckons you must care about me a lot.'

191

Grace rolls her eyes. 'She offered you money? How much money?'

'She never said a figure. I just told her I didn't want anything. She didn't push it.'

Grace sucks her lower lip. 'So how did you leave it? I mean, what next? Are you staying in touch? Is there any family you could contact? Pamela's parents, maybe?'

'All dead,' says Adam, shaking his head. 'Her dad was pals with Mr Jardine. That's how Pamela and Alison became friends. Moved in the same circles in Canning Town. Pamela's dad, I think his name was Archie – he died when Pamela was ten or eleven. Stabbed. A fight in a pub. Mr Jardine took care of his widow, or what was left of her. Paid her bills, kept her comfortable. It didn't stop her losing her mind. Drank herself batty. Threw herself in front of a train. Mr Jardine took Pamela in. He was doing well by then. Big house. Alison at private school. Business was booming. Pamela must have thought she'd landed on her feet.'

Grace looks unsure. 'With two dead parents? Living in a gangster's mansion? I don't know.'

'Alison said that Irons had a soft spot for her,' continues Adam, to himself. 'He'd been hurt. The injuries I told you about – they made it hard to look at him. Alison says Pamela used to go over to the cottage where he was convalescing – where he still lives. She'd talk with him. Read to him. She did drawings for him. First person who was ever kind to him, according to Alison. After what happened, after I was born, he couldn't deal with it. He went after the man who did it. After my . . . after my father . . .'

192

Grace watches as Adam dissolves in on himself. She reaches out to hold him and he flinches at her touch.

'I'm fucking rotten,' he whispers, as she wraps her arms around him and pulls him close.

'Adam, you're a good man . . .'

'Rotten all the way through.'

Twenty-Two

Irons lolls in the armchair in front of the dead fire, staring at the patterns on the wall. He has been sitting here for more than two hours. The drink in his right hand remains untouched. A cigarette has burned to dust in the ashtray on his lap.

Alison was gentle as she swung the club that floored him. Took the trouble to hold his hand and sit him down as she confirmed what he had known as he wrapped his fingers around Adam's and felt the familiar skin.

He's Pamela's boy. He's Dozzle's blood. He's the product of an angel and a demon and he's all grown up.

Irons had held himself together. Just growled, as she left, the only piece of advice that seemed important.

Don't tell your dad – it will finish him.

Irons has never been one to analyse or question. He is instinctive and direct. He knows, without thinking, the best way to dispatch a problem. Can claim a life without arousing suspicion, or ever biting his lip or scratching his head over the safest way to get the job done.

Now he examines his thoughts like a prospector panning for gold. Sifts through the

194

possibles, the various outcomes, the best and worst scenarios.

He thinks about his long association with the family. The blood he has spilled and the scars it cost him. He thinks of Pamela and what was done to her. His own part in it.

A name scuttles across his mind as his thoughts form and evaporate, twist and entwine. He thinks about Larry Paris, trussed up and smashed to bits and dunked at Dead Man's Vale. Adam hadn't done it, of that Irons was sure. But he'd paid him to look into his background. And something he found had made his death preferable to life for somebody. Irons drifts back through the years. Thinks of men long since turned to dust. Considers those left alive. The footballer, Ace. The councillor who pulled the strings Mr Jardine wanted to be pulled. Freeman of the city, now. There had been others, too. At the manor house. Strangers. People he didn't recognize and who flinched when they saw his face.

He chews at his cheek until he tastes blood. Hears his own wheezing breath as the cells in his lungs devour his living flesh and pull him closer to the grave in tiny, infinitesimal increments.

Adam, he thinks.

The boy was well named by the family that took him. Pamela would have liked it.

Irons glares again at the picture on the chimney breast. She did this. Carved this ugly, leering memory into the wall, hacking at the brickwork with her paintbrush until this leering, bug-eyed monster came to life. She painted it for him, so he would know whom to kill. It had never struck him as a good likeness of Tommy Dozzle, but Mr Jardine had promised him. Said that he needed to be left alone until they had completed their business. Told him that they would have their vengeance eventually, but that now was not the time. In all of their long years of friendship, this was the only command that Irons was unable to carry out. He took Tommy Dozzle to pieces. It cost him eighteen years.

Irons closes his eyes. He tells himself that he has only ever had one job. To look out for the Jardine family. To do what needs to be done. To sew the city up like a duck's arse and make sure nobody ever tried to unpick the stitches.

He knows what he must do. As much for the family as himself.

He needs to find out about the boy. Climb inside his life and judge him. His worth. See what the man sired by a monster had become, and decide, in Pamela's name, if he be allowed to live.

Twenty-Three

Victoria Park, Portsmouth
November 1st, 2.44 p.m.

Adam throws a branch, thick as an arm, at the crackle-glazed mirror of ice which covers the duck pond. It smashes the surface into irregular triangles, and as Tilly squeals with excitement, coffee-brown water splashes upwards. More mud begins to ooze through the cracks. The disturbance throws up some of the treasures from the pond's murky depths. A hypodermic needle, a used condom and an empty crisp packet, manufactured by a company long since in administration, rise to the surface, before sinking back down.

Tilly is wide-mouthed and amazed, her jaw hanging open beneath cheeks and nose pink with cold. She is wearing a bobble hat, scarf, padded coat, mittens and wellington boots, but is still feeling the chill.

The sun is shining brightly from a blue sky. The puddles in the pitted concrete paths are as frozen as the pond, and Tilly has slipped over several times, while running around the pond, chasing the ducks. None of the spills have been enough to cry about, but she is getting tired, and her nose is running, and will soon be in the mood for tears.

Adam returns to the plastic table and chairs by the café and sits down next to Selena.

'Best be getting back soon,' mutters Adam, watching Tilly chase a pigeon. 'She's cold. How are you? You look as cold as a penguin's toenails.'

Selena is huddled down inside her sensible coat, her face a charcoal drawing on white paper. 'I'm fine,' she mumbles. 'I'd run around, but my knees have locked.'

'You'll talk about this winter, one day,' says Adam. 'You'll tell your grandkids they don't know they're born, and that the winters when you were little would have killed them off.'

'Old people do that, don't they?' grins Selena, teeth chattering. 'When I meet your parents, will they tell me loads of stuff about the old days?'

Adam drops his gaze. He keeps trying to lighten his mood but even the most innocuous comment feels weighted with symbolism. He knows that Zara wants him to introduce her to his mum and dad. He knows, too, that she would have supported him these past weeks if he had let her know what he has been going through. But to do so would be to show himself vulnerable; to let her see what he really is, and it already hurts him like a burn when she opens the latest bill for the restaurant and he can do nothing to help save telling her to put it on the pile. He wants to fix everything for her, though whether it is for love of her or a need to measure up to some inexplicable ideal, he truly would not be able to say. He feels like his mind is stuffed to overflowing with things to worry about. It's been weeks since Bosworth hauled him in for questioning and he hasn't heard a solitary word about whether he's likely to face another grilling. He's had a couple of calls from Angus, asking whether he got anywhere with the note that Larry had left beneath his computer, but so much has happened that Adam hasn't felt able to open up about any of it. His world feels like it's been knocked off its axis. He cannot make himself do the things he knows to be best for him. He should break off contact with Alison. Forget the Jardines. Commit to Zara, or have the good grace to walk away. He should buy his mum a box of chocolates and tell her he's sorry he went looking for some other mother when she's only ever done her best by him. He should sit by his dad's bed and read him a cowboy story. He doesn't do any of the things he should. Just keeps sinking deeper, and trying to work out whether the bad seed within him has already flowered.

'You okay? You look all far away . . .'

'Lot on my mind,' he says, quietly. 'It's not easy, y'know. Being a grown up. Doing the right thing.'

'You do it really well,' says Selena, loyally. 'Mum isn't easy to be with. I love her, but she's hard work.'

'She's got a lot to deal with,' says Adam, and means it. He lets her picture flash in his mind and feels a sudden swelling of emotion, as if he has blown on an ember. He thinks of how he has been these past days; the distance between them; the restraint she has shown in turning a blind eye to his clandestine phone calls, his busy thumbs on the keypad of his laptop, his phone. He wants to pick up the children, take Zara by the hand, and lead them somewhere pretty and warm. Wants to make them see how much they mean to him. Wants to show them he can be a better man. He just can't afford it.

This is me, now, he thinks, as his spirits sink. *This is me forever.*

There are only two customers in The Basil Pot, and Zara, instinctively, is working out how much food they will need to order to make opening this morning worthwhile. When she considers the cost of employing the chef, and a waitress, she realizes that they will both need to order a three-course dinner and two bottles of wine for her to even start making a profit. He, a full-faced, bearded, mature student, orders eggs with hollandaise sauce on a toasted bagel. She, plain and homely, treats herself to blueberry pancakes with crème fraiche. A pot of coffee and a jug of tap water. Just over £11 for the lot.

Be a millionaire, she thinks, and somehow the thought is a prayer. *Leave me a grand as a tip.*

Zara wishes she were over the road, dressed in thick jeans and Ugg boots, ski jacket and bobble hat, snuggling up with Adam and watching their children play in the park. She wonders if she will make as much money today as the little brick-built café by the pond, selling its teas and its Kit-Kats.

The phone rings, and as she answers it, she finds the pause before she hears the voice, too long. Too uncomfortable. The second of anticipation, of not knowing if it will be a booking for a table of ten, or Sol asking for his money back, is interminable.

In the second of not knowing, she pictures Adam's face. His silence these past days. His coldness. His icy, distracted, passionless love-making. She knows it has got too much for him, now. She knows he will leave her soon, or worse still, ask her to leave him. She wonders if and when he goes, he will live with Grace, that perfect, sweet, sensitive ball of lard on the far side of town whom Adam has allowed to meet his parents and who can't seem to leave him alone; texting him a dozen times in the moments that Zara is supposed to have Adam to herself.

My best friend, Adam had said, when they first talked about her. *It was just one night. It's not her I want. It's you.*

Zara wonders when he started believing his own lies.

Adam and Selena sit quietly, listening to Tilly squeal and point out the grey squirrels which play in the bare branches that form a canopy over the pond. In his pocket, Adam's hand closes around his telephone. It is almost a permanent fixture in his fist. Each time it vibrates, he asks himself who he wants it to be. He fears new revelations, new slashes at his open wounds, but he also fears their healing. He wants to telephone Alison and ask more questions, but no answer he has yet received has made him feel any better and he doubts he could tolerate more pain.

Jordan runs up, muddy water dripping from

soaked trouser legs. His face is a mask of hurt feelings.

'One of my new friends said he didn't want to play with me any more,' says Jordan, panting, pointing randomly in the direction of the swings.

'The swine,' smiles Adam. He pulls him onto his knee and hugs him. 'That's people for you – thoroughly disappointing. Anyway, it's his loss.'

'But he was really mean,' continues Jordan.

'People can be mean sometimes. Blame jealousy. It's because you're funny and clever and handsome. I get the same treatment.'

'He said my sword was rubbish.'

Adam turns Jordan to face him. He likes the feeling of comforting the lad. Knows he would miss it, and so much else, if he were to walk away. 'What sword, mate?'

'I made a sword out of a tree . . .'

'You do me good, mate, you really do. Would other, less brilliant, people think your sword was just a stick, do you think?'

'Yeah, it was my sword and he said it was rubbish . . .'

'Well, what does he know? I bet it was a great sword. Where is it now?'

'I left it by the swings.'

'You'd better go back and get it then before somebody steals it. It could be valuable.'

'Thanks, Adam.'

Adam realizes he feels better. Watches as the boy runs off, and feels the heat of Selena's smile as she stares at the side of his face. He blows a raspberry, pleased to be feeling a little more familiar to himself. He wonders, idly, whether people will ever think of him as Jordan's real father. Whether he will ever call him Dad. The absurdity of it all hits home. He feels at once foolish and disloyal. He's had a good upbringing. His parents love him. He doesn't need any more than he has. He closes his hand around the phone again, and calls Grace. He's going to tell her that he's decided to stop searching. Going to tell her that this has gone far enough. He knows who he is. It's time to start living right.

By the third ring, the impulse to do the right thing has devoured itself. He knows himself incapable of stopping now.

'I need to know what he looks like,' he says, before he can stop himself. 'I need to know if his face is anything like mine.'

Twenty-Four

The Basil Pot, Bridge Street, Portsmouth
4.09 p.m.

The old man sips his glass of hot water and lights
an untipped cigarette that he has extracted from
a crumpled packet. When he strikes the match,
Zara finds herself afraid that the strange aroma
which engulfs him might be methane, and that
he will explode, damply, like a compost heap.

'You're sure that's all you want,' she asks the
man, and her voice is still teary, like a violin
string wound to the very brink of snapping.

'Coffee gives me heartburn and tea dries my
mouth out,' says the man, with what sounds like
a London accent. 'Hot water does me fine.'

'Makes me think of drinking my bathwater,'
says Zara, with a girlish smile.

'I've never drunk your bathwater,' says the
man. 'I wouldn't know.'

Zara dabs again at her eyes with the neat white
handkerchief that he handed her as he picked her
up off the floor and steered her to the nearest
table. Her eyes are seamed red and she knows
they will be puffy tomorrow. She says so to the
man, as he sucks another inch off his cigarette,
and then extinguishes it between forefinger and
thumb.

'You're a looker,' says the man, and a dribble

of pinkish liquid runs down his chin. A piece of his lip has peeled off, attached to the cigarette.

'Not today,' says Zara.

'Well, you're prettier than I am.'

Zara picks up her second glass of vodka, but puts it down again before it reaches her lips. She doesn't want to drink or smoke or eat or be held, or not be held, and she feels her skin prickle again as the enormity of it all presses down upon her.

'Whatever it is, can be fixed,' says the man, as he spots the dampness returning to her eyes. 'You must have a nice young man who can make it all better.'

Zara blinks and gives in to another sob. She hates herself for showing weakness like this, but she can't seem to stop. She feels mummified with ribbons of misery, and this big old man, with his sores and his wounds and his strange smell, seems a kindly soul who genuinely wants to listen. She felt strength in him as he picked her up. She saw tenderness in his face, and a competence, a knowledge, like a transfer stuck over the mismatched lenses, the black and white eyes. His face, almost cartoonish in its appearance, does not repulse her, but intrigues. She, with her piercings and paints, her shaved head, her short skirts, finds herself admiring his uniqueness; a compulsion to touch the shiny, gnarled skin that clings to his skull like a melted carrier bag.

So she tells him. She tells him that she has a man whom she adores in a way she didn't think was possible, and that he has ridden in on a white charger and given her and her family everything they could wish for, but that she fears it is all becoming too much for him, and she has done the sums and knows that he can't afford to keep looking after them all like this. And she tells him about Grace, and how she hates herself for not being able to accept that she is just a friend. Then, in a voice wrung free of tears, she tells him of her money woes. The bailiffs. The bad people who want to take her dream.

The man sits, and smokes his way through the packet. He nods, and smiles, and soaks up what she says. He asks gentle questions about her man. Is he a good father? Is he happy? Is he a violent man? Does he ever hurt you? What are his family like? Is he local? Does he see much of his mum and dad?

Zara, lost in her own story, her own woes, does not see pinpricks of flame dancing in his eyes.

As he gets up to leave and tells her it will all be OK, and she steels herself and treats him to a kiss on his least fetid cheek, she fancies she can smell something new emanating from his ruined skin. Hiding among the corruption and the earth and the damp leaves and the cigarette smoke, she can smell the faintest whiff of burning. And flesh.

On the street, outside the restaurant, Irons sees his breath turn to fog on the air. It is black, like a thunder cloud, and rises upwards on the breeze like smoke from a fire, like dust from a death camp.

Irons coughs, and feels wetness on his chin. He scowls, and zips his jacket up to the top. The

206

zip tears a half-inch of skin from the loose skin at his Adam's apple, but it does not bleed, and he does not feel it. He sets off towards his car, parked a few streets away, on a street of Victorian terraced houses, where people carriers sniff the bumpers of Minis and Suzuki Swifts.

Irons doesn't like this city, with its wet, chilly air, its heat-haze of some undefined gloom. It is adding to his mood. He finds himself thinking about his home. He can almost feel the soft cushions of his favourite armchair around his tired legs. Irons is not one to indulge much in regret, or want, but he feels somehow shaken by the past few days, and there is something about his own fireside, his own pictures, his own surroundings, that seems somehow soothing.

Irons reaches the Hilux and climbs inside. Lights another cigarette. Feels the smoke warming him through, clinging to his bones, adding another layer of varnish and tar to muscles and organs that he sees as those of a corpse preserved in peat; hardened and solid by damp earth, silence, and time.

He feels displaced.

The boy that was conceived in anguish and given away in disgrace, has tumbled back into his life in a swirl of dead leaves, on a maelstrom of memories.

The boy he allowed to be born, is here, alive, now.

He is trying to find a way to act like the automaton that he has always been. To be the ruthless, immovable monster that carried Franco Jardine up the food chain. But he is asking questions of

207

himself. Doubting himself. Deconstructing his truths. And amid it all, his visions of her face, his mess of questions, lies, secrets, he finds himself catching the faintest trace of Zara's perfume in his nostrils, and for the merest second, it overshadows the gunpowder, the damp leaves, the cigarette smoke, the corruption, the decay. He breathes it again, and it seems to soften his bones. It is a feeling he remembers, too fleetingly, and he wants to feel again.

Twenty-Five

November 2nd, 9.36 a.m.

The same carriage, the same train, the same window. Same landscape, beyond the dirty glass, but this time it's lit by a low sunlight that adds a sort of candlewax sheen to the houses, fields, estates, hills, swishing by, swishing by . . .

Grace sips her coffee and, surprising herself with her boldness, reaches out and closes her warm hand around Adam's cold fist. He looks across at her and smiles, then strokes her wrist with his thumb. They have a conversation like this for the next few minutes, sitting in silence, communicating only by these faint, delicate, tender touches. Both have their eyes closed.

Adam has an air of unfinished business about him, this time. He doesn't look angry, but there is something about his posture and his jiggling right leg that suggests he is feeling a lot more focused, this time. He wants answers. He wants knowledge. He's absorbed what he was told last time, and now he wants to plug the gaps. It's reasonable, he tells himself. It's not much to ask, is it?

'You really think she won't mind me coming?' asks Grace, pulling a face. 'I'm not really a part of all this.'

'Yes, you are,' says Adam, giving Grace what she wants. 'You're my best friend and you're Tilly's mum, and you keep my brain from meltdown. I can't do this without you.'

'And she's sure she can do this? It's going to be hard for her too.'

'She said I deserved it. She's strong. She'll be fine.'

'And her boy? And her dad? He doesn't know?'

'She says her dad would go crazy. And if her boy turns up, I've got a few things to say to him anyway.'

They nod, and smile again, and then retreat into their own thoughts.

Adam sits and concentrates on breathing.

Today, Alison Jardine will take him to the hotel where his father raped his mother.

He will see where the rotten seed was sewn.

Alison's waiting as they emerge from the station into the weak sunlight, leaning against the bonnet of a blue Rover 75 – the kind that looks like a Jaguar, but isn't. She smiles when she sees Adam, but it flickers as it becomes clear that he is with the curvy, Indian-looking girl who walks two steps behind.

Adam strides forward, and this time, as though he has been thinking about it, doesn't hesitate. He wraps his arms around Alison, who holds back for a moment, before responding in kind. They hold each other, warm and tight.

Grace stands awkwardly to the side. She looks around and sees nothing about the landscape that

210

makes her want to stay, and nothing that makes her desperate to leave. It's a car park, like any other, and it's as cold as bloody England. She's pleased she's wearing tights under her jeans and a vest beneath her striped cotton jumper, though the denim jacket is offering little protection against the wind, which is piling up her hair on one side, like a dirty snowdrift.

Adam and Alison separate themselves and share a look, then Alison turns and gives Grace a glance. There is something appraising but not unkind in her gaze.

'Alison this is Grace. She's Tilly's mum.'

Grace shakes Alison's gloved hand, and wishes that Adam had found a better way to describe her.

'He needed a friend,' says Grace, by way of explanation. 'This has all been quite a shock.'

'It's nice that he has people who care,' says Alison, softly. Then she looks at the car and says, 'Shall we?'

Adam gets in the front, Grace in the back. It's comfortable, and tidy, save an open notepad with scribbled directions on the front seat.

Alison settles herself in the driver's seat and then looks at Adam.

'I'm doing this because you asked me to,' she says, earnestly. 'If you want to turn back at any moment, just say.'

'I'll want to all the way there,' says Adam, looking at the floor. 'But I won't let myself. Maybe it is like playing with a scab. I don't know. I just need to see. I need for it to become real.'

'I've spent more than thirty years trying to make it a bad dream,' she says. 'I've never known which compartment of my brain to put it in, so it's bled into everything.'

'Well, I'm in your nightmare now,' says Adam. 'I need to wake up.'

Twenty-Six

12.58 p.m.

A fast eighty in the outside lane, slowing down to pass through market towns and yuppie villages, then foot down again, on grey roads bisecting green hills.

Silence in the car, laying over its occupants like a dust sheet.

'Tell me about him.'

Alison seems surprised and asks him to repeat himself. He does.

'Who?'

'Him. The rapist.' He can't bring himself to say *father*.

Alison takes her eyes off the road to look at Adam. Grace feels the car swerve.

She talks in a way that suggests she has been rehearsing what to say. 'Look, you've got to remember I was a kid when this happened. All I knew was that this creepy bloke from one of the firms we worked with had tried some stuff with me that he shouldn't have done – and then he went and did the same thing to Pam. There was never any doubt who did it. Thomas Dozzle. Razzle-Dazzle, he went by. A nobody. I can't even picture him.'

Adam looks down at his shoes. 'I can't stand this,' he whispers.

'Whatever badness might be in you is cancelled out by Pamela, I swear. She was clever and kind and lovely and what happened to her was the worst thing anybody could imagine. Don't ask more questions than I can answer about Dozzle. He got what was coming to him. It was months later I found out Pam got pregnant but the baby – you – was going to a safe place. I knew better than to ask any more and I made such a mess of being her friend. Her face scared me, that's the hardest part. Dad had plans – he was going to set her up, take care of her, give her a place to get well. But she was dead within days. An infection, so they said, though I don't know if that's what I really believe. Dad was so angry and upset. I heard people talking and I heard bits and pieces, and the next thing I heard that Dozzle had been killed and that was why Irons was in prison and we were tightening our belts. And we wanted to do right by you. Irons would have taken you in, but he couldn't – not inside.'

'Irons?'

'Yes. I thought you knew that. Dad didn't want it that way. He wanted Dozzle to face up to what he'd done. Irons went Old Testament on him. He went to prison for it. Didn't offer a word in his own defence. Could have gone to a hospital instead but wouldn't cooperate with the shrinks when they tried to test him. Didn't speak for the whole time he was inside.'

Adam grinds his jaw. 'Your dad didn't want it that way?'

'He wanted to hear him admit it. To face up to it.'

'So there was doubt,' says Adam, quietly. 'It might not have been him. The person who did this – who made me . . .'

Alison focuses her eyes on the road.

Softly, as if the words were written in water, she says, 'I don't know.'

Twenty-Seven

Lathon Grange Hotel, Maidenhead
1.33 p.m.

They sit in the car park. Adam is breathing hard, half-moon scars in his palms, staring at nothing. Alison watches Adam, chewing on her thoughts like gum. Grace turns around to look at the big Georgian manor house with its mullioned windows and red brick and its giant plant pots standing either side of an open pair of double doors.

Adam says nothing. Just glares, his guts full of fire and snakes.

'What do you want me to say?' asks Alison, and those who know her as the boss of a criminal organization would be surprised to hear the little-girl-lost tone of her voice. She remembers stepping out of this car more than thirty years ago: high-heeled shoes crunching over the smooth gravel pathway. She remembers their laughter, their excitement. Pamela pointing out Thomas Dozzle at the corner of the dance floor, and giggling. She remembers running up to her father, and him breaking away from the circle of big men in expensive suits, to dance with her and tell the DJ to change the song to something she might prefer. She remembers him doing the same to Pamela – his other little princess.

216

Here.

In this house, in the middle of nowhere, so long ago.

Adam turns. Gives a half shake of his head, and looks back down at his shoes.

They sit, silently, their breath starting to fog up the windows of the car.

'We shouldn't be here,' says Grace, and it's as though she's made a decision. 'It's no good for either of you.'

Adam looks up, eyes heavy, breath controlled. 'Just show me where it happened, then we'll go.'

They climb from the vehicle without another word. Alison leads them down a gravel path and into the neat walled gardens at the rear of the converted stately home. She starts lighting a cigarette while the one in her mouth smoulders, forgotten.

'There,' says Alison. She doesn't seem to know how to stand; how to arrange her face. Just waves at the stone barrier, jewellery clanking, and scowls at the foulness of the world. 'Over that wall.'

Adam stands on the damp grass, with his hands in his pockets so as to stop himself reaching out for Grace, who is leaning against a tree trunk, under a weeping willow.

'She came outside for some air,' says Alison. 'She'd been enjoying the party but we think she wanted to cool off. We don't really know what happened next.' She pauses, caught up in guilt and regret. She shakes it away. 'The doctors said she was struck with some kind of blunt instrument, probably a mallet. It wasn't metal. Then he carried her here, through the woods.'

217

Adam looks at the drystone wall, its lichen covered rocks stacked up like mouldy cakes. He pictures a girl in a party dress being hoisted across its rough surface, followed by a man who can still leer and snarl, despite being faceless, a shadow, a coil of smoke in black jeans and a gas mask.

'The van was parked down there, in a little layby. He got her in, and did it. She was gone for at least a few hours so we know he took his time. I think they found her here. Naked. Shivering. Wouldn't speak. They must have thought she was dead.'

Adam walks to the wall and peers over. It's just a road. No white markings or cats' eyes. No street lights. A field beyond a low wall at the far side of the road. Trees on this. He lets himself imagine a van parked up on the muddy crescent moon of tarmac, but again, the image is cartoonish and abstract. Rocking, lights flashing, as if its occupants are riding a rodeo bull.

As Adam peers over the wall he feels a sudden warmth at his waist as Grace slides her arm around him. 'You OK?' she whispers.

'Peachy,' he says, then feels bad about it, and pushes himself against her. 'Thanks for being here,' he adds and cocks his head, a dog who's heard a noise.

'I belong where you are,' she says.

'It's bollocks,' says Adam to Alison, who approaches from out of the woods, the wet grass turning her fawn boots a dark, chocolatey brown.

'What is?' she asks, as she draws close enough to him to smell the whisky and antacid and empty belly of his breath.

218

'He had a van here, did he? Dozzle? Parked up and waiting? That doesn't make much sense – at a party, where people knew him . . .'

Alison feels coldness in her belly. She knows this trip isn't for her, that she must be the strong one, here, now. But if she had come here alone, she would be shaking and crying and picturing the things that she knows must be infesting Adam's mind, as he stands, cold and motionless, at her side. He is asking the questions she would ask, picking at the threads which she would tug. Saying what she would say, were she not Daddy's girl.

'That's what they said,' she says, quiet, eyes closed. 'They reckon he'd had his eye on her and planned ahead.'

'It's bollocks,' says Adam, and Alison knows she has always agreed.

They walk back over the grass, Grace a few steps behind, feeling like an infidel, an interloper, until Adam remembers she is there and pauses for her to catch up. He seems to be thinking, hard. It is as though his thoughts are written in Braille on the inside of his skull and he is using his brain to feel them out. It hurts, this much thinking. It hurts, this much pain.

Alison wonders what is appropriate. She thinks about reaching out for him and holding him close. Taking his mind off it all with questions about his own family, his own life. She wants to tell him that this is hard on her, too. That she was Pamela's best friend. She who saw the transformation.

'I don't know what to do next,' says Adam,

trudging over the wet grass, ducking under the bare trees. He turns to face her, stopping short. 'I don't know if I'm happy or sad or what to fucking say . . .'

Alison glances at her watch, then plays with the big costume pendant at her throat. She doesn't know what to say. Doesn't know whether to bark, bite, or roll over and let her tummy be tickled.

Adam, watching these minute gestures, this distracted fiddling, looks at the wrinkles at Alison's neck, at the loose skin, the puckered flesh, and somehow, despite it all, the horror of this place, its vile history, feels a pang of want, a whiff of desire.

He shakes it away, revolted by himself. Sees the rotten seed inside his chest, and wants to gouge it out.

Looks at her, and realizes she is staring at him in just the same way.

Twenty-Eight

Dysart Avenue, Drayton, Portsmouth
2.08 p.m.

He's still a handsome man, thinks Pat, cutting the cake into eighths. He looks his age, but there's a cheekiness to him, like that newsreader, who gives you bad news with a twinkle in his eyes that suggests he may not be wearing trousers beneath his desk.

She's known him forty years, seen him shrink five inches in height and go up a waist size, but Mally Santinello still makes Pat Nunn giggle. Still a catch for somebody, she thinks, and can't help but contrast it with the way her own partner has aged.

Matured like wine, not cheese, she thinks, and wishes she had the courage to say it.

Santinello's lounging in the kitchen, leaning back against the sink, best china cup in his hand. The saucer, complete with an untouched biscuit, stands on the drainer. He's framed by the kitchen window: a canvas of wet grey skies and shaking leaves.

'Leave it, Pat,' he says, soothingly. 'Don't waste it.'

'Nonsense,' she says, plating up a slice. 'We don't get much of a chance to entertain.'

Santinello takes the plate and puts it down next

221

to the saucer. He takes a bite, nods, then takes a slurp of tea to wash it down. Pat watches, as though waiting for the man from Del Monte to give his opinion, and unfolds a grin as he mutters approval. She retreats to the far work surface and busies herself wiping up crumbs and picking microscopic flecks of nothing off the carpet. She wishes she were better dressed. He'd warned her he might pop around today, but she has had a busy night with Billy and it had gone out of her mind. She has only given her grey curls a quick once-over with a hair brush and she's dressed in a thin jumper with matching cardigan and a sensible pair of dark blue trousers. She worries she looks like an old lady. Certainly she looks tired, with the darkness beneath her eyes seemingly drawn there in charcoal. Her pinafore is rolled up and shoved in the drawer full of used carrier bags, where she hastily shoved it when the doorbell rang.

'Are we going into the front room?' asks Santinello, who looks rosy-cheeked and healthy in his fawn trousers and expensive sweater, his hair gelled back so it still looks dark and full. 'Or shall I pop straight in and say hello?'

'I think he may be a bit tired for visitors right now, Malcolm,' she says, apologetically. 'Wasn't the easiest night.'

'No better?' he asks, sympathetically.

'Ups and downs,' says Pat, and it's important to her that she never once thinks of herself as moaning. She wants to be a good wife. She thinks she always has been, by and large. Snapped at him a few too many times, perhaps, and she was never too keen on trying new things, like holidays abroad or fancy meals out, but she's always kept a nice home and made sure he had his tea on the table and no dust on the TV screen, and she never once blamed him for his little problem, which was more of a blessing than anything, all things considered, after the stories she'd heard from the other mums about what their men did when their blood was up . . .

Santinello puts a hand upon hers as they stand at the sink, gazing at the garden. 'You're doing a great job,' he says. 'Our age, we should be relaxing on a beach somewhere, not plodding on in bloody Portsmouth.'

Pat looks at him, and for a moment, wonders if he meant just the two of them. She likes the feelings she gets when Mally stops by. She's always looked forward to his calls. His wife, God rest her soul, was a glamorous thing with curly blonde hair and a thick London accent whom Pat always felt outdone by when the four of them sat at the top table at the company parties. She'd never felt able to talk to her, not really, and though she'd shed a tear or two at the funeral, it was always Mally whom she felt most able to open up to. If asked, she would say he has a way of listening that makes people feel compelled to go into every detail of their story. That he is genuinely interested. He's a good man. She's always cited him as proof that you don't have to be a nasty piece of work to succeed. She remembers telling Adam, perhaps more times than she should have, to look to Mr Santinello for a role model.

'Started out with nothing,' she'd say, as he sat

at the kitchen table trying to get through his homework without having to think or write anything down. 'Near as dammit, any road. Built up the firm to what it is now. And do you see him splashing his money around? Showing off? He's a good man. Done a lot for this family. Done us all more good turns than I can count and he won't even accept a thank you . . .'

Pat bends down and is ashamed by the creak in her knees. She opens the cupboard and removes a dustpan, then straightens up. 'No rest for the wicked,' she says and unlocks the back door.

As she steps outside, she feels the cold gust of wind and rain upon her face and at the same moment a soft warmth envelops her wrist. She turns, suddenly, and sees Mr Santinello, smiling into her eyes, his palm upon her bare forearm, and holding out the other for the dustpan. 'I can do that,' he says. 'You just stop for a second.'

With only a moment's resistance, Pat hands him the dustpan, and the vague feeling of relief that enters her drags with it other dormant emotions, and she experiences a sudden rush of uncontrollable feeling; a mix of sadness and self-pity, anger and exhaustion. She totters for a moment on her feet, her mind awash with images of Billy, last night, lashing out on his bed, pissing himself, shitting in his pyjamas; sitting there on the bed in slippered feet and nothing else, tugging at himself, glaring like she was a stranger.

Santinello catches her and with a surprising strength, moves her effortlessly into the cheap plastic chair on the wet patio. He kneels down before her, and Pat notices, despite the pounding in her head and the spots before her eyes, that his knees don't crack.

'Look at the state of me,' she says, pulling a handkerchief from her sleeve and dabbing at her eyes. 'I'm just a mess . . .'

Santinello shushes her, still crouching down, his hands upon her knees, his eyes on hers. 'You're a little trouper, Pat,' he says, softly. 'You're doing us all proud.'

Pat allows herself to whine a little more, so that she will hear more of these encouraging words, and is rewarded with a symphony of compliments.

'Nobody should be going through this, Pat,' he says. 'It's hard enough for me as his friend. You must be having a nightmare of it. That man in there isn't the Billy Nunn I know. That's somebody who just looks a bit like him. Billy's gone, but his ghost comes back once in a while to remind us of who he was. And that's what we have to cling on to. The memory of who he was . . .'

Pat nods along, as if in time with music. She knows what he is saying to be true. She knows she is a widow to a man who has not yet died. She hates herself for it, but there are times when she wishes he would just slip away. Die. That she could be left to grieve for the strong, upright, steel-backed man she has shared her life with, instead of tending the sickly old cripple who barely remembers her name and is growing angrier as his body becomes weaker.

'. . . you remember the way he used to joke. Would wind the lads up like nobody's business.

That big guy. The one we used on the jobs up north. Wouldn't do what your Billy was telling him and thought he knew it all. Ted, or something. So your dad welded his toolbox shut and then glued it onto the bonnet of Ted's car, like it was a mascot for a Jaguar or something. He was so much fun. And strong, too. Wouldn't take any nonsense. That's why he was top dog. Soon as I met him I knew he could run the show for me. More than a foreman, he was. Could price up a job in seconds and never skim a penny off for himself. And even after the accident, he ran the office like he ran a worksite. Real easy going, but you didn't cross him. Never took any sick leave. I couldn't ask for a better friend or a better worker. That's the Billy we should all remember . . .'

Pat hears the words wash over her, and each blink, wet with tears, becomes longer than the last, until she feels herself starting to give over to sleep.

'. . . and the family you raised together are a credit to you. He was a bloody good dad, and you can see in Adam's eyes how much he means to him. How much you both do . . .'

Pat shivers, and she finds herself unable to clamp her mouth shut before it blurts out disloyal words about the man asleep on clean sheets in the spare room, wrestling with demons, oxygen mask by his pillows, his wretchedly thin face turned to the flickering portable TV screen in the corner of the room.

'His mind's ruined everything,' she sniffs. 'He doesn't know who he is any more and when he does come back, it's to say something horrible. He's pulled the rug out from under Adam's feet and I'm left to pick up the pieces.'

'Now, now,' he coos, and his face gives a sudden lurch as he fancies for a second he can smell something rotten. He shakes it away. 'Everybody's making allowances. Last time I saw him he didn't even know who I was. Time before that we were laughing about some of the lasses who used to work in the Portakabin at the site office on that job in Slough. Ones who were so daft you couldn't even wind them up. He comes and he goes.'

'But to tell him that. To tell Adam where he came from . . .'

'I know, I know,' says Santinello, grimacing as he imagines how such a truth must feel.

'Adam's face,' she says, recoiling from the memory. 'To be told like that. We should have told him long ago . . .'

'You did what you thought was best. You're his mum. Billy's his dad. Adam knows that. When I saw him he seemed like a proper chip off the old block. A good man. And that daughter of his is a beautiful thing. He's done you proud and you've done the same for him.'

'They told us it was up to us,' she continues, as if in a witness box, mitigating furiously. 'Whether we tell him or not. Billy didn't want him knowing and I agreed. He was a baby when he came. Nobody else could say they were his parents. The lady from the agency said we were so lucky to be chosen after such a short time on the register, but we were perfect for each other.

227

Good people. Proper jobs. Billy's burn was a problem but he was on the mend and you'd given him the office job. We wanted children so much and by the time he got to an age where he would have understood, there didn't seem any benefit in telling him. He didn't look different. He was just like us. Like him, more than anything. It didn't matter. Even when it came to filling out the medical forms and stuff, they'd told us just to do our best. It was different back then. They just let you get on with it. He was my boy and he was a good boy at that. It didn't matter where he had been before. For him to find out like that. For Billy to just blurt it out and say we weren't his real parents . . .'

'That wasn't Billy talking, Pat. That was just this person he's become . . .'

'But I should have made it better! I should have lied and told him Billy was making it up. Or given him a hug and said it didn't matter. But I just got cross and told him to drop it, and there's just this great big thing between us now, this wall of things that have been said that can't be taken back!'

Pat dissolves in on herself, and Mr Santinello pats her back. He likes Pat. Always has. She's a bit highly strung and she does like to get herself worked up, but he knows she's going through difficult times. She and Billy don't deserve to grow old in this way. He knows he has been fortunate. He's in good health and he's got enough cash in the bank never to have to remind himself of his mortality by queuing at the post office for his pension. He has a nice home, and he's never

228

bored. He misses his son, who severed ties when his wife died, but he's not short of companionship. He can keep himself warm at night whenever he chooses. He feels bad that Pat and Billy have been reduced to this. He, a stranger to himself, jerking and fouling himself towards death. Her, exhausted and sickly, whining and lonely. He holds Pat until he feels her get hold of herself, and gives another sniff. The smell that troubled him has vanished. He can detect nothing but fresh air and the promise of more rain.

He feels a profound thump of relief.

At his age, the stench of death is a terrifying thing.

Twenty-Nine

2.29 p.m.

Irons stands at the foot of Billy Nunn's bed. The light of the TV screen casts bizarre colours upon his face and illuminates the pale sheets, so it seems to writhe with creatures and bawdy images.

The room smells of medicine and ointment, TCP and excrement. Perfume adds a sickly hue to the textured scents that colour the air.

Moving silently, Irons steps closer to Billy's face. He bends down and examines the man. The lights make it hard to discern anything familiar, and he sees nothing about the old, sickly man that requires further investigation. Quickly, his eyes are drawn to a patch of hairless, scarred tissue that is visible through the unfastened buttons of his striped pyjama top. Irons cocks his head and examines the wound. It appears old. It smells faintly of the same cream that Irons used to plaster his own face with.

This is who raised him, he thinks. *This is the man they gave Pamela's boy to.*

He returns to the door, satisfied the conversation in the garden will yield nothing more. He sifts through the new information that dances like a paper chase in his mind, looking for something meaningful. An indicator of what to do next. He can only find proof of a nice family. Ordinary.

Down to earth and no more miserable than anybody else. Doing their best for a lad who they gave a home, unaware they were letting something at once beautiful and poisonous into their lives.

Irons opens the door and walks quickly along the hall and out the front door. He only notices that the wind tearing at his face contains rain when he spies the droplets upon his glasses.

He has left the cul-de-sac in moments, unseen and unheard, and feels a strange pang of relief at having found out nothing unpleasant. He does not know how we would react were he to find that Pamela's boy had been given to unkind people.

The Toyota door closes with a click behind him as he clambers inside the vehicle. As he starts the engine he fishes his telephone from his pocket. The family phone contains three missed calls, all from Alison. He deletes the message and puts the phone away. Then he reaches into the other side of the great leather jacket. It contains a text message from his new friend. The one with the shaved head and the kind eyes. The tattoos and the failing restaurant. The one made tiny by the weight of pain upon her shoulders. She is asking if he remembers her, and whether he wants to talk.

Inside himself, a light no larger than a match-head seems to flare into life. It sends tremors through his system and he has to hold himself with both of his giant arms to stop himself giving in to a tremble.

He finds himself wanting to talk. To share his feelings with somebody else who knows how it feels to love Pamela's blood.

Thirty

Lathon Grange Hotel, Maidenhead
3.30 p.m.

The hardwood floors are almost black, save for a scuffed area by the bar which blooms with trodden-in chewing gum. The heavy, crushed velvet curtains look like matted animal pelts, and the tables and chairs are varnished to different mahogany hues. The lamps on the walls are skewed at angles, knocked by inconsiderate dusters and not put right. It's not much larger than a good-sized living room, but the layout is chaotic, and despite there being no other patrons, the trio still feel cramped as they sit on backless stools and lean forward to hold their drinks. Another pint for Adam. Vodka and tonic for Alison. Orange and amaretto for Grace. The young girl in the white blouse and black skirt behind the bar had never heard of Grace's preferred tipple, and it had been left to Alison to direct the barmaid's finger until it was pointing at the correct bottle.

The lounge bar has the bearing of a toff who's gambled the family millions away. It puts Grace in mind of a liver-spotted lord of the manor, clad in moth-eaten smoking jacket and paisley cravat, living in one room of his crumbling mansion, eating beans from the tin and watching a portable TV.

She reads the blurb on the back of the laminated menu, trying to find something to do with her eyes other than watch the sparks crackle between Adam and Alison. She feels hotly uncomfortable. A spare part. They are talking from beneath heavy eyelids, their voices soft, breath husky and sometimes tremulous.

'It's hardly recognizable,' says Alison, again. She seems stunned at the decrepitude of this building that stood dumb witness to an event that changed her life. 'We were in the big hall, which must be the other side of the reception and through those double doors, and that was like something out of a fairy tale. Big chandeliers, beautiful parquet floors. Every tablecloth was pretty as a wedding dress. I know Dad had arranged for it to be extra-special that night but it really was a place to be. I was a kid, of course, and the mind does edit your snapshots when you send them down to storage, but this might as well be a different building.' She stops talking, and stares into the surface of her glass. 'I don't know how I feel about that. I don't know how I would have felt walking through the door and things being exactly as they were.'

'It just leaves my imagination,' says Adam, gently, turning away to stare through the leaded windows and gale-tossed bare branches scrawled into the purple and yellow crayon of the sky outside. 'Maybe if I could have seen it as it was, I could just paint her face on it. Put you there. Maybe it would have made a difference. Maybe not. It's so difficult to know what to tell your brain to do. What's the right thing? Should I let my mind wonder? Let it take me over? Is that the way to honour her? She's gone. She'll never know me. Even if I could speak to her, some-where, somehow, I wouldn't know what to say. She's a name and a story. Something terrible happened to her, but I don't even know what she looks like.' He sighs, looking across at Grace, as though hoping to find instructions written on her face. 'You know what my dad says. That I fall in love with every woman I meet. That I feel I've got to save them all. Maybe this is just . . .'

'Adam, this is a massive thing for everybody,' says Alison, cutting Grace off before she can speak. 'This is something that's been inside me since I was a girl. Something hidden and horrible and buried away. There hasn't been a day when I haven't wished I could just smash down the walls we built up around what happened that night. We bricked it up. Bricked her up. But we blocked off the light. It's been shadows ever since.'

They sit and brood, listening to the rain and the wind, watching the sky darken, the drinks go flat. They consider ordering food, but haven't the stomach. A group of pensioners poke their heads into the bar, see nothing to intrigue them, and leave. They talk of business. Adam explaining what he does. Where he finds his contracts. The difficulties he has getting the bigger firms to pay up. They discuss sunbeds: Adam's aversion, Alison's addiction. Grace mentions she's plan-ning to go home to Malaysia for Christmas and Alison says she once spent a fortnight in the Maldives and thought it was paradise. Didn't care for the food, but the people were so polite.

The conversation turns to their surroundings and they criticize the layout. Make suggestions as to how they would decorate it differently. Alison looks at it appraisingly, and Grace realizes there is nothing to stop this woman from making an offer on the place, and the knowledge reaffirms her discomfort.

Adam stands, pulling his phone from his pocket. There are six empty pint glasses on the table before him, but other than a thickness to his voice and a heaviness to his eyes, he seems none the worse for drink. He nods to the women and heads for the door, gesturing at the phone.

'Girlfriend?' asks Alison.

'Dad,' replies Grace, feeling a sudden thrill at knowing him so well, at being able to read his face, his thoughts.

Alison nods, understanding. 'It must have hit him like a brick,' she says, leaning forward. 'I really didn't expect him to know absolutely nothing. It's been such a cloud over our lives that the thought of somebody who was so much a part of all that not knowing about it is so hard to take. Then again, what good would it have done him? Sounds like he was raised by good people. He's turned out a good man. I'm only seeing him in extreme circumstances, but he's got his head screwed on. Clever, you can see that. And good-looking . . .'

'Does he look like her? His mum?' Grace jumps in quicker than she intends. Her words come out garbled and impulsive. She realizes it sounds like she doesn't want anybody else noticing Adam's looks.

235

'She's in there somewhere,' Alison says. Then, as if for bad: 'I suppose if I stared into his eyes long enough I could spot her.'

They sit quietly, staring at the sooty sky beyond the glass, cushioned from further conversation by their own thoughts. Finally, Grace says, 'That's what he's finding hardest. The thought that all these people he doesn't know anything about are somehow a part of him. His mum sounds lovely, but even if you find out Mother Teresa is your grandma, what are you supposed to do with that information? Go and look at lepers and see if you feel an overwhelming urge to help them? He kind of got into this out of curiosity. Just a basic need to follow a story to its next chapter. Neither of us were thinking of this, but he can't put the genie back in the bottle now he knows what he knows. And that's not much. He knows his mother was a little girl. He knows his dad was a rapist. And now he's involved with a family that most people have only read about . . .' She stops, colour draining from her face.

Alison looks for a moment as though she might take offence, then smiles and reaches across to touch Grace's leg. She seems pleased that Adam has somebody who cares for him so much and feels overcome by a sudden liking for her. 'I can't pretend we're not known,' she says, instantly effervescent and sparkly. 'To be honest, I don't think I'd like to be anonymous. I've always been Mr Jardine's daughter. It's not often I have to book a table. But that whole gangster world you see at the pictures is a nonsense. We still get people ringing up and offering to change our gas

236

suppliers. You still need to remember a password before the bank will let you transfer funds between accounts. You try telling somebody in a call centre your daddy is Franco Jardine and see what difference it makes. None at all. Try going up to a chain pub and telling the spotty little manager they could be protected from any harm for a small fee each month, and see how far you get. They give you the phone number for head office. Dad used to have a few rough edges once upon a time, but they were different times. You need a degree in computers just to tape a programme off the telly these days. Then, you could just get by with a bit of swagger in your walk. Dad brought me up knowing we were a family which some people were afraid of, but he knew that those people didn't deserve to live the easy life.'

'It is exciting though,' says Grace, in an enthusiastic whisper. 'The thought of walking in to a restaurant and people nudging each other and then the manager coming out and saying your dinner's free. It probably isn't like that, but the thought of it . . .'

'It can be like that, if you go somewhere that has a bit of history. If the owner made his money in the sixties. But trust me, you don't get served any quicker in Starbucks for having my last name.'

'Did you change it when you got married?' asks Grace, and there are two spots of darkness on her cheeks. She's a little flushed, suddenly enjoying this chat and hoping Adam will take his time.

'I didn't get married,' says Alison, shrugging. She pauses, unsure how much to give away, then seems to make up her mind. 'I haven't always been on top of my game. For a long time I was a bit of a wild child. After Pamela . . . well, things were different. Dad had always wanted me to be at a normal school, but that changed after what happened. I went off to a boarding school full of little princesses, and every one of them had a mum or dad who had heard of mine, and all the kids had been told to be polite to me, but not get too close. So that was my life for years. Polite, but no real friends. Acquaintances, but no intimates. Same at home. Dad still gave me everything I wanted, but the house of comings and goings, and big men in suits, it all went away. We rattled around in a house too big for us and filled with memories we didn't want. I hit seventeen and went crazy. Found out just how far you could go with a last name like mine. Behaved the way my silly boy is behaving now.'

'Timmy, yes?'

'Yes. His father's son. Bloody idiot. I met his dad when I was still in my teens. Young, dumb and hard as nails. Didn't take any crap from anybody. Not the best looking, but all man. Or what my idea of a man was, back then. Didn't give a damn what my dad thought. Didn't back down even when one of Dad's lads had a quiet word in his ear. I ran off to be with him. I still had a nice allowance from Dad and we lived pretty decent. Then a while down the road I got pregnant. Dad and me buried the hatchet and me and Dean, that's Tim's dad, we moved into a nice family house down the coast.'

'Sounds nice.'

'It was a farce. I was still off the rails. Dean was drinking for England. I didn't know what the hell to do with a baby. I had nobody to confide in. No friends. So I had him, and we shuffled on. A few years back, Dean walked out, and I've been putting myself to better use ever since. I like working with Dad. I like what I've become.'

'It must be daunting, telling all those men what to do, though,' says Grace.

Alison giggles, and it sparks Grace into a fit of conspiratorial laughter. 'It's great fun,' she says. 'Sometimes I make them do things just to see if they will. There's one lad at the pool hall. I caught him with his hand in the till and I made him staple gun it for every penny he had taken. Said I would tell Dad if not. He did it. Looked like he was a robot from the wrist down by the time he'd finished. I wouldn't have said a word, that's the funny thing. I don't tell Dad anything. Not at his age. It'll either upset him, or I'll feel daft for not being able to sort it myself.'

'He's in the dark about this, then?' asks Grace, starting to collect the glasses together to take back to the bar. 'About Adam.'

Alison nods, her brows knotting. 'Totally. There was maybe a time to ask him about any of this, but I missed it. He doesn't need to know Adam and I have met. He doesn't need to know any of it.'

'It's going to be hard,' says Grace. 'We've only got the memories of a child to go on.'

They sit on the edge of their seats, considering one another. It occurs to them both that without acknowledging it, they have silently decided to search for answers about Pamela's rape, and Adam's birth. They have agreed to dig down into the past.

'How much do you remember?' asks Grace. 'In real terms. Where do I start?'

Alison stands and smooths herself down. She takes a handful of glasses to the bar and plonks them noisily on the counter. The barmaid is nowhere to be seen, so Alison opens the hatch on the counter and walks behind the bar. She reaches up and pulls down the nearest optic. It's brandy. Posh stuff. Three tumblers from below the till. She walks back to Grace, sits down, and pours them each a measure. Adam's glass remains empty.

'I know who not to bother with,' says Alison, eventually, sipping her drink. She remembers herself, and clinks glasses with Grace, whose lips tingle as she downs the unfamiliar drink. 'I think of that night and there are huge blurs in the picture. Half the people who were there are just nobodies. They mattered enough to be there, but my family can be counted out. Some of the businessmen too. They had a van, that's the thing. This is somebody who prepared . . .'

'That's what I keep coming back to,' she says, then, dutifully, 'Adam too. If they'd just done it on the spur of the moment, then . . .'

'I know. These are the things that have been eating me away. They said it was Dozzle, so that's what I accepted.'

'But it can't have been, can it? The way it

happened.' She pauses, unsure if she should continue. 'Do you think it might have been you they were after?'

Alison looks down into her glass. Downs it. Pours another. 'I think Dad does. I think Dad could almost understand if it was me. If it was to make a point. If it was for leverage. But to do Pamela. It's the kind of thing that could have happened even if she had never met us. Maybe that's what makes it harder. Not knowing if it was something that happened to her because she came into our lives. Not knowing whether this was a result of her being my friend, his princess . . .'

They stop, and Grace wonders if she can see a dampness in Alison's eyes.

As they sit, quietly, thinking themselves sluggish, Adam comes back into the bar. His face is pale but red at the cheeks. His eyes are glistening and his jacket is damp. He's been standing in the rain, listening to his mum, hearing about Dad's funny turn in the night, when he fancied he could hear burglars and started swinging, wildly, in the dark. Knocked Pat down and hurt her side. Said she was fine, but there was blood in her wee this morning . . .

Adam pours himself a brandy, raises it, salutes, and downs it.

'Everything fine?' asks Grace.

'I feel like doing star jumps,' he says flatly.

'Your dad?'

'Oh he's fabulous.'

Adam sits down, heavily.

'We were talking about that night,' says Alison, putting a hand on Adam's.

241

'Shocker,' he says, blunt and cold.

'I do remember a couple of Dad's old contacts,' says Alison, not stopping. 'Dealt with one myself up until quite recently and he's friendly enough. He'll have been at the party here, I'm sure of it. He's an old boy now but he could remember something. We could be subtle, of course. Mention the importance of keeping it all between ourselves. Leonard Riley. And the footballer. Ace.'

'Riley,' says Grace, thoughtfully. 'The chap from the stadium? Alderman, or something.'

'Very good,' says Alison, impressed. 'You been doing your research?'

'I'm good at it,' she says, and tries to make it sound modest. 'That's what I did, before Tilly came along . . .'

'How did I come out of it?' asks Alison, with a smile.

Grace looks sheepish and guilty. 'There wasn't that much about you,' she says, and isn't sure how to read Alison's expression. Already her mind is racing. Already she wants to pull out her phone and call King Rat. Perhaps even see him. Find out the truths that are hiding among so many lies.

They drink the brandy and smoke cigarettes, and nobody bothers them, because they look fiery and intense, and they reek of alcohol and cigarettes, and they are talking of horrid things. They mention names not spoken in more than thirty years. Councillors, policemen, businessmen, footballers. They make decisions, without acknowledging them. Alison will pick up the bill at the end of the session, and book them rooms.

242

They will sleep fitfully and drunkenly, in sleeps peopled with killers and rapists, babies and each other. The tab for the night will set Alison back more than £400. She will pay it willingly, unaware the gesture is unnecessary. Her father has owned this hotel since 1974.

Thirty-One

Chinatown, Wardour Street, London
8.07 p.m.

Yellows and reds, gold and green, a child's drawing of Bonfire night made neon-real. Dragons, stencil-curves, grinning dogs and paper lanterns.

A wet street sticking into the centre of London like a needle into a vein.

A smell of satay sauce and egg rolls, ripe on a grey sky.

Adam and Grace, sitting in a booth. It's all ornate chairs and perfect white tablecloths. The classier kind of cheap lunch. Serves camel hump, but takes American Express. No knives and forks, but they serve London Pride. Authentic main course, followed by sticky toffee pudding and a deep-fried Creme Egg.

'Are you nervous?' she asks, for the thousandth time.

'I don't know what I am,' replies Adam, and he's telling the truth.

It's been a week since the hotel. A week in which Adam and Grace have barely been apart. A week of playing detectives. Talking in excited voices into mobile phones. Turning it into a game, somehow. They've got names and numbers, now. People to see, places to be. And by losing themselves in the hunt, they've managed to distance themselves from acknowledging the nature of the quarry.

'He'll come,' says Adam. 'Would you say no to Francis Jardine's baby girl?'

Ace, Alison said they called him. Charlie Howell. Quality striker, back in his day. Started at West Ham and would have made the first XI if it wasn't for Martin Peters being better. Four seasons at Stoke City and sixty-four goals, then a year at Palace, chasing long balls, hitting brick-wall defenders, snagging a brace against United, then off to Sunderland and Bristol Rovers to become a folk hero. Champagne superstar. Eighty goals in four seasons, then a kick to the knee, and over the border to Hibernian.

'I don't know why I'm so hungry,' says Grace, as she peers at the laminated menu in its leather wallet, and decides the mixed starter for two is not so much a title as a challenge. She sips at her mineral water, and looks across at Adam, who is staring at the door. 'He'll come,' she says, gently.

'I know he'll come,' says Adam. 'I just don't know what I should think when I look at him for the first time.'

'There is no right and wrong. You'll know when you see him. You'll know if it was him.'

'Will I?' asks Adam, turning away from the door to stare at her intently. 'Will I really know? Or do we all just assume that we'll feel a connection? Does blood sense itself? Do genes sniff each other out? Or do we just rut and fuck, and then take care of the little sod that the nurse puts in our arms? Animals don't always recognize their own children.'

245

They sit in silence, watching the clock above the door, the gentle rain against the window, the big cars cruising by outside. Waiters come and go, bring more drinks and prawn crackers. Grace eats, Adam drinks. He fields a phone call from Zara. Tells her he is busy in a meeting.

The doors open, and a plump man in a grey suit and golfing jumper, white hair and black eyebrows, opens both doors, and eases through the gap. Alison follows, pushing her hair from her eyes, sexy in black tights, knee-length black dress and open raincoat, flushed at the cheeks, damp at the cleavage.

Adam feels a stab of recognition, a sudden jolt of familiarity, and for a second he wonders if his blood is speaking to him, if it is sensing the nearness of its own kin. But in an instant the face becomes black and white, pixilated, younger, and he realizes he knows this man as a football fan and nothing more.

The waiter, in his fancy patterned pyjamas, approaches them as they enter and asks if they want a table for two. Ace looks set to answer, before Alison steps in and whispers something in his ear. He looks puzzled for a moment, then shrugs, and Alison leads him over to Adam's table. Adam stands and extends a hand, which Ace pauses before shaking. Close to, he looks younger. A good ten years beneath his true sixty-six. He has a heavy drinker's complexion, a waxiness to his cheeks and nose, but in poor light, it could be mistaken for the bloom of youth.

'I didn't realize we would be making up a four-some,' says Ace, turning to look at Alison. He'd been surprised when she rang, but pleasantly so. Took him a second to reconcile the confident, womanly voice at the end of the line with the precocious, flirty little girl who used to be the fruit bowl of her daddy's eye all those years ago.

'This is Adam,' says Alison, gently, placing a warm hand on Ace's sleeve. 'And his friend, Grace. I don't want you to be cross with me, but they really wanted to meet you and I said we were old friends.' Alison's voice is flirty, naughty, as though she's admitting that she ate an extra slice of chocolate cake. Ace produces a smile, then gives her a gentle slap on the wrist.

'Naughty girl,' says Ace, with a noise that sounds almost like a sigh of relief. 'Just wait until I see your father.'

'He'd like that,' says Alison. 'He's often asking after you.'

'How is the old bugger?' asks Ace. 'I read about that court case he was at. Brought the house down, didn't he? I had tears in my eyes when I read it, laughing so much I was. What were they thinking, summoning a man like Franco to court? Beats me.'

The waiter comes over and Ace orders a bottle of red wine for himself and Alison. Amaretto and orange juice for Grace. Whisky for Adam. The drinks come fast, but nobody says cheers before they raise their glasses.

'Man after my own heart,' says Ace, smiling, gulping his wine. He starts to talk, trotting out choice anecdotes about names from the past – the sort that bring the house down when he gets a booking for an after-dinner speech.

247

Grace sips her drink and watches Adam. He nods, now and again, out of politeness, but she can tell he isn't listening. He's staring a hole through the man in front of him because he doesn't know what else to do. She looks across at Alison, and sees that she, too, is watching Adam. They catch each other's eye, give the ghost of a smile, then return to their menus. Neither of them knows how to raise the subject that brought them here. Neither of them knows how to ask Ace the questions that have been without answers for almost thirty-five years.

The waiter takes their orders and returns ten minutes later with the mixed starters. Grace and Ace get stuck in. Alison picks. Adam drinks.

Then the main courses, piled high on the white tablecloths. Bowls of multi-coloured meat and veg. Tureens of boiled rice. Prawn crackers. Chopsticks for everybody. Even Ace is an old hand, and doesn't need the knife and fork that the waiter offers him.

'Been eating this stuff for years,' he confides, quietly, to Adam. 'You not hungry, son?'

'Thirsty,' replies Adam, and knocks back another double. Orders another.

They eat. Scatter rice across the table. Munch on feathered king prawns and diced chicken, crunch bean sprouts and veiny strips of onion. Ace talks the most. Asks questions of Alison. Doesn't wait for answers. Calls Grace 'sweetheart' and stares at her chest.

'How do you know the lovely Alison here, then?' asks Ace, using a prawn cracker to scoop up an errant piece of carrot in a purple sauce.

248

'She was a friend of my mother's,' says Adam, and the two women pause, to look at him. The moment seems to stretch, like dough, before it tears and snaps, and Adam looks up from his glass and stares at the man across the table.

'Oh yes?' says Ace, slurping down the last of the second bottle of red wine and looking around for the next. 'Can't have been one of her school friends, though eh? You must be thirty-five if you're a day.'

'Near as dammit,' says Adam, looking back down at the amber liquid in his tumbler, looking at his untouched plate through the distorted lens of the glass. 'Pamela Garner. My mum. You might have known her.'

'Doubt it, son,' says Ace. 'She mentioned me, has she? Football fan.'

'Not sure, mate. Didn't have the pleasure of getting to know her. Gave me away when I was a baby.'

Ace looks at Adam, and his smile fades for the first time in an hour. He tries to make his face sympathetic, but doesn't know what's appropriate. Funny thing to tell a stranger, he says to himself. Hope he's not going to get maudlin.

'Sorry, lad. Or maybe not. Maybe she did you a favour. You could be living the dream. What do I know? Eh?'

Grace gives a little laugh, out of politeness, while Alison opens her mouth to speak, but can't think of anything to say. Ace looks from one face to another, then turns to Alison, smile fading, and says, 'Am I missing something?'

Alison steels herself with a sip from the new

249

bottle of wine, then turns to face him. 'This isn't easy for me to say, Ace,' she begins, falls away, sighs. 'Look, do you remember the celebration party? After Dad got off. That place in the arse end of nowhere . . .'

Here it comes, thinks Ace. Be sure your sins will find you out, old son.

'What do you remember about that night?'

Ace's face crumples into a frown of puzzlement, and he looks across at Grace, seeking an ally. Thinking, quickly. Sweating. Images and memories tugging at him, like he's running through line after line of damp laundry.

'Not bloody much,' he says, and there's a tremble there. 'It was a good turnout, I remember that. Lot of faces, lot of friends. Your dad was on form. Had the place booked for days before the end of the trial, didn't he? Knew they couldn't get him. That's because he was bloody innocent, I said. Told my manager that, too, when he said I shouldn't go to the party. I said he's innocent, mate. And he's my friend. My biggest fan. I'm going to toast his health, and toast it I did. Toasted it until I couldn't see straight.'

'So you were pissed and saw fuck all,' says Adam, suddenly finding something specific to be angry about. He latches on to a feeling of having wasted his time, and focuses himself on that. 'You going to say you fell asleep in a corner somewhere and missed all the fun and games at the end, too, are you?'

'Fun and games?' begins Ace, and he looks again, from one face to another, trying to work it out. 'Look, son, I don't . . .'

'Don't call me that. Don't ever use that word around me.'

'What? Sorry, sorry. Look, I don't understand.'

'You don't? You don't remember Alison's friend? The girl in the white dress. Went outside for some fresh air and not all of her came back. You don't remember somebody slipping away from the party, throwing her in a van and raping the fuck out of her?'

The other handful of diners look around as Adam raises his voice. Ace seems to get smaller in his chair. His vision is spinning, like he's going the wrong way down a plughole. He's falling backwards more than thirty years . . .

Thirty-Two

1971

A parquet dance floor. Balloons and party hats, poppers and streamers, chicken legs and champagne.

Him, in a white suit and pink tie, curly hair and moustache.

Ace.

It's not long after midnight, and he's had more than too much to drink. He's chatting up a tasty thing and her sister, sitting on a crushed velvet bar stool, one elbow in a puddle of bitter, a cigarette in his mouth. Feeling fuzzy, but he's used to that. He's looking around, lazily, head lolling, considering his options. He'd prefer a redhead, given the chance. He's no doubt it can be arranged. He wonders where Jardine's got to. He hasn't seen him in a while. Not since that bloke in the leather jacket whispered something in his ear and they all fucked off out of the dance hall.

Where's that other dirty bastard? Councillor Whatshisname. Riley. Can't relax, that one. Kept asking, *Are you sure there's no snappers here, no photographers, no journos. Great friend of mine, Mr Jardine is, but I have a reputation. An image. Can't be seen . . .* All that bollocks. Silly bastard.

Ace sits, drinks, smokes, chats. He's nodding in time with Cliff Bloody Richard, trying to say something witty, but he can barely hear his own voice over the sound of the amplifiers, so when the permed brunette in the flares and boob tube laughs at his jokes, he knows she's lying, but eager to please. He doesn't mind the combination.

He looks around for familiar faces. Those two coppers have buggered off long since. The politicians too. Riley's probably shot his bolt and clambered back into the council Roller. Mostly family and close friends now, still tipping the good champagne down their necks and picking at sausage rolls. He wonders if he's being anti-social. Wonders if all the A-list are having a separate little party somewhere else, and he's managed to lose it. He doesn't want to upset anybody. Place like this, men like these, it could be fucking lethal.

He promises the brunette he'll see her later, and slides off the bar stool and onto the carpeted area around the bar, which is spongy with spilled ale. The disco lights and the smoke and the pounding bass are making his head hurt, and he has to make a conscious effort not to stagger as he walks to the door from the dance floor. Beery faces belch hellos and best regards as he fumbles at the door, and escapes into the long, cool corridor. The lights are low here. Comforting. The carpet clean, the off-white walls and timber beams seem wonderfully English, and he feels a sudden burst of patriotism, a love of his country and a passing regret that he hasn't yet been called up to play for them, and never will. Not even Franco can do that, he thinks. Not with the file they've got on you at the FA.

He totters off down the corridor, looking up at the oil paintings on the wall, the stern men in fancy dress, the English roses with warm cleavages and ringlets. Then into reception, a nod to the girl on the front desk, and out the double doors onto the steps. The cold hits him with a sobering punch and he feels for an instant as though he might be sick. He screws up his eyes, balls his fists, bumbles down the steps and onto the shingle of the car park. Leans his hand on the low wall. Plenty money here tonight, he thinks, looking at the flash cars, the moonlight bouncing off gleaming metal, greased with fine rain. Stick with these lads, Ace. Bit shifty, but decent people. They love you. They'll see you right. Then the sickness comes again, and he half runs, half scurries, into the trees that line the car park. He vomits, narrowly missing his shoes. Throws up a vile rainbow of wine, champagne, peanuts and chicken legs. Chunders until he's empty and the world spins, and the bark of the tree trunk that he's leaning against cuts into his palm. Wipes his mouth. Feels better. Turns away.

And sees him.

On the grass, arms and legs splayed, like a starfish. A handle sticking out of the oil-black mess at his throat, like a cigar from a grin.

Irons.

Ace stumbles back and sits in the puddle of sick. He retches, but there's nothing left.

And then there are voices. Coming closer. Angry shouts, and hissed curses. Get out of here, Ace, he tells himself. It's fuck all to do with you. He's on his feet, cursing the white suit, wishing

254

he could just blend into the darkness, melt away, disappear. He scampers from tree to tree, flattening himself against the trunks, heading away from the house, the voices, dimming, now, as they get further away. He breaks into a sprint that takes him suddenly into a clearing, and a low stone wall. Runs to it, thinking, simply: hide. Looks over the wall, places his foot on a loose brick.

Looks up.

Sees a face. A plump, round face, shiny with sweat. A face he knows. A face that turns, looks down, at the thing in its arms. A lifeless, pure-white mannequin, carried like a sack of bones, head back, throat exposed, breasts like fairy cakes, skin, dark in places, too dark, oily dark, slick at the face, the thighs. The face looks up again, and Ace, with footballer's instincts, ducks down. Thinks. Dismisses. Decides.

Turns, and runs.

Through the trees and past the voices, a white streak against the darkness. Finds his keys, fumbles with the door of his rented MG. Climbs inside. He fancies he can hear Irons's name. In his mirror, he sees the shape of big men, dressed in darkness, emerging from the treeline. Into reverse, a spray of gravel, then gone. Sitting in sick, empty and pissed.

None of your business, Ace, he's thinking, rubbing the sweat from his face. *You're a footballer. Fuck this. You were drunk. Lose the memory. You were seeing things. Stick to football, keep your head down, say nowt . . .*

He's never really been the same man since.

* * *

255

Here, in the warmth of the restaurant, sweat glinting on his pink skin, he sits silently trying to order his thoughts. His hands are shaking. He tries to feel angry at being ambushed, but can't. They have a right to ask these questions. Christ, if the police had investigated back in the day, they wouldn't have to. Jardine dealt with it his way, and here, today, it still isn't settled.

Best tell them, Ace, he thinks. You don't owe anybody anything. Least of all him.

'I saw him carrying her,' he says, quietly. 'I saw him holding her in his arms.'

'Who?' asks Alison. 'Who did you see?'

'Riley,' he says, staring into his lap. 'Alderman Leo Riley. Freeman of the City.'

Thirty-Three

The man sitting in the chair is fiftyish, and the strands of hair that garland his bald head are swept back into a greasy ponytail. He's wearing a loud shirt beneath a cream suit jacket, open to the nipples, revealing a tuft of curly grey hair. He's smoking a roll-up as though it were a Cuban cigar. The office is bare. One cheap metal filing cabinet stands against the far wall, and a rack of metal shelves, containing empty ring-binders and manila files, blocks the light from the lone, high window. The walls are painted cream, but there is a yellow patch, like damp, above the man's chair. A new cloud of nicotine spirals upwards and adds its own mottling to the pattern as the man breathes out to expose large, unnaturally white false teeth.

He stands, while Grace makes herself comfortable: his gut a great capital D.

The man extends a hand. It's the one holding the dog-end, but he doesn't seem to think this is impolite. Grace shakes it, and is surprised to find the palm is dry rather than sweaty. He gives her another grin and sinks back behind his desk. His chair is hard-backed and made of cheap wood. It looks like it's been nabbed from a chain pub.

257

The desk doesn't match. It has the air of a charity shop purchase about it.

Grace begins to speak, but the man holds up a hand. 'Pleasantries first,' he says. 'Bacardi, Coke, or Bacardi and Coke?'

Taken aback, Grace starts to say she'll have nothing, she's fine, then remembers her manners and asks for whatever he'd recommend. He gleams and reaches into his desk drawer. Pulls out two mugs, a bottle of Bacardi and some cheap cola. Pours them both a slug of alcohol then tops them up. It doesn't froth. Grace wonders how long it's been there.

'You're right,' says the man. 'You look even better in the flesh.'

'Flattery will get you everywhere,' says Grace, and wonders if she should have.

'Said the stamp-collector to his wife . . .'

Grace looks confused, and wonders where she's supposed to sit. There's only one chair.

'Philately,' he explains, with the air of a man who's had to spell out this gag before. 'Stamp-collecting. Philately will get you everywhere . . .'

'Oh,' says Grace. She laughs politely.

The man gives her an appraising gaze, nods, sucks through his teeth, and downs his drink. Then, as if remembering his manners, he stands up and offers Grace his chair. Unsure what is the correct way to respond, she accepts, and sinks into the chair, untouched drink in her hand, flinching as the warmth of the wooden seat eases through her trousers. She wonders how many of this man's farts have rippled into the varnish over the years.

He flicks the off switch on the computer before he goes over to stand by the door. Grace has a brief image of a screen full of text. Her eyes have time to take in the word 'shooter' and 'slag' before the screen disappears into darkness.

'It's Brian, by the way,' he says, his tone friendly. 'I'm sure I can trust you to keep it to yourself, and I feel a bit of a prat you calling me King Rat. It's nice to put a face to your name. I was glad you called back.'

'This is your full-time job, is it?' she asks, unsure how to begin so just letting the conversation flow.

'Oh I've got a few plump digits in a few fat pies, love,' he smiles. 'But this is the bread and butter. Published six books last year. Couple only available via email, but people will pay. Everybody loves a glimpse at the seedier side of life, don't they? Love reading about people with bigger balls than their own, if you'll excuse my Urdu.'

'Anybody I would have heard of?'

He gives a conspiratorial wink. 'They tend to be published anonymously. Confessions of a Number Two, that sort of thing. Diary of a hired gun. People who used to do bare-knuckle boxing with the Krays, that sort of thing. Some old boy who did a stretch for being on an armed raid with Mad Frank.'

'It all sounds very exciting,' says Grace, and she realizes as she says it that were she trying to win his confidence this would be the perfect line to use. As it is, she's genuinely interested by what he does.

'Oh it is, love,' he says, looking pleased, and

259

resting his buttocks on his hands, back against the wall. 'It's good fun in the shadows. Warm down here in the underbelly, you might say.'

'And you don't get any bother? You publish a book slating some big-time criminal and there's no comeback.'

'Oh I've had the odd quiet word in my shell-like, but everybody knows I'm not doing any real harm. Nobody's reputation's suffering. And the people my lads write about are already in the public eye, or too bloody old to get themselves het up over stuff that doesn't matter. I steer clear of anybody still playing the game.' He stops, and considers for a moment, his eyes finding Grace's. 'Like your Mr Jardine, for example,' he finishes.

Grace doesn't know how she should react, so she reaches into her bundle of stuff and pulls out her notepad and pen. 'This OK?' she asks.

'Help yourself,' he beams, expansively. Grace gets the impression he spends a lot of time in his own company and is pleased to have somebody showing an interest in him. She imagines he gave himself his own nickname. She starts to wonder whether he knows anything at all. Whether she's come to Bethnal Green for nothing more than a sticky cocktail with a slimy man who publishes pulp fiction about yesterday's criminals.

'So,' she begins, 'as I explained, I'm coming up against one or two brick walls. I've heard some of the whispers about Mr Jardine and his methods, but I'm really interested in what happened after his murder trial. Why he slipped out of the limelight, that sort of thing . . .'

For a moment, he's silent, sucking in his cheeks,

listening, pondering, scraping memory banks. It's as if he's wondering how much he needs to say to impress her. Whole truth, he decides. What little there is of it.

She gives him an encouraging smile and decides to start with an easy one. 'Probably best if I got some biographical information about your good self,' she says, brightly.

He relaxes and gives another big grin. He starts rolling another cigarette, absent-mindedly, in one hand. He doesn't even look at it as his fingers go about their work. 'That's a book in itself,' he says. 'But if you want the basics, then here you go, love. I'm fifty-six, but I don't look a day over fifty-five. I'm not married, got no kids I know about and I live in a bloody bed and breakfast because my credit rating is so bad I can't even get a flat. I've been to prison four times for obtaining money by deception, which essentially means I'm a bright spark who knows how to get people's cash out of them. Not a bad forger neither, which is where my services were used by the occasional household name. Sub-contracted, of course, but close enough to the power to be able to say I knew the big boys. Last stretch I did, I was in a prison cell with a murderer for a while. Doesn't normally happen but anyway, the place was overcrowded and I was an old hand and they put me in with him. High profile, he was. None too bright, neither. Amount of people I'd done time with and the faces I knew, he was always keen to impress me, so he told me all about what he did and why he did it. When I got out I sold the story to the papers. All anonymous, of course. Next thing I got a call from this publisher saying they could turn my story into a book, but I'd have to pay for the privilege. I had a better idea. Set myself up as a publisher. Churned out a couple of bad lad memoirs, and I've been doing the same ever since.'

'Good money?' asks Grace.

Brian waves a hand. 'Oh yeah, I'm rolling in it.' He says it without malice. He seems a good-natured fellow, aware of how silly some parts of his life story sound when laid bare. Grace has no doubt he's an accomplished liar, and suddenly finds herself deciding that he writes all of the books himself. Makes up old hit-men and bruisers and sells their life story.

Grace smiles at his little joke and decides to get this over with quickly. 'Yours was one of the few websites to mention Jardine by name,' she says, trying to hint that she's impressed. 'And you were such a joy to talk to the other day. So, what do you know about him and his operations?'

'I know he's not a well man. Not long for this world. But the name's in good hands with that daughter of his. Copper at SOCA has an itch in her bits to catch a big name but I don't see her getting Alison while Effie's alive.'

'You mentioned that name before,' says Grace, cautiously. 'I think I've worked it out. It's not Effie. It's Fe. The chemical name for Iron. Or Irons.'

'Well, you're a clever girl,' smiles Brian. 'I don't want to get on the wrong side of that one, no matter what. He knows how to hurt. Your Larry Paris – the way the coppers found him, that's Irons all the way through. Somebody was trying to set him up, though it looks like Alison's put all that to bed now. Kukuc won't be coming back, I tell you that much. And with her contacts, all the names she knows, going all the way back to God knows when, too many people need her for her to be at risk. She's good at this. Daddy's girl. The apple doesn't fall far.'

Grace is suddenly aware of the scratching of her pen on the notepad in the silence of the room. She looks up. He's sitting there, expectant, like a dog waiting for a treat.

'This is all very helpful,' she says, and he smiles, seemingly mollified. It's replaced by a sudden flash of sadness, suggesting a sudden realization that he hasn't got much more to tell her.

'You got what you need?' he asks, clearly hoping she hasn't. She smiles, politely, and wonders why the hell she's doing any of this. The answer, insidious, disloyal, creeps in from somewhere dark.

Because he's Tilly's father. He's in her. And you want to know all that you can to keep her safe . . .

Flustered, Grace nods and stands up. She feels unsteady on her feet. Her head is swimming with information, but she doesn't know what to do with it. She doesn't know if she's been told lies, or half-truths. She feels suddenly unintelligent and naïve. She feels silly. She looks at herself, stood here in a grim little office above a pizza shop, talking to a con man, pretending to be a journalist, listening to stories about a man whose name is on the birth certificate of the man she loves. She imagines telling Adam what she has found out, and realizes it is nothing. That Franco was a bad man. That he bowed out after something horrible happened in the 1970s. That Alison runs the show. That Irons was a psycho's wet dream. She knows only that she has not found out enough to justify this dangerous trip. To meet a man she met on the Internet. She suddenly knows she won't even tell Adam that she's been here. That she'll slip back into the car and go home. Home, to play detectives and enjoy the adventure and the excitement and the closeness of Adam's skin, and not to let herself get too close to the raw unpleasantness of it all.

'So you'll be in touch?' asks Brian, as he sees her to the door. 'You get anywhere, there could be a book in it, though you're probably best off going to one of the bigger houses. Bit small fry, here.' Brian says it with a jaded sadness. An admission of who he is. He bounces back with a flash of a smile. 'Only way is up, though, eh?'

Grace surveys the man in the doorway as she steps back on the fire escape. Were there time, she would like to get to know him. To unpick his life story and find out which twists and turns in the path of his life led him here, to this grotty office, writing lies. She smiles and shakes his hand, and shivers in the wind as she makes her way back to the car, her head full of criminals and rapists, liars and murderers, pictures of crying kingpins and bleeding assassins in her mind.

She wonders if this is how it feels to be Adam.

She shivers.

It's not from the cold.

Thirty-Four

The Prince, Parkgate Road, Battersea
5.12 p.m.

There's been a pub here, on the corner of Parkgate Road, since 1866. It faces Battersea Park and has a kind of faded majesty about it, like a ninety-something war veteran dressed in his uniform and medals on Remembrance Day. It's old, but it can still doll itself up for a special occasion.

Adam hasn't ever been in before. Hopes he'll get a chance to bring Zara next time they take the trip across. She'll like this, he reckons. He'd admired the big red tiles and the fancy, cream-coloured awnings as he'd followed Alison inside, trying to make small-talk with the two men who kept conspiring to remain two steps behind him.

Even here, at the bar, they're off to one side, watching Alison as she reclines in a booth, her espresso cooling on the table-top, and talks to a small, frightened Maltese man who has asked her here to discuss something he didn't feel able to chat about over the phone.

One of Adam's minders is Jimbo. As far as Adam can tell, Jimbo's main function is looking the part and keeping his mouth shut. Adam's had a glance at his knuckles. He's no fighter, that's for sure. Adam hates himself for considering such a toxic, macho scenario, but he's confident that

265

if push came to shove, he could wipe the floor with him. The other minder is a young, wide-eyed lump called Luke. He's a cheery sort. Dropped out of training for the Royal Navy because of girl trouble and has been getting into mischief for a while now. Pulled a few Post Office jobs and took a hammer to a fruit machine in a casino off Trafalgar Square. A concerned uncle has called in a favour with a minor player in the Jardine organization. He's doing fetch-and-carry work for Alison now. Standing still and looking tough, as the situation necessitates. He's chattier with Jimbo, who barely managed to throw half a dozen words his way on the drive from King's Cross. Been no chattier with Grace, neither. Dropped her off, as requested, in some ghastly triangle of Stepney Green, then carried on across the river to meet up with the boss.

Adam, nursing a pint of London Pride, is feeling a prickle of embarrassment. He feels like a spare part. Doesn't know why they've asked him along, or why Alison is stone-walling him. He's coming to the conclusion he may have misjudged the tone of this particular get-together. He winces as he thinks back. He'd been overfamiliar in his greeting, trying to make her laugh, telling her he'd missed her, thanking her for going to the trouble of sending the Mercedes, complete with pretty-boy drivers. Tried to give her a hug and a kiss and ended up with the arm of her Stella McCartney glasses scratching the corner of his mouth. She'd stayed on the phone while he prattled on about nothing, looking irritated and rich in her Magda Butrym kitten-heeled boots, khaki jodhpurs and brown leather minidress. She was always business. No warmth in her greeting. Just a rich woman, standing on a street corner under an umbrella held by a tall, black man, his eyes scanning the street and the nearby park for signs of impending trouble.

'You won't have one?' asks Adam, hoping that Luke will trade the sparkling water for something a little livelier.

'No he won't,' growls Jimbo, beside him. He's sipping green tea from a big cup and saucer; the antioxidant benefits of the beverage undermined a little by the crust of white powder around his nostril, and the open bag of pork scratchings on the bar.

'I will, then,' says Adam, grateful he won't have to shell out for three drinks. He taps his glass, and the barmaid, with her big hoop earrings and choppy red hair, does the honours. He smiles at her as she pours the pint and gets nothing back in return. She keeps looking past him, to where Alison is deep in conversation with the small, bald-headed man.

'You seem stressed,' says Adam, feeling an urge to put his hand around hers as she puts the drink down. She's shaking a little; a muscle ticking, like a clock, in her cheek. 'Are you okay?'

Her smile, when it comes, is a frightened grimace. Adam wants to tell her it will all be okay; that whatever is worrying her, it can't be that bad. She waves him away when he tries to pay. She did the same with his first pint too.

Bored, listless, he leans against the bar. Plays with his phone. Sips his drink. Occasionally, he tries to catch Alison's eye, but whatever she's here for, it's more important than him.

A text message beeps through. It's Grace – chin deep in bullshit and still doggy-paddling through more of it, thanks to King Rat's extraordinary reserves of gossip and conceit. He imagines her, sitting opposite the author and supergrass, pretending to be a professional, sifting through his memory banks for information about Leo Riley; Ace Howell – about Larry Paris, where this all began. He realizes he doesn't like it. He's starting to feel as though he has absolutely no right to be here and even less to have dragged Grace, the mother of his child, along for the ride. His thoughts start to speed up. He becomes aware of where he is; what he's doing; the absurdity of following this path. They left Tilly with Grace's neighbour, Maxine, and left Portsmouth as if making for the border. He'd even thought about asking Zara to look after her – to keep an eye on his daughter while he goes looking for answers about a parentage that she does not even know has been in doubt.

He sips his drink, misery descending like rain. Catches sight of himself in the glass behind the bar and sees his father looking back at him. He shakes it away, angry with his own mind for conjuring up such an impossible projection.

He realizes he's no longer listening to the quiet chatter in the bar. There are only half a dozen customers in the big, wood-floored bar, and they're taking an overwhelming interest in newspapers, phones and their own shoes. From behind him, he hears Alison's voice growing louder.

'. . . nothing to do with us, you fucking know that, Albert, but if he's got himself done in then that's a sadness but it's not a reason to lose your bottle – you told me you had him sewn up. He was going to sign. Scared him bad enough to turn his hair white, that's what you said . . .'

Adam strains to hear more. The smaller man's voice is accented, wheedling, scared. '. . . but he thinks that if you would do this to Nicholas then perhaps that is the future for all of us, and with your father so unwell . . .'

Beside him, he sees Jimbo and Luke grimace in unison.

'What was that about my father?'

'Alison, please, how long have we done business together? I have nothing but respect for you and your family. But nothing lasts forever. Your father is old, and you, well, you are a business-woman, aren't you? That's how you want the papers to print it – your father spent enough money trying to prove he wasn't a gangster. People are getting scared. It's too big, Alison. An Olympic village? It's, well, it's hard to see how you can keep a hold of it . . .'

Adam glances up from his drink and catches sight of the barmaid. She's glancing at the door. She's terrified. She's waiting for something. For someone.

'And these other rumours. This private detective, trussed up like we're back in 1968. Christ, Alison – my niece has shown me posts on that fucking Facebook from your boy Timmy, bragging that the Jardines are back in business, running London like they always have. It's

269

embarrassing. I don't wish it on you, but it causes those who were onside to have second thoughts. Even the Freeman has gone quiet. Times change. And the mob coming out of Canning Town are ruthless. I don't know if you want what's coming. I can get you a sit-down with him, maybe carve up the good bits, put a few things to rest, then you can enjoy a retirement, eh . . .?'

Adam hears desperation in the man's voice. Changes his position so he can watch the trickles of sweat run down his glossy pink face. Alison's eyes are a blowtorch, melting him to the bone.

'All you had to do was what I told you,' hisses Alison. 'It's a goldmine. You just need to put your doubts to one side. If you stay onside then the others will too.'

'How can I? Your man, your monster, we don't know if he still exists, Alison. And these past days when it's all been going to shit, you've been out of the picture. Been up to "personal business", whatever the hell that is. It gets the old geezers talking. They fall back into old prejudices. You're a woman, you're all hormones and *feeelings* . . .' he says, making the word sound revolting. 'I can't tell you how to run your side of the firm but this was the wrong time to take your eye off the ball . . .'

Adam senses a change in the quality of the air. Everything slows down. The lights seem to crackle and fizz within the bulbs.

And then he is raising his hands, shielding his eyes, as Jimbo takes five brisk steps across the floor and brings a metal-tipped wooden hammer down on the top of the Maltese man's shiny dome. It cracks like glass. Jimbo brings it down again. The fat man falls forward, blood and skull forming an archipelago on the table top.

Alison sits back in the booth. Adam becomes aware of a screaming behind him; the barmaid, pressing herself up small behind the till. He swivels back to Alison. He realizes he isn't scared. Isn't even excited. He just wishes he hadn't seen this. Hadn't heard the sound of hammer on bone.

He locks eyes with her. Watches her drain her espresso, emotionless. She flicks her eyes towards the door. He doesn't need telling twice. Walks away, hearing the *thunk* as Jimbo drops the hammer on the floor, and pulls out a mobile phone. As Adam bangs out into the street, he hears him asking for the police. Telling them to come quick. Telling them that a man in a black hood and a black mask has just smashed in the skull of Alfredo Bussutil. That his boss is a witness. She can tell them everything.

Rain on his face, a chemical tang in his nostrils, Adam starts to run.

As he'd stared into her eyes, he'd seen nothing but darkness.

It had felt like looking into a mirror.

Thirty-Five

The Bat and Ball, Waterlooville
1.14 p.m.

Irons pinches out his cigarette between forefinger and thumb and turns to look at the blazing oak fire that sits halfway along the back wall of the main bar. The flames fold in on themselves, turn inside out, like material caught in crosswinds. The light bounces off the brasses that hang from the dark oak timbers, cast shadows on the old black-and-white photographs. For an instant he remembers the kiss of the flame, the sensation of his skin turning to glue, dribbling onto his chest, into his ears, like candlewax among the hairs. Transformed by fire, reborn in agony, anointed with a cross of sulphur.

Close up, and in this light, Zara has started seeing a strange, unexpected beauty in Irons's face. She can only liken it to the way that the grain in a wooden table, when studied, can suddenly grow perfect and sensuous, more dramatic than any deft brushstroke or sculpted alabaster. Or the way that the patterns which swirl in a cup of coffee as the milk goes in can some-times be mesmerizingly elegant, like a galaxy viewed from God's platform.

In places his face is a raw, scrubbed pink; a baby with nappy rash. Here and there the flesh puckers,

272

in deep, scarred tunnels. At the jawline the skin is almost leather. It looks as though it has melted and dripped away, and what remains has been glued back down then varnished. The skull, so utterly bald, seems to have been sanded down, rubbed too close to the bone. But his eyes, one black and shark-like, one the head on a flat pint, seem to hold her gaze in a way that no pristine set of blue irises has ever managed. Despite his age, his scent of wet leaves, his alabaster hands, the baby smile, Zara finds herself thinking of her new friend as an attractive man. She reproaches herself for flinching the first time he took her hand.

'We're not going to have to argue about the bill again, are we?' she asks, as she drains the last of her double espresso then settles back in her hard wooden seat and places a cigarillo between her lips.

'No argument, pet,' says Irons, leaning across the table and lighting it. 'I'm paying, you're saying thank you.'

Zara pulls a face of mock indignation, then smiles. 'But you don't eat,' she says. 'A bowl of gravy and a few slices of bread isn't going to make you a big strong boy.'

'It's served me fine up until now,' says Irons, as he lights another cigarette and takes a sip of water, swirling it around his toothless mouth.

They sit and smile at each other across the table, and both feel strangely comfortable. Zara wonders what the other diners think of them. She, with her shaved head, short skirt, knee-length boots and sloppy jumper. He, melted, remoulded into something monstrous, powerful in his black

273

jumper, black jeans, leather coat. Father and daughter? Lovers? The thought makes her giggle.

'You reckon they think we're at it?' asks Irons, reading her mind and nodding in the direction of the four elderly ladies, clothed head to toe in Laura Ashley, drinking their sweet sherries in the snug by the fire.

'Do you think they know what "it" is?' replies Zara, and they smile afresh.

This is the third time Zara and Irons have been out for lunch together inside a week. Two days after he found her crying in the restaurant, they bumped into one another in the cash and carry. Irons had offered to pay for Zara's trolley-load of booze, but she refused, despite the screaming inside. Instead, she accepted a cup of coffee in the crappy canteen, and found herself again filling him up with her misery. Him, listening, questioning, caring. Telling her his own stories. Explanations. He's looking into his family tree. Spending his days in libraries and archives, visiting graves and gazing at addresses that have played a part in his life. On Wednesday night he came to the restaurant, dabbed up his Roquefort cheese and red wine sauce with a complimentary roll, and left the steak untouched. Pushed his plate away and insisted Zara join him. It wasn't busy, so she agreed. Spoke a little more, then a lot. Unburdened herself of just a little baggage. Then all of it. Found herself growing more and more comfortable in the company of this curious bruise of a man.

His treat again, today. Sunday lunch in this well-to-do country pub. She, digging into turkey from

274

the carvery, summer-fruit pudding and a bottle of house red. He, a bowl of gravy and half a bag of bread. Glass of water and a packet of cigarettes. Eating slowly, methodically, like it's a chore.

'Another?' asks Irons, as Zara drains the last of her red wine.

'No, I'd best behave,' she replies. 'Adam's coming home tonight, all being well, and I want to get the kids bathed and into bed before he does. Wouldn't mind an early night of my own.'

'Business must be going well then,' says Irons. 'Working on Remembrance Day.' His poppy is so pristine in his leather buttonhole that the old ladies at the nearby table are wondering if his disfiguration occurred during the war.

'Seems to be,' says Zara, nodding enthusiastically. 'I miss him like crazy but he's doing what he always wanted to do. He phones me as often as he can and I think after this trip he'll be home a lot more often. The kids are lost without him, especially Selena.'

'How are the money woes?'

Zara stares at the dribble of red, already turning to treacle, in the bottom of her glass. She doesn't like thinking about it, but she knows that she came here today to talk about this very thing. 'I've got a week, tops. I spoke to the people at the law centre and they said I've got a case but the only way I can prove it is to go through arbitration, and that's going to cost more than I've got. There are moments when I just want to chuck it all in.'

'Do you really think Adam will let you fail?' asks Irons. 'Is he that kind of man?'

Zara wipes her eyes with the heels of her hands, smearing her make-up. She looks fragile and far-away. 'He's been through so much with me already. I'll be dragging him down with me and that isn't fair. He's making a go of his own business but not enough to subsidize mine. He's got a temper. I don't know if he gets it from his dad, but when he's angry he doesn't think . . .'

'You still haven't met them, then? His parents?'

'No chance. His dad's getting worse and worse, by all accounts. He sounds a decent sort from Adam's stories, but who knows? And his mum just sounds like a neurotic. God knows how she'll cope when his dad dies, which can't be long. I know it's hitting him hard. I think that might be what's wrong with him. I hope it is. I don't want it to be me.'

'He probably doesn't want your impressions of his dad to be a dying man losing his mind. He's probably protecting you both.'

'Maybe,' says Zara, and then thinks about it, and finds herself nodding. 'You could be right. I know his dad's been a big influence to him. He was a man's man, by all accounts. I told you, didn't I? He was a builder, out on the road, until he was, erm . . .' Zara shifts uncomfortably, pulls a face, searches for a word that isn't rude.

'Burned?' prompts Irons, and gives a smile that splits his scarred face. 'You don't have to sugar-coat it, pet. I've got mirrors. I'm a car crash, I know that. And fair play to you, love, you've managed to spend a good bit of time with me without mentioning it.'

Zara starts to say that it's none of her

business, that she doesn't need to know, but she's longing to hear his story, to listen and nod and pay attention as he has for her, and distract herself from her own problems, if only for a few more moments.

'You don't have to tell me,' she says, and drops her eyes to the table.

Irons looks across at Zara, the gentle, pale lines of her face, the stoop to her shoulders, the tiny buds of her breasts, the passion and anger in her belly, and realizes that he is truly fond of this woman. She is becoming more than a source of answers. She is more than a doorway into Adam's life. He is enjoying her company.

'Your scars,' she asks, her voice a whisper. 'Did somebody hurt you?'

Irons feels a tightness across his chest. His vision, split into light and darkness, suddenly blurs, as though twisted sheets of cellophane are being held in front of his eyes. The effort of telling the story has hit him harder than he expected. Memories are fighting in his mind. The black eye seems to become even darker.

At length, he looks down at his hands. 'I made a mistake. I deserved what I got.'

'Nobody deserves that,' says Zara, softly.

And he hears it. Hears her. The voice, in his head, silent these past forty years – muted by the crescendo of crackling flame as the fire devoured the petrol and began to work its way through his face.

You let me down. You let him in. You need to make it right.

Thirty-Six

The Cenotaph, Westminster
November 11th, 12.22 p.m.

The snow falls in great fat flakes, like cherry blossom drifting from April trees. It throws a lace veil over the borough.

Freeman Leo Riley leans on his walking stick and feels the chill seeping into his bones. *Cold to the marrow*, he thinks. It used to be just a phrase, when he was young. Now he knows its true meaning. Knows how it feels to see your own skeleton as nothing more than a collection of icicles, held together with sagging skin.

He feels old, today. He stands by the kerbside, watching the traffic, weight on his stick, fighting the urge to tremble. Gridlock in front of him, shops behind. Cold and wet and dark and miserable. He glances to his left. Some young press officer with blonde hair and a flat chest is holding a large golf umbrella over his head while he waits for the car, but it's doing nothing to stop the billowing flakes of snow, and his coat is growing heavier as the water soaks in.

'Shouldn't be long now,' she says, cheerily, pulling a face against the cold. 'Always the same on Remembrance Day.'

Riley gives her a nod and a grunt.

'Did you enjoy the service?' she asks, shivering.

'Very uplifting,' he says. His voice is rich and deep, and doesn't tremble. It never betrays him. 'Far fewer veterans this year. Fewer every year, to be honest. I hope your generation doesn't ever let this tradition die out. It's a duty.'

'Oh no,' she says, shaking her head. A snowflake is melting on her long eyelashes. 'No, this is important to everybody.'

No it isn't, he thinks. Doesn't bloody matter at all. We do it because we've always done it. I'm only here so people don't think I'm dead. I haven't listened to the Remembrance Service in fucking years. I'm freezing and I need a piss and a sandwich . . .

'You must have better things to do on a Sunday, though,' Riley says, turning his face into the wind to get a better look at her. Victoria, she said she was called. 'You got a nice young man waiting for you at home?'

'Oh he's having a look around the shops while I'm here,' she says, grinning. 'I'll meet him when I'm done here.'

'You get a day off in the week for this?'

'Hopefully,' she says, with a cheeky little smile.

In front of them, the traffic starts to move a little quicker. The noise of windscreen wipers beating away the plump flakes of snow and of wet tyres swishing over dark tarmac is a soft accompaniment to the sounds of families and young couples filling the pavements and spilling out of the great glass shopping centre behind where Riley stands. He can hear grumbles about the weather, the traffic, the midweek result at White Hart Lane. Miserable bloody day, he

279

thinks. And him, stood with a little girl, waiting for a car that should have been here twenty minutes ago. He's getting cross.

'Here it is,' says the girl, suddenly, pointing down the street to where one of the big black civic cars is pulling out of the traffic and easing across to the kerb.

Riley feels relief flood through him. A minute or two and you'll be in the warm, he tells himself. Quick drive, then into the civic hall for some grub and back-slapping. Few glasses of wine, sausage roll or two. Maybe even get a mention in somebody's speech. Then home, bit of telly, back rub from Urszula, quick toss, wash his hair in a cup of her piss, if she can squeeze one out, bed.

The rear door opens and a young man with glasses and dark hair steps out, rubbing his arms and pulling a face at the girl. Another bloody press officer. 'Can you manage?' he asks, taking Riley's arm.

'I'm fine,' he grunts, and takes the cold metal of the open car door with his hand, using it to push himself off the kerb and onto the comfortable leather seats. The heater's been on, and the warmth of the car is delicious.

He sits back as the Mercedes pulls away from the kerb and back into the traffic. All the cars have headlights on full beam. It's just gone lunch, but dark as bedtime, and Riley can see his reflection in the tinted windscreens. He looks every one of his eighty-one years. A lot shorter than he used to be, too. He sees himself as some hunched little wizard, wrapped in an overcoat and ceremonial robes. A horseshoe of white hair around a liver-spotted skull. Wrinkles that could have been put there with a pizza wheel. Wet eyes, still fine for long-distance but useless close to. Neck like a turkey. Urszula has to stretch the skin almost to his ear before she can shave him.

'Should be a good spread,' says the young man, cheerfully. 'My first one of these dos, actually. Starving, I am. Banquet room, they said. You be OK with the stairs? Course you will, we've got that whatsit. Chairlift. If you're taking the chair, that is. You looked pretty light on your pins during the procession. Horrible day for it though, eh. Honestly, I can't believe it. On the council for donkey's years, weren't you? Alderman, freeman, now this. This borough owes you a lot, I'd say. I was made up when they said I'd be looking after you for the day. Sorry about the delay with the car but we had to drop the mayor off, and then the traffic was terrible. That's one for the council, eh? Get the bloody city centre moving. Oh, sorry, my phone's ringing . . .'

Riley sits and lets the words wash over him. He concentrates on warming his body through. What's the boy saying? Deserves it? Course he fucking deserves it. He built this city. Never taken a bloody penny on the side for it, neither. Sometimes he wishes he had. Wishes he'd pocketed the envelopes that were offered alongside the perks. The hospitality. The warm bodies and instructions to never say no. Could use the cash now though. Urszula isn't cheap. Council pension, war pension, nest egg from the sale of the big house where he used to live before the stairs

281

became a burden. Just about enough to pay for his dalliances with Magda, but not much reward for a life of unstinting service to the community, sweet as she is. She hasn't got the paperwork, of course, but she's a good little carer. Polish. Blonde. Nineteen. Mouth like a plunger. Expert hands. Does as she's told, and doesn't object to a man with a temper, and curious ways. Fucking terrible English, though. Not much of a receptionist, neither. What had she said last night? Alison Jardine ringing for him? Bollocks. He hasn't spoken to the Jardines in years. Spent force. No point. Did each other some good turns, once upon a time, but things change. Change spectacularly, sometimes.

No, he'd told Urszula, *you've got it wrong. Never mind, pet. Come here and let me sniff you . . .*

An annoying ditty is chirruping inside the car, and Riley turns to look at his companion, who is struggling with his pocket. He pulls out a mobile phone, flips it open, and the music stops.

'Hi, Wayne Dunning. Oh hi. Hmm. Yes. No, he wouldn't be. Right, of course. Well he's with me now, actually. OK.' The lad turns to Riley with his hand over the telephone. 'Journalist looking for you. Wants to do an article about your legacy – about the Games and how it's men like you who paved the way. All go, isn't it? You want to talk to him?'

Riley gives an exaggerated sigh, but reaches for the phone. He's always liked talking to the Press. He was making a name for himself as a safe pair of hands before the phrase 'public relations' had even been invented. Knew how to play the game. Kept reporters happy, and his own image whiter than white. It's come in handy, once or twice, having a journalist onside. One or two pictures that wouldn't have looked good in print have disappeared over the years thanks to a tip-off and some friends on the picture desk.

'Freeman Leo Riley. Can I help?'

There is a pause, and then a voice, full of venom, says, 'I know what you did.'

Riley sits silently in the big comfortable car. Considers his responses. The voice at the other end of the phone is going to have to be far more specific.

'That's good,' says Riley, thoughtfully. 'Maybe you could let me in on the secret.'

'1971,' comes the voice, thick with drink and emotion. 'Jardine's party. I know.'

Riley nods, slowly. He's not worried. Mightily intrigued, but a long way from worried. He's always been the cleverest person in the room and his mind is the one part of him that has improved with age.

'What a strange thing to say,' muses Riley. He moves his tongue around his mouth, considering. A smile crosses his face as he works through the list of people who might have reason to make this call. 'Can I look forward to our continuing this conversation in person? I just need an address.'

There is silence at the other end of the line. Riley listens to the windscreen wipers. The tyres. The chatter outside. The tic-toc of the indicator as they turn onto the road leading to the reception. His mind, still sharp, goes into auto-pilot. Decades of thinking on his feet have taught him never to be rattled. Never be surprised. He races through the possibilities. Who knew? Jardine. His monster, probably. Whoever picked up the pieces. Who else? That phone call. Maybe Jardine had said something to his daughter. Old, by now. Maybe his mind's going. His lass might have a boyfriend. A son. Have the family still got money? Relax. Always relax.

'I'm not sure I understand,' he says, calmly. 'Could you repeat that, please?'

There is another pause, then the voice says, 'Fuck you. You know what I'm talking about. You know what you did.'

'I'm afraid there's been some confusion,' says Riley. 'Where are you getting your facts?'

'You were seen. Carrying her. Naked and bleeding.'

'Really? By whom?'

'Fuck you.'

'No, if an accusation has been made then I deserve to know by whom.'

'Don't give me that politics shit. I'm not really a fucking journalist.'

'No? Then who are you.'

'I'm what you left behind, you dirty bastard.'

Riley ponders for a moment. Somebody saw you, he tells himself. Kept their mouth shut about it long enough, haven't they? What they blabbing for now? Money? Clearing a conscience? Or are they thinking you and Jardine can't harm them any more. That you're old and knackered? Silly bastard.

'Can I assume that this call has something to do with the Jardine family? I understand that somebody has been trying to get in touch with me.'

'You were running scared. Wouldn't ring her back. This was the only way to get you.'

'And now you have me, what do you want?'

There is a pause. The sound of mental gears changing. Then the voice says, 'To put things right.'

The line goes dead.

Riley takes the phone from his ear and looks at it. Says hello once or twice, just for show, then hands it back to the young lad. 'Bad line,' he says. 'I'll never get the hang of those things.'

He sits back in the chair and closes his eyes. Thinks back. That night. Middle of nowhere, then right at the lights. The big house and the brandy and the shiny cars. The dark woods and the fine rain. Sees himself, with a young girl. Him, pissed, in the dark. Her, wanting it but not knowing it yet. That shadow in the trees. The streak of white with the bundle in his arms. The flash of light, that suddenly illuminated a bare torso, dark trousers. Mosquito, ink-black eyes. And the patterns on his skin. Playing cards. The aces and eights: the Dead Man's Hand.

Jardine had sorted it, though. That was what he did. It was what friends were for.

He feels somehow exhilarated by the call.

Could Jardine be doing this? A man like that doesn't get attacked by conscience, does he? Not with all the things he's done. The bodies he's put in the ground would fill a fucking forest. One

285

slag. One laughing bitch thirty-odd years ago? Wouldn't matter a fuck to Jardine. No. He's not behind it. He's as involved as you are. And he said he would sort it out. That's a promise you keep. He's still younger than you, too, Leo. Probably still in good shape. He was at that court case flexing his muscles not so long ago. And the monster's out now, too, isn't he? They still owe you. Half their empire would have fallen down if you hadn't greased their wheels. Let them sort it out. Find out who did it, then explain how things work. You're Leo Riley and you built this city.

He turns to the young lad. 'Sorry son, I'm feeling rotten. You're going to have to take me home.'

Without waiting for a reply, Riley turns back and stares out of the window. Watches the snowflakes; a billion white bees.

Going to be a funny old day, he tells himself.

Going to have to relive some old memories.

And say hello to an old friend.

Thirty-Seven

Derby Road, Stamshaw, Portsmouth
November 11th, 7.11 p.m.

Adam can taste garlic. It feels like there's a bulb of the stuff decomposing in his chest. He pulls faces as he lays on the sofa, in jeans and a vest, bare feet in Zara's lap, holding the sheaf of papers in an outstretched arm, reaching into the large triangle of half-light which shines through from the kitchen.

Adam reaches down and picks up his whisky, bending the crumpled papers against the glass as he does so. Takes a swig. Fumbles around till he feels the bottle. Unscrews the cap, takes a gulp. Pulls a face. Closes his eyes. Nods at something Zara's telling him. Smiles, wriggles his toes, like a good boyfriend should, as she strokes them.

He's trying hard. Tilly has come down with chicken pox and neither the nursery, nor Grace's put-upon neighbour, will continue to look after her while she's contagious. There wasn't much discussion about returning. He and Grace, both eager to be good parents, got on the first train back home, but it was a sense of duty, rather than desire, that saw them leave London. They would never admit it, but their first thoughts upon hearing their little girl was poorly, were for themselves. The hiatus in their adventure. The stepping off the path, even for a moment. Their hearts melted when they saw Tilly's face, of course, with its pubescent constellation of pus-filled spots and mucky scabs, her sulky pout, her scalp too sore to comb, but their attention to her every whim has been motivated as much by a desire to remove the inconvenience of her illness as by a need to ease their daughter's suffering.

'. . . so maybe like, a kind of evening brunch, if you get me – like waffles and donuts and bananas and Nutella and stuff, but with cocktails – kind of that late-evening sweetness vibe, y'know, I mean it could be mad but what if it takes off, though of course then you've got to pay to publicise it and who has the money to do that . . .?'

Adam holds the papers to his face again. They're crumpled now, folded in the shape of his back pocket. Reams of printed pages, pictures, cuttings. Every word he could find on Riley. Every spit and cough.

He re-reads the feature from the council's website, a profile on council legends padded out with background on what an alderman does.

> Alderman Leo Riley isn't as quick on his feet as he used to be. He walks slowly, with a frame, and his hearing aid has a tendency to play up, so he asks you to speak slowly and clearly.
>
> The picture on the wall behind him when we meet in a small, comfortable room at the Freeman's Guild, is a photograph of himself as a younger man. It shows a stocky man with a ruddy

complexion and thick, wiry, grey hair. It bears little resemblance to the slim but dapper gent who now sits in the high-backed leather chair, dressed in a brown suit over a blue jumper and Party tie.

'It cleared off over the space of a few weeks in the 1970s,' says Alderman Riley, with a laugh, as he points to his bald scalp. 'Must have been the heat of my brain that burned it away.'

As an ex-Lord Mayor, Leader of the Council, Chairman of the Regional Development Board, former magistrate, and a dedicated councillor of some fifty years standing, Alderman Riley clearly misses being close to the centre of the action, and looks forward to the occasions he can represent his old neighbourhood as an Honorary Alderman – an office bestowed on those who have served the city with distinction.

As a councillor, one of Alderman Riley's main interests was improving the health of his constituents. When he first stood for election Public Assistance Institutions (workhouses) still existed as the only form of social care for unmarried mothers, the elderly and people with learning dis-abilities, and many of the constituents on his inner city ward lived in unsanitary, overcrowded conditions. He takes pride in knowing that many of the initiatives he launched and oversaw had a direct effect on his community.

Perhaps Alderman Riley's biggest contribution to the Borough has been in the arena of sport. The lifelong football fan has ensured major resources have been pumped into sporting provision in communities across the city. He is rumoured to be in line for the ultimate honour when a new football stand in the community centre at Upton Park is named in his honour, and was heavily involved in the failed bid to host the 1988 Olympics in London.

Alderman Riley has always kept his personal life private. He was briefly married as a young man but since then says he has been happier on his own.

'Sometimes I think it would be nice to have lots of grandchildren running around but I was always too busy to start a family,' he says. 'Maybe I missed out, maybe I didn't. I feel like this council is my baby and I've loved watching it grow.'

The paper becomes a ball in Adam's fist.

'. . . but then he said the phone wouldn't scan through on the machine because it wasn't a recommissioned one, so the deal wouldn't work, and he had to scrap the whole thing and get me to phone somewhere in bloody India to tell them I didn't mind him scrapping it, then phone the other company for this code, and . . .'

Adam watches her lips move, the glint of the stud in her mouth, the soft pink of her skin, the fine lines of her face, the slope of her breasts beneath her borrowed shirt.

'. . . so now we're on the same network it's free between our phones, so you can call me whenever and not have to worry about it . . .'

Adam smiles at her, feeling something briefly bloom inside him. She sees it, and the light that fills her eyes make him feel, briefly, like a man capable of creating happiness in somebody else. He wants to sit up and kiss her neck. To gently knead her soft earlobes between his forefinger and thumb, the way she likes.

'. . . he's got bad burns,' she says. 'Really bad. Over his whole face. Like that man in the Falklands War. His whole face is just one big pink scar.'

Adam's arms stiffen around her. His breathing halts. His chest stops rising. The hands that were stroking her bare skin freeze, motionless.

'Adam?'

He doesn't speak.

Then, faintly, his breath comes again.

'Yeah?' he asks, and it's almost nothing. Barely a sound. He coughs, then, louder: 'Yeah?'

'Yeah,' says Zara, somewhere between confusion and relief. She feels Adam's fingers begin to caress her skin once more but there's a tremble there, as though he's cold. 'He came in the restaurant a wee while back. We got chatting, like I said. Hit it off. He's been a good pal, actually. It can't be easy for him, people staring all the time. I told him, I'm used to it. We've had a bit of dinner. People must have thought we were a right odd couple, but I got the impression he was lonely.' She falls quiet, expecting a response. She's puzzled. Surely he's not jealous? He's never shown any signs of it before, she thinks. Never seemed to worry about her straying. She finds herself strangely pleased. Feels tempted to milk it. 'You don't mind, do you? He's not exactly my type.' Then, for bad: 'He's big, though. Striking looking. His face is quite beautiful, close to.'

Adam's hands continue to stroke Zara's skin, but there's no warmth in the touch. He rubs her flesh rhythmically, without feeling.

'What's he called?' asks Adam. His voice is almost the light, bouncy sound he aims for, but not quite. There's damp in there. A November breeze.

'Ray,' she says, turning her head to smile up at him. 'Don't think he said his last name.'

'What do you talk about?'

'Oh, this and that. The restaurant. The kids. What he's up to.'

'Me?'

'Bits and bobs. I know how you get, so don't worry, I didn't tell him about anything that matters.'

'Tilly? Did you tell him about Tilly?'

'Why?'

'Did you?'

'Adam, I don't understand . . .'

He stands up, and steps into the patch of light emanating from the kitchen.

He's shaking. Selena, in her chair, opens an eye and shrinks back in the chair. Jordan begins to wake up on the floor.

'You don't understand! You've no fucking idea!'

He starts rubbing his forehead, muttering to himself. He turns away from her, stiff-backed. 'Irons,' he's saying, tossing his head from side to side, as though shaking water from his hair. 'Here. Now.'

'Darling,' she says, timidly reaching an arm up to him. 'Darling, talk to me . . .'

Adam shakes his head, pulls open the door to the lobby, and yanks on his boots. Cold against his bare feet. Pulls a jacket down from the hook, opens the door and steps outside.

He barely feels the cold, or registers the ink-black, cloudless sky, scattered with stars, scented with the metallic tang of snow.

Thinking: *Irons.*

Thirty-Eight

Candy's Pit Cave, Portsdown Hill, Portsmouth
10.14 p.m.

The hollow in the rock face is an ink-black mouth; a toothless rectangle in a great white wall of scars. Adam likes it here. Has memories, good and bad. Likes the smell of the tree roots as they break, slowly, through the rock-strewn earth. It's a place where teenagers find refuge; to skulk in the damp and the darkness and to suck on aerosols and one another. The sun went down hours ago, and if it weren't for the perfect chalky whiteness of the cliff-face, the cavern would be all but invisible. Even if it were so, Adam would be able to find his way here. This is a place for sanctuary. It's where he used to come when he was a teenager; to sit and think and to wonder what he was for; what he was meant to be – why he was clever enough to see how little he mattered, but insufficiently wise to do anything about it. Where an older, bolder woman had taken his virginity before he really knew that it was something to treasure. Elaine, her name was. Vinegar and cider on her tongue; the taste of talcum powder and roll-on deodorant on the skin of her doughy, motherly breasts. He supposes it would be called abuse, these days. She'd have gone to prison if she was a bloke and he was a thirteen-year-old girl. Truth is, he's grateful to her. He's been after that feeling ever since. Has wanted nothing more than to feel like a legend for making a strong, confident, sexually-experienced woman scream like a happy hyena as she rode him.

He sits squeezing the phone in his hand, legs drawn up, backside cold on the cold floor. The only light in the cave is from the screen of his phone and the glare of the cigarette that he smokes, angrily and joylessly; the tip gleaming brighter with each swirling gust of wind.

He knows all about this place thanks to Dad. To good old Billy Nunn. Always good for a bit of trivia, Billy. Read a lot when he was off sick with his injuries. Gave himself a brain the size of Hulk Hogan's bicep, according to Santinello and the lads who worked for and worshipped him. First pick on the pub quiz teams – beating the buggers with the buzzers whenever father and son sat and watched *Blockbusters* and *Krypton Factor*, eating tea from trays on their knees, thanking Mum each time she bustled in with a fresh pot of tea or a tray of biscuits. God how he wishes he could reach back into his memories and make himself say something kind. Something thoughtful. How he wishes he'd given his mum a cuddle around the middle and told her she was brilliant. Wishes he'd not tried so hard to piss off his dad, too. He can hear his voice, now, drumming at his head like rain on a tin roof. Talking to him like one of the lads – trying to get a bit of respect from a lad who didn't know how lucky he was.

Candy's Pit Cave? You don't know the story?

Bloody hell, what are they teaching you? Thought you were tipped for an A in History? There were tea gardens at the top of the cliff above the quarry. Lovely spot, run by a local woman. Did I tell you that it was Napoleonic prisoners who dug the cave? Christ, I'm no kind of father. Anyways, there was a tramp turned up one day, best part of a hundred years ago. Had a brown bear cub with him – taught it to dance for money and it made the lady who ran the tea room a few quid so she let them both stay. Candy, its name was. Buried nearby, so I'm told. Be a treat for the archaeologists, won't it . . .

Adam tugs at his hair. He'd been trying so hard. It wasn't settling, he'd explained as much to himself. He wasn't picking a simple life over an interesting one. He loved Zara. Loves her. She makes his skin warm and quiets the noises in his head. And now Irons has been slithering around her, asking questions, sucking the honey from her tongue – checking him out even as Alison pretended to be his friend. The cheek of it. The nerve!

He texts her again, more insistent this time.

I KNOW WHAT HE'S BEEN DOING. I WANT TO SPEAK TO HIM, ALISON. NOW!

For once, he doesn't feel guilty for his tone. He feels betrayed. Tricked. Christ, how much of what she's told him has been a lie. Has she been manoeuvring him around, keeping him out of harm's way, feeding him stories about old footballers and London freemen, just so her hired killer could get close to his family?

The phone vibrates in his hand. He drops it, curses, listening to it bounce around on the stones.

'Adam? What's going on? What's wrong?'

He wants to hang up. He isn't sure he can find the words to explain himself.

'You're upset, I can tell. What's happened? Is Tilly okay? Have you heard something?'

Her voice hardens, her patience fraying.

'Adam, I don't know what's wrong but that isn't how people talk to me. Isn't how they text me. Take a breath. Where are you?'

He swallows, his throat hard. Throws his cigarette and sees a shower of sparks.

'I want to speak to Irons,' he growls, petulant. 'He's been talking to Zara.'

'Zara?' asks Alison, sounding surprised. 'She's your girlfriend, isn't she? Well, if he has there'll be a good reason. He's one to trust, not to fear. Is that all that's wrong? Seriously, he can keep a secret. He's good at what he does.'

'I thought we were on the same side,' he says, quietly. His head is spinning, his gut sour.

'Of course,' she says, a laugh in her voice. 'I've enjoyed our little trip down Memory Lane. It's done me the world of good spending time with you. She'd be proud of you, I'm sure. It's really helped me see what I've been missing. I hope we carry on being in one another's lives.'

'You sound like you're sort of . . . I don't know . . . breaking up with me, or something,' he mutters, appalled by himself. 'I'm sorry about losing my temper. Alison, look, this isn't my world . . .'

'I'll ask Irons to call you, don't fret. This number, is it? Okay. Love to Grace – we'll speak soon.'

The line goes dead. He sits holding it in his hand like something dead. His skull feels like it's caving in. He doesn't know what he wanted to happen, or where it's all gone wrong. Should he not have called Leo Riley? She'd given the nod, hadn't she? Or had her boy told her some fibs – got jealous at her spending time with some interloper and dripped poison in her ear. Perhaps it was Zara. What had she told Irons? He shakes his head, alone and angry, as his thoughts drift down familiar paths. He's simply not lived up, that's the problem. Exciting at first, but the novelty never lasts. He hasn't lived up to expectations. Couldn't sustain her attention . . .

The phone buzzes in his hand. He answers without meaning to.

'Mr Irons, it's Adam, look, I know you have a job to do . . .'

'Close the hole in your face, lad,' mutters Irons, down the receiver. 'Just listen and learn, yeah. First up, you don't upset Alison. That's not me threatening you, that's me explaining things to you. Doesn't matter what your mother meant to me, I have a job and I do it well and I don't ever want her to tell me she's pissed off with you to the point of violence. And secondly, yeah, I've been talking with your girl. Had a shufty at your mum too. Even ran the rule over your poor dad. Doesn't look well, does he? But I reckon we did all right by you, lad. The Nunns seem like they gave you all you could have asked for.

298

And I reckon you've done okay. Maybe gone wrong a few times, maybe not matched the potential, but you've got love in your life and that matters a lot, so on balance, I'm going to put you down as being more of Pamela than you are of the other fucker. So I'm going to help you . . .'

'Mr Irons, I . . .'

'And there you go again, talking when you should be listening. I'm going to put things right for your missus. She's been through a lot with you away and busy with other things. She doesn't need the stress of bailiffs and bankruptcy and all that bollocks. She needs a fresh start. All I want from you, is a yes or a no.'

Adam swallows, his mouth all whisky and tar. 'A yes or a no?'

'Do you reckon she'd get over it? Losing the restaurant, I mean? You reckon she'd be okay after the tears had dried, if the debts weren't there any more and she had a few quid to play with? You reckon it might do you some good in her eyes if you came in like a white knight on a charger and told her that the worst of her worries were over?'

Adam, as instructed, keeps his answer simple. 'Yes.'

'I'm going to do you both a good turn,' he says. 'In return, you do me one. You stay away. It's not personal. I think I might even like you, given time. But it's painful. It's getting in the way. It's making my skin sore, truth be told. All I need from you, is to make sure there are people who can vouch for you, and for Zara, all night tonight. Call a friend or two. Invite Grace over. Report a fire – do what you like. But you'll need an alibi. And on Friday, I'll want you to act all bashful and heroic when she finds the "insurance pay-out" in her account. And I'm putting insurance pay-out in inverted commas, all right?'

Adam lights another cigarette. He's so far out of his depth he feels like he's drowning.

'Yes,' he says, quietly.

'Good lad. That'll do it then. Get yourself away home. You'll catch cold otherwise.'

Adam begins to speak. Irons cuts him off.

'I don't know what to believe,' splutters Adam, desperate now, a mad grin twisting his face even as his eyes fill with tears. 'Riley. Ace. Dozzle. Who did it? I mean, which one of them is half of me? I can't untangle it. I'd rather it was you. I swear, I've thought about it, and you're the best of them, and you're a killer!'

He stops talking, his words echoing back off the cave. Hears the old man breathing.

'She'd have liked you, I reckon,' says Irons, at last. 'Your mum, I mean. She'd be pleased with what you are. That matters more than anything else. I did years for what I did to Dozzle and I've never thought I got it wrong. Riley's done some terrible things but if it was him I'd have already fucking killed him. And Ace is just a silly bollocks. Truth is, Dozzle wasn't all that bad before he did what he did. If you're going to worry about what you're made up of, focus on your mum. Dozzle's dead. There's nowt else for you to uncover. You've done okay, all told. And if it counts for owt, if I were your dad, I'd be pleased as fucking punch. Now, be lucky . . .'

A moment later, Adam is alone in the dark, staring at a dead phone, wondering if he has just made a deal with the devil, or embraced a guardian angel.

Thirty-Nine

Songbrook Manor
Somewhere between Saffron Walden and
Bishop's Stortford, Essex
11.16 p.m.

Illuminated in the doorway of the big grey house, framed between the columns, floating in cold, black air . . .

A short, unremarkable man.

An ex-jockey perhaps, or a washed-up bantamweight.

Old, certainly. An antique, inelegantly tended. A sculpture of a Chinese fisherman; varnish cracked and details chipped.

Skeletally thin, too. Legs like lengths of rope, knotted at the knees.

His face, cadaverous. Pinched and hollow; candlewax marbled with a violet network of capillaries.

Large, old-man ears and clean-shaved cheeks. A thin moustache, like a liquorice bootlace, clinging to his upper lip; bottle-black.

Glasses, thick as church windows, in unfashionable frames.

Bags like segments of satsuma beneath wet eyes.

He has lost the fight with his nostril hair. Stopped trimming it a decade ago when it became clear there was an infinite supply.

One of his hands is curved completely inwards, the middle finger reaching almost to his wrist, as though taking a pulse. Arthritis.

He is wearing jogging trousers, a fleece-shirt and a harlequin-patterned jumper under a baggy suit-jacket, because he has been told to keep out the chill.

He was handsome, once. And strong. Still feels it, though, despite his frailty. Still got something firm and confident in his chest. He's storing his fight as if in a camel's hump, for when he needs to throw his fists again.

A haunted-house mannequin, a ghost-train puppet.

Franco Jardine.

The old man stands still, concentrating on holding his bones together. It feels like his skeleton is made of glass and he's driving over a rutted track. Only sheer force of will keeps him alive.

He's done one or two bad things in his long life, has Franco. Hurt people, when they've asked for it. Sent men to slit throats and break limbs. Hasn't helped many old ladies across the road. Wasn't there, when the girl he called 'princess' was being hurt beyond enduring.

He's hurting, as he stands here in the cold. He spends most of his time sitting down, these days. Napping. Dozing. Waking up to read a book or watch a film or have a chat with Timmy or Alison. Spin a yarn. Tell a tale. Sometimes take a call from Irons. Or one of the snooker-club boys. Coppers and councillors with old age dribbling into their voices. Maybe talk himself into shuffling down the hall to the window that faces the city. Open it wide, lean out, and take a lungful. Search the breeze for the trace of the city. Fill himself with it, and survive another day.

The pain in his joints comes from arthritis, they say. Bad. Near-terminal, the pain. Enough to cripple a lesser man. Enough to paralyse a horse. Enough to lay low Franco Jardine, but not to keep him down.

His leukaemia's still going to get him, but it's finding him a tough opponent. He gave up on the chemotherapy after two weeks, and decided to fight it with Mackeson's stout and Embassy cigarettes instead. A year on and it's working. Should be dead. But he isn't. And he isn't planning on it any time soon.

There's a glow to the old man as he stands in the patch of light and listens to the car rolling over the pebbles of the driveway. A certain effervescence. An air of being more alive than he was yesterday.

Anger? Perhaps, in the way he runs his tongue over his lips. Locks his jaw.

The call was a surprise. Until this afternoon, Franco hadn't heard from Leo Riley in years. Hadn't missed the dirty bastard, neither. He'd been useful, once. They'd made a lot of money together. Wined and dined with men in expensive suits and silk ties. Sat side by side in the executive boxes at Upton Park. But it had been a long time since he'd felt a compulsion to call him up and talk about the old days.

Franco isn't one for whimsy. His memories are too often peppered with scenes that an old man should not have to relive, and so he maintains a distance from the faces that used to surround him. The business runs itself these days. Mostly legitimate, give or take. The snooker clubs and the fruit machines make more in a year than he could snatch from a dozen armed robberies. His doorman agency uses muscle more profitably than the protection rackets ever did. Alison does a good job running the books. The bouncers are always keen to make a little more money when muscle is required, but by and large, the name Jardine is enough to settle disputes.

And then there's *Irons.*

He hears the car come closer and gives his teeth a more solid click as he thinks about what he's going to have to do. He didn't like being taken unawares. Didn't appreciate hearing that voice, wheezing down the phone line, bringing with it a flood of buried thoughts and compacted memories. Didn't like what he'd said, neither. Didn't like being told that Alison had been making a nuisance of herself. Digging up things he'd told her to leave well alone.

He waits for his daughter. He wishes he were the kind of man who could fool himself. Talk himself into another frame of mind. Convince himself he believes something when he doesn't. But he's single-minded. Always has been.

Here, now, waiting for the car to pull up, Riley's words still crackling in his ear, he knows that some of this is his own fault. He wishes Alison had listened to him, of course. That she'd been strong enough to do as she was told and forget all about Pamela. But she wasn't. She hadn't.

Hadn't done as she was told. She hadn't swallowed down the pain. She'd hidden it, and let it fester.

As the car pulls up, Franco feels the tug of old memories. Smells the wet grass and sticky champagne, the cigars and brandy, the Brut and wet wool. That night. When his eyes betrayed him and he cried in front of the lads.

All the things you've done, he tells himself. *So much bloodshed.*

But keeping her alive is what you'll go to Hell for.

There's only one other car in the big gravelled parking area at the front of the house, and Alison has her pick of the spaces as she swings the Rover in a lazy arc, the lights sweeping across the front of the house.

She pulls up in front of one of the conical evergreens, her mouth opening and closing as she lip-syncs to the track on the CD player. It's a song by one of the new girlie bands, and although she'd like to punch each member of the group until their perfect, twenty-something faces resemble lasagne, she has to admit it's a catchy tune. She glances down at her phone, hoping he'll call back, and telling herself she doesn't give a damn either way. He'd pushed it a bit hard. Been a little over-zealous in his choice of language. She may have to slow things down a little. She's fond of him, but she prefers herself.

Switching off the engine, she reaches across to the passenger seat and scoops up her folders, laptop and handbag. It's been a hard day, doing the rounds of pubs, clubs and pool halls, signing forms, making decisions, authorizing acquisitions. There was a lot to catch up on, after the past few days. She's been a bit slack. Let a few contracts rot and allowed some cheeky monkeys to take the piss while she's been consumed with Adam, Grace, Pamela. Set them straight today, though. Back on an even keel. Her hands smell of money. The backs of her knees are wet with sweat. Inside her black, knee-length boots, she senses her feet are damp and swollen; black specks between her toes, like dots of old oil on deep-fried chips.

Rolling her neck to relieve the tension in her shoulders, she steps onto the gravel and shivers into the slicing, cold air that whips across her face. She's only wearing a white blouse and A-line skirt. She's looking forward to a bath. A bowl of noodles and a dollop of tiramisu. Maybe phone Adam back and let him apologize. She's been putting it off all day, not sure if he wants to speak to her.

She approaches the house. For years she has downplayed the splendour of the property, been modest about its luxury, but under the moonlight and against the canopy of rain-lashed darkness, she knows it to be an impressive creation. Late Victorian, all high chimneys and corrugated columns, rooftop gargoyles and wrought-iron railings. Landscaped gardens, curving pebble drive. The comma-shaped lake an oily mirror, rippled by raindrops, laid flat on the neatly-trimmed grass.

Then she sees him. Sees the small, fragile man in the too-big clothes.

Her father.

She fights with herself. Tells herself that she's a grown woman. That she makes the family millions; that she's orchestrated nearly as many broken bones and severed limbs as he has, and all in a world covered with cameras, mobile phones and computers. She's got no reason to be afraid. She almost manages to make herself believe it.

Giving a frown of puzzlement, she climbs the stairs to the front door, feeling an ache in her calves as she does so. She wags a finger. 'You shouldn't be out,' she says. 'It's freezing.'

'I can tek it,' says Franco, and one half of his face twitches, like Bogart. It's not a smile. He doesn't suffer himself to smile unless it's truly warranted, but she's pleased to see that at least he isn't scowling, snapping at himself, a dog with a tick, snarling at the pain that holds him hostage.

'The doctor will have your guts for garters,' says Alison, leaning in, brushing his cheek with her lips. She smells the gravy of his lunch, the Irish stout, the cigarettes and cod-liver oil. Loves it like Chanel.

'He can bloody try,' says Franco, and grimaces as the pain in his knees takes hold for a second, then passes, at his command.

'We in?' asks Alison, nodding at the door. 'Or you fancy a jog?'

'Don't get funny.'

'Me? Never.'

She looks at her father and gets the sense

something isn't quite right. He's stiffer than usual. More tightly wound. His lips are dry as brown paper.

'What's wrong?' she asks. 'Timmy hasn't been playing his music again, has he?'

Franco looks at her. Hard. It's the searching, knowing look that has flash-fried opponents and adversaries for more than half a century. He turns it on his daughter. His searchlight glare. Eyes like a serial killer, face of stone.

'Dad?'

Her voice is extinguished like a candle flame.

And she knows. Knows, instantly, she's been found out.

At once, she's a naughty schoolgirl, caught with a boy. A teenager with a can of lager in her room. She feels a quiver in her belly and a shake in her legs as she meets his gaze, tries to defy it, then fails, and looks down.

'I had a call from Leo Riley this aft,' he says, softly. 'Hadn't heard from him in years. Took me back a bit, it did. Had some interesting things to say.'

She can't find a suitable retort, so gives up. 'Yeah?'

'Yeah.'

Alison looks up again, trying to focus her attention on the spot between her father's eyebrows so she doesn't have to look him in the eye. He's never hurt her, of course. Never done more than give her a telling-off or tell her she can do better. She knows all she's done is upset him, but that, in itself, is enough.

'Yeah,' he says again, and his glasses amplify his grey-green eyes. 'Very interesting.'

The silence stretches out. The echoes of Franco's wheezing, phlegmatic voice hang on the air like pegs on a line. For a moment, the old man stares at his daughter sternly, as though she's only got a C in her maths test, or been told off at school for swearing. Then he gives a shake of his head that sends his glasses a little way down his nose.

'You're a bugger,' he says, eventually, and gives the softest of laughs.

Alison breathes out, slowly, as if filling a balloon. Rolls her eyes and gives an extravagant yawn, for no other reason than her body needs to stretch out, assert itself, prove it's more than the hunched, scared, guilty figure it has spent the last minute portraying.

'Look, Dad, I was going to . . .'

'Don't bother,' says Franco. 'I've got the gist. Let's go inside.'

Together, Alison taking her father's arm, they step inside the giant double doors and into the hallway. Only one of the chandeliers has been lit and the black-and-white tiles are full of shadows and weak light.

'Riley's the councillor chap, isn't he?' begins Alison, more for the look of the thing than any real conviction her father will buy what she's saying.

'Yes,' he says, a note of sarcasm entering his voice. 'The councillor chap. Yeah.'

Alison feels a pressure on her arm as her father steers her down the corridor. Turns left, towards the west wing, where the servants used to live, when the world allowed such things. His hand, a useless claw, its fingers fused, is firm upon her skin. He seems to have a direction in mind, and she knows better than to question it. She feels excitement. Guilt. Naughtiness. Like she did when her dad used to tell her, with complete certainty, who was worth a flutter at the dogs on a Friday night, back when she and Timmy's dad used to like their nights out, their steak dinners, the sensation of dirty cash in their pockets and purses.

'It wasn't anything sinister, Dad,' she says, softly, and the words are all but swallowed up by the enormity of the house, the cold of the hallway. Even now, she is wondering at the wisdom of living here, in this vast mausoleum that has seen so much suffering and stood dumb witness to a grief that could flood the coast with the weight of its tears.

'Dad.'

Jardine pauses at the foot of the stairs. It is a cold, narrow flight, uncarpeted and little used. Dark and dusty. The hallway at the top used to lead to the quarters of the senior waiting staff, but has been used for little more than storage and overspill since Jardine bought the place from the drunken toff whose family had let it fester since before the war.

The moment stretches out, like chewing gum.

Alison, staring at her dad.

He, eyes closed, preparing himself, as if gathering breath and strength for the ascent, and the revelation he will make along the way. He has resisted all calls to install a stairlift or elevator and will continue to do so. He will die in the

311

knowledge that he has never had to be carried to bed.

'Dad?'

Jardine looks at his daughter, trying to slow the heaving in his chest. His tongue flicks out, like a snake's, and he adjusts his teeth. Considers his thoughts. Puts a foot on the bottom step, a hand on the varnished banister, and hauls himself up.

'Don't talk for a second, love. Just listen, eh pet? There's a good girl.'

Alison smiles, well-meaningly. She's cold, but doesn't want to give in to the shiver in case she knocks her father off balance. He nods and begins to speak. His words grow fainter and more pained with each stair, but he feels a lightness enter his step as he sets down a burden he has carried, and not acknowledged, for more than thirty years.

Forty

'She was like a daughter to me, you know that.
It's a cliché, yeah, but I can't think of any other
way to describe it. Hasn't been a day that I haven't
wished things were different. Good girl. Never
expected. Grateful, but not feeble with it, you
hear me? When you became friends I liked it.
Liked what she brought out of you. And when I
saw her drawings, I was blown away. You know
me, love. I'm not one for that sort of stuff. I like
a nice picture, same as anyone, but there was
something about what she could do that made
me feel like smiling. She could have gone far,
love. Then it all went to pot, didn't it? That night
happened. She got hurt. I should have spoken to
you about it all then. Spoken properly, I mean.
But how do you? How do you tell a kid her best
friend's had those things done to her? So I kept
what I could from you. While she was healing.
I kept her out of your way, and then she had her
nipper. That nurse, she was more surprised than
anybody. Wanted to live, that kid, even though
nobody thought he would. I did what people did
back then. Believe me, there were those who
wouldn't have blamed me for chucking him in
the river. Bad blood, Alison. You saw what he
did to her. Made Irons look like Audrey Hepburn,

313

she did. Tommy Dozzle. He'd done those things to her. Torn her apart, and now she's left with his bastard in her arms? She couldn't look after it, could she? And I knew somebody who could make things right. I should never have let Irons have a look at the thing. I'd never seen him soft like that before. Cooing like he was a puppy. I swear, a part of him was away in fairyland. He said he'd do the cottage up – he'd help Pamela raise him. Can you imagine? Both of them, half a face each? Poor sod. I said no, of course, but what does he do? Loses his mind. Goes after Tommy Dozzle, despite all he'd been told. He finds where the lad's hiding, and he walks in there and fills the place with blood. You don't want to know what he did to the lad. Leaves me right in it – my best man, locked up and looking at serious time. I had bigger things to think about than playing Happy Families. Like I say, I had contacts. A man who'd done some work for me, who I trusted – he said he knew a family that couldn't have kids of their own. Good people. Kind people. People a long way from this life, love. He had connections – no questions would be asked. So I signed the forms. Said goodbye to it without even looking at the little bastard. And when Pamela wakes up, I'm there to tell her it's all going to be OK now. That it's taken care of. She looks at me like I've stolen her soul and tells me she wants her baby. She was a child, Alison. A child who went through things nobody could imagine. I told her the baby was gone. That it had gone to a good home, and that Dozzle was dead and Irons was going to prison, and that it

314

was time for her to begin again. I've never heard weeping like it. Never seen tears like that. It was like I'd reached into her and taken the only thing she cared about. I didn't understand it. So I tells her to stop crying. And she did. Dried her tears – but she must have already decided what she would do. Broke my heart when I found her. Only time I've heard Irons cry was when I told him she was dead. Dozzle did it. He's that lad's daddy. Irons killed him, and she killed herself when she realized Irons had given his life to a prison cell because of it.

'Irons took the cottage when he came home. I haven't been in there since. You've done good. Timmy's a good lad, underneath it all. Irons is home, where he should be. We're fucking winning, love. Then it all comes back. I get a phone call from somebody who I haven't thought about in years and he tells me he's had a call from some lad saying he knows what happened that night. I'm feeling a bit fitter today, Alison. Did some ringing around. Got Timmy on the mobile and, God bless him, didn't he have a story to tell me. Some private detective making a nuisance of himself, brown bread and bloated in Dead Man's Vale. Said he'd shown them I was still up and about and capable – silly bastard. They're all pieces of a picture, pet, and I filled in the gaps. I reckon laddo's back. That little bastard, the seed of that rapist, is dribbling in your ear and trying to get something out of you. Or maybe me. Well, I tell you something, sweetheart, I hold my hands up. I've done things wrong, and misjudged big decisions. I've maybe even

315

let you down. So I'm going to put it right. I'm talking to you like an adult. I'll answer your questions. I'll let you see inside Pamela's heart. We'll remember her. Toast her memory. And then we'll let the wound heal, and forget her. Like we should have done a long time ago. There's just one thing I'm rigid on, pet, and that's this boy. This chap on the phone to Riley. He's gone, pet. He's out of your life. He's salt in your wounds and he's nothing to do with us. His daddy was Dozzle. Dozzle's dead. You don't see him again. You say goodbye, and it's over. I can't solve this the way I normally would, because there might be something in him that's Pamela. He can't be cut out of our lives. So you'll just have to tell him he's not welcome here. You think Riley did that to Pamela? You should have asked me, pet. Or Irons. He was otherwise engaged that night, sweetheart. He was in the woods with one of the girls that the lads brought to the party for entertainment. I know this, because he beat her half to death. He came out of the woods like a madman, naked, covered in blood, gibbering some nonsense about a devil, a creature with a tattooed chest and eyes of glass, and for a second, I thought it might have been him. But he showed me what he had done, and I made the problem go away. That's what I do. No matter the circumstances, I make problems go away. Riley's a dirty, ratty, little pervert, but he's not your friend's dad. Your friend's dad is in the ground. Now wipe your eyes, love. It's a lot to take in, I know. We should have spoken about it a long time ago. I should have been there to hold you. I am now, pet. I am now.'

Jardine stops at the door and releases the pressure on Alison's arm. His breath is dust and ground glass, caught on the faintest of breezes.

Although they are not touching, he can feel his daughter shaking. The shivers of her sobs are like blows against his skin. But he can take blows. And not fall down.

With his good hand, Francis Jardine turns the handle of the bedroom. Flicks on the light. He almost loses his balance as Alison grabs him in an embrace that takes the wind from his lungs, and squeezes a tear from his old, dry eyes.

He almost tells her that he loves her, but can't quite be that man.

Some things are best left unsaid.

Forty-One

The Basil Pot, Bridge Street, Portsmouth
11.09 p.m.

Irons is parked in a side street, engine on but lights off. He is returning to himself. Stepping back into his tattered skin. Feeling the strength in his hard bones, the capability in the biceps and pectorals. The sensation of ragged flesh from neck to scalp. He has watched these last minutes as a spirit, floating above the mortal remains, elevated and apart.

He will miss Zara.

He does not indulge in regret, but wishes he had got to know Adam a little. Perhaps answered some of his questions. Told him about his mum. Pamela. The girl who saw the beauty underneath, but couldn't spot her own.

Irons wonders if he will see the boy again. He would like to know if there are traces of Pamela in him. Would like to explore him. Look inside.

He lets out a sigh as the phone in his pocket gives a faint trill. He recognizes the number. Answers to a scared, breathless PC Jon Goodwin.

'They've got a print off the wire he was wrapped in. Larry Paris. It's a partial but they're running it. It's not Adam Nunn, they ran that first of all. Not Kukuc either. Have I helped? I hope I've fucking helped. Are you there? Hello?'

Irons looks at his watch.

Three.

Two.

One.

The Basil Pot ignites in an orange fireball. The windows blow out and fly as a billion knives to rattle and smash against the metal shutters of the shops and bars across the street.

In the darkness, lit only by the sodium yellow of the streetlamps, the tongues of flame appear as a crimson and purple blanket, lifting, rolling, curling through the ruined frontage of the building that was once Zara's dream.

Irons pulls away from the kerb without looking back.

He would like to say goodbye to Zara, but regret is an expensive luxury, and Irons lives within a budget.

He does not feel anything when he considers returning home. He misses the pictures. The urn. The sense of being close to her. But he carries her with him, under his skin and behind his eyes, and knows she will not begrudge him these few days away, watching over her son.

On the street, lit by the flame, a snowstorm of paper falls to the wet tarmac, edges crisping, words fading. Unpaid bills and a poor handful of receipts.

Zara's dream, up in smoke.

Debts, cremated.

Dust to dust.

Part Three

Part Three

Forty-Two

Dysart Avenue, Drayton, Portsmouth
December 25th, 7.28 p.m.

Pat is hanging up Mr Santinello's coat when she hears the car. She turns and squints through the frosted glass of the front door. She ignores the spyhole. Billy once made her watch a film where somebody got shot in the eye while peeping out to identify a caller, and she has never felt comfortable using it since. She recognizes the sound of the engine as Adam's new sporty little number, and she feels a little dancing sensation in her full tummy as she starts to unlock the door, the wind snatching the party hat from her permed grey curls as she steps into the cold.

Her smile fades as a young, dark-haired girl gets out the passenger seat. Adam climbs out the driver's door a moment later. He's wearing a new suit. Looks thinner. She puts it down to the new haircut, which she doesn't approve of. Told him he looked like a skinhead when he arrived a few days ago to bring presents for her and Billy. He'd told her the hairstyle was in fashion. That he'd needed a change. Looked at her, curiously, then grabbed her round the middle, rubbing the soft fuzz on his skull against her cheek and making her laugh. She'd told him off but enjoyed the rush of colour to her face. The flash of fire in his eyes. The momentary bubble of life that tore through the house. She'd smelled whisky on his breath, but hoped the sudden outburst of fun had come from a deeper place than the bottom of a glass.

'Mum, Selena. Selena, Mum.'

The pleasantries are conducted on the doorstep. Selena offering a hand, and Pat taking it, then pulling her in for a hug. Selena saying, 'Nice to meet you,' and Pat telling her she's a pretty girl and asking whether she got all she wanted for Christmas and telling her not to let Adam boss her around. She plays the role of an indulgent grandmother. Slips into it like a pair of slippers. Pat wishes she had a chocolate bar in the pocket of the pink tabard she wears over her best blue trousers and cream jumper. She thinks a good grandmother should never be without a treat.

They pause at the door to the living room, as Pat and Adam exchange a look. *In here? How is he? Going to make a show of himself? She's only young.*

'He's having a good day,' says Pat, brightly. 'Polished off a good dinner, he did. Mr Santinello, sorry, Malcolm, he always brings him out of himself.'

'He's here, is he?'

'Oh yes. Had his lunch at the golf club but came round mid-afternoon. We watched the Queen's speech together. Had a bit of a natter. We didn't think your dad was going to still be awake by the time you got here, but he's on fine form.'

They open the door and step into the living

room. Survey the colour and light in a room the size of a small kitchen.

The Christmas tree is shop-bought, ready-decorated, and stands on a coffee table by the French windows, which act as mirrors against the darkness. A handful of cards adorn the mantelpiece and some tassels of tinsel have been draped above family photographs and Lake District watercolours.

Their arrival is greeted with a good-natured cheer from the two old men, who sit side by side on the sofa. They look like adverts for different lifestyles. Billy is almost yellow, his cheeks sunken, eyes almost black. He's a frail, delicate thing, in pyjama trousers and a golfing jumper, still with the tag hanging out at the neck. Santinello, by contrast, looks as though he's just stepped from the pages of a catalogue of fashions for the over-sixties.

'Don't mind these two,' says Pat, fussily, enjoying the sound of laughter and naughtiness in her small, cold home. 'They've been talking about the good old days and drinking some of Malcolm's lovely wine. Anyway, what can I get you both?'

The two men see Selena standing behind Adam and both start to get out of their seat. It's the instinctive politeness of old men in the presence of a young lady, and it looks like it might kill Billy. He gets halfway up, nods, then slumps again, satisfied his duty is done. Santinello is out of the chair with the speed and grace of a young man. He's all smiles.

'And who's this pretty young thing?' he asks,

twinkling a little. Up close, there's wine in his smile. It looks sinister against his slicked, dark clothes, as though he's a vampire dressed for a town council meeting.

Selena extends her hand and says her name. He takes it, bends down, and kisses the back of her wrist. Looks up, and smiles. 'A pleasure,' he says. 'You must be Adam's latest girlfriend,' he teases.

Selena looks to Adam for help, not sure what to say, but he's staring at the half-empty carafe of red wine on the floor by the vacant seat and not paying attention. Pat steps in. 'He's a devil, this one,' she says. 'Always been a one for the ladies, he has. Could charm the birds from the trees.'

Santinello bows to Pat. 'Guilty as charged,' he says. 'Not a patch on Billy, though,' he adds. 'Honestly Adam, if it wasn't for your mother, he'd have been in an early grave from exhaustion. Although running from the ladies was almost as tiring as giving in to them, eh Bill?'

Their eyes all turn to the man in the chair. He's staring at the surface of the drink in his hand, his toothless gums worrying at his bottom lip. It makes a sound like tearing sandpaper. The motion seems to take on its own momentum and soon his whole jaw starts oscillating, until it looks like he's moving a toffee around his mouth. He looks as though he should be on a park bench, mumbling to himself. And this is one of his better days.

'Anyway,' says Santinello, to break the sudden silence. 'Merry Christmas, and all that. I saw the pearls you got your mum, Adam. Very nice. The wine's keeping me busy at the moment. Turned out really nice, for a first attempt. You'll have some, won't you, Adam? And your young lady, here.'

Adam gives a smile and puts his hands in his pockets.

'I'll get some glasses, then,' says Pat, and there's a spring in her step as she leaves the room. It's starting to feel like a proper family day. She's been dreading it, of course. Hadn't expected Billy to still be alive. Had only bought a turkey crown from the butchers and a few veg from the late-shop. But Billy had woken with a brightness she hadn't seen in months. Woke before her, and made a pot of tea. Brought it into her bedroom on a tray. He'd given her quite a start when she woke and found him standing there, a tea-towel over his arm and saying 'mademoiselle'. For a moment she was as confused as he had been. Wondering what was real and what was imagined, what was memory and what she could trust. He'd asked her how Christmas had sneaked up on him. What they'd got the lad. Whether she liked her present, opened the night before, as was their way. She worked out quickly that he'd been talking about the pendant she had received from him some twenty years before. Dutifully, now as then, she told him she loved it. That she'd maybe wear it this evening. He went in and out of his senses, after that. Sometimes he was a young man, full of self-confidence, telling her the life they were going to have together. A moment later, middle-aged and angry, desk-bound, house-bound, impotent and burned. Then an old man, taking

327

pleasure in making things for the neighbourhood kids, revelling in his image as a sweet old boy with a taste for mischief and pockets full of sweets. They had a pleasant day. Talked of a son who was so many different ages, but never less than the centre of their worlds. The boy they'd longed for but couldn't have, and who was given to them in a bundle of blankets, because Mally Santinello had contacts in the city, and her husband's record for some silly misdemeanours in his youth meant they couldn't adopt through the proper channels, much as they'd tried to explain it away to the busybodies in the suits. A misunderstanding. A girl who didn't take no for an answer and made up nasty, spiteful things to get him back. He would never have hurt anybody, not really. Not her Billy. Oh no. Not like the way she claimed. He was a gentleman. Mally understood that. He brought them Adam. It cost them their savings and they had to downsize the house, but he'd been worth it. He was *their* Adam. Their son. Pat and Billy's boy, all the way through.

In the living room, Adam tells Selena to take a seat and she slips politely into the armchair by the window. She starts looking at the books on the shelves. Histories of Britain. Biographies of the Royal Family. Cookbooks and true crime stories. Cowboys, by the bucket-load. She imagines Adam's dad reading these to him when he was a boy, and smiles at the image.

'What's this I hear about a full-time job, then?' asks Mr Santinello, sitting back down. 'You tired of being your own boss?'

'An offer I couldn't refuse,' he says, then laughs, too loud, at his own words.

'What's he say?' asks Billy, looking up and nudging Santinello.

'The new job, Bill,' he says. 'You were saying before. Landed on his feet again.'

'Who's that?'

'Adam,' he says. 'Your boy.'

'My Adam? Don't be daft, Mal.'

'Oh, right, my mistake . . .'

Billy suddenly looks up and flashes a smile. 'Don't think I'm that far gone yet,' he says, and starts laughing. The others join him, relieved and surprised.

'Still got your sense of humour,' says Adam, pleased with his dad.

'And I've still got my hair,' he adds, nodding at Adam's shaved head. 'You one of them bovver boys now, are you?'

'I just like it,' he says, suddenly feeling seventeen and having to explain to his dad why he wanted a motorbike. 'You never liked the long hair.'

'No, that were a bit nancy, but there's a happy medium. It's always been the same, Mal,' he says. 'Always extremes. Panic or calm. Angry or happy. Taking over the world one day, not a farthing to his name the next. And girlfriends? Can't just say hello and goodbye, this one. He's fallen in love more times than I've changed my socks.'

'Not often, then,' says Mr Santinello, and the pair laugh. They have the look of two experienced workmen picking on the site apprentice. They seem ready to send him to the storeroom for a 'long stand' or some striped paint.

Selena laughs along, and her giggle sees all three turn their heads in her direction.

'Which one's that?' asks Billy.

'This is Zara's daughter, Dad,' he says. 'My step-daughter, I suppose.'

Selena smiles, uncomfortable in the spotlight, as Billy gives her the once-over. 'Nice,' he says. 'Bit big around the middle, but she's going to be pretty. Nice knockers, eh Mal?'

For a second, Selena wonders if she's heard correctly. The look on Adam's face tells her she has. She doesn't know if she should laugh or storm out. She knows the rules are different for old people. That people of a certain generation can be given allowances for saying certain things.

'Don't,' he says, his mood darkening. 'Don't you dare.'

The two old men on the sofa laugh and nudge each other. They seem happy. Good old boys. Cracking jokes and winding people up. Were it not for the wrinkles and the old bones, they could be stood on a building site, wolf-whistling at the schoolgirls and office workers below.

'I think we'd best be on the road,' mutters Adam. 'I've had a long day, Zara will be wondering where I am . . .'

Pat looks crestfallen as she returns to the living room with a tray of mince pies. 'No, Adam, please stay for a little while. You might not get another chance with your dad.'

'Another time,' he says, shuffling backwards. 'When I've got Tilly.'

He glances at Selena. She's sat where he left her. Her knees are drawn up. Her arms around herself.

'Adam,' says Santinello. 'Don't be sour, lad . . .'

'We've got to go,' says Adam flatly, and Selena stands, quickly.

'Busy bee,' says Santinello.

Adam looks at his father. 'Bye Dad,' he says, softly.

Billy grunts. Opens his eyes. Looks at them both. 'Pretty lass,' he says. 'Bit chunky, but nice tits,' and then he's laughing again.

Adam takes Selena's hand in his, and they walk to the front door. The cold grabs them as they step into the darkness.

He looks at her, face lit by streetlamps. Her nose is running slightly. He feels a paternal rush of blood; an instinct to hold a handkerchief to her face and say 'blow'. Instead, he says, 'See why I haven't brought you before?'

Selena smiles at him as they get into the car. 'They're a naughty pair when they get together, aren't they?'

'Always have been,' says Adam, fumbling with the gearstick, swearing, and finding reverse. 'They didn't upset you, did they?'

'No,' lies Selena. 'They're just old boys, aren't they? They were a bit rude, though.'

'Yeah?'

'Asking me how old I was. Whether I wore those thongs they saw on *Top of the Pops*. If I was old enough to shave my legs. Whether I called you Dad and if you were bathing me before bed.' She pauses, realizing that she feels more upset than she had first been willing to admit.

'Selena?'

She closes her eyes. 'They were egging each other on.'

Forty-Three

Lower Drayton Lane, Portsmouth
9.13 p.m.

'I think it's bedtime, Tilly.'

'No. Shurrup.'

'Tilly, you've had a lovely day. Father Christmas has been very kind. You need to sleep . . .'

'No. Shurrup. Watch Po.'

'Sweetheart, Po isn't on.'

'No. Po.'

'Tilly, it's bedtime.'

'Daddy. Daddy watch Po . . .'

'It's not called Po, you halfwit, it's Teletu . . .'

'Haffwitt. Mummy say me Haffwitt.'

'Oh shit, Tilly, no . . .'

'Shitt. Shitshitshit. Haffwit shit.'

Grace closes her eyes, wondering if there is an award she can apply for, convinced she's at least a contender for the title of Worst Mother Ever.

She's had a few drinks. Endured a carb-heavy, methane-rich Christmas lunch at the posh hotel. Brought home a tinfoil parcel full of leftover pigs-in-blankets and the bulk of the second bottle of wine that Mum, Dad and one of her aunties had ordered from the bottom of the menu. They turned down her offer to come to her for lunch and she'd been grateful for that kindness. She's spent the last hour sipping Bailey's, eating cold sausages, and dipping After Eights in her Tia Maria.

'Daddy?'

'No, babe, you saw him this morning, remember? You were at Daddy's last night. You opened your presents there this morning. You met your Auntie Zara. Didn't like her much did you, I can tell.'

'Zara nice. Lena. Nordon.'

'Well, you'll hate her in time, I'm sure.'

'Daddy now.'

'No, he'll be at home. With them.'

'Shurrup.'

Grace sighs. Picks up her phone and hopes there'll be something to explain why he's been so quiet. She knows something happened while she was seeing King Rat, and that things aren't right between him and Alison. Knows, too, that Zara's restaurant has gone up in flames and that he's suddenly got cash in his pocket. He got her a hamper full of her favourite things: brownies, muffins, sugared almonds, all pretty and luxurious in a wicker basket that looked like it should have been hanging off Little Red Riding Hood's arm. But he's been evasive whenever she asks him. Speaks to her in platitudes and unfinished sentences. Whatever it was he needed her for, he doesn't seem to need her any more.

'See. Daddy!'

There is a gentle knocking on the double-glazed panelling, and Tilly runs from the living room, leaps up and pulls the handle down. She's big enough to do that now, thinks Grace. Better start locking it. She'll be off. Running down the street in her Dora slippers, looking for Daddy.

Adam bends down and scoops his giggling daughter into the air as he steps inside. Blows a raspberry on her tummy. Wriggles his hand up her T-shirt and tickles her under the chin. She screams with laughter and kicks her feet. Adam pretends to put her down, then scoops her up again.

'Where's my kiss?' he asks her.

Tilly puckers her lips and presses them against Adam's.

Grace pours herself off the sofa. He saw her in worse states at university, but she's self-conscious about her mum-tum and wants to check she hasn't got a finger of Kit-Kat down her cleavage.

'Adam? I didn't think we'd be seeing you . . .'

He enters the living room, looking like a cracked reflection of the man she used to know. The sadness in his eyes is ocean-deep.

'Needed a kiss from my girl,' he says, quietly. 'That's Tilly, by the way. Not you.'

'Ha! I taste of turkey and Tia Maria.'

'I'd best take your word for that,' he smiles.

They stay silent for a spell. He presses his head to Tilly's. He suddenly looks very tired.

'New Year soon,' he says, quietly. 'New start.'

'Yeah. Same resolutions as last time for me.'

'I made mine early. Tried to keep them. Tried to stay away.'

Grace smiles, kindly. 'I've done what you asked. Haven't pried. Didn't call King Rat after we got back. Didn't reach out. Certainly didn't go looking for headlines about incidents that happened in Battersea while you were with her . . .'

335

'The restaurant,' says Adam, not really listening. 'I did well out of that. Made a deal.'

'Yes?'

'I'm trying, Gracie. But something in me just keeps dragging my thoughts back to them. I don't believe them about Dozzle. And I don't know if what I saw in London excited me or disgusted me. I feel so fucking lost.'

'Daddy haffwit.'

They smile at that. Adam holds his daughter tighter. 'I want you to know how grateful I am to you. You've never judged me. The seed of that man, it's in me, so it's in our daughter. And you've never looked at me any differently.'

'It never occurred to me to,' says Grace, tears pricking her eyes. She wishes she had the right words. Can't do much more than offer him an After Eight and a place to dip it.

'I'm going there,' he says, to Grace. 'I should go home. Should curl up with people who care about me. Or stay here. Or take a walk to the cave and brood for a bit. But I'm going there.'

'To see Alison?'

'To see him.'

Grace hesitates. 'Irons?'

'He knows more than he's told. He came here. Looked into my life as if he was trying to come to a decision about whether I was worth saving.'

'He gave you money,' says Grace. 'I'm only guessing, but those are nice shoes . . .'

'I don't know if I deserve it. Zara does. I don't know whether he came to the conclusion that I'm somebody he was right to let live.'

Grace stares at him, holding their daughter,

336

love and sadness flooding out of him. She wants to hold him, but fears she will crumble if she moves.

'If I told you not to go? If I begged you not to risk it? Told you think of Tilly – of me . . .'

'I'd do what you asked.'

'Is that why you came?'

He smiles. 'You know me better than anybody.'

'I won't ask that of you.'

He nods. Kisses Tilly on the head. 'Love you.'

'Daddy shittt.'

The laugh, as he puts her down and turns away, is not enough to distract her from the tears that fall down his face.

She doesn't let her own tears fall until she hears the car start up and drive away.

She decides to let Tilly stay up as long as she wants.

Holds her tight, on the sofa, and weeps silently into the back of her neck.

Forty-Four

The girl looks like a hot-water-bottle cover: an empty skin awaiting fluff or air. She lolls in Timmy's lap, arms about his neck, head on his shoulder – both slowly sinking into the cushions of the big Chesterfield sofa.

Her eyes may be out of focus, floating in booze, but Irons can still feel them upon him as he loiters, uncomfortable, in the bay window, a full can of lager in his hand. He wants to go and hide behind the Christmas tree. The flickering of the lights is giving him a headache. His lungs are burning. He can feel his cancerous cells eating his good ones. It is all he can do not to cough out his cigarette like an arrow from a catapult. He glances in the girl's direction and then away again, grateful for the privacy afforded him by the sunglasses.

They have retreated to the warm, high-ceilinged billiards room and have each found a comfortable spot to drape themselves as they work their way through the traditional tipples: port, bitter, Tia Maria. Irons is grateful for the low light. The deep, burgundy curtains are pulled shut. Even so, he can feel her staring. Can still feel himself being scrutinized, held up to a lamp for examination;

338

autopsied by this skinny slip of a thing who reeks of a perfume that's worth more than she is.

Irons looks at his feet. Tries to find patterns in the thick carpet. At the squares of illumination on the baubles that hang from the plastic branches. He doesn't want to look at the girl, in case their eyes meet, and she looks away, revolted and giggling, as if she's just popped a treat into the slobbery lips of a carthorse.

Timmy seems to sense Irons's discomfort, and pulls his girl's face to his; tongue snaking out of his mouth and plopping between her open lips like an indecisive lugworm emerging from damp sand. She returns the gesture and the big living room, with the glowing fire and the Norwegian spruce and the bare chandeliers and racehorse prints, is suddenly full of the sound of slurping teenage mouths.

He's hot, in his big coat, his hat, scarf and jeans, but he's not taking any of it off. Doesn't want to stop. Doesn't want to be here. Or any-fucking-where. More than a month since he pressed a doorstop of cash into the boy's hand, and the scars are deeper than ever. Pamela, more distant. The sores on his face starting to weep like frightened children. He feels like he's breaking apart. Dying. And he finds that he cares.

Irons hears footsteps and Alison re-enters the room. She's holding an armful of presents, wrapped in blue paper covered in what looks like snowmen, but could be badly drawn Christmas puddings.

'All the best,' she grins, and reaches up to place a peck on his cheek.

Irons braces himself for it, telling himself not to pull away. They have gone through this little ritual every year since his release. Alison, planting a kiss on his scarred features, handing him a gift and saying thank you for all he has done, is doing, will continue to do, for her, for Timmy, for Dad. He, smiling, trying to think of things to say, feeling his skin prickle and his socks fill with sweat, giving it just long enough to be polite, trying to find the words to say thank you. Always desperate to leave. He appreciates the kiss, the gifts, the gesture, the affection, but he doesn't know how to gift-wrap his own gratitude and his isn't a face built for beaming smiles, so he just mutters and tells her that if she wants anything herself, she just has to ask.

'I got some people in to do the tree. Would have loved to have done it myself but who has the time? And Timmy's too old to be draping tinsel.'

He endures the burn of memory. He sees them as they were. Himself and Mr Jardine, young and strong and fearless, laughing with the lads as they struggled into Santa costumes and held Pamela and Alison on their shoulders so they could put their pretty baubles at the top of the tree; the smell of sap and sawdust mingling with cigar smoke, wood smoke; whisky and Brylcreem. He can see her, arm stretched out like a sculpture of a ballerina; a porcelain angel in her hand. Sees her smiling. Sees the way the fire dances on the dark lenses of her smiling eyes.

'Looks grand.'

'You okay?' she asks, quizzically. 'You don't look well.'

Timmy gives a nasty snicker of laughter. 'Ha! When does he fucking ever?'

'Don't you dare,' hisses Alison, glaring at him. 'Not today.'

Irons puts his can of lager down on the dresser by the window. He creases his lips into what he hopes is a nice expression, and starts gently unwrapping the gifts. A fountain pen. New Zippo lighter. A fleece scarf.

'It's the same one they use on the Arctic expeditions,' says Alison, pleased with herself.

Last, a book on birds native to the local coastline. There's always a gift like this. Something educational and instructive. A hobby guide. He wonders if Alison truly imagines him and her father, sitting on a hillside, sharing a flask of tea and a pair of binoculars, staring out at the flocks of guillemots and razorbills and talking about the footie.

'Very thoughtful,' he mumbles, flicking through the pages. 'I'll give it a go, definitely.'

'Excellent,' says Alison, beaming, looking relieved. She turns around to see if her father has come down to join them yet. He hasn't. He won't. 'Right,' she says, clapping her hands. 'Are you going to stay for a nightcap?'

Irons doesn't know why she bothers. She knows he'll politely decline. Make an excuse about having some place to be. He'll promise that next year, they'll all sit down for dinner together. He'll apologize for not having made it to lunch, despite his earlier assurances he would do his best.

They have the conversation.

She smiles, and pretends to believe him.

341

He tells her to have a good time. To pass on his best to Franco, along with his hopes he's had a good day. Gives her his word they'll all go out for a drink to see in the New Year together. Fucks off, holding his presents, and feeling a blush in his burned face.

Pulls at the door handle and feels cold air on his hot face.

Blinks, slowly, in the darkness, the soft rain: the smell of Christmas and money.

Glares through the woods in the direction of the cottage. Clocks the single yellow light: a pale patch of yellow on the black velvet evening.

Knows.

There's a feeling in his gut he can't place. It's almost one of reunion.

Of joy at finding something feared lost.

Thinking: *Adam.*

Back.

He wouldn't fucking leave it alone.

And now he's going to get the whole, ugly truth.

Forty-Five

11.55 p.m.

'Tea?'
  'Whisky.'
  'None of it.'
  'Wine.'
  'No.'
  'Anything?'
  'Tea.'
  'Tea, then.'
Adam leans against the cold wall of the big, farmhouse kitchen, and inhales the scent of dead flowers. It's a clearer, crisper scent than the odour which emanates from Irons. Less of an insinuation and more a genuine presence. He turns, slightly, to follow the scent and his shoulder nudges the light switch, casting an orange glare over the bare flagstones, the deep, red-stained sink, the vase of half-dead flowers.

Irons turns from the kettle, his ravaged face suddenly brought into sharp relief. He looks like an iced cake, left out in the warm for too long.

'You want it off?' Adam asks, jerking his head at the light.

'Leave it,' says Irons with a shrug, and pours the boiling water into a brown mug, puts his finger in and squashes the teabag against the enamel. Pours in milk without being asked and nods at it.

343

'Tea.'

Adam doesn't move.

They stand at opposite ends of the kitchen, surveying each other, searching the signs and maps and scars and clues in each other's faces.

They survey each other for another minute, before Irons nods. He pulls the cord from around his wrist, and lays it on the table. There is a clunk, as his other hand hits the wood, and as he removes the giant palm, a blade winks up, lying on its side: a fish out of water.

'Boy Scout,' says Adam.

'Always prepared,' says Irons.

More silence. Then: 'You've got a funny way of staying away, lad. Think I was quite clear you shouldn't be showing your face in this part of the world.'

'They let you show yours . . .' begins Adam, then stops. There's no bravado in him. No strength. Part of him wonders if he came here for a confrontation he cannot win. If he wants to offend this killer, and to see if he can find peace at the end of his knife.

'I can't,' he says, softly. 'I couldn't, I mean. I don't know what I want or what to do next. I can't just close the lid on it all. The things I've heard. When this all started I just wanted to know a bit about my background. Answer a few questions. I wanted to know about my biology, I suppose. If there's a history of anything interesting. Christ knows what. Being good at football, maybe. Boxing. If we were into maths or English. If there was a predisposition to cancer. Just the stuff you take for granted when your parents are who they say they are. Then I hear this name Francis Jardine, and my life suddenly has roots in shit and blood and all this horrible stuff. I meet you, and Alison, and you tell me where I came from. What he did. What she went through. You tell me he's dead and so's she. Or maybe he isn't. Maybe he's still out there. Nobody wants to talk about it, nobody knows anything and everybody's scared of upsetting people who already seem like they're dying inside. And now I've got the money and the problems have gone, but it doesn't matter, because I know the world isn't like it was before. I feel like a baby whose been left in front of the TV and a horror movie's come on. It's got under my skin. I don't know if the way I'm acting is because of my blood, or if my brain is telling me this is who I should be, or if I just think it's a good excuse to bitch and whinge and feel sorry for myself and do whatever nasty shit I feel like doing. I could live another fifty years, and I can't live them like this. With these thoughts. I can't be a dad. I couldn't even be a son.'

Adam's arms look as though he is conducting an orchestra as he gesticulates, wild and desperate. Finally, his hands encase his face, and he slides down the wall. He doesn't feel there's enough whisky in the world to drown what he's feeling.

Irons looks at the boy on the floor. Then at the doorway through to the living room. He pictures the image on the chimney breast, the patterns of light that dance on the polished brass of the urn. Gives the thought a nod.

And begins to unfasten his shirt.

Adam looks up. His eyelashes are tangled

345

spider-legs, the lenses of his eyes hazy and sore. He seems to be looking out through a swarm of flies. Black dots dance in his vision. Puke swims in his gut.

Irons holds his gaze. His words, heavy footsteps on dry leaves.

'She sketched me once,' he says, distantly. 'She just sat me down and sketched my face. Every scar. Every broken bone. She was a diamond. An angel. She came into our lives and she lit us up. Lit me up. And I don't light easy.'

Irons stops. Lost in himself. Staring at nothing. He gives a slight nod of his head and motions for Adam to follow him to the living room, flicking the light on as he goes. He stalks to the fireplace, giving a pursed-lip smile to the urn, the rose, the pictures on the chimney breast. He turns back to where Adam stands, red-eyed, open-mouthed, gazing at the vile pornography on the bare brick.

'She became part of the family,' he says, softly, talking as much to himself as to his guest. He has never said these words out loud. Never even acknowledged them in his mind. 'Franco had always wanted more kids, but that wasn't to be. Then suddenly he had this other little girl. Quiet. Grateful. Happy. Talented. Everything you could want. Her and Alison barely fell out. Always said her pleases and thank yous. I used to pick her up sometimes, when she was still living with that useless excuse for a mother. I always used to bring one of the big motors, because it made her a bit of a princess down that estate where she was living. I used to look forward to that time together. She would talk to me like I was a normal man. Like I hadn't done all the things I'd done. Told me about painters. Her favourites. Different styles. What they meant. She loved paintings of flowers. Henri Fantin-Latour. Not easy to say with no teeth. French guy who did flowers. He was the one she liked most. She gave me a book on him once. She was a beautiful soul. Saw the beauty in everything. Everyone.'

He stops again. Holds up a hand as Adam begins to speak. He feels like he's excavating himself. Digging down through rock-layers of memory; dragging out his feelings in an avalanche of bone.

'Then Franco got pulled. A silly so-and-so and his mate tried to do one of our bars. Silly in itself, but even sillier when Franco was in there at the time. They did a proper job on the place. Took everything in the till and made all the punters chuck their wallets and watches in a bag. Franco too. Didn't know him. Didn't know what they were doing. They got picked up quickly enough, of course. Couple of my lads found them in a B & B. I was on my way to solve the problem, when Franco gets a rush of blood to the head. Goes there himself. His temper was up. By the time I got there, they weren't breathing. Franco was. Hard. I went spare at him. No point having me and exposing yourself, I said. He just told me this one was his job, not mine. Wouldn't even let me get rid of them for him. Bundled them in his car and took off. And didn't he go and get pulled for speeding? Our whole world looked like falling apart. He was on remand for months.

Alison and Pamela, terrified they were going to be left on their own. Me, trying to keep things together. Every other outfit for miles around trying to get what was Mr Jardine's. Worst of the lot, the blooming Dozzles. Gypsies who settled down. The type who keep an old car engine on their front lawn. Lived in squalor. Fat, nasty, ugly people one and all, but hard as nails. I don't say that lightly. Wouldn't back down. Would take a beating and come back for more. Lose an eye and blink the problem away. Felt entitled to a good share of this area and with Franco away, it was hard to keep what was ours. Had a few scraps, we did. People got hurt. So we gave them a wee bit of what they wanted, and I took on the youngest, Thomas, to look after some of the pubs and clubs on our patch. Wasn't much more than sixteen, but a tough kid. Only dapper one in the family. Looked like a Teddy boy. Born in the wrong time. And temper? By Christ he couldn't keep it in check. Cost us more money than he made. Got his own back on people who didn't pay on time by bombing their pubs. Even the ones we owned! I hired him out once or twice, bit of muscle work, but he didn't have much in the way of finesse. I don't like to use such words, but he was an arsehole. Randy little git. Nasty, arrogant and dangerous. Didn't blink very often. I reckoned once Franco came out, I'd solve the problem permanently, but it was all about containment in his absence. Keeping things together. That's what I did. By the time of the trial there were no witnesses left. His barrister arranged the hearing around the date we'd already booked the celebration party. We knew he was getting out. We hired this gorgeous place out west. Belonged to somebody Franco knew. Football chairman. I went over and inspected it before the big night, just to check it out. Took the girls, actually, just for the run. The owner was having the place tarted up. Painted, banners hung, all the usual. Workmen crawling over the place like ants. The girls loved it. Cheered them up no end. Then word comes through he's been acquitted, and it's party time.'

Irons looks down at his feet. His gaze flickers back to the urn.

'She came in her best dress. In the big car, with Alison. Danced her little socks off. Had the time of her life. Reckon that was the last time she smiled . . .'

'Look, I don't . . .' begins Adam, and stops when he realizes his throat is too dry, his insides too nauseous, to finish the sentence. He sips his tea and feels it burn his dry lips. Sloshing and blending with the whisky in his chest. He wants to vomit. Throw up his insides and fill himself with something better.

Irons looks away again, back at the chimney breast, as though the words he needs are painted there. His fingers have stopped fumbling at the buttons of his shirt. They fall back to his sides.

'I'm pretty good at knowing people. I look into their eyes and see what they're capable of. What they are willing to do. I looked in hers and knew what she was. She was one of those paintings. Her insides were a watercolour. His weren't. Dozzle. I knew they were black, but I didn't know how dark. That night, we were at the party. All hugs. All smiles. Dozzle didn't have much to do. Just keep an eye on the door. Keep the Press back. Behave himself. Couldn't do it. Had to play the big man. Had to try and get one over. So he goes off for a kiss and a cuddle with Alison. She was only fifteen. And she was a Jardine. Lad committed suicide when he touched her. One of the boys heard a commotion in the cloakroom. Should have told me, but he went to Franco first. Was all I could do to stop him from killing the lad there and then. Don't get me wrong, Franco's the cool head, but that temper had put him inside and we'd only just got him out. I did what I do best. Sorted it. Told Mr Jardine to go back to the party. To leave it to me. I was going to take him somewhere quiet and keep him there until all the pretty people went home. Until we could think about what to do next.'

Irons's tongue darts over his ruined lips. He closes his eyes, immersing himself in the horrors of three decades before.

'I took him outside. There were still some work vans parked up at the service entrance from the people who'd tarted the place up so I figured I'd bung him in one of them. Put him out of harm's way. I never got the chance. I was barely on the grass when I saw her. Your mum . . .'

'Don't call her . . .'

'Pamela, barefoot on the grass, staring at the stars, smiling like it was Christmas morning. All the venom went out of me. All the darkness I had to do. That I had done. Suddenly all I wanted to do was watch her. Next thing I can't breathe.

Cheeky little bleeder's only stuck a blade in my throat. I couldn't even speak. Just dropped. I've been covered in blood a lot of times but it's always warmer when it's your own. They found me a while later, and by then, it had happened. She'd been taken. And hurt. Somebody had done such horrible things to her, and I was lying on the grass, breathing blood.'

A shiver seems to pass through the room, wrapping Adam in a cold chill, then making Irons sway. He reaches for the mantelpiece for support, then balls his fists, trying to soothe himself.

'I was out of action for an age. They didn't tell me what happened for weeks. Franco was sorting it out diplomatically. They had no doubt it was Dozzle. I suppose I didn't either, once the idea was put in my head. I didn't stop to think about it. Didn't ask the questions. Who else was there? Who had the opportunity? Just fixed it in my head it was the lad. Then Franco tells me she's pregnant. Having a nipper. Born out of that. I shut myself down. Concentrated on getting well. Speaking again. I wanted to see her, but she'd seen enough ugliness. He sent me away. Bit of hurting work on the coast. Then you pop out. And I don't give a damn about keeping the Dozzles onside any more. I do what needs to be done. I go to the boozer where they're all giggling and having a laugh and playing pool and wearing silly bloody Christmas hats, and I take them down. Put my foot on the young lad's neck and take his face. Blow the rest of it off with a shotgun. He was begging, but I've heard begging before. Saying it wasn't him, but they all say that. Trouble was, his eyes said he wasn't lying. That's why he'd stayed low. Heard about what happened to her. Knew it was a death sentence. But once I'd pulled the trigger I couldn't get any more answers. Maybe that's why I pulled it. Hoped I could convince myself it was over. The right man had died. But I didn't convince myself. I got sent down and spent most my lifetime in a cell. Thinking about it. Over and over. That and nowt else. Closed off. Shut down. Caged.'

Irons suddenly spins back from the fireplace. He tears at the buttons on his shirt and exposes his bare chest.

Adam visibly flinches.

On the pink and hairless canvas of his broad chest are concentric circles of scars. Ugly, risen, like a procession of bald caterpillars following one another over a grotesquely pale canvas. They spin inwards, growing fresher. Smaller. More bloody. They remind Adam of African ceremonial scars. What was the word? The one from the documentary channel. Keloids, is it? Not knowing how to articulate his feelings, how to react to this abomination of tortured flesh, his mind retreats to the safety of the question, busying itself with trying to remember the word for what he is witnessing.

'Eighteen years inside, son. Done for manslaughter, because Franco got me a good brief, but I done somebody else while I was inside and the stretch kept stretching. I didn't care. I was in my cell when word came that she'd done herself in. Her heart was broken.'

Irons shakes his head afresh. Begins rubbing

352

his hand over the wrinkled, ridged skin on his torso.

Outside the cottage the wind picks up and the bare branches suddenly bend to scratch at the windowpanes like fingernails. A gust of wind surges down the chimney and a handful of petals fall from the rose. Irons, his reflexes abnormally fast, catches them as they fall, scooping them into his palm.

'She left her mark here. Chose this place to end it all. Left me this picture. This present, to remind me what had happened. I've tried to cover it up but it's still under there – the picture she left to show us all why she'd done what she'd done. A picture of a man in a gas mask, fucking a little girl. Look past the big brushstrokes and you'll see it. Then you'll never not see it.'

Another petal falls, and Irons doesn't even try to catch it. He reaches up and touches the brick; tender, as if cupping a cheek.

Adam's bones ache as he rises to his feet. He is swaying, slightly. Cold. His mind full of pictures of the final moments of a woman he once lived inside.

'I've looked at this picture every day I've been out,' says Irons. 'Tried to find something about him that looks like Dozzle. Or Riley. Or Ace. Even Franco. I don't know who did it to her. I don't know who took her life or created you. I don't know how to live the rest of my life, so I don't. I function. I take care of business. I kill. I'm Franco's monster. The only person who ever made me feel anything else is dead, gone, and burned to dust.'

Adam walks, unsteadily, to where Irons stands. Together they examine the picture.

'His chest,' says Adam, through a closed throat and dry lips. 'What's that on his chest?'

'Dead Man's Hand, son. You know your Wild West? Wild Bill was holding it when they shot him. It's a tattoo. Playing cards held in a fist.'

'He had this on him? The man who did it?'

'I've been there, lad. Called in favours from every tattooist out there. Nothing. Done everything you and Alison have tried. Damn sight more besides. All you can do is live with it. Tell yourself it was Dozzle, and try and live. I don't see much of her in you, but that doesn't mean you have to be him.'

'The urn,' says Adam. He closes his eyes, and gulps, noisily, painfully. 'Is that Pamela?'

Irons turns to look at Adam. He stares through him. Through the sepia of his eyes he sees a boy who has suffered, but can take more.

'Pamela's here,' says Irons, stroking his chest. 'In me.'

'Yeah, yeah,' begins Adam misunderstanding. 'Her ashes, I mean.'

'So do I.'

Silence falls as Adam, through the confusion and the tears and the pain and the hurt, stares at the scarification on Irons's chest.

Without saying anything, Irons pulls a small blade from his trouser pocket and finds the tail of the freshest scar. Eyes locked on Adam's as he digs the blade into it, and tears it an inch further into his skin. There is the sound of paper tearing. Irons reaches for the urn, picks it up with one hand, and shakes a tiny amount of grey ash into his palm.

'No, don't . . .' begins Adam, but Irons is already pulling back the flap of bleeding skin. He smears the grey powder into the wound.

'She's with me. Always,' says Irons. 'I keep her alive. Keep her with me. I kept myself alive through dreaming of her. I can still dream. But one day she'll seep inside me properly, and I'll feel my heart thump like it did when she kissed my cheek. When she smiled. You're part of her too. You understand, don't you?'

For the first time, Adam can see a human emotion in the old man's face. It is a desperation. A hunger. A need to be understood.

Irons needs Pamela's flesh and blood to forgive him for not being there.

For not protecting her.

For not even killing the right man.

Adam's knees are buckling. He feels weak. Sick. Lethargic. Angry. He tries to turn it on Irons, and can't. He feels pity. Compassion. He can feel his own heart beating and sense his own tears on his cheeks and wonders how it must feel to know that only one person can make you human, and that person has suffered and died.

He gazes again at the wounds, the bleeding tail of the innermost circle on the giant's chest, and wonders if he could love anybody that much. If he could take their remains and grind them into his skin. To wear them like a shadow, stitched within, never without.

Adam has no claim on Pamela.

He has no right to be here. To hijack somebody

355

else's pain. To stumble into an agony that has been alive as long as he has.

Suddenly Adam does not want to be here. He wants to go home. Any home. Grace and Tilly, Zara and Selena and Jordan. Mum and Dad. He wants to leave this place with its blood-soaked chimney breasts and scarred killers and its lies and secrets and its old men who've made a living from pain.

He turns, tears pricking at his eyes.

He won't let himself take a last look. At this place. At him. Where she died, and he built her shrine.

He is out the door and into the cool night before he even realizes he is moving.

Licking his lips as they start to sting. Feet pounding on the wet leaves.

Running for home.

Forty-Six

Adam's vision is shattered glass. Sea spray. A storm viewed through a migraine. He can barely see the branches that claw at his face, nor feel the dribbles of rain that slip-slap down the boughs to drench him, as he stumbles over damp leaves; his feet kicking up an aroma so reminiscent of the man he has left in the cottage, it makes him gasp.

The desire not to be here is overwhelming.

The need to be home, any home, consumes him so utterly that for a moment, he wonders if he can force himself away from this place through sheer force of will.

His chest, he's thinking, as his boots find the path. *Your mother was burned to dust and insinuated into the skin of a killer. Her resting place is in the flesh of a man who makes his living claiming lives. Get the fuck out of here, Adam. Find somewhere to cry. Get yourself home.*

Adam pictures Zara, curled up, hugging her knees, sitting in front of the telly with a hot drink, coloured by Christmas lights, waiting for him. She'll be chewing the skin of her wrist, practising the smile she'll use when he walks in.

He tries to imagine telling Grace what happened. It makes him gag. His skin prickles,

357

rises, protests, as if he's trying to get through a mouthful of something disgusting. He closes his eyes and begs for her not to speak of it. Not to mention it. Not even to think of it. He knows it is an action that won't be repeated. He has fallen as far as he is willing to go. He has looked inside himself, seen what he could become were he to let himself fall, and now wants to abandon the pursuit. He wants to go home. Back to the banality he had before all this began. He wants normal problems. Normal stresses. Wants to get irritated by the simple things. Wants to hold Billy Nunn's hand and say, 'I love you'. Call him 'Dad'.

The lights of the house suddenly wink through the trees and Adam emerges from the woods and onto the gravel of the forecourt. The wind is picking up and the lights that shine great circles on the mansion catch the movement of endless leaves as they dance on the breeze.

Adam reaches into his pocket with cold fingers and pulls out the keys to the car. The sudden gusts of wind, now unimpeded by the canopy of trees, cuts at the damp patches on his cheeks, and he wipes himself clean, gulping back the little choking sounds and staggered breaths that wheeze up from his throat. Staring down, he watches his boots kick up little puffs of gravel and dust.

He looks up, heading for the car, abandoned in the centre of the driveway.

Timmy is sitting on the bonnet. The door is open and the faint light by the mirror illuminates the shape of a teenage girl in the driver's seat.

Adam is maybe ten paces away when he stops walking. He stares at Timmy, who is dressed in his new white tracksuit. Against the darkness, feet up on the hood, he looks like a floating ghost.

Timmy's face creases into an ugly mask of surprise.

'What the fuck you doing here?'

Adam blinks, slowly. He shivers and looks around himself taking it all in. It looks for a moment as though he has just woken up in this place. He is exhausted. Utterly drained. But there is a snarl in his voice when he speaks.

'Get off the car,' he says, just as the wind drops and the rain begins to fall. It's gentle at first, but grows quickly into a downpour, which makes a pleasing sound as the water bounces off the array of cars in the driveway, and, more distantly, drums against the surface of the pond at the side of the house.

Timmy smiles and gives a jiggle of his shoulders. He looks inside the car and smirks at the girl, then turns his attention back to Adam.

'What are you doing here? It's Christmas.'

Adam takes three steps forward. 'I know. I'm going home. Get off the car.'

'This yours is it? I was just admiring it. 1.7?'

'1.5. More economical. Nippy as fuck. Get off the bonnet. Get your girl out of the car.'

'Was just having a look. Mate of mine's thinking of getting one like this. I prefer the Golf, like. This is a bit of a girl-car, innit?'

'Just get off.'

'Don't be a twat about it. I'm saying, it's a nice motor. Just not my type.'

Adam moves forward again. The rain is starting to run down his face. His suit is wringing wet. His face, sickly white. He looks like a drowned man, resurrected for vengeance. He is growing impatient. All he can think of is leaving this place. Going home. Getting free.

'Please move,' says Adam, and closes the distance between himself and the car. He puts a hand on the open door and peers in at the young girl in the driver's seat. He remembers her face from before. From the bathroom. When all this seemed exciting and he didn't know he'd been shot from a rapist's cock. 'Do me a favour, love. Get out.'

Timmy slides down the bonnet. Although he is grimacing at the rain, he doesn't seem in any rush to get inside. He looks confused. A little confrontational. 'Does my granddad know you're here?' he asks. 'Or my mum?'

'I've been seeing Irons,' replies Adam, and finds himself starting to tense. His cheek twitches, almost imperceptibly. *Who does he think he is? On top of all of it? All this? Some little turd who tried to have you done over, asking questions you don't want to answer?*

'What about?'

'None of your business,' snaps Adam, and suppresses a shiver as the cold rain seeps through to his skin.

'My house.'

'No it's not.'

'Fucking good as.'

'No it's not.'

Adam is bone-tired. His words are weary. He feels like he's swaying slightly. He's full of drink

360

and food and vile knowledge; secrets, delusions, fantasies. He wants to go home.

'Don't get smart.'

'Or what?'

'You can't touch me. Not here. Not at Franco Jardine's.'

'You're a prat, son. Now get her out of my car or we're going to fall out. Didn't work out so well for you last time, did it?' Adam doesn't sound like himself. He's shaking. Trembling. He sounds pestilent. Weak. He doesn't like it. He feels as though he has been robbed of what he was. That all the things about himself that he liked have been replaced by fear and insecurity. He doubts his own strength.

'You look like you're going to fall down,' sneers Timmy.

'Then we'll both be on the ground,' says Adam, and he locks his gaze on the younger lad. Even now, up close, he sees nothing of Alison in him. Sees nothing decent, neither.

'Let me take the car for a bit of a spin, eh? I'll see what it can do.'

'I know what it can do.'

'Bet I'm a better driver.'

'He is,' says the girl, grinning, as she pulls her feet up and holds her legs, there in the driver's seat, nodding encouragement.

'Yeah, you probably are.'

'No, honest, I am.'

'I'm not arguing. I don't argue. I'm asking you very nicely to fuck off.'

Timmy's face scrunches into anger and he steps forward, his finger up in Adam's face.

361

'I dunno why you're here, mate, but you don't talk like that. You don't mug me off in front of my lass.' He's raging, hands flailing. 'You don't know what I'm capable of. What I've done. Last bloke who thought he could play me found out what happens when you fuck with the Jardines. Put a mallet through his skull – watched it come apart like a boiled egg. You don't come here and . . .'

Adam's left hand closes around Timmy's throat before he can finish the sentence, and he lifts him from the ground, slamming him down, back-first, on the wet bonnet of the car. The girl swears and edges back in her seat, hands to her face. Adam lifts Timmy again and thumps him down once more. The boy's hand is clawing at Adam's but the grip is firm.

Were he to squeeze a little tighter, Adam knows he could kill the lad. He suddenly seems solid again. He can feel his blood thicken. He can feel glorious rage, thundering like a cavalry charge into his skin and bones. He suddenly wants to hurt somebody. Something. Anybody. Everything. To be a normal man, who takes things out on those who happen to be around . . .

'Stop it!'

Alison's voice cuts through the blood which thunders in Adam's ears. It is a shriek. Shrill, sharp, like a crystal glass being smashed on rocks. He turns, his hands still at Timmy's throat, the skin soft, peach-like, beneath his fingers. He looks up, from beneath heavy lids, his mouth slightly open, his teeth bared, the muscles in his arms standing out through the drenched suit which clings to his torso. A noise like a hiss escapes his lips.

'Adam!'

Alison stops, midway across the forecourt. A dark hole appears in the centre of her pale face as she recognizes the man who is throttling her son on the bonnet of a car, here, at her home, late on Christmas day.

He has shaved his head. Thinned out on the face. His skin is a garden statue. Grey-green. The only light left in his eyes is rage. If there was ever any Pamela in him, it's gone.

She rushes forward again, suddenly angry. She starts pulling at his arm and is surprised at how much strength she can feel in those arms. She remembers the last time they touched. She is suddenly Jardine's daughter. Angry. Capable. Appalled her home has been violated, her kin touched. She wonders where Irons is. How he has allowed this. The angry man, throttling her only son, becomes any intruder. Any stranger. Any business rival who needs to be removed.

Alison's thoughts are not of her son. They are not the concerns of a mother. They are the venomous curses of a gangster's daughter, abused by a nobody who has dared to take them on.

He sees the change in her. Her face is a black cloud, changing shape and form under the onslaught of a harsh breeze. In an instant, the shock on her face is replaced by a snarl of anger. Outrage.

He can feel her clawing at him, and he squeezes harder, just for bad. He had been ready to let go, but he's not in the mood for yielding.

There is another pressure at his back. The young girl is squealing, pulling at him, begging him to stop. He likes it. He feels powerful. Strong. He has the power to take life. The capacity to inflict pain. Or the mercy to spare. Staring into Timmy's purple, open face, he wonders if this is how it feels to be Franco. Irons. Billy Nunn. Big, capable, enduring men. Unencumbered by fear. Conscience. Doubt. Misery.

Men who can. And do.

He leans forward, puts his weight on his left hand . . .

The gunshot is a thunderclap. Even the rain seems to fall silent in the few seconds after the colossal bang, that sends a great squawking flapping procession of birds into the dark sky.

The quartet on the bonnet of the car throw themselves sideways as the spray of shot thuds into the side of the car like a handful of stones. The window of the driver's door shatters; cobwebs, splinters, fractures running outwards from a central point. A dozen tiny holes appear in the door.

On the steps, outlined by the yellow light of the hallway, stands Franco Jardine.

Forty-Seven

2.18 a.m.

Smoke coils upwards from the long barrel of the shotgun in the pale, wrinkled hands.

Jardine can feel himself growing taller. Stronger. He feels as though he has injected himself with something. Snorted a line of rage.

He knows only that a tall, handsome man has entered his property. Hurt his family. He knows that Irons must be dead, for otherwise, this man would already be a deflating corpse.

Franco Jardine doesn't believe in forgiving his trespassers.

He shoots them in the stomach and watches them bleed to death.

Adam sees a little old man holding a gun three sizes too big for him, swaying on the breeze, damp from the rain, ridiculous in huge jam-jar glasses and a bottle-black moustache. He's wearing a Christmas sweater, jogging trousers and a crepe paper hat. With the steam rising from the gun and his clothes, he looks as if he's just been dug up and left to slowly decompose beneath a warm bulb.

The anger hasn't gone. The adrenaline still fills him.

He stands up and looks around. Alison is

climbing to her feet. The girl, feeble, hugging herself, on the wet gravel.

Timmy is on his knees, retching, coughing out insults and swear words.

'Leave him alone,' cries Alison. 'Who the fuck do you think you are?'

Adam's face creases into a smile and his laughter is a hollow, joyless thing.

'I'm Adam Nunn,' he says, kicking Timmy again. 'My mum was a little girl. My daddy was a rapist. A gangster had me adopted because he couldn't stand to look at me. And it was the best thing that could have happened. You're all fucking mad. No wonder Pamela did what she did. You failed her that night. All of you. And you kept on failing her. She did what she did because it was better than living her life on the path you all put her on.'

Adam reaches down and picks up Timmy by the back of his tracksuit. He hauls him to his feet, then embeds his fist in his stomach. He doubles over, like a folded sandwich. Adam knees him in the face.

'How can you do this?' shrieks Alison, darting forward. 'After everything. You're nothing like her. You're all him. You're Dozzle.'

'Dozzle?' bellows Adam. 'You're believing that now, are you? Daddy's told you not to ask any more questions so you stop? You've got what you wanted. You got to dip back into Pamela again, say you were sorry, and move on. What about me?'

On the steps, Franco is struggling to aim the gun.

The words are hitting him like tiny fists.

366

Pamela's boy.
Here.
In his home.
Hurting his blood.
Screaming at his daughter.
Here, as a man.
A man who looks nothing like Dozzle.
And everything like somebody else.
The gun becomes too heavy for his hands.
His heart is being squeezed beneath giant hands.

'He's had enough,' says Alison, though there is no affection in her words. She is not trying to save her son. She is trying to make sense of what is happening. Pamela's boy, turning on Franco's little girl.

She turns to her father, standing, motionless, on the steps. 'Dad!'

She doesn't recognize him. He is weak. Old. Hopeless. Ineffectual. A pensioner, wrapped up against the cold. The gun in his hands seems to be pulling him forwards.

In a moment of anger and desperation she runs to him and grabs the rifle. The barrel is warm from the first shot. Her eyes meet her father's as she drags the gun from his grip.

He coughs out two words.

A duo of gargled syllables, dredged up from the blackest shadow of his bile duct and spat out in a spray of red-flecked spittle.

Alison hears what he says. She doesn't understand. Her fingers are shaking, but it is through anger, not fear.

367

She grips the gun and runs back down the steps. The fury has chilled her skin.

Adam holds Timmy by the hair. His mouth is bleeding. His nose plastered across his face. His new tracksuit an artist's palette of crimson and claret.

He looks up and sees her coming. Holding the gun. Turning it upon him.

He flashes her a smile as she takes aim.

Then slams Timmy's head through the car window.

Another ear-splitting thunderclap. Another squeal of birds.

Then a thud, as a crow falls from the sky and lands on the damp gravel.

Adam and Alison turn their heads to the treeline.

Irons stands there, a blob of pitch against the jet of the forest.

Alison looks at the gun, lying on its side a few feet away. There is a dint in the barrel where the knife struck it. The knife, having ricocheted off, turns slowly, on the bonnet of the car, like a bottle being spun at a school disco.

Timmy slowly slides down the car door. Glass in his hair. Smaller shards stuck in his forehead. Cage bars of blood run down his face.

Irons stalks forward.

He has made his choice. Saved Pamela's boy, at the risk of Jardine's girl.

He can feel his heart beating.

He fancies that if he were to rub his hands over his face, he would feel nothing but smooth skin.

Dozzle? Riley? Ace? It doesn't matter.

He knows who the boy's mother was.

And that is enough.

The fight goes out of Adam as he looks down at the teenager at his feet.

He looks around as if waking from a sleep.

He is standing in the shadow of an expensive house. His hands are covered in blood and glass. Alison Jardine is standing nearby, massaging her hands, breathing hard; her face somewhere between a snivel and a snarl.

Irons is walking across the gravel. He has stepped into the illumination being cast from the house, but he has grown no lighter.

The man who must be Franco Jardine is leaning against one of the columns at the front of the house, clutching his chest.

Adam looks at him. Locks eyes on the little old man who sent him away.

'Go.'

He looks up.

Irons is beside him, hauling Timmy to his feet as if he were weightless.

'Go.'

'But . . .' begins Adam.

'This is the end of it.'

'All this.' He gestures, feebly. 'What I've done.'

'We've all done things we shouldn't.'

'He's Franco Jardine . . .'

'The person he'd send after you is me. And I'm not coming.'

369

'What about you?'

'He owes me.'

'What about Alison?' he says and looks up. She is still standing there, looking at her father as he gasps for breath. She is making no move to help him. Or her son. She looks as though everything she has ever known has just been made a lie.

'She'll understand. Eventually.'

'But . . .'

'Go.'

He climbs through the open door. As he closes it, more shards of glass erupt from the broken window and rain in his lap. He looks up again, his lungs full of honey, his whole body shaking.

Irons is already walking away.

Adam reverses carefully, and turns the car. He is tensed for the sound of a gunshot. The explosion of a tyre. The smashing of a rear window. Even an explosion, from beneath the chassis. None comes.

He drives down the dark driveway, his eyes two white circles in the mirror.

He sees Irons stoop to Jardine. He picks him up like a child, and carries him indoors.

The yellow light dwindles to black.

Alison, a statue.

Slowly sinking into the ground.

Her father's words still rasping at her ears.

Two words.

The Wop.

Part Four

Part Four

Forty-Eight

Songbrook Manor
January 11th, 2008, 11.04 a.m.

The footsteps sound clipped and businesslike as they resound on the bare flags of the hall. It is hard not to liken the sound to the ticking of a clock. The beating of a heart monitor. The steady metronome of a life nearing its end.

Here, now, in this place.

This place with its smell of damp clothes and spilled medicine, ointment and phlegm.

Here, where thick white bedsheets are made extravagant maps by piss stains, dribbled tonics and the bloody coral reefs of sputtered breath.

Here, where Francis Jardine lays like a skittle on the covers of a wrought-iron bed, surrounded by gilt-edged frames and plum-coloured walls, indecipherable tapestries and ornate maple furniture.

Here, where a gangster sucks in oxygen through the gap between his skeletal lips, and hisses a blackened, poisonous mixture of carbon dioxide and bile into the greasy cloud of spit-infused misery that hangs above the bed like a canopy.

The footsteps are brusque.

The crisp, wooden clarinet quality of the sound tells of expensive high heels, expertly worn, leading up black-stockinged calves to a tailored

373

dress and jewellery chosen for understated extravagance.

Pissed off at life and unsure how to be anything other than Franco's daughter.

Unsure how to forgive a dying man for a moment of weakness that tore the scales from her eyes, and replaced the rich oil painting of her father with a shaky line drawing of broken weakling.

The footsteps grow louder as they near the bedroom.

They reach a zenith without a pause.

Continue on.

She has seen all she needs to.

Sniffed more than she can stomach.

She has changed seats and wiped spit and puss from a sandpapered chin.

And now she's done.

Irons sits by the bed, cut in two. The light from the lamp only covers the lower half of his body, like a shawl pulled up to the waist of a seafront pensioner. It illuminates his dark trousers, his black shoes, crusted with mud and broken glass. His torso and face drown in the puddle of darkness. His eyes are two glasses of soured milk, each crowned with a pitted olive.

This is the deathwatch.

Irons has not left the room since he laid Franco upon the high, comfortable, double-mattressed bed so many days ago. He has eaten only the mush that he could not spoon through the cracked mouth of his employer. Drunk the water which ran down the scratched slate of Jardine's face.

He has shut himself down. Become a watchman. A carer. Protector and nurse. Become what Mr Jardine needs him to be. As he has always done.

Irons will not himself wallow in the sadness of the moment. He has experienced enough death to know that tears do not help.

He sits in the darkness, watching his friend breathe; each gasp more difficult than the last.

There had been some brief talk of taking the old man to hospital, but neither he nor Alison had seriously expected the other to condone the suggestion. Their reticence had nothing to do with any desire to help him see out his days in his own home, but rather a reluctance to allow anybody to see what the man with the most powerful name in the north east had allowed himself to become.

That Jardine still lives is almost miraculous. His skin is garish and clammy, like a marble statue exposed to lichen and rain. His mouth, toothless, the grin of cartoon worm. His eyes are closed, but in the moments when they flutter open, the pupils are black, flecked with deep red, like pieces of shit forced from a cancerous bowel.

It is unfinished business that powers Francis Jardine. A detestation of leaving things unfinished, or injustices unrevenged.

He should be dead. His heart is barely beating. The cancerous tissue eating at his flesh has grown hungrier and he is fighting with everything he has left not to be completely devoured. He can feel himself crumbling. Breaking apart. He is a sculpture of compacted ash, left out in a storm.

In his lungs is a flaming sunflower, its petals glowing hot, searing his insides, making each second of life more painful than the last.

It is the fire of having made a mistake. Of having spent more than thirty years believing the correct blood had been spilled.

In a brain lost in time, in a body that has outlived its usefulness, Francis Jardine remembers the men he knew. Their faces are indistinct; a watercolour painted too damp. Colours blend and features intermingle.

Ace Howell, eager to please, crippled with debts, dancing like a barrel-organ monkey to whichever tune was playing.

Riley, strutting like a peacock in the council chambers and shivering like a girl, naked and blood-soaked, begging for help, forgiveness; justifying a moment of raw and unleashed fury by snivelling about his years of good deeds.

And among it all, green eyes and felt-tip jawline.

Dark hair.

Pale fingers and ink.

A man from then. Before. A fleeting glimpse of a passenger on his and Riley's money train.

A man who he spotted in the crowd, that night, in 1971.

A face he saw again, days ago. Standing there.

Jardine coughs and feels the spray of blood rain down upon himself. Senses movement. A sensation of silk upon his chin.

His eyes roll open and lock upon those of his killer. His friend. His monster.

Irons.

376

He looks out through red-seamed eyes. A grape-vine of blood. It lends a more terrible aspect to the scarred and inhuman face, looking down, inches above his own; grey beyond the burns, painted beyond that, pink and innocent so far beneath.

The moment lasts.

A union of memories. Regrets over words unsaid. Laughter at a moment shared. Fear, at what one will be without the other.

He speaks so softly his lips do not part.

'Riley,' he says, in a voice snapping bird bones. 'Pamela . . . Riley's man. Inked . . .' He falls silent. 'The Wop.'

The words wheeze and flutter, rise and cool, to form droplets of water on the leaded glass.

Inside the prism of the orb, a swirl; a rainbow of lurid greys.

The hint of a face.

A last command.

Forty-Nine

Thackeray Road, East Ham, London
January 14th, 9.25 p.m.

Freeman Leo Riley holds the toilet seat with his knotted left hand and squeezes a few drops of pinkish piss from the shrivelled crayfish tail in his right. It trickles over his fingers.

He looks up to watch himself in the mirror above the sink, and his reflection bounces back garish and bright, overly illuminated by the pristine white walls, the powerful bulb, the reflective tiles around the Victorian bathtub. He's not upset by the picture. He has always accepted himself as unattractive, but he knows that there are ways to make these things unimportant. He has never been deterred from achieving his goals by the absence of a movie-star smile. He knows that cash is an aphrodisiac. Power enough to loosen any pair of knickers. And fear a crowbar to stubborn legs.

As he examines his reflection, he hears the telltale patter as the stream of piss misses the enamel bowl and splashes the linoleum floor. Without changing his expression, he purposefully redirects the flow, and forces a cupfull of liquid onto the floor, where it pools. Tucking himself back into his pyjama trousers he looks at the puddle. He gives a vague thought to the possibilities that the opportunity presents. Make her sit in it, perhaps? Soak it up with those silly grey jogging pants she likes to wear. Make a damp map of Africa on her arse. Tell her to strip naked and mop it up in rubber gloves, on her knees, back-arched, tiny tits pointing at the floor. Oh the possibilities.

He fastens his dressing gown and shuffles over to the sink. Lathers himself with the expensive, scented soap on the porcelain dish.

Despite the way he intends to spend the next few hours, he cannot raise any excitement. The Viagra only gets him half-hard and it has been a long time since he experienced an orgasm that was worth the shortness of breath and blinding kidney pain that accompanied it.

He continues to allow himself his extravagances only because he cannot imagine how else to live. He has retired from public life and politics, but not from himself. His hunger is the same. His tastes. His peculiarities. He may have slowed down, but he still likes to fuck somebody until they cry.

From the master bedroom comes the sound of the brass band. Urszula doesn't care for the CD, but he finds the music stirring. Patriotic and fitting. He imagines it as a fanfare ahead of his performance.

Looking at himself, he pictures Urszula in the neighbouring room.

Bitch better be doing as she's told, he thinks. *Best be wearing the new stockings with the wartime seam; the red high heels and the school-girl gym knickers. Cost good money. Weren't easy to come by. Better be grateful. Better be smiling. Best not fucking cry 'til I'm good and ready . . .*

The sound of trumpets and euphoniums fill the bathroom as he opens the door and the soft red light spills in. His feet find the thick cream carpet, and he walks into the large, crimson-painted bedroom with its mirrored ceiling, its ornate brass bed, its 1920s glamour postcards in varnished black frames.

He looks up and sees Urszula. Tears are cutting channels in her make-up. She's standing by the bed in jogging suit and winter coat – the lingerie and high-heels untouched on the quilted blanket.

'You fucking . . .' he begins, with a snarl full of malice and contempt.

The words catch in his mouth as the cord fastens around his neck.

Leo Riley rises to his tiptoes, hands clawing at the constriction around his scrawny throat. His eyes bulge, pupils swivelling like the eyes of a mad and frightened horse.

He feels a forceful shove to the back of his knees, a draft on his bare belly as his gown falls open. He leans back to try and relieve the pressure, and feels another shove, pushing him forward, cutting off the airway.

'Go,' comes a voice.

Riley's eyes fix on Urszula. She is looking past him, at something behind.

Her gaze travels down.

There is a malice in the goodbye she smiles.

Then she is running for the door.

Riley senses something behind him. He can

smell piss and posh soap. He can hear his own heart. Feel flecks of frothy spit upon his lips.

The shadow moves.

A darkness seems to stretch out and elongate, block out all light, then withdraw, shrink, and take form before him.

He blinks and takes it in.

Him. Jardine's monster.

Steam rising from his black jacket, his bald head, his burned face.

His anger a physical, tangible thing, that seems to engulf his massive bulk in a black tar.

Riley can't scream. Can't breathe. He fears closing his eyes in case they never open again and he goes to his death with Irons's face seared upon his irises.

'Mr Jardine's dead.'

A pause.

'Tell me what I don't know.'

The response is guttural and strangled, squawking and base.

Irons jabs a gloved finger up Riley's nostril, and tugs down, putting fresh pressure on his throat.

'I know you made each other money. I know you put contracts the way of companies he had an interest in. I know you got rich from his name, and the things I did for him.'

A pause.

'I don't know why Mr Jardine used his last breath to send you to your grave. I don't know what you did to Pamela, but I know you brought somebody into her life that ended it.'

A foot in Riley's gut, pushing him back, slackening the rope.

'If I asked you to tell me where to find The Wop, what would you say?'

A pause.

'You think you're going to get a statue after I'm finished?'

A snarl. A glimpse into a bright red mouth and a blackened gullet.

'Talk to me . . .'

The soft trilling of a phone inside his coat. Irons growls to himself, pissed off at the intrusion. He was just starting to enjoy himself. He glances at the screen and decides it's worth the delay. Listens to the voice of PC Goodwin, nervous, breathless, in his ear.

'. . . we're done, yeah? This has to be the end of it. It's going to come crashing down. The partial – they ran it through juvenile records. It's his fucking grandson, do you hear me? Timothy Francis Jardine. The DCI's putting an operation together and they're going to be going through the family business with a fucking microscope. You know the boy better than me but I swear they'll offer a deal and he doesn't seem the type to stay loyal, no matter what he's done to get in his grandad's good books. Fuck, it's all going to come out. I need triple what I'm getting. More. You'll take care of me, yeah? The stuff I know, you don't want to be thinking I'm a risk, I'm not, but still . . .'

Irons ends the call. He shakes his head, his disappointment in the police force absolute. He cannot fathom why it took them so long to work out what he'd known himself the moment he looked into the lad's eyes and saw something far uglier than himself staring back. Mr Jardine had given him a going-away present. Had allowed him to do something useful for the family, and to take a life that didn't matter. He'd let him kill Larry Paris with the same grandfatherly largesse that other people might allow a teenager to drive their car.

'Please . . . I didn't . . .'

Irons returns his gaze to Riley. Looks at things he has done to him while his mind has been elsewhere. It is a long time since anything has turned his stomach, but the thing he has transformed Riley into is enough to make his guts heave.

Irons concentrates on breathing. He slows his heart. Soothes the vibrato in his limbs. His anger buzzes inside his skin like a swarm of bluebottles, but he holds it in. He knows how to use it. Where to send it. Where to go.

Later, he watches Riley die. Sees his tongue slide from his mouth and flop onto his chin, slug-like and ugly.

Irons goes about his decoration of the body with the sound of his own blood rushing in his skull. Occasionally he stops, removes a glove, and reaches inside his shirt to stroke the scarring upon his skin.

He thinks of the big old hotel where they'd had the party. Franco had brought in Riley's favourite cash-in-hand builders to tart the place up.

The firm was run by a man who made a mint for the pair of them with bodged work and estimates that always undercut the other tenders for local authority business.

383

A slick Italian.

A man who might still be alive.

Who raped Pamela and shafted them all.

A man who looked so like the boy, that it stopped an old man's heart.

A man called Santinello.

Fifty

The Laburnums Care Home,
Holybourne, Hampshire
January 19th, 1.03 p.m.

The nursing home is set back from the main road, shielded from the wide, quiet street by bare trees planted close enough together for their branches to intertwine, so that visitors' first impressions of the large Victorian building seem to arrive through a black veil. It's an apt image for a place that makes its living offering end-of-days care. Red-bricked and high-roofed, set in two acres of landscaped gardens and decorated to the standard of a decent bed and breakfast, Mally Santinello considers it to be a decent enough place for his old friend to die, and well worth the money he insisted Pat accept to ensure Billy sees out his days in comfort. The investment is a paltry one. Mally knows that had Billy been a man more like himself, he could have fleeced him royally over the years: skimming from the business, and demanding cash to keep his trap shut.

Santinello's shoes make little noise on the driveway as he walks up to the visitors' entrance, hands in the pockets of his expensive, three-quarter-length coat. He's not cold, although it's a bright and bitter day, but he's never quite known what to do with his hands when they're not full. He supposes that's always been his problem.

The car park is half-full. He notices a sporty little thing parked next to a 4 x 4 and spots the baby seat in the back. Wonders if this is Adam's vehicle: the nippy little thing Pat had told him about. Doing well, she says. New job. More colour in his cheeks. Laughing like he used to. Visiting his dad every day. Reading Westerns to him and calming him down when he gets upset. Once upon a time, Mally would have popped home for his silver Mercedes and driven back here, just to park it next to Adam's and make the little prick feel shit about himself. Show him he may be raising his game, but that he's still no success. No big-shot. No Mally Santinello. But these days, Mally doesn't feel the urge to show off. Doesn't need to buy a drink for every man in the bar or treat himself to a new vehicle with a personalized number plate each Christmas. He's a lot more at ease with himself than he used to be. Content in his wealth. Proud of himself. Reconciled to his mistakes. And besides, he likes young Adam. Sees a bit of himself in the lad. The same drive, the same winky twinkle that helped him secure the deals that made him rich, all those years ago.

As he enters the warmth of the reception area and smiles at the familiar face behind the desk, Mally wonders about the nature of fortune. Wonders how much luck a man makes for himself, and how much is foisted upon him. He wonders if he'll end up in a place like this. Gaga

386

and piss-stained, coughing himself into the grave, surrounded by faces he doesn't recognize in a world that wants him gone.

Mally gives a polite knock at the open oak door then pokes his head into Billy's room. Adam is sitting at the foot of the bed, reading a story about some Indian scout taking on some tribe of baddies. Adam nods a smile and Mally indicates the lad should carry on. There's no sign that Billy is listening to the tale, but Mally doesn't doubt that Adam feels better for having something to do, and doesn't want to stop his flow. He listens for a while, to the stories of the gunfights and knife-fights and beautiful girls in frilly dresses, and watches Billy die. He's hooked up to a drip, fastened inside pale blue pyjamas and mummified by sheets and a crocheted blanket. A TV is on in the corner of the airy, high-ceilinged room, the sound turned down, a colourful programme for kids flickering odd lights onto the cream walls. There's little about the man in the bed Mally recognizes as Billy Nunn; the tall, capable, funny fucker who helped him build up the company, stood by his side through it all, and who bailed him out of the shit without judging, or having to be asked.

Eventually, Adam reaches the end of the chapter, and closes the book. He's dressed casually, in combat trousers and a fashionable jumper. His hair is growing back and he's clean shaven. He's looking better than the last time Mally laid eyes on him, and he's pleased to see Pat was right: he's thriving.

'Day off?' Mally asks, quietly.

'Week,' he says. 'Felt a bit bad asking for time

off so soon after starting, but it's important, isn't it.'

'Definitely, son, definitely. They OK with you about it?'

'Oh fine. They understand. And I've been putting in the hours. Knackered, to the tell the truth, but it's a good knackered. You know that feeling, where you've put in a good day's work?'

'Oh yes, nowt like it. I know he'd be proud of you.' He nods at the figure in the bed. 'And you're doing all any son could do for their father.'

'I hope so.'

Mally takes off his coat and hangs it over the side of the chair, then sits back down. 'Any more news from the doctors?'

'Just more of the same. Can't be long left, but they said that weeks ago.'

'They just don't know, do they?'

'No.'

'Do they think he's suffering?'

'They say not, but when he has his moments and comes to, you can see he's in pain. Couple of days back, he was himself for a good few minutes. Knew me. Asked about Tilly. Mam. He was cracking jokes. Then he was gone again. Back inside himself. Next time he came to he was younger than I am now. Angry and upset and giving shit to the nurses.'

'It must be hard.'

'It is.'

They sit and talk about Adam's job for a while. The weather, and how the nights are drawing out. Football, and where the England manager is going wrong. They agree that if

Billy was a dog, the vet would have put him to sleep by now. They share stories about the man in the bed, and sometimes remember to include him in the conversation. Once in a while, he wakes up, and mutters. Adam has to stifle a laugh as he notices one of Billy's ears has folded over and stuck fast to the side of the face he has been laying on. He rights it, dutifully, and returns to his position.

'That young one not here today?' asks Mally, as he says yes to the offer of a cup of tea from the middle-aged carer who pokes her head around the door and smiles at the men in the room.

'Tilly? No, she's with her nan.'

'No, I meant that nurse. Red-head. One who was here on Friday.'

'Oh, you mean Helen? No, I haven't seen her.'

'Cracker, that one. If I was twenty years younger . . .'

'You'd be ninety-seven.'

They laugh at that, and Mally hears Billy's speech patterns in the jokes that Adam starts to crack. Soon they are laughing, chuckling, getting on, like grown men should. The moment makes Mally feel nostalgic. He remembers Billy, before the accident, and the rapid-fire one-liners he used to throw at the other men on their works crew. Used to have him in stitches.

'You still haven't picked up those photos, by the way,' says Mally, picturing the collection of black-and-white images that have been laying on his kitchen table for months.

'Oh, sorry,' says Adam, sipping at his tea. 'I keep meaning to, but you know how it is.'

389

'I do, lad, I do. But they're just going back in the cupboard if you don't want them.'

'I do want them, I've just been up to my eyes . . .'

'They might do some good, is all I'm saying. Your dad looks happy as Larry in one of them. Laughing like somebody's tickling his whatsit. I would have given them to your mam, but I don't know how fondly she remembers those times, when he was away on the road, before the accident and before you came along. She could be a bit funny about things like that. Never really liked it.'

'I understand. Blokey times.'

'Exactly,' says Mally, nodding his appreciation that Adam understands.

Adam pauses and looks at his watch. Pulls a face. 'Your place isn't far, is it?'

'Five minutes on foot. Ten in that fridge on wheels you're driving.'

Adam smiles. Looks at his dad. 'Cool. Shall we give it another half hour here, then pop to your place?'

'Lovely,' says Mally. 'I'll crack open a bottle, if you're up for it. And the cleaning lady's made another bloody tiramisu.'

'Just like mother used to make?'

'Not a bit,' he laughs.

'She a looker?'

'Tastier than her tiramisu. I'll let you draw your own conclusion.'

The house isn't particularly fancy, but Adam can tell from the quality of the cars parked up at the other sprawling properties in the neighbourhood that it would set him back the best part of half

390

a million pounds if he were to buy it in today's market. It's a bungalow with a converted attic, set in neatly tended gardens. The last of the daylight bounces off the glass conservatory, the roof of which is just visible as Adam parks the Suzuki on the criss-crossed brick driveway. Gives a whistle. He feels a moment's irritation, that his passenger lives hale and hearty in such luxury, while his father, his right-hand man for half a century, withers away in a nursing home, but he is trying to stop thinking negative or unkind thoughts, and tells himself that Mally deserves his success, and that he has never been slow to share it with the Nunn family.

Mally opens the double front door and they step inside. There is a smell of tomatoes and basil, and a gentle warmth that makes Adam feel instantly comfortable and drowsy. The inner doors open into a large, open-plan living room. It stretches forty feet to the far glass doors, which flows into the conservatory. A large kitchen stands beyond the door to the corridor, which Adam assumes leads to the bedrooms. It's tastefully decorated in creams and terracotta. There is a large, leather, three-piece suite in the centre of the room, facing a giant entertainment system: a plasma screen TV at the centre of the shiny silver ensemble. The art on the wall is surprisingly modern. Impressionist red faces on blank canvases. Silhouettes of large, topless women overlaid on different coloured backdrops. A picture of a young man that Adam surmises to be Mally's son, smiles out of a gilded frame on the mantel-piece above the glossy, wood-effect fireplace.

'Make yourself comfortable,' says Mally. 'Wine? Sandwich?'

Adam considers the offer of the wine, and then shakes his head. He's drinking to a strict schedule, these days. It's a deal he's made with himself. A pint and two doubles with his lunch. A bottle of wine after dinner. Nip before bed. He knows it's too much, but argues that if he sticks to drinking merely excessively, he will be able to keep it in check better than if he allowed himself to binge.

'Just water for me, please.'

'You sure?' asks Mally, and he seems surprised.

'Honestly,' says Adam, and sounds too firm. He makes light of it. 'I tried a drop at Christmas and if I remember rightly, it's too easy to polish off a vat of the stuff.'

Mally smiles, appeased. 'Right, you wait there. I'll be back.'

Adam sinks into the sofa, his eyes on the blank TV screen. He takes deep breaths, wanting a cigarette, but concentrating on the nicotine patch on his forearm, along with a mental image of Tilly's face and voice. Her nose is wrinkled. 'Daddy smelly,' she'd said, and Adam hasn't sparked up since. He's living as well as he can. Has given himself over to Zara completely. Can't be in a room with her and not hold her close. Texts her every moment of his working day. Has even let her meet Pat, a brief hello and a kiss on the cheek on the doorstep; Zara dressed demure and delicate in long gypsy skirt and a fur-lined denim jacket. He is no more certain of his love for her than he is of anything else in his life, but he knows that making her happy makes him feel

392

better. Jordan too, silly daft lump that he is. And Selena. Smiling more, now. Content with the playful thumps on the arms and giggling head-locks they share. Their chats on the way to school and as they take walks down the waterfront after tea. Father and daughter. Best of friends.

Mally returns with an old brown envelope in one hand and a glass of red wine in the other. 'Here we are then,' he says, handing the envelope to Adam and sitting down in the armchair, facing him. 'Good days, them,' he says, and Adam looks at the slick, polished, nimble man of seventy-eight years old who sits close by, and hopes that he will age as well and as gracefully as he has. He has comforted himself, as he has watched his father withering and dying, that even if dementia is hereditary, he is not at risk. It is a crumb of comfort, against the famine of knowing that he is not Billy Nunn's blood.

Adam reaches into the envelope and takes out the photographs. Leafs through the first dozen. Building sites, mostly. Cement mixers and out-of-shape men in overalls, smearing cement onto bricks like paté onto toast, or carting wheel-barrows up planks and over puddles. He sees a few faces he recognizes but couldn't name. Pulls appreciative faces as he works his way through the bundle. Sees his father, perhaps forty years old, caught off-guard, feet up on his desk in the Portakabin, tie and checked shirt, paperback Western in his hands. Mally leans over. 'Got him a treat that day,' he says, indicating the picture, and sitting back down, smiling.

More pictures. Black-and-white again, now.

Blokes. Eating butties and drinking flasks of tea. Hard hats and high-visibility vests. Mally and Billy, side by side, cutting a ribbon to open a new block of flats in Southampton, fresh-faced and smirking, Billy's fingers ever so subtly curved into a V-sign at his side.

Next photo.

A face he knows.

Adam's face twitches in confusion and he feels acid climb into his chest.

Mally leans over again. Looks at the image. 'Aye, thought you might spot that one,' says Mally, breezily. He nods at the image of the tall, broad-shouldered man in a grey suit and hard hat, shaking hands with a more youthful version of himself. 'Not the way you'd want to go, is it?' Mally laughs.

Adam's brow creases. 'Riley?' he says. 'Leo Riley?'

'Well remembered,' says Mally, impressed.

'But . . .?'

'I've got the paper here,' he says, gleefully. He reaches down beside the chair and picks up a copy of the *Express*. Flicks through the pages. Holds up the paper for Adam to see. A picture of Leo Riley smiles out at him, under the head-line: **Kinky Sex Death of Politician**.

Adam snatches the paper. Skims the article.

A well-known politician who survived scandal enquiries which cast a cloud over a city council has been found dead in his home – apparently the victim of a sex game gone wrong. Leo Riley, eighty-two,

394

an Alderman and Freeman of the city, was discovered dressed in stockings and suspenders at his home on the outskirts of the city. He appeared to have accidentally asphyxiated while hanging himself from a doorframe, dressed in the kinky gear. A colleague said last night: 'To think this is what he will be remembered for is a tragedy. There was talk of a statue being put up of Leo but now his name will be a laughing stock . . .'

Adam feels a numbness prickling into his chest and limbs. The world beneath his feet seems to be sloping. His balance is skewed.

'Always was a funny bugger, that one,' carries on Mally, unaware of his guest's discomfort. 'Your dad had him pegged as a dodgy so-and-so the minute he clapped eyes on him, but you make allowances when it helps your wallet, don't you?'

'Dad knew him?' Breathy. Aghast.

'Course he did. Your dad was my number two, wasn't he. Was better at pricing up jobs than I was. I hope he gets a moment's respite so I can tell him about that dodgy bugger going out dressed in bra and knickers. He'd laugh his head off.'

'But when?' Adam is stumbling over his words. He grabs Mally's wine from the table and downs it, unthinking.

'Easy, lad,' says Mally, smiling, but puzzled. 'I know it's funny but what people get up to in their own home is their own business.' He laughs, as if realization is dawning. 'Don't be thinking we were into any of that funny business. It was strictly business.'

Adam forces himself to breathe. Calm down. 'What was the deal?'

'Oh that was back in the glory days, when we were building things up,' says Mally, stretching, enjoying the memory. 'He was on the council and had the say on who got the contracts for building work. There was some other daft bugger on the council lining his pocket with brown envelopes, but Leo, God love him, had a bit more scope. Brought in outsiders with no connection, and gave us the government grants to build all these new community and housing projects. He took a cut, of course, but even with the three-way split, we made a mint.'

Adam is breathing through his nose. He can smell blood. Damp earth. Corruption. 'Three-way?'

Mally leans forward, enjoying sharing these old war stories. 'Oh aye. Bad lad from Canning Town. Name you might have heard of.'

Adam says it under his breath.

'That's right, Jardine. Real thing, he was. Used to be a big name, once upon a time. Saw off the Krays, so they say.'

'They do.'

'Aye, we were close, once upon a time. Not friends, but friendly. Moved in some nice circles, he did. Had a lot of people in his pocket, but not me. We were partners. And who's done the best in the long run, eh? We're all much of an age, but Riley's there in the paper in his glad rags, and last I heard, Jardine was rattling about in some bloody castle up north. Little old me, here, living the good life. Fate's a cruel mistress, as they say.'

'When was this?' asks Adam. He is still looking at the photo of Riley, his eyes blurring, the roar of the ocean in his head.

'We did business for about ten years, I reckon. Last I saw Jardine was when he came out. Got let off and had a bloody great party to stick two fingers up to the coppers. Called me when he was still inside, before he'd even been cleared, and asked me to get a crew up to the hotel and make it presentable for the shindig. Can you credit that? Your dad did as good a job as ever, mind. I didn't tell him it was Jardine, though. Jardine called me a wop whenever we met, but it was good-natured. Your dad didn't like it, mind, so I just brought him with me the once. That was Billy, though, always had my back . . .'

Adam turns to the next photograph, moving as if in slow motion, Mally's words crashing into and over him. He feels swirled and battered, a piece of driftwood amid thundering surf.

He sees his father.

Laying on the grass outside a half-finished apartment block. Jeans and work boots.

Tussled hair and youthful smile.

Bare chest.

A tattoo, livid among the scattering of chest hair.

Aces and Eights.

Dead Man's Hand.

Adam feels his chest cave in. His vision turns black then red. Mally Santinello's words become a high-pitched vibration rattling his skull.

'. . . aye, they were the days, right enough. Couldn't have done it without him, your old fella. Happiest times of my life, when we were on the road. He sorted me out plenty times. Once, we were down south and I got myself into such a state over this one young lassie. Real head over heels. Made an arse of myself and he really took care of me. We were a right couple of likely lads in those days. If he hadn't loved your mum so much he could have been a real bad one, but he was never up for my sort of caper. It was always me had the van a-rocking,' he says, with a conspiratorial leer. *All boys together.* 'Was hellish what happened. When he lit that cigarette and burned himself inside out . . .'*

Adam feels himself sliding onto the floor. He feels drunk. Enraged and hollow. He bites into his cheek, jaw locked, sweat beading his forehead.

Mally stands and heads for the kitchen to replenish his wine, still talking of past conquests, victories, joys.

'What he said to you – I know it must have hurt. But I'm pleased you've took my advice. Seen past it. Moved on. A dad and a father are different things and he's been both to you. Wish I could tell you the strings we had to pull but it all worked out. Honestly, it's good to get this off my chest. It's been doing me in. Pat wasn't sure if I should get involved but after that slipper puff came knocking, well . . .'

'Who?' he whispers.

'Fat lad. Loud shirt. Got himself done in. Had the damn cheek to put a note through my door,

398

to ring me up and ask me about what I remembered about that shindig donkey's years ago – like
I would tell him! Shook me up though. Had to
go through nearly four decades of boxes to find
the right number. Sent him away with a flea in
his ear, then made a call to the old man, warning
him he'd be on his way. Didn't work out too well
for him, the daft sod. What did he think was
going to happen? You don't turn up at a
warehouse run by the Jardines and start asking
questions – least of all when the old man's sent
his own flesh and blood to sort the problem out.
Made a statement, so I heard. Did him over just
like his grandad used to do. Honestly, this is
doing me good. If I'd known you were so staunch
– if I'd known you could understand how the
game is played – I could have been putting
help and info your way for years . . .'

Adam slithers to his feet. He can feel his blood.
Feels it moving around him.

He stumbles for the door – Santinello's voice
drifting into silence as he hears the thumping of
his pulse.

Only one destination on his mind.

Fifty-One

2.29 p.m.

Mally Santinello opens the fridge door, and removes the bottle of home-made red. He's feeling good. Loves spinning a yarn and remembering better days. The boy seems impressed, too.

He removes the cork and breathes deep. Sweet and fragrant. Blackcurrants and vanilla. A hint of elderberries. Something else, perhaps. Autumnal. Earthy. Like mud on the knees of your best trousers.

He frowns, puzzled by the new aroma.

Begins to turn . . .

A ligature fastens at his throat and he gasps as his airway is cut off, and he is pulled onto his tiptoes.

He tries to say, 'Adam?'

The sound is a strangled gasp.

Irons slams the old man's face into the fridge and hears the cartilage in his nose break. The body in his arms goes limp.

Irons doesn't worry about the evidence he is leaving. He doesn't care. He is learning how it feels to be angry. To act in rage. To take a life for the pleasure of it. He has her with him, now. Can feel his heart beating. Can feel her, in his blood, at his side. *Pamela*. She would never have asked him to be avenged, but he has no other gift to give.

He drops the body on the kitchen floor and reaches for the golden urn that he has placed upon the work surface. He cradles it like a child, and looks down at the man on the floor.

The Wop, Franco had called him. The man who helped build the shittiest bits of a shitty city, grew rich, then scuttled away with his dick wet and his hands red.

He looks at the face, but even through the blood, sees little of Adam about him. None of the similarities that so tore into Franco on Christmas day.

He frowns, trying to slow his heart, calm the burning in the blood. Looks at the urn. Its smooth surface. Its precision and tranquillity. Pictures the treasure it contains, and rubs a hand across his ruined face, then down to his scarred chest.

He kicks Mally in the ribs, but not too hard. Tries again, but the old boy doesn't stir. He fills a glass of water and splashes it on his face. Mally gulps and coughs into life.

'You raped her,' says Irons, softly. 'The girl at the party. You took a shine to her when you were tarting up the hotel, and you took her, and you raped her.'

'What?' splutters Mally. All of his nightmares fuse into one shape. His mind fills with images of a Southampton scrubber, on her knees at the back of the pub, his hands in her hair, gripping too hard. Her tears hitting the pavement. She was one of many, but he never liked them too young. Not like his pal. Not like his mate, who loved to scare them first – to wear the mask his daddy brought home from the war. 'Please! They wanted it . . .'

'She was a child.'

401

'She was old enough!' he screams, and tastes his own blood.

'She was an angel. You tore her apart.'

'Who? Which one . . .'

Irons kicks him again. 'Pamela. Pamela Garner.'

'No . . . no, look, I've done right by you all, haven't I? Got the boy a good home? Never done you any trouble. Never said a word when that ponce detective came asking questions and hinting he knew more than he did. I've done right by the lass – and her boy. Kept him on the straight and . . .!'

He never finishes his sentence. The urn comes down on his skull. He falls into unconsciousness by the third blow.

There is little of his face left by the time Irons cuts it off and stamps on it.

Irons takes his time over his work. There is no sound, save for Irons's occasional mutterings. Anybody watching would hear him cooing to the dented urn. They would see a man content, at peace.

Putting the world right. Putting things in order. He's done most of what he wanted to. Even sent a few quid to Larry Paris's widow by way of apology and reported Jon Goodwin to Professional Standards. He's never liked bent cops.

He's nearly finished. Nearly ready to say goodbye.

He's doing right by the only person who ever really mattered.

Truly, truly blissful in his ignorance.

Fifty-Two

The Laburnums Care Home, Holybourne,
Hampshire
January 19th, 4.33 p.m.

Adam stands above his father's bed and looks at him through tear-streaked eyes. Billy is staring back up at him, confused but half-smiling; eager to please but oblivious to the identity of his visitor.

Adam considers the thing in the bed. Considers what it is to be a monster. To be inhuman. To commit acts so terrible as to render the doer somehow alien; somehow *apart*.

Adam sniffs back snot. Sweat is prickling him beneath his clothes. His chest is heaving, head running with perspiration. He is grinding his teeth as if to powder.

He has tried to find his anger on the journey here. Tried to turn the key in the lock of his rage, but it will not come. He feels just a numbing disgust. An unfathomable guilt; that a man he knows so well, could have once been responsible for such savagery.

He tries to picture it, but the image distorts. His father, a young man, with a face like his own, rutting in the back of a van. A girl, naked and crying. Her face: Selena, Tilly, Zara, Alison, Grace, Pamela, Pamela, Pamela . . .

Gripping the foot of the bed, he sways, vomit rising; his face a medley of jaundice-yellows and slate-greys.

So many questions.

How many?

How many more?

Why?

Dad, why?

He knows, as he looks upon the old man, fragile as a spider's web, breathing as if through sand, that he will not kill him. Knows it is not in him. He will not squeeze the drip. Will not smother him with a pillow. Will not pull the knife from the plate of untouched dinner on the bedside table and cut out Billy's heart.

Nor will he love him. Will not tell Tilly her granddad was a great man, full of jokes and strength and silliness. Will not hold the sadist's hand as he dies, soon, in a room stinking of his own piss. Will not ease his passage into death with words of comfort about his contributions in life.

Adam feels simply broken. All his life, he has believed the man who raised him was his father. Then it was taken away. The knowledge has been handed back with a force he can only liken to the agony that bore into the little girl who once carried him in her belly.

Adam wonders if there is any life to be lived after this. How he should react around those who love him. If he should turn icy eyes upon his mother. Tell Grace. Tell Alison. Tell him.

Irons.

He considers the giant, scarred brute. Decades

spent in prison in Pamela's memory. Living to be her work of art. Prolonging his life, so she can live on. Thinks of Alison. Jardine, in his cold, empty castle. Dozzle, beneath the ground. Riley, his name destroyed. Ace, never without fear. Pamela, dust in an urn, beneath a tribute painted in blood.

And he pictures the people he loved before this began. People untouched by any of this. Pure and good and normal and burdensome and outlined in light against the blackness of his mind. Somehow glorious and golden amid the things he has seen and unearthed.

And suddenly, he needs warm skin upon his. Needs Grace's hand in his palm. Zara's lips on his forehead. Tilly hugged tight to his chest. He wants no more of this. No more ugliness. No more death or violence or secrets daubed on crude surfaces in blood and brains.

He looks at his father, his eyes closing again. Six stone of bewildered, withered, emaciated insect.

Can think of no gesture to make. No sneer. No nod. No hand upon the bedclothes nor a muted goodbye.

He hears Tilly's laughter. Sees Grace's smile. Traces Zara's portrait in his mind.

Walks from the room, into the light.

Pushes open the doors, and sees him. Ratty and pale-faced and grinning like a corpse.

Timmy Jardine.

Doesn't register the sound of the gunshot until his head hits the floor.

Then he is patting at his chest, his guts, his

head, his thoughts a dizzying carousel of gaudy colours: desperately looking for the hole in himself, his face dripping with warm, wet blood.

He scrambles back. Looks down at his feet. Timmy: a furrow from the back of his head all the way through to the front. He's still got his cap on.

Adam stares towards the road.

Irons puts the gun beneath his own chin.

'No . . . no!'

Irons gives a nod; polite and businesslike.

Closes his eyes.

Pulls the trigger.

Adam watches the old man crumple like a pack of cards. Sees the top of his head come off as if an explosion has taken place within his skull.

Adam reaches down and picks up the gun.

Turns his back on the damply steaming bodies.

Walks back through the doors.

Thinks: *Dad.*

He will never know whether what comes next is an act of mercy or revenge.